D0018014

WITCH BLOOD

ANYA BAST

BERKLEY SENSATION, NEW YORK

THE BERKLEY PUBLISHING GROUP
Published by the Penguin Group
Penguin Group (USA) Inc.
375 Hudson Street, New York, New York 10014, USA
Penguin Group (Canada), 90 Eglinton Avenue East, Suite 700, Toronto, Ontario M4P 2Y3, Canada
(a division of Pearson Penguin Canada Inc.)
Penguin Books Ltd., 80 Strand, London WC2R 0RL, England
Penguin Group Ireland, 25 St. Stephen's Green, Dublin 2, Ireland (a division of Penguin Books Ltd.)
Penguin Group (Australia), 250 Camberwell Road, Camberwell, Victoria 3124, Australia
(a division of Pearson Australia Group Pty. Ltd.)
Penguin Books India Pvt. Ltd., 11 Community Centre, Panchsheel Park, New Delhi—110 017, India
Penguin Group (NZ), 67 Apollo Drive, Rosedale, North Shore 0632, New Zealand
(a division of Pearson New Zealand Ltd.)
Penguin Books (South Africa) (Pty.) Ltd., 24 Sturdee Avenue, Rosebank, Johannesburg 2196,
South Africa

Penguin Books Ltd., Registered Offices: 80 Strand, London WC2R 0RL, England

This is a work of fiction. Names, characters, places, and incidents either are the product of the author's imagination or are used fictitiously, and any resemblance to actual persons, living or dead, business establishments, events, or locales is entirely coincidental. The publisher does not have any control over and does not assume any responsibility for author or third-party websites or their content.

WITCH BLOOD

A Berkley Sensation Book / published by arrangement with the author

PRINTING HISTORY
Berkley Sensation mass-market edition / March 2008

ISBN: 978-0-425-22043-6

BERKLEY® SENSATION
Berkley Sensation Books are published by The Berkley Publishing Group,
a division of Penguin Group (USA) Inc.,
375 Hudson Street, New York, New York 10014.
BERKLEY SENSATION and the "B" design are trademarks belonging to Penguin Group (USA) Inc.

PRINTED IN THE UNITED STATES OF AMERICA

10   9   8   7   6   5   4   3   2   1

To James, who is my heart

Acknowledgments

Many thanks to Lauren Dane, Megan Hart, and Jody Wallace for reading through and helping me iron out the wrinkles. Every writer needs people to give them the unvarnished truth about a book. I value you all very much.

Thanks to Brenda for being her wonderful, caring self. Who would have thought that our strange first meeting in the eighth grade would have developed into a lifelong friendship? I'm so glad it did. I'm a better person for knowing you.

ONE

❦

How to Catch a Warlock 101. Isabelle could teach that class.

Club music thrummed through Isabelle's body. Eyes closed, she swayed her hips, dancing more to the ebb and flow of the subtle emotions around her than to the beat. Intoxicated by the sea of euphoria and lust, she allowed the seductive, primal weave to free her for a few blessed moments.

The trap she'd set for the warlock also trapped her.

A man's hands grasped her waist. A lean, muscular body pressed against hers from behind. She knew that touch, those hands and the subtle, woody scent of his expensive cologne. It was the warlock she hunted. The one who thought she was a woman just like any other. Her eyes came open, the moment of serenity vanquished by his presence.

Anyone able to see her face would've glimpsed revulsion pass over her features before her lips curved into a coy smile. She snuggled back into Stefan Faucheux's arms. He rocked her back and forth, changing the sway of her body to the beat of the music. Luckily, Stefan had no empathy. He couldn't sense how much she abhorred his touch.

Somewhere nearby a camera flashed, then another. Paparazzi. The media fawned over Stefan, an ultrarich playboy. Any woman he dated was a source of particular interest. Isabelle had managed to stay on Stefan's arm longer than most. She was the mysterious red-haired, green-eyed woman about whom no reporter could find much information. Isabelle had paid a lot of money to ensure that was so. She'd worked hard to make certain she interested Faucheux for a while, too. A lot of planning had brought her to this night.

Of course, the photographers didn't know she was a witch and Stefan a warlock. Those were secrets best kept from the non-magickal population. That was the only thing the Coven and the warlock-controlled Duskoff Cabal could agree on. The non-magickals greatly outnumbered the magickals and, historically, showed a lot of bloodthirstiness for those perceived to be different.

Stefan moved his body with hers in a teasing semblance of sex that made her stomach roil. Soon, this would all be over. That was the only positive thing about having to suffer his closeness.

Isabelle pasted a smile on her lips and closed her eyes again. She thought of deep, rushing streams furrowing their way through the earth, the recesses of the ocean, where the water lay still and silent, the gentle eddies and ripples at the edge of a lake. Her power rose in response to the mental stimulus, just a little. It bled off a bit of her stress, blunted the sharp edge.

Stefan's arms tightened around her and he nuzzled her throat. More cameras flashed. They'd be on the front page of every tabloid in the country by tomorrow. She'd probably be touted as pregnant and making plans for a wedding. The Lady only knew what stupidity they'd come up with.

And then the *other* story would break. The darker one. The far more violent one.

Soon, she assured herself. Tonight. Because she was not a woman like any other and today was no ordinary day. It was time Stefan Faucheux paid for his sins.

Emotion welled in her throat for a moment. She'd barely had time to grieve. These days she was running on rage, sorrow, and little else.

Use it. Don't let it use you.

Immediately, the sudden swell of vulnerability faded into cold resolve. It was a lesson she'd learned long ago and learned well. She'd had lots of practice stuffing away her pain, transforming it into a far more effective force. Her emotion had become a well-honed weapon.

He leaned into her, spoke into her ear loud enough for her to hear over the pounding music. "Time to leave, *ma cherie.*"

It was, indeed, time.

Anticipation coursed through her, leaving a tingle of sweetness that warmed her more surely than Stefan's skill with fire could ever do. Stefan was a fire witch, one of the more powerful of those she'd encountered. Though he couldn't claim the title *witch* anymore, not technically. He'd betrayed the Coven, broken the rede too many times to count. Now he was a low-down, dirty warlock.

Her own ability resided in the realm of water. That meant she and Stefan were direct opposites magickally. It had complicated her plans somewhat. Normally fire and water had a natural repulsion, whereas fire and air had a built-in attraction. Isabelle had had to work double-time to snare her quarry because of that, especially since she couldn't hide her abilities from a warlock like Stefan. He had a nose like a bloodhound for different types of magick.

He took her hand and led her through the crowd toward the door. The photographers detached themselves from the partying throng and followed. She could see them scuttling like crabs out of the corner of her eye. Stefan's bodyguards flanked them, not allowing anyone to get too close. Earth charms helped. He'd had several created that compelled people to keep their distance.

They made their way out of the club and the heavy doors closed behind them, not quite blocking the bass of the music, which seemed to make the entire club throb on its foundation. The early morning chill raised goose bumps on her bare arms and legs. She took a moment to inhale the fresh, not-quite-clean, air of the city, ignoring the surprised whispers and gasps of those in line to enter the club.

"Come, darling," Stefan said, placing a proprietary hand at the small of her back and guiding her toward the limo. "*La limousine attend.*"

She flashed him a ditzy smile. "I love it when you speak French, Stefan. It's so sexy."

Stefan didn't know it, but she understood every foreign word he spoke to impress her. She'd been a child of the world, growing up as a temporary resident of many countries, and spoke both French and Italian fluently.

He stopped her in front of the limo, tucked her hair behind her ear, and leaned in to whisper, "I will speak it to you until the sun comes up, if you allow me, *ma cherie*."

She moved her head and placed a lingering kiss to his neck. "Then send your bodyguards away." Isabelle dragged his earlobe between her teeth and he responded with a shiver. Cameras flashed in abandon.

He spoke a few words to the warlock muscle near him while the driver opened the door for her and ushered her in. Regulating her breath, as she always had to do when entering a small area, she climbed into the cool interior of the limo and sank down onto one of the leather seats. Isabelle had a moment of unease when the dark closed around her like a velvet fist. Close spaces weren't her thing.

Stefan sat down next to her. As soon as the door was closed, he was on her. But not coarsely, or clumsily. That was not Stefan. He was a perfect gentleman until he decided not to be.

He slid his hand to her waist, tilted her chin toward his face and pressed his lips to hers. Suave, undemanding, seductive. His fresh breath invaded her mouth as his tongue sought entry.

She suppressed a shudder and placed her hands on his broad shoulders, the fabric of his suit cool against her palms. She hesitated, unwilling to allow him a deeper kiss. He pressed the issue and she yielded, using every ounce of her willpower to not push him away.

Outwardly to the non-magickal world, Stefan was a benevolent social icon, known for his goodwill and his generosity. In reality, as head of the Duskoff Cabal, the violent little club warlocks kept, he pillaged and plundered his way through witches as though they were his personal stockyard, slaughtering here and there when he felt like it.

Like any sociopath worth his salt, Stefan was a charming, handsome monster. The world should thank her for what she was about to do, even though she'd had to turn her back on the Coven Rede to accomplish it.

He leaned in toward her, burying his nose in the curve of

her neck and sliding a hand past the hem of her short, black Versace. "We're finally alone," he whispered, "as you requested." The car pulled forward, rocking her against his body.

She tilted his face to hers and kissed him, pressing herself into the curve of his body. She cupped his groin through his black pants and felt his hardness. "So we are."

"Then why so shy? Tonight you will not escape me, Isabelle," he breathed against her skin with his smooth French accent.

Part of her plan had been to tease him sexually. It had been a little like taunting a starving tiger with a slab of meat, but she'd been successful. It had hooked him, made him want her more . . . and allowed her limited intimate contact with him. A definite plus.

She raised an eyebrow. "I think it's *you* who won't escape *me*, Stefan." If only he knew. She unbuttoned his pants. "Take them off."

He grasped the hem of her skirt. "You first," he purred.

"Noooo, you," she shot back coyly.

He shook his head. "Take off your dress for me, Isabelle." His voice held a thread of steel and his eyes had a brutally cold glint in them.

Her sly, sexy smile faltered. Damn it! This was not going the way she'd envisioned it. In her head, she'd been fully clothed when she brought him down. Having no choice unless she wanted to raise suspicion, she allowed him to draw her dress over her head, leaving her in only a lacy red bra and panty set and her shoes.

"Mmm," he murmured in appreciation right before he pressed his lips to the swell of her breast. *Oh, yeech. Yeech, yeech, yeech!*

She yanked him forward by the waistband of his pants and kissed him roughly, biting his lower lip hard. He jerked a little and she tasted blood. "Off now," she commanded.

"I adore a woman who likes it a little rough."

Then he'd love her.

He slipped his shoes and pants off. She glanced down and lifted a brow as if in sexual anticipation. He gave her a cocky smile, the smile of a man who's sure he's about to get laid. How wrong could he be? He was about to find out. She reached out and took him in her hand.

And she squeezed. Hard.

TWO

At the same time, she flooded her body with magick. It exploded from the center of her chest with a warm pulse. Power shot down her arm, centering in her fingers. They tingled and twitched as she fought to retain the heavy burst of emotion-drenched magick. The water in his groin responded instantly to her will, the molecules jumping to do her bidding. They grew cold, then even colder.

Stefan's eyes bulged out of his head and shock took his expression from arousal to terror in under a quarter second. A soundless scream erupted from his mouth, his lips forming an O of unvoiced pain.

"I thought you liked it rough, Stefan?" she asked through gritted teeth. She had him right where she wanted him. She'd known she'd had to get him by the balls . . . literally. There was no other way to trap a warlock as powerful as he was. She'd needed to get close enough to get him in a susceptible position, without his hired muscle present, make him let down his guard and then take advantage of his vulnerability.

She squeezed the soft flesh of that vulnerability in her hand a little tighter. "Awww . . . not having fun? I'm sorry." She twisted until he gasped. "*Really.*"

Stefan made a gurgling noise somewhere in his throat.

"Does it frighten you to stare into the eyes of your own mortality, Stefan? Do you ever wonder what happens to us when we die? Do we blink out like a light, or do we live on?"

She paused, tilting her head to the side. "Is death only another life? Hmm . . . what do you think?"

"I don't . . . know," he gritted out.

"I think you're about to find out."

"Who . . . are you?" His lips formed the words, but there wasn't enough breath to give them life. She eased up a little. He'd pass out otherwise and it was too soon for that.

"That is not the relevant question at this juncture. The real question is about Angela, Stefan."

Confusion clouded his eyes.

Oh, that was the *wrong* answer. Power flared down her arm, making her fingers ache. His head snapped back in pain and she forcibly eased up on him.

"Angela?" he gasped.

"Angela Novak. The last witch murdered by your demon." She clamped down harder. "You can't even remember her name?"

His lips peeled back in a grimace. "Not . . . my . . . demon."

"Well, no. Maybe not technically. Your father, William Crane, raised the demon that killed Angela. Crane and his minions. But your father is dead and you've taken his place at the head of the Duskoff. The Duskoff is the reason the demon exists in this dimension. Therefore, the Duskoff is responsible for Angela's death and the death of Melina Andersen, the first witch the demon killed."

"But I wasn't with the Duskoff then."

"Oh, spare me. You've done enough horrible things to warrant this, Stefan, and don't try to tell me you wouldn't raise another demon if you could."

"No," he whispered, his head falling back from the pain.

"No? What do you mean, Stefan? Wasn't it you who was going to sacrifice those four witches last winter to pull a demon through? If it wasn't for the Coven, you would have succeeded. That alone makes you deserving of punishment." She cocked her head to the side. "And aside from all that, what about Naomi Nelson, that earth witch you roasted when you were eighteen? What about Robin Taylor—"

He pulled his head forward and focused on her. "I can help you. Help . . . help find the demon. Right the . . . wrong."

He was making bargains now, was he? How dare he try.

She opened her mouth to respond, but heat flared white-hot against her palm. They both cried out in pain. Isabelle snatched her scorched hand away. Damn it, she'd lost focus for a moment and he'd taken control from her.

Stefan rolled to the side, his hand between his legs, cupping his privates. Her hand hurt like she'd been holding it over a flame, but he had to be in more agony than she was. He'd burned himself in a very sensitive place in order to unseat her.

Isabelle raised power as fast as she could, despite the pain. The air crackled as Stefan also drew magick to defend himself. In the same moment, the entire limo lurched to the side. Isabelle slammed against the opposite seat and cried out as her back twisted. The limo came to a swerving, squealing, smoke-under-the-tires halt. She fell to the floor of the limo, her face contorting from the pain searing down her leg and through her lower back.

She glanced up through her tangled dark red hair, seeing Stefan kneeling on the floor of the vehicle in front of her, looking as though he might retch. Outside the sounds of boots pounding on pavement and shouting reached her ears.

Fighting through the discomfort, she resumed drawing magick and directed it at Stefan. Sensing the swift buildup within the confines of the limo, his head snapped up and he also tapped power. The air snapped with electricity from their combined efforts. It was a magickical showdown and they were both battling through injuries.

But his were worse.

Isabelle shot her hand out in a near unconscious effort to increase her power, commanding the water in Stefan's body to do her bidding—to freeze.

The limo door opened. Confusion and fury from the unknown observers pressed against her empathy. The intense emotions around her settled like a bitter wine on the back of her tongue, but she focused all her attention on Stefan.

"No," came a commanding male voice. "Stop it now."

She ignored the order. Stefan's spine snapped back as she intensified the freezing process. She had him now and, dear

Lady, it had to hurt. It was nothing compared to what the demon had done to Angela, though.

Her sister had died the one way she'd always feared, by a demon's hand. Angela had had nightmares about that since she'd been a child, after one of their "uncles" had related to them how demons killed their victims.

Isabelle had been the one to find her body, but she still couldn't bring herself to visit those memories. Not in detail. Her mind had blocked them and she was grateful for that.

In front of her, Stefan keened.

Funny, Isabelle thought she'd feel satisfaction when this moment came, perhaps a release and a lifting of the heavy emotion that had weighed her down for so long. But she felt none of those things. She only felt sorrow.

"This is for Angela, Stefan," she said woodenly. "This is my sister saying hello from the grave."

Where was the fulfillment she thought she'd feel? Where was the righteous justification? She stared into Stefan's eyes, watching pain explode his pupils. Her magickal grip faltered. She couldn't do this . . . Damn it!

From her left, a man approached her. "Isabelle," he said gently. "He's the scum of the earth, but he didn't kill your sister."

Her face contorted, her eyes filling with tears. "He did. He's the head of the Duskoff. Without the Duskoff, the demon wouldn't exist."

"I'm asking you for the last time. Stop."

This revenge, once a red-hot, pulsing, living thing in her heart and mind, now tasted bitter and cold.

Still . . . *Angela*.

"I can't," she whispered. "I can't stop."

The man threw himself at her, breaking her hold on Stefan. Pain cut up her spine and down her legs, making her cry out, but she still fought the heavy weight on top of her. He pinned her down, struggling to gain control of her limbs. Exhaustion and her back injury forced her to go passive. Her magick sparked and died in her chest, spent like a candle burned too long. She made a choking sound of grief.

He stared down at her, his face shadowed by a long fall of

blue black hair. Thomas Monahan, head of the Coven. The hair branded him. She didn't even need to see his face.

She winced and let out a small sob. "It's because of him, because of the Duskoff, that my sister is dead."

"He won't get away with what he's done, Isabelle," came his low voice. "But his punishment can't be like this."

"How do you know my name?"

Behind them she could hear witches subduing Stefan. The limo rocked with the motion. "You said you're Angela's sister. I can only assume you mean Angela Novak, the water witch who was killed by a demon a couple of months ago. That makes you Isabelle. We're on the same side. If I let you up, will you be good?"

Her mouth snapped shut and she nodded.

He moved away from her, Monahan's face—set in handsome, brutal lines—finally coming into view. She glanced around the limo's interior, seeing Adam Tyrell and Jack McAllister, both fire witches she was well acquainted with. The two men restrained the injured Stefan, who wasn't fighting anymore. He knelt with his hands between his legs, looking like the only battle he could wage was against unconsciousness.

"We are not on the same side," she growled at Thomas. "You are preventing me from—"

"Taking your revenge. I know."

"I didn't kill her sister," spat Stefan.

Thomas cast a look at Stefan that reminded Isabelle of how a cat might regard a worm, beneath his bother but something interesting to play with. "In general I'd prefer Stefan dead," he drawled, "but we need him."

Cradling her injured hand, Isabelle only glowered at him through her hair in response. She sought Monahan's emotions, but got nothing more than a flicker. Either she was too tired to sense them or he was hellishly repressed.

"Ah, Isabelle? Not that I mind the view, but . . ." Adam looked at her pointedly, helping her remember her state of undress.

She glanced down, registering her lack of clothing. In her rage, that little detail had been lost. Hell. Could anything more go wrong?

Making sure Jack had ahold of Stefan, Adam tossed her dress to her and she gingerly slid it over her head, wincing at the pain in her back.

Thomas jerked his head at Stefan. "Incapacitate him for transportation."

Jack stared down at Stefan—his expression dangerously dark. For a moment Isabelle wondered what he'd do. The warlock had tried to kill Jack's girlfriend last winter.

Jack glanced pointedly at Stefan's privates. "You should see a doctor about that." Then he punched him—hard. Stefan slumped to the floor of the limo, unconscious.

"You could've just drugged him," said Thomas with a twist to his lips.

Jack glared down at Stefan. "That was one option."

"You could've just let me kill him, too," Isabelle added. "That would have been much less trouble for everyone. I know I would have been far happier."

Thomas turned and regarded her with eyes that seemed blacker than obsidian. They were unsettling, yet beautiful, and they matched the hair that swirled around his shoulders. The man truly did look like a witch—a very, very wicked one. "Really? That would have made you happy, Isabelle? Tell the truth."

She glanced away from him, suddenly feeling far more naked under his gaze than when she'd been undressed.

The head of the Coven was better looking in person than he was in his pictures, like some beautiful fallen angel, although the rough-hewn lines of his face saved him from the more perfect type of male prettiness. His sensual, lush mouth seemed at odds with the rest of him, set with deep lines on either side. He had a powerfully built body, long of leg and broad of shoulder. Every inch of that massive body had been pressed against her and it had hurt. Her back twinged with the memory and she grimaced.

"So how's it going, Isabelle? Long time, no see," said Adam as though they'd met up by chance at Starbucks or something.

Her lips turned up in a smile. Grinning at Adam Tyrell was something you had to do because of his charm, especially if you were female. Even under these circumstances, she couldn't help it. "Not too great, Adam."

"Get him out of here," Thomas growled at Adam. He turned to Jack. "Can you heal her back and hand?"

"Isabelle's hand and back, yes. Stefan's dick, no. My hands aren't going anywhere near that."

"We'll let Stefan heal on his own, I think. It's the least he deserves."

Adam heaved Stefan out of the limo and Thomas followed, casting one piercing look at her over his shoulder before he went. "I want to talk to you. Don't disappear."

She narrowed her eyes at his back. Asshole! He had no right to order her around. She'd left the Coven. Hell, what she'd just done made her a flat-out warlock. Thomas Monahan held no power over her.

"Give me your hand," said Jack.

She unlocked her jaw and raised her hand, shifting gingerly on the floor of the limo and snagging the heel of her shoe in the carpet.

He took her hand between his palms. Jack was a fire witch and, therefore, could heal. She'd always found it odd that the power resided in such a destructive element. Her hand grew warm, tingled, and the pain receded. When he released her, the skin was pink and healing quickly. He jerked his chin at the seat. "Sit down with your back to me."

Carefully, she pushed up and slid onto the seat. Ripples of pain shot through her back and down her legs. She blew out a careful breath as nausea swamped her.

Jack sat behind her and placed his palms along her spine, one above the other. His hands, completely businesslike on her back, grew warm. Her twisted back improved immediately. "I don't remember your hair being this dark a shade of red or your eyes being green, Isabelle."

"I colored my hair and I'm wearing contacts."

"All the better to stalk your prey, hmm?"

"I guess. Stefan prefers redheads."

"Good disguise. None of us recognized you in the tabloids. We didn't know who you were, or that you were even a witch.

It wasn't until tonight, when we saw you up close, that we realized your identity. All we knew was that this evening Stefan's flavor-of-the-month had finally convinced him to shed his bodyguards for sex."

She let out a small laugh. "You guys were piggybacking my seduction as a way to take Stefan hostage?"

"Yep. We were watching, waiting for an opportunity. You gave us a surprise when we opened the limo door. Never saw that one coming." He paused. "I'm sorry about your sister. I understand why you went after Stefan."

She had a million questions, but they all caught in her throat. They were questions for the head of the Coven, anyway, not Jack McAllister, Thomas's right-hand man. "I hunted the demon for a month and couldn't find it."

"We've been hunting it, too, without any luck."

"I went after the cause for the demon's existence instead." She swallowed hard. "I just . . . needed to do something, and Stefan can't be allowed to bring any more of those creatures into our world."

Jack slid away and she turned toward him on the seat. Her back still ached, but the worst of the pain had faded.

"Isabelle, I get that. I do. But you should have come to us instead of playing vigilante. We'd always planned to take down Stefan and we're going after the demon." Jack shook his head and *tch tched*. "Bad, bad girl."

"So what's new?" she muttered in response. Angela had always been the good one. Isabelle had always been the one getting into trouble.

He must've known she wasn't asking what was new *with him*, but he answered that way all the same. "I'm going to be a father." The words were spoken with such pride that she smiled.

She fussed with the hem of her skirt, happy to change the subject. "I heard that. Knocked up that little air witch of yours."

"Mira."

Lady, the look in his eyes when he said her name. Such love. Such devotion. A man had never looked that way while speaking *her* name, at least not that she knew of, and Isabelle had to admit that a part of her regretted it.

"That's right, her name is Mira," Isabelle answered. "Everyone's hoping she'll turn up with a baby air witch of her own." Of all the elemental witches, air was by far the rarest and most powerful. "What do you think, air or fire?"

"I think she'll take after her mom and be an air witch. We're going to name her Eva, for Mira's mom if it's a girl. David, for her dad if it's a boy."

Eva Hoskins, maiden name Monahan. She had been the air witch who'd been sacrificed in the circle that had brought the demon into existence over twenty-five years ago. Four witches—one for each of the elements—had been killed to bring in the demon who had murdered Angela. How poetic one of their names should be spoken on this night.

She patted him on his shoulder. "Good luck to you both." She scooped up her purse from the floor of the limo and exited the vehicle.

Isabelle found herself on a darkened side street in a commercial part of town. The front of the limo had been rammed in by a Hummer. Behind the limo was another car crash, a tangle of metal where sedan had met heavy SUV. The sedan had been the vehicle carrying Stefan's muscle.

She cast a glance at Stefan, whom they were lifting into the back of Thomas's car. Thomas stood nearby. He stared at her across the distance, his black-as-sin hair spread over his shoulders, his expression intent. Then he crooked a finger.

Oh, no. Hell would freeze over first.

Isabelle gave him a little wave and walked away.

"Isabelle," he called after her. "I need to talk to you."

Ignoring him, she turned a corner and pulled on her remaining magickal reserves, scraping the very bottom of her capacity. Isabelle gathered water molecules from the air, condensing them around dust particles and cloaking herself in the resulting thick fog. By the time she heard his footsteps behind her, she'd disappeared, leaving him standing in zero visibility.

Thomas swore loudly and Isabelle smiled. She needed to talk to him, but she wasn't about to do it on his terms.

THREE

SHE LOOKED BETTER AS A BLONDE.

Thomas stepped into the Coven library, a room that also served as his office and took stock of the woman sitting on his desk, one of her long legs swinging. He'd been expecting Isabelle Novak to show up sometime.

In order to figure out how no one had recognized her while she'd been beguiling Stefan, he'd had Jack show him pictures of her when she wasn't all glossy and polished for Stefan's liking. Now she looked more like herself. She'd changed her hair back to its natural color, a strawberry blond, and wore a pair of faded jeans, a black knit top and a pair of scuffed black boots.

Normally she wasn't this gaunt. Thomas suspected she'd purposely lost weight in order to insinuate herself into Stefan's world. Or perhaps grief had shaved some pounds off her. In his opinion, she looked better with a little more weight on her.

Her hair was long and glossy, framing an oval face with porcelain skin and large brown eyes. Her mouth was full, expressive. She wore nearly no makeup and did little to her hair beyond brush it. She had a natural type of beauty that required little embellishment and seemed to care nothing for fashion. Yet she possessed a manner that screamed self-confidence.

Not only was she gorgeous, she looked innocent. Yet Thomas knew better. Miss Isabelle Novak had a reputation for trouble. The research he'd done on her had revealed that right away. From even her earliest days in grade school, Isabelle had left a trail of trouble behind her—getting into fights, talking back to teachers. Her older years revealed a passionate, impulsive woman who couldn't stay in one place, couldn't hold a steady job, couldn't form relationships.

She was also a strong water witch. Thomas could sense the strength in her from across the room. Ripples of volatile emotion, the ebb and flow of psychic power—they were the hallmarks of the water witch and they were impressively palpable in Isabelle Novak.

He closed the door and spoke as he turned toward her. "Violence is an easy way to mourn someone you've lost. Don't you think it's better to save a life in order to honor a life lost?"

She stood, pressed her hands together, and bowed. "Buddha, I'm pleasured to make your acquaintance." She straightened and put a hand to her hip. "I didn't come here for a lecture."

She was pretty. Too bad she was such a pain in the ass.

Thomas squelched his annoyance and walked toward her. "You need to look at the big picture. He can help us—"

"Help us? When does that man start helping anyone but himself? When does he do anything that's not in his own best interests? And when does he pay for his crimes, Mr. Monahan? *When?*"

"Call me Thomas."

"Mr. Monahan, Thomas, whatever." She waved her hand, dismissing his overture. "Are we going to wait for Stefan to die of old age, then? Should we let him get away with everything he's done?"

"Of course not."

"Really? The non-magickals aren't going to touch him, so it falls to *us* to do it, his peers. Yet I haven't seen the Coven or the Council acting to take care of it. Wasn't that one of the reasons why the Coven and Council were created to begin with? Aren't you guys supposed to be handling the warlocks and punishing crimes?" She slammed her hand down on the desk. "He doesn't deserve to live his life any way he sees fit, Thomas."

"If you're finished ranting, can you sit down and listen? I have things to explain. Do you want a drink? I have just about anything you can order in a bar and you look like you could use one."

She shook her head, whirled, and paced to the far floor-to-ceiling window and the high bookshelves that framed it. "I wasted a month of my life preparing to make Stefan pay for what he did to Angela and you come rushing in and snatch it all away from me."

He took his gamble, remembering the quiver of hesitation he'd sensed in her that night and the apprehensive look on her face. She'd been pissed as hell, but unsure about actually killing Stefan. "How did it feel, almost taking his life?"

She turned without a moment's uncertainty. "Horrible! It felt horrible. Cold and empty and not at all like I thought."

Of course. Isabelle might want justice for her sister, but she was no murderer. "You hunted the demon, Jack tells me."

"I hunted the demon for over a month after I f-found Angela." She shook her head and hugged herself. "I could find no trace of it anywhere."

"So you went after the person you perceived to be responsible for the demon's existence."

She nodded.

"Please sit down, Isabelle." He nodded at one of the soft leather chairs in front of his desk.

She hesitated a moment, her eyes flashing and probably a few sharp words poised on her tongue. It was clear she didn't like authority and perceived him as such. Still, she swallowed what she was about to say, walked across the room and sank into the chair.

Thomas sat on the edge of the desk in front of her. "It is our intention to catch and kill this demon, Isabelle. The Council has had a directive to apprehend Stefan ever since the incident last winter. We've been watching him for a long time, waiting for him to relax and let his guard down. You helped us to finally get him. He's in Gribben now, in *prison*. We're not going to let him out. Ever."

"Jack told me, but—"

"*But* Stefan needs to stay alive. At least for now. He can help us apprehend the demon by providing information. The Duskoff are the people who have had the most interaction with demons. They've studied them in order to understand the creatures they're using. After he's helped us, he'll stand trial for his crimes, along with the thirteen other warlocks who participated in the circle last winter at Duskoff International. They will be tried and punished. That means either life imprisonment or death."

She snorted and crossed her arms over her chest. "I'll believe it when I see it."

He sighed. "Don't make the mistake of thinking you're the only one who wants to see Stefan pay. And don't think you're the only one who wants that demon dead."

"What did Stefan do to you?"

"Well, he tried to kill my cousin last winter for starters."

"Mira Hoskins."

He nodded. "And the first witch the demon killed, Melina, she was someone I knew." He paused. She had been an old lover. It had been a long time ago, but Melina had been special to him. "She was a good friend. She had kids, a husband."

Isabelle was silent a long moment before she spoke. "Do you think the demon picked her on purpose? It's a strange coincidence she should be an old friend of the leader of the Coven."

"That's exactly why we need all the information from Stefan that we can gather. We don't know how or why the demon is picking his victims at this point. We don't know much of anything beyond the fact that the demon is killing witches."

She chewed her lower lip, deep in thought. "Usually the demons the Duskoff raise have their fun and go home. They don't stick around for twenty-five years hiding, then all of a sudden pop up and start killing off witches."

"We've just noticed the demon never returned to his dimension, but the Coven archivist is going through old newspapers and finding evidence the demon hasn't been *hiding* at all. We think he's been killing humans for sport the entire time. We just never noticed him until he started targeting witches so heinously."

"Yeah, *heinous* is one word for it." Her hands tightened so hard on the arms of the chair they turned white. "He's been killing the witches in some kind of demon ritual, hasn't he? He's stealing their power for something."

"We think so, but we're not sure. All of this is reason to use Stefan to gain information. He knows more about demons and their world than we do and it's imperative we find and kill this demon before he murders more people."

"So you think we can find him." Her tone was caustic. "Thomas, that demon has disappeared. I've moved heaven and hell trying to locate the monster. I have dedicated every waking breath to it since Angela was killed. All I want in this universe is to rid the world of that thing and prevent any more witches from being murdered."

He folded his hands together. "And maybe with Stefan and the Duskoff's information, we can accomplish that."

Her mouth snapped shut. "You're the boss, I guess. You're the head of the Coven, after all. You must know best." Her tone clearly said she didn't believe that.

"I'm sorry for your loss, Isabelle, and I understand your need to punish someone. However, we need to put our emotions on hold right now and proceed rationally."

"Yes, empathically I can tell you're good at that. Putting your emotions on hold."

"And I don't need any empathic ability to tell you're not."

She turned an interesting, angry, shade of red. "You think I'm not acting rationally?"

"No, I was speaking in general terms, about all of us. We all want revenge, Isabelle. We all want to punish this demon, but we need to make our moves carefully."

"But you believe I don't have a good handle on my emotions."

"You strike me as a passionate person and I think you're grieving. But I believe if you consider what Stefan can bring to us in the long run, you'll see that we need to keep him alive, no matter what our hearts want." He paused. "Anyway, I don't think you have a revenge killing in you, Isabelle. That's a compliment, by the way."

Thomas had never seen such warm brown eyes go so cold, so fast. Her beautiful face tightened as she stared at him for a long moment before speaking. "I see your point but that doesn't mean I have to like it. By the way, I don't appreciate the psychoanalysis, since I never asked for it."

"I call things the way I see them," he answered with a shrug.

She stood. "I like you, but you're kind of a prick. Do you know that?"

"So I've been told. Numerous times."

"I'm sorry you lost an old friend."

He glanced away, his jaw tightening. "Me, too. I'm sorry about your sister."

She walked to him, so close he could see the pain in her eyes when she answered softly, "Thank you."

They stood in silence for a moment. The woman had beautiful eyes, like melted chocolate. They were back to warm again. She leaned forward, so close he could smell her musky perfume as she cocked her head to the side. "Do you even have pupils?"

He blinked in surprise. "Last time I checked."

She stared into his eyes for a moment and her lips parted. Her head dipped a little closer to his and her gaze dropped to his mouth. For one wild moment he thought she might kiss him.

For the next wild moment he thought he might kiss her.

Where that impulse came from, he wasn't sure. Maybe it was the water-earth attraction affecting him. Earth and water had a natural sexual attraction sometimes, as did fire and air. It lasted until the magicks found a balance. He'd felt that artificial pull toward Isabelle ever since the limo.

Or maybe it had simply been too long since he'd been with a woman.

She straightened and backed away, breaking the strange, momentary spell. "Did you even notice I was nearly naked in the limo?"

He cleared his throat. "There were other concerns." He paused. "But, yes, I noticed. It would have been impossible not to notice." Those long legs, that flawless pale skin and the fullness of her breasts swelling from her silky demi bra. Thomas might be head of the Coven, but he was a man first.

A satisfied little smile flickered across her lips. "Good." She turned toward the door.

What a strange woman. "Stay," he said simply before she could leave.

She turned back around slowly, wearing a questioning expression.

"Stay here at the Coven for a while. Work with us. Help us deal with Stefan. Help us find the demon."

Isabelle Novak possessed abilities uncommon to most water witches. Not only could she manipulate the water in a man's body—a deadly skill she'd demonstrated readily on Stefan—she could access moisture memory, tapping into the water of a given area and replaying recent events. She could be valuable to them.

She pursed her lips and thought about it for a moment. "You'll make me play nice."

He smiled. "I'll make you play effectively, not necessarily nicely."

"I want to be in on any official Coven communication with Stefan. Any contact you have with him in Gribben, I want to be present."

Thomas rubbed a hand over his chin for a moment, thinking over the issue. "I don't see why not."

She considered him, worrying at her lower lip between her white teeth. "Give me time to tie up a few loose ends and I'll come in."

Absurdly, he wondered what kind of "ends" she meant. He knew she wasn't married, but did she have a boyfriend?

Damn it, why did he care?

He nodded. "Just tell them who you are at the front gate and Douglas will meet you. He manages the house. When you return there will be a room ready for you."

"And a prisoner to torture." She clapped her hands together and rubbed them with glee. "If we play good cop, bad cop, can I be the bad cop?"

"After what you did to his dick, Stefan probably thinks you're the baddest thing around."

She smiled broadly. "Now I can die happy."

Lady, what had he just done?

FOUR

ISABELLE ENTERED HER SISTER'S POSH CONDO IN Lincoln Park, the rich scent of vanilla and roses enveloping her as soon as she stepped within. She'd been staying there since Angela had died and still burned her sister's favorite candles every morning in a vigil of sorts.

She set her keys down on the bar that separated the gourmet kitchen and large living room and glanced around at the homey furnishings. The place was decorated in calming blues and silvers, filled to bursting with overstuffed couches and chairs, soft throw blankets and plush area rugs covering the shining hardwood floors. Soothing modern artwork adorned the walls, pastel colors swooping and arcing across the canvases.

This place was Angela. It embodied her very spirit—cool, composed, emotionally centered, and sensitive. It didn't really suit Isabelle's personality, but she wished it did. She wished she had a few more of her sister's qualities, rather than their mother's. Angela must have inherited her easygoing calmness from her father, whoever he'd been. Angela's father hadn't been the same as Isabelle's. Their mother, Catalina, got around.

Isabelle slipped her shoes off and unstrapped the small, pretty knife with the copper blade she wore sheathed to her wrist. Laying it on the counter, she ran her finger over the swoops and whorls engraved in the handle. Angela had given Isabelle the knife after a trip she'd taken to Peru. Isabelle had been wearing it to demon-hunt ever since Angela's murder. Not built for anything more than looks, it was really just a symbolic gesture. A nod to her sister.

After fishing a pint of Chunky Monkey out of the recesses of the freezer and grabbing a spoon, she padded across the area rug in the living room to the window that overlooked the heavily tree-lined street below. There she stood and contentedly picked out the chocolate chunks from the banana ice cream while she watched a woman with a stroller walk by, men in business suits arriving home after a day at the office, and kids coming home from school.

Normal people with normal lives.

Angela hadn't been killed in her condo. Rather, the demon had followed her to her work, a law office, no less. Angela had been a defense attorney, specializing in the magickally inclined. Witchdom had such professionals across all aspects of society, helping hide their existence from non-magickals—the normal people with normal lives.

Knowledge of their existence only brought fear and burnings, history had shown that amply enough. There weren't enough witches in the world to fight against what might happen if their existence was discovered. Elemental witches were woefully outnumbered so they did all they could to hide.

Since both bodies murdered by the demon so far had been found by witches, the Coven was handling the crimes internally, within witchdom, and would do so for as long as possible. There was no need to involve non-magickal authorities, who would have no way to pursue the killer or investigate the paranormal crimes. The non-magickal police force would only end up hindering things.

Earth magick cleaned up the site and the victim was reported missing to the non-magickal authorities. Rites and burials were performed by the victim's magickal kindred. Most witches made out special wills with the Coven that were handled within witchdom as well. So when a witch died as violently as Angela had. . . .

Isabelle closed her eyes, unable to make her mind go there. She still couldn't bring herself to remember what she'd found when she'd entered the law office to pick her sister up for a late dinner. Her mind went white when she ventured any-where close to those horrible memories.

Hungry no longer, Isabelle set the ice cream container on the windowsill in front of her.

Angela had been her only relative of consequence. Not only that, she'd really been Isabelle's only friend. Their mother was still alive, but she didn't know where Catalina was or how to get into direct contact with her.

Catalina wasn't the warmest of mothers. She flitted around the world, hopping from one meaningless relationship to the next. She didn't even know her eldest daughter had died yet. Isabelle had left messages with some of her mother's male friends in Europe, but who knew when she'd contact any of them?

No, there was not much mother-daughter affection be-tween herself and Catalina. The only way their mother knew how to express her love was through money. Catalina had set her daughters up nicely in that way, but true motherly guid-ance, compassion, or caring lay beyond her grasp. Isabelle had heard her mother express sentiments of love for them a few times in her life, but she wasn't sure Catalina really meant it. As they'd been growing up, her older sister had filled the place for Isabelle where their mother had been absent. Most called Catalina a *charming free spirit*; Isabelle called her de-tached and selfish.

And yet, these days Isabelle seemed to be much like Catalina, a fact she'd only become aware of recently. The last person Isabelle wanted to turn into was her mother. The very thought gave her hives. It had been why she'd been in town to visit Angela. Isabelle had been seeking counsel from her calm, steadfast sister. Counsel Angela had never been able to give.

Without Angela, Isabelle felt adrift.

Although even in death Angela had given her an anchor. In her will, executed by the Coven, Angela had left her condo, all her belongings, and financial assets to Isabelle.

Isabelle turned and glanced around the living room. Now she had a *home*. She hadn't had an actual residence since . . . ever. In childhood she'd never known what it was like to live in the same place for more than a year or two at a stretch.

In adulthood, Isabelle had always prided herself on being able to pack all her belongings into a suitcase. She lived in hotels and rented villas wherever she traveled. Having this condo meant she could no longer do that unless she sold it. Selling it, since it had been Angela's, was out of the question.

So, in a way, she was no longer free.

At the thought, her throat closed up and her heart pounded. A memory swelled. Closing her eyes, she took a deep, hitching breath, relegating that old pain to the same place where her sister's mangled body lay. The deep recesses. The small, dark places she never ventured. It was better that way. Far safer.

Isabelle stayed away from small, dark places.

Isabelle shook her head and swore under her breath. She did not need this self-indulgent shit right now! It was time to pack a bag, pay some bills, and get a good night's sleep. Tomorrow she was leaving for the Coven.

After stuffing the ice cream container back in the freezer, she pulled a duffle bag from the hall closet, laid it on the bed in the master bedroom and started packing.

When Thomas Monahan had offered her the chance to come to the Coven and aid in finding the demon, Isabelle's heart had leapt into her throat with joy. She'd acted cool and a little reserved in accepting the offer, but there had been no chance in hell she would've turned him down. The Coven had far more resources than she had on her own.

She shoved some clothes into the duffle bag and then stood there, her mind suddenly awash in thoughts of Thomas Monahan. He was an interesting man, the head of the Coven. Unyielding and a control-freak. She could see *that* in every inch of his ultrafine, muscled body, even if she hadn't known him by reputation.

And Thomas Monahan had *quite* the rep in the witch world. Protective to a fault, stubborn, quick to temper, and totally devoted to his responsibilities. From what she'd heard, the man didn't have a life outside of his job. He'd devoted everything, every aspect of himself, to the Coven.

In witchdom, he was famous, or infamous, depending on one's particular point of view. A witch didn't cross Thomas Monahan and get away with it. Plus, he could be very Machiavellian in his protection of the Coven. That's why she didn't like that he had control of Stefan. She wanted Stefan punished, but if Thomas saw a more pragmatic path, a deal to cut that might help the Coven, Isabelle worried he'd take it. That's why she'd made Thomas agree she be there during any Coven dealings with Stefan. She wanted to make sure nothing like that happened.

She couldn't believe she'd been the one to allow them to finally capture the head of the Duskoff. Seems she'd been working with the Coven all along without knowing it.

She finished packing, paid some bills, and finally turned off the lights and snuggled into bed. Angela's bed. Despite everything, Isabelle had been sleeping better here than anywhere else she could recall. Maybe because Angela's energy still clung to this apartment, to these pieces of furniture, the blankets and sheets that now covered her. She'd miss the place when she was at the Coven.

With Thomas Monahan. His face flashed into her mind as she closed her eyes: his full mouth, his blacker-than-black eyes. Monahan was a good-looking man and she was not immune. Normally, a man like Thomas—controlling and single-minded—would turn her off. In the past she'd gravitated more toward artistic types: painters, musicians, and writers. But Thomas Monahan wore those type A qualities strangely well. He intrigued her. As a result, she found herself powerfully drawn to him, more than the natural water/earth magnetism should engender.

Earth witches were plentiful, so she frequently ran into male earth witches to whom she was attracted on a physical level. It was a phenomenon she'd grown used to dealing with and it usually faded quickly once a balance of magicks was found. What she felt for Thomas Monahan was far, far stronger than anything she'd experienced before.

She wondered if he felt it, too.

Remembering the hungry way he'd looked at her in the library earlier that day, Isabelle decided he did.

But how to deal with it? She'd gladly sleep with him if that would help. Isabelle had a feeling one night with that particular witch would blow her mind. She'd like to find out if her hunch was correct. Yet they'd be working together, so maybe it wasn't the best notion she'd had all day.

Not that she was having particularly good notions lately.

Sighing, she tried to calm her mind enough to sleep. She tuned into the water in her body, sensing it like the ocean. She concentrated on the rise and fall of her breath and the gentle rush of the blood through her veins. Eventually sheer fatigue dragged her under with heavy hands. Her body relaxed into sleep.

But nightmares caught her instantly.

The smell of must and mothballs stung her nose. Did spiders have a scent? She swore she could detect the fragrance of their frail, dry bodies in the recesses of this place, where fabric brushed her cheeks, and hunger gnawed at her stomach. Despair and sharp-edged fear overwhelmed her and she clawed and beat on the door until she was too weak to do it any longer.

Still no one came.

"No!"

Isabelle sat straight up in bed with her heart pounding and tears streaming down her face. Grief twisted cold and empty through her stomach, weighed heavy in her chest. The sensation made her dizzy and sick.

Just like when she'd been a child.

Breathing hard and shaking, she glanced at the clock. She'd only been asleep ten minutes. Isabelle drew her knees up and covered her eyes with her hands. REM didn't happen that soon after one fell asleep. How had she dreamed?

Especially about that.

A whimpering sound reached her ears and it took a second for her to realize it came from her. She hadn't had those dreams in years. Lord and Lady, she thought for sure she'd gotten past all that. Frustrated with herself and her weakness, she squeezed her eyes shut, banishing the memory to the recesses of her mind.

This had *to stop. The past was the past. Period. Move on, Isabelle.*

Her heart rate slowly returned to normal and Isabelle became aware of a smell amidst the vanilla and lavender, a scent that shouldn't be there—a dry, earthy fragrance, almost like incense but a little more acrid. A little like how she'd imagined spiders might smell when she'd been a child. It was faint, but definitely there.

Movement out of the corner of her eye. A large shadow, darting.

She turned her head just in time to see a figure flit across the bedroom balcony past the sheer curtains and beyond the sliding glass door . . . no *through* the sliding glass door.

Isabelle threw the blankets back and lunged out of bed. She reached the patio door in a few long strides. Whipping the curtains to the side, she looked past the pane of glass to the dark sky. No one stood on the balcony. Nothing there.

She fumbled with the lock, slid the door to the side and stepped outside. The warm wind whipped around her bare body as she examined the balcony. The condo was on the fifteenth floor. The only place for the figure to have gone was straight up to the balcony above. She gazed skyward, but saw nothing.

There had been *something*, though. She knew she hadn't imagined it. Unless the dream had shaken her so badly, she'd hallucinated. But was it possible to hallucinate a scent? And a scent as strange as that? Like earth, but not of *this* Earth.

Isabelle shivered, despite the warm air. She stood for a moment, staring out into the darkness. Somewhere in the distance, thunder boomed.

A storm was coming.

FIVE

❦

THOMAS WAITED IN THE RECESSES OF GRIBBEN
Prison for Isabelle to arrive. Micah, his cousin, stood near him.

The building was named for the Coven director who'd had
it built on the sprawling Coven-owned lands. The Council had
decided long ago that witches who harmed others could not
be allowed to roam free in non-magickal society. First, they
posed a threat to witchdom by calling attention to themselves.
Second, non-magickals were ill-equipped to protect themselves
against a witch with a will to harm.

The Coven had a contingent trained to deal with those who
broke the rules they called witch hunters. Wayward witches
were tracked down and killed outright by Coven hunters if
they posed an immediate danger to others. Witches guilty of
lesser crimes or only suspected of violence were caught and
brought in to stand trial. If the witch was found guilty, he was
housed in Gribben, an underground facility with wardings and
spellcastings cemented right into the construction by some of
the best earth witches to ever live.

Here, no witch could use magick—not the tenants, not the
caretakers or guards, not even visitors. Working here was no
treat, so the employees tended to be witches with little inherited magick, who noticed the loss less. In addition, they only
worked part-time to limit their exposure to the place.

Thomas hated being in Gribben. Crossing the threshold
first made him nauseous, then, as his ability to tap his power
vanished, he began to feel like a piece of melba toast—dry,

flavorless, and easily breakable. It was probably how the non-magickicals felt all the time.

Some of the prisoners went mad from being imprisoned in Gribben and he could see why. The threat of imprisonment here was a very effective incentive to not break Coven law. Because of that, they didn't have a huge problem with offending witches. Only the most incorrigible or crazy ended up in Gribben.

Warlocks, witches who had publicly turned their back on Coven law and made a career of breaking the rede, often found protection within the Duskoff Cabal. The Duskoff was as organized and as powerful as the Coven. Therefore warlocks were difficult to catch. Still there were about twenty warlocks within Gribben's walls . . . along with their leader, Stefan.

"Where the hell is she?" muttered Micah, glancing at his watch.

"What's the matter? Got dust to get back to?"

Micah was the Coven archivist and self-appointed researcher. Thomas's cousin had always been a bookworm and had graduated top of his class at MIT, though at first glance he defied the stereotype of a book geek.

He had the same body that all the males in his family possessed—strong, broad-shouldered, and tall. Micah looked more like a well-built surfer than a scholar. His dark reddish brown hair hung a little past his collar and sharp green eyes and handsome face attracted women, though he didn't know what to do with all that female attention. Womanizer, his cousin was not.

"I just want to get this over with and get the hell out of Gribben. I can't believe you're letting the woman who tried to kill Stefan in cold blood help question him, by the way." Micah shook his head of shaggy hair. "Where does that get productive?"

Thomas shifted and leaned against the wall. "Her attempt wasn't made in cold blood. Trust me, this woman doesn't know the meaning of *cold*."

Micah lifted a copper-colored brow. "So you think she's hot, huh?"

Thomas ignored him. "I suspect she has a hell of a temper,

isn't someone to mess with, and I think she's grieving. I also believe there's something else going on with her, but I'm not sure what."

"What do you mean?"

Thomas shook his head. "I don't know yet. Her records only went back so far. The mother is a wealthy drifter, looks like. She travels all over the world, befriending men of means."

"Prostitute?"

"Maybe not an outright prostitute, but a woman who hunts rich men for money and trinkets. There's no record of a father for either Isabelle or Angela. Either their mother doesn't know who fathered them or it's because Isabelle doesn't have a complete set of records in the archives. I actually thought I'd get you to do some more research on Isabelle and her mother, Catalina Novak. Can you do that? Dig a little deeper than what's there now?"

He shrugged. "I can try."

"I get an intuitive hit off Isabelle. She's got secrets and I think they're the kind deep hurts are made of."

"Why do you care? I mean, why snoop into her past? Why is that relevant?"

Thomas rubbed a hand over his chin. "I want to know what we've just invited onto our team. If she's got a bunch of unresolved issues that are going to muck up our investigation, I want to know about it. Anyway, I don't think Catalina knows her daughter died yet. I thought maybe you might discover her whereabouts while you poke around for information."

"I'll keep an eye out. But that still doesn't explain why you're letting her help question Stefan. She's dragging in a bunch of baggage."

He studied his cousin. Micah's mother, his aunt, had been killed by a warlock when Micah had just been a child. "You have your own issues with the Duskoff and you're here."

He glanced away. "Don't we all?"

"Look, Isabelle spent a long time hunting the demon and struck out, just like us. Her sister was the second witch killed. She has a right to be here."

"Yeah, well, I have a right to not like it," he mumbled.

They looked up at the distant sound of clicking heels on the concrete floor. Isabelle turned a corner and walked toward them, dressed in a scoop-neck red top, faded, close-fitting jeans and a pair of red boots with heels. She wore her hair loose and long, little makeup, and no jewelry.

"Damn, you were right about her being hot," Micah said under his breath.

"I never said that."

"Yeah, whatever. That's why you're practically drooling on the floor right now."

"It's just the water-to-earth attraction. That's all."

Micah gave a derisive snort. "Uh-uh. I think I'm feeling it, too."

Dark circles marked the smooth skin under her eyes and her face was a shade paler than normal. "This place is horrible. It's so bad my skin wants to walk away without me." She shuddered.

Thomas frowned. "You look tired. Are you all right?"

She glanced at him, then at Micah. "I didn't sleep well." She stuck her hand out toward his cousin. "I doubt Thomas will introduce us, so, hello."

Thomas fought the urge to grind his teeth. "Isabelle, this is Micah. He's sort of our official historian and record keeper. We don't know much about the demons, but out of everyone in the Coven, Micah knows the most."

His cousin shook her hand. "Nice to meet you."

"Pleasure. Now, let's get this over with. I've already been in Gribben way too long."

They passed through the set of swinging doors at the end of the hallway and allowed a guard to let them through another set, giving them entrance into the cell block. All the small containment rooms held just one prisoner each.

The chambers were uniformly bare, with only a bed and small bathroom apiece. There were no bars. The place was set up more like a psych ward in a hospital than a traditional prison. The inmates were allowed little to no contact between them and they were never allowed to go outside, not for the entirety of their terms, since outside meant beyond the charmed walls.

"Has anyone ever escaped this place?" asked Isabelle, her

gaze eating up the austere, depressing surroundings with interest. "Bribe a guard? Escape into the ventilation?"

Thomas shook his head. "There have been attempts, none successful."

She glanced up at the white walls and shivered. "If I were an inmate here, I'd spend every second of my time trying to get out."

"*You'd* probably succeed, too."

She gave him a coy glance, big brown eyes warm beneath long ginger-colored lashes. "Flatterer."

Accompanied by two armed guards, they walked to a room at the end of a long corridor and stood in front of a metal door with a viewing slit in the top. One of the guards produced a key and led them inside.

Stefan sat on the bed wearing light gray Gribben prison clothes and soft-soled shoes. He appeared so harmless when he was powerless, just like any other silly, millionaire playboy who'd been naughty and been thrown in county lockup. His pretty boy face wore a morose expression, his shoulders slumped. In a word, he looked humiliated.

Was it an act, or was he genuinely suffering under the burden of having his magick removed? Stefan was an extremely powerful warlock and Gribben tended to be harder on them.

Or maybe he was feeling the injuries Isabelle had dealt him. He'd still be able to sire children, but the doctors said it had been a close thing. The thought of Stefan being a father sent chills through him. Perhaps Isabelle should have been more thorough.

Isabelle and Micah hung back by the door with the guards while Thomas took a few steps into the bare room, the heels of his shoes sounding on the concrete floor. Despite his approach, Stefan only had eyes for Isabelle and they sparked with pure murderous hatred.

Thomas walked into his line of sight, blocking Isabelle's form and forcing Stefan to move his gaze to Thomas's face. He did, slowly.

"Do you know why you're here, Stefan?"

"Because of that bitch." The words were low and clearly pronounced.

"Wrong."

Defiance flared across his face, hot and unrelenting. His blue eyes seemed to burn in his ashen face. It made it clear that, though he may be suffering under the effects of Gribben and from his injuries, Stefan was not down for the count, not by a long shot.

"Do you really think you and your Coven could have taken me, Monahan? I wouldn't be here if it weren't for that bitch of a witch."

"I'd be happy to try and freeze it off again, Stefan," said Isabelle, "if you're not happy with my first attempt."

Stefan bolted toward Isabelle, but the guards aimed their guns at him. The cold, metallic sound of their weapons being repositioned and aimed rooted Stefan in place not far from his bunk. Stefan had no magick to call and he knew it. He slid slowly back to his original spot, his baleful gaze centered on Isabelle.

"If you can't resist goading him, Isabelle, I'll ask you to leave," said Thomas in a low, icy voice without turning around.

"Sorry." She didn't actually *sound* sorry, however.

"Stefan, you're here because you tried to kill four witches in a demon circle last winter and because you're the head of the Duskoff, the organization responsible for the demon currently residing in our dimension."

"I was a child when that demon was birthed. I bear no responsibility."

Thomas ignored him. "You're also here because we need information." He paused. "If we didn't need that information, I would've let Isabelle kill you."

"You want to know about the demon, the one who will not go home," replied Stefan. "If I tell you, will you still kill me?"

"If you cooperate, you buy your life."

Stefan laughed harshly and looked up. "Right. You would not kill me here. Not now, when I am stripped of my magick and defenseless this way. That is against your precious code of conduct. *Harm ye none.* But you don't understand I would rather *die* than stay here in this magickless place. To imprison me here *is* to *harm*, you fool."

Thomas blinked slowly. "You brought it on yourself. Think of it as karma."

"I will not give you anything without receiving something in return."

Thomas had anticipated this, but it made his blood heat all the same. Being divested of his magick had stripped Stefan of his usual bravado, though it was clear that he still possessed his will . . . and his gall.

He took two steps forward and yanked Stefan up by his shirt front. "Didn't you hear me?" his voice shook with emotion, trembled with the restraint it took not to punch Stefan out cold. This warlock had nearly killed his cousin last winter and Thomas took threats to his family very seriously.

"I guess I didn't. Explain it again." A sneer saturated the words.

"You're alive only because of the information you can give us. You will tell us what we want to know without any concessions on our part." He let go. Stefan sat down hard on the bed. "You have no leverage here. You have no *power* here."

Stefan didn't say anything. Didn't even look at Thomas. He simply stared past Thomas at the wall, barely banked rage in his eyes. Stefan looked ready to snap and Thomas wondered for a moment if he would attack him in an attempt to commit suicide by prison warden.

Micah stepped forward impatiently and broke the tension. "Why didn't the demon go home, Stefan? Usually they're yanked through the doorway created in the Duskoff's demon circle, they serve the warlocks, have their fun, and they return to their world. They don't want to spend their entire existence here. So why has this one stayed?"

There were many dimensions that existed alongside Earth, accessed only when an area of the matter that created reality was sped up to the vibrational rate needed to create a breach. When the Duskoff cast a demon circle and sacrificed four witches, one for each of the elements, they used the witches' raped magick to change the frequency of matter to open such a door.

The magick of the warlocks who cast the circle resonated with a specific demon somewhere past the doorway, one that was as malicious and self-serving as the warlocks themselves. Plus, the more powerful the witches sacrificed, the more powerful and evil the demon.

The spell cast by the warlocks dragged the creature through the doorway against its will, essentially kidnapping and enslaving it for a negotiated period of time.

The demons, however, didn't like this place and certainly didn't want to reside here when they had a better-suited environment back home. Historically, they'd come, wreak havoc, shed blood, and go home. The doorways worked that way—demons could return to their dimension once they'd come through, but demons could not, at will, enter this dimension unless a doorway was deliberately created on this side.

The demon they now searched for had been raised in the demon circle that had killed Thomas's Aunt Eva, a powerful air witch who had also been Mira's mother. This demon had elected to reside in this dimension for over twenty-five years.

"I am happy to tell you why it stayed." Stefan gave a short, harsh laugh. "No, I am *proud* to tell you, because this demon is the worst of the worst. The Duskoff raised a magnificent, powerful creature." He raised his gaze and smiled. "It is a credit to our ability."

"What do you mean?" asked Micah.

"We pulled through not just a demon, but a monster. A demon so terrible, who had committed so many atrocious acts in his own dimension, that they shut the door on him."

"Wait a minute. Are you saying this demon couldn't go home even if he wanted to?"

Stefan leaned forward, a satisfied smile playing on his lips. "They don't want him back. This is his prison, his punishment."

SIX

ON THAT COMMENT, THE WHOLE CELL DESCENDED INTO silence for several moments.

Thomas drew a breath. If they hadn't known the demon was bad to the bone already, now they sure did.

"I don't understand why trapping the demon here would be considered a punishment," said Isabelle, finally. "Why wouldn't he want to stay here? Wouldn't this be a big playground for him?"

Micah turned to her. "We suspect the beings we refer to as 'demons' live in a world not much different from ours. They have a culture, a society, laws, everything we have. They mate, they have little baby demons they raise to become big, bad demons. It's their *home*. Here they're just aliens, without freedom, family or friends. Think about it. Would you want to spend your life completely alone in a foreign world? This demon is essentially in exile."

Isabelle hugged herself. "It's just strange to think of them that way, as anything more than primitive monsters."

Micah pushed a hand through his hair. "We believe their society is fairly complex, but we don't know for certain since no human or witch has ever been through a doorway that we know of."

"But we know they have prisons, just like we do," said Stefan tonelessly. "In this case, the Duskoff pulled an inmate from one of them. It freed him. I'm sure he has been contenting himself here well enough."

Contenting himself. Yes, killing people.

"How long has the Duskoff known the demon still resided on this side of the doorway?" asked Thomas. His voice sounded wooden to his own ears because he suspected the Duskoff could've stopped the demon long before now . . . if they'd bothered to try.

Stefan looked up, focused his gaze on Thomas's face and laughed bitterly. "Since it stole our library."

"Explain."

"We had a collection of books—ancient texts on demons the Duskoff has possessed since the Middle Ages. The demon divined the location of the books and came one night. He broke through our magical defenses and stole them all."

"How long ago?" His voice sounded like the lash of a whip in the small room. His fingernails dug into his palms as he fought to restrain himself.

Micah had found at least thirty-five murders of non-magickals the demon may have committed, aside from the two witches, in the time since the Duskoff had brought him into this world.

Stefan blinked, and then gave a slow, self-satisfied smile. "Twenty years ago."

"You bastard!" yelled Isabelle right before she rushed him.

Thomas was tempted to let her go, but he stopped her for her own safety. Stefan had at least a hundred and ten pounds on her, all muscle. She got in one nice punch that whipped Stefan's face to the side before Thomas was able to grab her around the waist and wrench her backward. He swung her around easily as she threw punches in the air, yelling about the murders that could've been prevented if they'd known.

But, of course, Stefan didn't care about that.

Stefan just laughed as Thomas held Isabelle tight against him, allowing her a chance to calm down. She quieted and pushed angrily against his arms. He released her and she stepped away, glaring.

"Soyez gentile, Isabelle! Be nice or I won't tell you where the backup library is," Stefan said, holding a hand to his face where she'd landed her punch. His cold gaze contradicted the amused little smile he wore.

"Why would you tell us where the backup library is?" asked Micah.

Stefan lowered his hand so he could appear offended. "I am not a monster, Micah. I want the demon defeated as well."

Micah snorted. "Yes, that's why the Duskoff did nothing and told no one when they discovered the demon had remained."

"Get me to a computer. Allow me access to the Duskoff's system and you will have our library. We digitized before the books were stolen." He paused and shifted his gaze to Thomas, his tongue stealing out to lick the trickle of blood at the corner of his mouth. "In return, I want you to kill me."

Thomas smiled. "Please, that's too good a deal for us. What game are you playing?"

He shook his head. "You don't understand. I know the Coven wishes me to suffer; therefore they may choose to give me life imprisonment. I would rather die than be imprisoned here in Gribben until the end of my days. So, the deal is simple. I will hand over the digitized library and you will ensure that my trial is short and the sentence I am given is death."

Thomas considered him. In Stefan's place, he might very well be asking for the same thing. "Okay, but you don't die until this is over, until the demon is caught, killed, or vanquished."

A muscle in Stefan's jaw locked. "Fine."

"Micah, you deal with the computer. Stefan doesn't touch it; he only tells you how to access the info."

Stefan opened his mouth to protest and Thomas shut him down with a look.

Micah nodded. "So the bottom line is that we have a demon on the loose, one trapped here against his will. In all the history I've studied, I've never read about something like this. I'm trying to imagine this demon who has been shunned by his people, since his people can only be considered brutal in the best light."

"So we hunt it down and kill it," answered Isabelle. "Seems simple to me."

Micah snorted. "Simple? Can I visit your planet sometime? Must be a nice place."

"I know demons are hard to kill but trust me, honey, I'll kill this one or die in the attempt. What I don't understand is why he's all of a sudden killing witches after so many years. Why attract the Coven's attention *now*? It's almost like he's playing with us, baiting us."

"Maybe he's bored," Micah answered.

"Are you done with me?" Stefan asked with a healthy dose of bitterness. A bruise was already blooming on his face from Isabelle's punch. "I would like to be left alone so I can get a head start on serving my sentence."

"Bored?" Isabelle chewed her bottom lip, completely ignoring Stefan. "No. That's not what I feel in my gut. There's a purpose to these killings. There's a reason why he's targeting witches right now."

Thomas felt it was something more, too, but it was just an intuitive hit. There wasn't anything solid to pursue at this point. He looked at Stefan. "How do we track him?"

Stefan's lips peeled back from his teeth in something that wasn't quite a smile. "Track him?" He gave a short, sharp laugh. "Please. The creature is tracking *you*. He will find you long before you'll be able to find him, unless you get lucky and surprise him. Otherwise, there is no way to track a demon. Not physically. Not magickally."

"That's very comforting," muttered Micah.

"Actually, I feel much safer in here than out there," continued Stefan. The words fell flat, since they were accompanied by a glum look on his face. Stefan couldn't even fake it.

"Oh, I'm sure if the demon set its sights on a nice, spicy fire witch, this prison wouldn't stop him," answered Thomas with a smile. "I'm sure our wards and spells would have no effect on him at all if he really had his heart set on you. Demon magick isn't witch magick, after all."

Stefan smiled back. This time he looked like he really meant it. "He won't be coming after me. Demons hunt their hunters. Did you not know? It is in their nature to do so. They stalk and toy with them. Sometimes they even develop an emotional attachment to them. It's no fun for the hunter, of course. No one wants a demon fixated on them."

Thomas looked at Micah and made the question plain in his expression.

"Some of my research seems to point to that, yes," answered Micah. "A demon's reaction to aggression is different than ours. They don't have fight or flight. They don't run; they turn around and stalk. This one is probably crazy from exile to boot."

"Great."

A sly expression stole over Stefan's face. "First, they shoot you full of venom, rendering you paralyzed and mute, yet aware. After that, they take your magick, drinking it from the center of your body. Then, they peel your skin off and slice you open to consume the juicy parts—the liver, kidneys, and heart. Last, they crack your bones for the marrow."

Yes, he'd seen the remains twice, up close and personal.

So had Isabelle.

Thomas glanced at her. She'd gone sheet white and stood stock straight with her arms crossed over her chest. "Are you all right?" he asked her.

She nodded once, her body tense. "I'm fine."

"Oh, yes, I forgot," Stefan said in a sugary-sweet tone. "Our lovely Isabelle has already seen a demon's handiwork for herself. It was your sister, yes?"

"This demon will die," she shot back.

"Such bravado! You're so sexy when you're being stupid. Nice sentiment, *ma cherie*, but I look forward to the news of your demise."

"As I look forward to the news of your sentence being rendered, Stefan. Until then it heartens me to know just how much you're suffering here in Gribben." Her lips parted in a wide, sincere smile, though her face was still pale as parchment. "In fact, that knowledge makes me happier than killing you."

"Great," Micah put in. "Well, that's established, then. Thomas, I can take it from here. I'll set Stefan up with a computer and obtain the texts. Why don't you get Isabelle out of here? She talks tough but looks like she's about to hurl on her pretty red boots."

"Good idea," Thomas answered.

Micah, as the Coven archivist and researcher, had the most business trying to get information from Stefan anyway. Micah would pass what he learned on to him.

Isabelle protested, but Thomas took her by the upper arm and led her toward the door. Her face was now a pale shade of green, but the woman didn't seem to know when to stop.

"It's been a pleasure, Stefan," muttered Thomas as the guard opened the door for them. "As always."

The door shut with a metallic thump behind them.

Isabelle stumbled. He caught her and guided her to a nearby wall where she splayed an open hand to brace herself.

"I'm fine," she snarled, pressing her forehead to the wall.

"You're not fine."

She winced and cradled the hand she'd injured when she'd punched Stefan. "It's just . . . I don't like remembering. Doing is fine. Hunting is great. Remembering is . . . not good."

"That's natural. You're grieving, Isabelle."

She closed her eyes and dragged in a breath.

Thomas knew that she'd found her sister since he'd been called in to the murders of both victims. The bodies had been . . . partially consumed.

When he'd first reached Angela Novak's kill site, it had been difficult to understand what he'd been looking at. Gradually, as his mind had fought to comprehend, the images had become clear—mangled, torn muscle, gobbets of matter no one wanted to examine closely. Blood absolutely everywhere. No longer human-looking, just so much meat and bone.

Isabelle had been there before him. She'd been the one to notify the Coven of the murder before she'd disappeared, presumably to hunt the demon.

Even worse than the scene was the knowledge both Angela Novak and Melina Andersen had been conscious until they'd succumbed to their injuries. Demons trapped their victims in a kind of venom-induced stasis. The paralyzed witch could feel, but couldn't speak, scream, or move.

While the victim lingered, the demon worked slowly, drawing out the killing. First the creature took the magick, psychically cracking the witch open like a coconut to drink the milk within. After that came the flaying of the skin and the extraction of the juiciest organs.

Knowing how that person had been treated as nothing

more than a bit of livestock, a plaything, was worse than anything else.

Worse than the cleanup. Worse than the sight or the smell.

Isabelle gave a short, bitter-sounding laugh. "Grieving seems like such a light, simple word to use for what I'm feeling."

Thomas shuddered, imagining finding his sister Serena the way Isabelle had found Angela. He placed his hand on her back to console her, but then removed it. Giving comfort didn't come easily to him. "Take a deep breath and let it out slowly."

Turning to lean against the wall, she drew in a shaky lungful of the stale Gribben air and slowly exhaled. "I just want to . . . *need* to do this," Isabelle continued. Steel backed her words.

"I know." He took her injured hand and examined it. It was nothing that wouldn't heal. He wasn't so sure that could be said about her other wounds.

He glanced up at her and found her staring at him in deep concentration. Absurd, inappropriate sexual awareness sparked, tightening his muscles. Her cheeks had regained their healthy color and lips were full and lush. He imagined several things he'd like to do to those lips in a span of a second.

Fuck.

He dropped her hand and turned away. "Come on, let's get out of here."

"I thought you'd never say that."

Thomas guided her away from the wall and down the corridor. He could understand how she felt and, even though he'd asked her along for the ride, he wasn't totally sure she should be on this mission.

From what he'd gathered from her records, Angela had essentially been her only family. Perhaps Isabelle would endanger herself in her quest to avenge her sister. He had the sense that maybe she didn't think she had much to lose these days. An attitude like that would make her reckless, a tendency she'd already shown anyway.

They didn't need reckless.

He didn't want to see her get hurt, either. Isabelle getting hurt, her fire snuffed out, would be a tragedy. He didn't know her well, but there was something about her that drew him to her. Maybe it was simply her personality, which he found in turns compelling, messy, attractive, and exasperating. Maybe it was the wildness and impulsiveness he sensed in her.

They made their way through the security checkpoints to the elevator that would bring them to the main floor of the prison. He punched the button to call the car, but Isabelle headed for the door leading to the stairwell instead.

She glanced at him, hand on the door knob. "I don't like elevators. I'll meet you up there."

He frowned at her. "It's fifteen flights up."

"What? Can't do fifteen flights, old-timer?" With a grin, she disappeared beyond the doorway.

"Old?" he murmured to himself. "I'm not old." The elevator door opened, but he just stared at the interior of the car, frowning. Leaving the elevator, he sprinted after her, taking the stairs two at a time until he'd caught up to her.

Her laugh echoed down the stairwell. "I knew you'd chase me after that comment." She quickened her pace. "I bet I can beat you to the top."

He increased his speed to match hers. "Since I'm an old man and I'm exerting myself, I need some incentive for this. What will you give me if I win?"

She laughed again. "You're pretty ripped for an elderly person. As for what you'll get if you win, it will be a surprise." She quickened her pace, not even out of breath.

He shot after her, keeping right on her tail until they were at the top. By that time they were both panting hard. They jostled their way to the door, elbowing each other out of the way. It was close, but Thomas got there first. Isabelle brushed past him, put her hand to the knob, and started to pull, but Thomas pressed his hand to the door and closed it.

Bracketing her as she faced the door, he dropped his head and murmured, "I won," in her ear. "I want my surprise."

Isabelle turned, his body still crowding hers. He liked the

proximity, liked the heat her body gave off and the scent of
her light perfume. Thomas dropped his gaze to her chest, rising and falling quickly in her exertion, and wondered what
color her nipples were. Wondered what they tasted like.

Thomas wanted her stripped and spread on his bed.
Wanted to drag his hands over every inch of her skin, kiss the
backs of her knees and lick the sensitive skin at the base of
her spine. He wanted his cock tunneling in and out of her
slick, wet heat, wanted her wrists captured and pressed to the
bed while he drove himself into her fast and hard. He wanted
to feel the muscles of her sex pulse and ripple along his length
as she came. He simply wanted her. Wanted her with a base,
male urge that made his cock go rock hard.

She stared up at him with her lips parted in surprise. Isabelle was empathic, she had to understand the lust he felt for
her. He lowered his head to hers, knowing damn well this was
a bad idea.

Isabelle stilled, even her breath stopped as he brushed his
lips across hers. Once. Twice. Her hands grasped his wrists,
slid up his arms. He nipped at her lower lip and her breath
sighed out of her, warming his mouth.

It was the spark that made a fire roar to life inside him.

He dragged her up against his chest, hungrily pressing his
lips to hers and demanding that she open for him. She whim-
pered somewhere low in her throat and parted her lips. He slid
his tongue inside and let it war with hers. She tasted hot and
sweet, felt like silky heaven. He knew where else she'd feel
like silky heaven and he wanted to stroke her there until she
shattered for him.

More. He wanted more of her.

Damn it. He wanted her clothes off, wanted her bare flesh
under his hands. He wanted her legs parted, his cock pistoning
deep inside her and her moans and sighs echoing in his ears.
He wanted to feel the slick, hot clasp of her sex around his
cock and her bare breasts filling his hands.

At the moment, that was all he could think about.

Her fingers curled around his shoulders as she pushed back
at him, returning his kiss every bit as hungrily.

Beyond rational thought, he found the edge of her shirt and

pushed his hand past it, finding smooth, warm skin beneath. Lady, he wanted her so badly he'd take her right here on the stairs if she'd let him. Who cared they were still in Gribben?

Who cared about anything but *this*?

Her fingers found the buttons of his shirt, and then dropped to the button and zipper of his pants. She undid them and slipped her hand down, searching out the hard, ridge of his cock through the fabric of his boxers. She stroked him as he pressed against her palm, groaning in the back of his throat.

But noises past the closed door of the stairwell intruded. The guards shouted at someone. . . .

Isabelle broke the kiss, her lips red and swollen. "What's that?"

Damn it all to hell.

He made a frustrated sound, released her, and did his pants back up in a hurry. Then he opened the door to the commotion beyond. As he stepped into the hallway he got a glimpse of a familiar form arguing with the men at the security checkpoint just inside Gribben's front door.

The men let her through and Mira, his cousin and a powerful air witch, emerged past the checkpoint, flanked by guards. She staggered as she entered the non-magickal zone, put a hand to the area between her breasts and caught herself against a wall. "Goddess, that's horrible."

"Mira? What are you doing here?" he asked.

She looked up, peering through the tangle of dark hair that crossed her face. "I heard a whisper."

SEVEN

❦

A VOICE ON THE WIND, THE ONE MIRA HAD OVERHEARD via her air magick, had spoken of a man named Simon Alexander. A man that may or may not be a demon in disguise. An air witch could troll the air for certain spoken words, eavesdrop at a distance on conversations. Mira had been on constant alert since the first murder for any murmurings related to the demon and it had finally paid off.

Magick tingled down Thomas's arms and through his fingertips from the tattoo that also served as a magickal storage source on his back as he murmured words of power to secure a warding. Hours after Mira had heard the whisper, the Coven had secured the empty apartment across from Alexander's in order to do some surveillance work.

He'd brought Isabelle and Adam with him for the first shift. Theo, one of the Coven hunters, and Jack would take the second shift. Micah was busy sifting through the texts they'd received from the Duskoff.

"I can't believe Alexander's been living just a few miles from the Coven for the last ten years," muttered Adam. He finished with a shake of his blond head. "Fuck me."

Their investigation had revealed that Alexander was an accountant—or was posing as an accountant—for a chain of motorcycle dealerships and that he'd been living in the Lakeview area of Chicago for the last ten years. The Coven's sprawling campus lay near the northern portion of the Forest Glen area, only a short drive away.

"That's Emma's job," Isabelle replied with a grin as she adjusted the spelled listening device they'd use to eavesdrop on Alexander's apartment. Isabelle could have done it through the water running through an unwarded residence, but Thomas had amped up her ability to listen in remotely by spelling a simple surveillance system. It would also allow Adam and himself to monitor Alexander as well, even though they were not water witches.

Whether Mira had caught the communication by chance, by pure dumb luck, or because the demon had deliberately blown it her way was a matter of debate. The fact that they'd been searching so long for a sign of the demon, only to have one pop up now, was ample cause for suspicion. Still, they had to take the chance it was legitimate. Too many lives were at risk.

"It's not Emma's job anymore," Adam answered with a grin. "Now it's Elizabeth's." Despite the fact that Adam smoked too much, drank too much, and the fact that he was less than classically attractive—with a nose that had been broken one too many times and a head full of spiky blond hair—women found him irresistible. Lots of women. And, unlike Micah, Adam knew *just* what to do with the attention.

"You're such a slut." Isabelle shook her head as she fiddled. "You go through so many women I can't even keep track. One day you're going to find one who breaks your heart."

"That sounds like a curse, Isabelle. Or is it a promise? Want to break my heart, baby?" He leered at her. "I'll let you try."

"You couldn't handle me, Adam," she shot back with a grin. He narrowed dark blue eyes at her. "Now *that* I believe."

Letting them banter, Thomas glanced around the room, sensing the walls, floor, ceiling, and doors to make sure he'd covered every inch with the warding. The physical space was bare, except for some tools the building maintenance crew had left. New caramel-colored carpeting covered the floor and the tang of fresh paint stung his nose.

Adam sat with Isabelle at a card table to adjust the equipment. Isabelle had her long jean-clad legs crossed and she'd hooked her hair behind her ears as she worked. Thomas had noticed she had an adorable habit of biting the tip of her tongue when she concentrated.

Isabelle set the headset aside and turned to Thomas. "So why do you think the demon has chosen to live so near the Coven?"

"Don't get ahead of yourself." Thomas smoothed out the last of the warding and grunted. "We don't even know if Alexander *is* the demon. If he is, he likely did it deliberately. It's too much of a coincidence otherwise."

"Maybe he got a kick out of being so close to us," added Adam.

"Maybe." Thomas murmured an incantation—words he'd imbued with his personal power. The last of his concealing wards snapped into place. "Done."

His tattoo tingled, tapped of some of the magickal energy he'd stored there. Fire, air, and water witches could just draw straight from the seats of their magick in the center of their chests, but earth witches had more preparation to do. Unless he used his magick to exert control over something directly of the Earth herself, like the ground or a tree, a charm had to be created beforehand. Earth witches had to anticipate the spells they'd need, cook them up, and transfer the pure resulting energy to their bodies to be accessed later. Because of the planning involved, earth magick was the least convenient of the four types of power, but also the most flexible.

Earth witches were the most stereotypical breed of the four elements. They were more what the non-magickals imagined when they thought *witch*. No one understood why earth witches were different, though there were plenty of theories.

"I hope the wards hold," said Isabelle, looking doubtfully out the window toward Alexander's apartment.

Yeah, so did he. They were in new territory with this one, having never done surveillance work on a suspected demon before. Alexander was at work now, which had given them some time to get the spells in place.

"I made the warding hard to detect," Thomas answered. "The upside is that if Alexander sniffs them out and comes after us, we'll know for sure he's the demon."

Isabelle raised a brow. "That's an upside?"

"Yeah, I'd rather not find out that way," groused Adam.

"We're about to know one way or the other because he's

home," murmured Isabelle. "I can feel it through the water in his apartment. That was none too soon."

Adam slipped on his headphones and Thomas went to a small table nearby and did the same. The shades were drawn on the windows of their apartment and the wards were locked down tight. From what they knew about demon magick, theoretically, the creature shouldn't notice their spying. According to Micah, demon magick and elemental magick were fundamentally different and one shouldn't be able to detect the other.

Of course, they really didn't know for certain.

Micah had successfully obtained the digitized books Stefan had provided and was feeding them information as he scoured and gleaned it. Unfortunately, this lead on Alexander had popped up so soon Micah hadn't had a lot of time to do research. They were flying blind and had to take as much care as possible.

They settled in to listen. Through the magickally imbued headset, they heard Alexander cough, blow his nose, go to the bathroom, open and close the refrigerator, pop the top off a beer, and then settle down on the couch with the sigh of one happy to be home from a long day at work.

The TV flipped on. "*Wheel . . . of . . . Fortune!*" sounded the television audience.

Adam looked over and gave him an eye roll.

Thomas took the headphones off and laid them on the table in front of him. "This may be a false alarm."

Isabelle slumped her shoulders. "When I tune in remotely to him, using the water in his body, he doesn't feel like anything more than a non-magickal human male." She paused and looked morose. "Not even a witch."

Thomas nodded. "If he were the demon, you'd know it."

Adam pulled his headset off one of his ears. "And I don't think he'd be watching *Wheel of Fortune*, if this was our guy. I don't think demons like Pat Sajak."

Isabelle sat up a little straighter. "He could just be playing with us. The demon has to be able to seem convincingly human. Otherwise witches would be spotting him all over the place. Maybe he knows we're watching and he's masking. Or maybe he's become humanized during his stay here and he's grown to like TV game shows."

Thomas and Adam only stared at her. "I think you're reaching," Thomas said finally.

"I'm just trying to think outside the box here, guys."

Adam leaned toward her. "Isabelle, I think outside the box with the best of them, but I still suspect he's a non-magickical human male just home from work with one hand down his pants and a beer in the other."

She tossed her headset to the table in front of her with force. "Damn it!"

Thomas considered her for a moment. "It's not over yet. Mira heard this man's name for a reason. He could be connected in some way with the demon."

"Maybe." Isabelle chewed the side of her thumb and slumped in her chair.

"I need to talk to Isabelle alone, Adam."

"Okay. I'll keep listening to *Wheel of Fortune*," said Adam with a sarcastic thumbs-up and grin. He placed the head-phones to one ear. "I think I know this puzzle. Buy a vowel!"

"Let me know if anything unusual happens or if he leaves."

Adam nodded. "Sure thing, boss."

Isabelle looked confused, but Thomas led her into the other room anyway. Only a long worktable stood in what would be the formal dining room. Wadded up painter's drop cloths lay discarded in the corner. She stood near the table, crossed her arms over her chest, and looked at him expectantly.

"I just want to make sure you're okay with all this," Thomas said. "I know you've been traumatized by the death of your sister and I need to make sure that you're not going to—"

She raised her eyebrows. "What? Freak out? Break down and cry at a critical moment?"

"I don't think you're the hysterical weeping type. I just want to make sure you're all right."

"I appreciate your concern, I really do, but I'm fine, Thomas. In fact, I'm more than fine now that I'm aligned with the Coven and helping to find this demon. And we will find him. This Alexander guy might be a dead end, but that doesn't mean we won't have other promising leads."

Relief swept through him. It was nice to hear her being positive. "I'm glad you feel that way—"

She uncrossed her arms and her expression softened. "Now what's with your hair?"

He blinked at the abrupt change of subject. "Excuse me?"

"I've established that you do, indeed, possess pupils, but what's up with the hair? I mean, it's beautiful. It's so long, glossy, and sexy. I want to thread my fingers through it every time I see you. But it seems strange on a man like you because you're all about work and never about play."

He blinked again. "My hair *is* about work, actually. It holds power for me. Earth witches don't hold magick in the center of our chest the way fire, water, and air witches do."

"I've dated earth witches, so I know you guys do that but I've never really understood how."

"My hair is charmed to hold a reserve of power for me, like you hold your magick in the center of your chest. Except we have to cook up the spells we'll need beforehand, draw the energy off them, and manually store it on our bodies in places that have been charmed to hold reserves . . . like my hair."

She nodded. "Yes, with one of the complicated earth spells that I'll never comprehend. Gotcha." She smiled and reached out to finger a tendril of his hair. "So your strength resides here . . . like Samson? If I cut it, are you less powerful?"

"That's not something earth witches usually reveal."

"That's . . . wild. And the whole thing makes an odd sort of sense." She dropped the hank of his hair. "You don't seem like the vain sort of man who would grow his hair this long for looks or style. It figures you'd have a purpose, a strategy. So, how else do you hold your magick?"

"I have a tattoo on my back. The ink is charmed to hold power for me."

"A tattoo?" A slow smile spread across her mouth. "Show me."

"You want me to take my shirt off." It was a statement more than a question.

She grinned and waggled her eyebrows. "Why not? Are you scared?"

He raised his eyebrows and pulled his suit jacket off.

She laughed and clapped. "Oh, yeah! Take it off, baby!"

Thomas grinned at her and laid his jacket on the table. The woman had that effect on him. He unbuttoned his shirt and slid that off, too.

"My, my, my, Mr. Monahan! What big biceps you have."

"Are you flirting with me?"

"Maybe. Why do you sound so surprised?"

Because women didn't flirt with him. Not ever. Well, occasionally a non-magickal woman might flirt with him in a store or a bar, but never a witch. Never anyone who knew who he was. Women didn't play with the heart and soul of the Coven.

Isabelle was apparently fearless.

He didn't answer her; he only turned around to show her his tattoo.

He heard her quick intake of air. "Oh, my Lady, it's gorgeous. Who did it?" Her fingers reached out and brushed his skin, making him shiver a little under her touch.

"An earth witch named Theo. His full name is Theodosius. He inks a lot of us because he's got the power and the artistic skill. You'll meet him soon, I'm sure. He's one of the Coven's best hunters."

ISABELLE TRACED THE LINES OF HIS TATTOO WITH HER fingertip. An angel marked his entire back, her wings arching up and covering his broad shoulders and trailing down his arms. She pushed his hair to the side to see the whole thing and dragged her fingertips over the exquisite artistry of the image. It was done in simple black, but with a high amount of detail.

Beneath the surface of his skin, along the marks the ink made, she could feel the pulse of the extra power he stored. Earth witches were certainly a different breed.

She let her gaze drop to his ass and bit her lower lip. The man was fine everywhere, from the top of his head to the tip of his toes. Could anyone blame her if she fantasized about licking everything in between?

He made her feel oddly safe, too, and she liked that. Isabelle could take care of herself. It was a specialty of hers, surviving. But once in a while it was nice to be in the presence of a man strong enough to take care of her for a change. Thomas was that man. When he entered a room, he commanded it. His leadership was something inborn, innate. It was magnetic, and all those around him reacted by falling in line.

Yes, she was powerfully attracted to Mr. Thomas Monahan. Most women considered him off-limits, Isabelle considered him fair game.

Isabelle lifted her hand from his tattoo, dragged it over his shoulder and down his bicep, losing herself for a moment in the bounty of male beauty spread before her.

He turned and she allowed her hand to trail on his warm skin as he did so. When he faced her, she pressed her palm to his muscular chest and looked up at him, letting her arousal shine in her eyes.

"Like I said . . . *gorgeous*," she murmured.

A small smile quirked the corners of his mouth. "That's supposed to be my line."

"Women's lib. Happened decades ago. What other abilities do you have?"

"I have some unpredictable PSI and basic empathic skills."

"Empathy, huh? What are you picking up from me right now?"

He took her hand and used it to pull her a step closer to him. That brought her flush up against his magnificent body. The look in his eyes dried her tongue as he slid a hand to the nape of her neck and lowered his head toward hers. "That you're attracted to me."

Her lips curved into a confident smile. "Likewise, I'm sure, Mr. Monahan."

The first touch of his lips on hers was a bare tasting, just a brush. Unlike the kiss at Gribben, this one was soft and undemanding. It made her legs feel weak. It promised that if she trusted her body to him, he would take good care of it. *Very good care.*

He walked her backward a step, so the back of her thighs hit the worktable in the center of the room. The table's feet made a squeaking noise on the floor as they bumped it backward an inch.

She sat down on the edge and he followed her with his mouth, the pressure becoming harder, hungrier. His tongue slid between her lips and brushed against hers lazily over and over, until that patient, thorough attention registered in an area of her body much farther south.

Thomas briefly broke the kiss. His warm breath caressed her lips. "You're right. I want you."

The words rolled over her, low, warm, and full of erotic promise. They tingled places that hadn't tingled in a while. She ached with the need for more. Damn it. She would've given anything for Adam to suddenly have to go out for a smoke . . . for an hour or two.

Isabelle nipped his lower lip. "Come to my room tonight. I promise I'll still respect you in the morning."

Just then the door slammed open. Adam looked stunned for a millisecond at the sight before him and then said, "He's moving."

HE MOVED FAST.

"What happened to sitting around and watching *Wheel of Fortune*? What happened to the beer drinking? What happened to the whole hand-down-the-pants thing?" asked Isabelle as Thomas guided the car down the busy street, trying to keep up with Alexander's Volvo.

Marrow-sucking demons didn't drive Volvos. They just didn't.

"I don't know," answered Adam from the back seat. "One second he was drowsing on the couch to the dulcet sounds of the spinning wheel, the next he was up and out the door."

"Maybe he's just off to pick up take-out Chinese or something," muttered Isabelle.

"If so, he's in a big hurry." Thomas made a hard left, causing her to grab the armrest for support.

It was much harder to follow someone in real life than in the movies. The follower had to keep a respectable distance behind the followee, while avoiding the traffic and stoplights that could easily cause a separation.

They followed him to a large building in one of the northwestern suburbs of Chicago. Staying well behind him, so as not to draw attention to themselves, they parked a good distance away in the large lot, concealing their vehicle behind some trees.

Alexander guided his Volvo into one of the parking spots in the overflow lot, near a blue SUV. Then he waited. He'd chosen an isolated place, with few cars or buildings nearby. It was far past the end of the normal workday.

"I don't have a good feeling about this," murmured Isabelle. "Is Alexander stalking someone here? Someone working after hours, maybe?"

"Like maybe the owner of that blue SUV?" Adam added.

"Adam, call Micah and see if we know of any witches who work at six hundred and one Amberlyn Drive," said Thomas in a low voice.

Adam flipped his cell phone open and talked with Micah in a muted whisper. He snapped his phone closed. "No one on record, but that doesn't mean much."

Not every witch registered with the Coven informed them of job changes and many witches weren't registered at all. They lived in the world like a non-magickal. Some witches didn't even know they were witches. Thomas's cousin Mira Hoskins hadn't known she was a witch until some warlocks had tried to snatch her to use in a demon circle.

They watched and waited until twilight tinged the sky myriad colors, shades of orange and red, then darkened from gloriousness into murk. Finally, footsteps sounded on the pavement. A middle-aged woman with short brown hair, dressed in business attire and carrying a briefcase, made her way across the parking lot toward the SUV. A girl of maybe seven years held her hand.

"They're witches," said Thomas. "I can feel it from here, two earth witches of middling power, mother and daughter."

Isabelle's breathing hitched and her hand curled around the door handle as the two figures disappeared momentarily behind the stand of trees that shielded their car from Alexander's view. "I *really* don't have a good feeling about this."

"Alexander could be her boyfriend," said Adam from the back.

"Yes, but he could be stalking them, too."

Her intuition screamed *stalk*. Her gaze fixed on the little girl. She carried a Hello Kitty backpack and wore a navy blue private school uniform. The child looked so fragile walking through the parking lot, so innocent.

Her gaze ate up the distance between themselves and Alexander. If Alexander was the demon, they were too far away to be effective quickly. They couldn't move the automobile, or they'd be seen. But . . . she assessed the terrain between the parking lots. There were many big trees for someone of her stature to hide behind. Thomas and Adam were too large to go unnoticed, but she could do it.

She turned to Thomas. "I want to go in closer."

Thomas gave a sharp shake of his head. "Too dangerous for you."

"Thomas, there's a little girl! We can't just hang back and hope she's not going to be hurt. Let me go. I can get over there without being seen, and I'll be closer if something happens. If it does, get your ass over there pronto."

Thomas chewed his lip, mulling it over.

Not able to stand it a moment longer, she opened the door slowly and eased out. "Goddamn it, I'm going."

"Be careful."

She rolled her eyes at him and slipped away.

From the car, she'd mapped out a way to get from point A to point B via cover. The campus of this office building was blessedly tree rich. As the woman and her daughter progressed across the pavement, Isabelle traversed from tree to tree, a path that brought her just shy of Alexander's car. There, Isabelle hid behind a huge oak and waited.

The dark-haired woman missed a step when she caught sight of the Volvo and kept her eyes on the vehicle as she approached. By now the couple had passed out of the blind spot the trees made and back into Thomas's line of sight. Isabelle hoped he'd seen that hesitation in the woman's step, which signaled her unease with the vehicle and the male figure behind the wheel.

Isabelle tensed as the woman and child grew nearer and the Volvo's car door opened.

"Simon," the woman called in a tired voice. "I don't want to do this right now." She remote unlocked her SUV, spoke low to the girl and the child ran to climb inside.

"Melanie," said Alexander with his hands out as if to stop her from fleeing. "I'm sorry, but I miss you and Katie. Just a couple minutes. That's all I'm asking. Just let me have a couple minutes to explain what happened."

Melanie hesitated, and then walked to him. They spoke in muted tones for a few minutes and then Melanie fell into Alexander's arms, crying.

Isabelle relaxed. This seemed like a run-of-the-mill domestic scene to her. She watched for a little longer, until she started to feel like she'd intruded on an intimate moment, and backed away to return to the car.

Backed away and hit something really big. She frowned. That tree hadn't been there three minutes ago.

Isabelle stilled. Her nostrils detected a scent she knew— that same dry, earthy, acrid smell that had lingered in her bedroom after she'd had the nightmare. Magick flared along her skin, first tingling and then burning. Sensing malice melded with incredible power, she whirled.

A beautiful blond-haired blue-eyed man stood there, wearing a long black trench coat, and an amused smile on his soapstar handsome face. Isabelle blinked in surprise as the man strode past her as though she didn't exist, toward Alexander and Melanie.

Demon.

This was the demon.

Dear Lady. The demon had been in her bedroom. Why hadn't it killed her?

EIGHT

SHE RAN AFTER HIM, RAISING POWER AS SHE WENT. Casting her arm out, she forced a powerful bolt of magick at the creature, with the intent of freezing all the water in his body solid. The recoil from the amount of power she'd released sent her careening backward to hit a tree trunk. Isabelle cried out as pain lashed up her spine and she struggled to focus on the monster striding away from her.

Throwing power at a solid brick wall would've had more effect. He continued across the parking lot toward the unsuspecting couple like nothing had happened. All she'd succeeded in doing was beating herself up.

Frantically, she cast about for other weapons to use and came up empty. She'd never dreamed her best weapon, her magick, would be useless.

She did have the small, pretty copper blade Angela had given her sheathed to her left wrist. It wasn't very practical, considering she'd have to get close to the demon to use it. The blade was more for looks, anyway, not for actual maiming. Also, according to Micah, a demon's blood was acidic, not conducive to stabbing wounds since she'd be in spurting and dripping range.

"Damn it!" She would have brought a bazooka if she'd known.

Isabelle peeled herself from the tree and ran at him as he grew near the couple.

"Mr. Boyle!" exclaimed Alexander with a confused look on his face. "Er . . . hey! Melanie, this is Erasmus Boyle—"

Melanie screamed and backed away. As a witch, she undoubtedly sensed that what approached them was not human. Boyle was hardly masking his nature.

Not knowing how else to slow the demon, Isabelle launched herself at Boyle's broad back, wrapping her legs around his rock-hard waist and her arms around his thick neck in an effort to choke him.

From behind, she heard the squeal of tires on pavement. Thomas. Thank the Lady.

The demon grunted, but continued forward like she wasn't even attached to him. He grabbed Alexander and threw him up and over the Volvo to land on the pavement on the other side. He landed with a sick-sounding thump and didn't move.

Melanie stood her ground, her eyes wide. She inserted herself between the demon and her daughter, who sat pale and staring in the passenger seat of the SUV.

Isabelle tightened her grip on the demon's neck, squeezing until she wanted to cry out from the effort, but the demon barely noticed her. She sank her teeth into the demon's ear, but quickly remembered the acidic blood and released it. Instead, she coursed magick up through her chest and down her arms, willing the water in the thing's body to boil.

Please boil, she prayed to the Lord and the Lady. *Please*.

This time she got a reaction, though it wasn't the one she'd been looking for. The demon backed up fast and hard against the Volvo. Isabelle's back made impact and her breath crushed out of her. Exploding pain clouded her vision white for a moment. Her grip faltered and she fell to the pavement at the thing's feet.

The demon just continued on as though he'd swatted a gnat.

As soon as she was clear, Adam and Thomas attacked. From her left came a pulse of power. The air sizzled as Adam threw a fireball at the demon, followed quickly by a rush of solid, powerful earth magick that felt as deep and wide as the Grand Canyon.

The demon blocked the fireball with one hand, extinguishing it, but Thomas's bolt rocked him to the right a little. That much magick would kill a witch or a non-magickal, but it only made the demon stumble.

The creature turned and shot alien magick at them. Thomas threw a barrier up in front of himself and Adam just in time, but the blast still made them stagger backward. The air rippled with the backlash of power. Oddly, it felt like earth magick, though the blast held that same dry-bitter dirt scent, the scent of demon.

Boyle turned back to Melanie. "I've come for your daughter, not you," he said in a deep, smooth voice with just a trace of a strange, inhuman accent. "Stand aside."

"The hell you're taking Katie!" Melanie pushed her palms against the demon's chest and funneled all her power through her hands.

Earth magick pulsed. Isabelle's ears popped and her mouth went dry with the taste of dust. The demon staggered backward, then gripped Melanie and threw her over the Volvo to land near Simon.

Katie screamed and clamored to the driver's side of the SUV. Isabelle heard the doors unlock and relock as the girl verified her perceived safety. Those locks wouldn't keep a demon out. Inside the vehicle, the child stared in the direction Boyle had thrown her mother and sobbed. Melanie wasn't getting up.

Isabelle shot to her feet, ignoring the wrench of pain across her chest where she thought she'd heard something crack. Her vision dimmed for a moment as she gathered her power again. She didn't have much in reserve, not that it mattered. Their magick was just an annoyance to him. Thomas and Adam took up the slack while she recovered by hurling blast after blast of magick at the demon.

With no clear way to reach the girl since the demon stood between her and the SUV, she joined the fray, tossing every trick she knew from her water magick arsenal, while she edged herself well away from Boyle's range.

The demon turned toward the three of them, blocking and parrying their attacks. He made a frustrated growling/gurgling sound deep in his throat. If she'd needed any reminder of what they were fighting, that completely inhuman sound provided it. It raised every hair on her body.

Thomas and Adam moved to the right and she moved to

the left, trying to get clear enough to make a dash for the girl. The men grasped her intention and began drawing the thing to the side more and more, farther away from the SUV.

The demon made the animal-like noise again and something on his hands flashed—he'd unsheathed some viciously long claws. Boyle turned toward her and images of how he'd used those claws on Angela swept through Isabelle's mind. Her knees went weak and her heart thumped faster.

She cried out under the demon's directed mental assault— Angela screaming, skin parting, blood spurting. A phantom pain in her chest flared, echoing what Angela likely felt when her magick had been ripped from its roots. Isabelle's knees gave out and she caught herself on the hood of the SUV, sobbing under the attack.

Bastard! He knew exactly who she was!

"Come on! Over here," taunted Adam. "You're neglecting us, you cute widdle demon, you."

The demon swung its head back to the men and the attack on her blessedly ended. Demon power crackled along her skin and that same dry/acrid scent filled the air. Her ears popped and her stomach heaved from the strength of it. The creature was raising a hell of a lot of power.

Adam charged him in a suicidal move if she ever saw one. He ran straight toward the demon, war cry pealing the air and fire ripping across the pavement on either side of him.

"*Aeamon*, you irritate me!" Boyle bellowed.

Judging by the strength of the magick filling the air, the thing had just been playing with them up until that moment. Now, Boyle was getting serious.

Thanks to Adam, he was also sufficiently distracted.

Knowing she only had this one opportunity, Isabelle shot to the driver's side of the SUV and motioned for the girl to exit. Inside, Katie froze. Her eyes went wide and she hesitated, as if thinking over the wisdom of leaving the vehicle.

Oh, no. Isabelle frantically mouthed, *Now!*

The girl unlocked the door and slid out into her arms, tears streaming down her face. Isabelle tapped the dregs of her reserves and used a quick burst of magick to influence the water around whatever was injured in her chest. It coalesced and soothed, eased the pain, as she picked up the child and ran as fast as she could without looking back.

Thomas called her name right before a blast of magick hit the men like a lightning bolt. The backlash of power rippled and rolled like a tidal wave behind her. Isabelle heard the rush of it, tasted it like dirt on the back of her tongue, but she couldn't outrun it.

It hit. She tripped and toppled face forward. Right before they made impact with the pavement, she twisted to break the child's fall. White-hot pain washed through her chest, making her vision spot.

It was nothing like the magick that followed it.

It seared her skin and filled her nostrils with sweet-burning yuck. Gasping, unable even to breathe, she rolled over onto her stomach and saw the girl sitting a short distance away, a look of horror in her dark eyes, her long chestnut-colored hair a tangle around her face.

"Run!"

The demon was coming.

"Run!" Isabelle managed to scream at her once more as a meaty hand closed over her ankle and pulled her backward.

Gravel scraped her skin where her shirt had ridden up. Her fingernails clawed the pavement as she attempted to find some kind of purchase to halt her backward slide into hell.

She was going to die like her sister.

Isabelle reached into her left sleeve and grasped the handle of the last tie to Angela she possessed in that moment. A pretty bit of artistic fluff disguised as a knife.

It came down to this; an earthly weapon to use against an unearthly beast.

Oh, this *so* wasn't going to go well.

The demon flipped her like she was made of aluminum foil and came down on top of her. He looked less human now, maybe because of the power he'd relinquished to defend himself.

And how had Adam and Thomas fared under that power, anyway? Lady, she didn't want to imagine.

Boyle's skin glowed with an unnatural reddish cast and his

eyes had bled to complete and utter black, disconcertingly like Thomas's. Then Boyle's lips peeled back and Isabelle got a glimpse of a double row of too sharp teeth bracketing a whiplike tongue.

Teeth strong enough to crack human bones for the marrow.

"I know you," he said in a low, soft voice, like a lover's. His gaze traced the lines of her face and bitter vomit crept into her throat. "I've been hunting you."

Images once again flashed through her mind of Angela's ruined body, but this time they came from her own subconscious instead of the demon's.

She choked down an anguished sob. "I've been hunting you, too," she gasped through the demon stench a second before she brought her fisted blade upward, straight into the thing's jaw.

The wound smoked and the demon screamed. She watched in surprise and horror as the stab wound opened even more, the flesh peeling away at the edges like burned parchment.

Blood dripped onto her chest, singeing a hole right through her shirt and burning her skin. Isabelle screamed and pushed herself away from him. In the melee, she'd forgotten about the blood.

She expected him to come after her, but the thing recoiled, screaming, and holding his jaw. Her realization came swiftly— for some reason the demon had trouble healing injuries made by her blade.

Looking down at the knife in her hand, she examined the beautiful, intricately etched copper handle and shiny blade.

Copper? Could it be?

Maybe she had a proper weapon after all.

Isabelle ripped her shirt off, trying to get the acidic blood away from her skin. While the demon turned away from her, nursing his injury, she wound the fabric around her right hand and wrist to protect her as she wielded the knife.

Just in time.

The demon turned and roared, his jaw nearly healed. The skin where she'd wounded him looked red and puckered but no longer smoked and bled.

She didn't waste a moment. She rushed the demon and stabbed him in the chest, in the leg, in the arm, anywhere she found available flesh.

More smoking, burning wounds. More demonic bellowing. More acidic blood that Isabelle danced to avoid.

The demon backed away from her, obviously in pain. He roared again, this time sounding like a wounded animal. Boyle lifted a well-clawed hand and then disappeared.

Quiet. Silence.

Isabelle stood on shaky legs, staring at the empty space in front of her with wide eyes. All of her injuries rushed up to meet her . . . just like the ground. The last thing she remembered was the vision of the newly starry sky above her head.

And then darkness.

NINE

✦

"ISABELLE?"

She winced as pain registered in her chest—a long, slow rip followed by a lingering throb. Her eyelids fluttered open and she saw Thomas's head blocking the stars. Ignoring the pain, she focused on the important thing. "Thomas, you're okay."

"So is Adam. Shields kept us alive, but not conscious. We've all been out for a while."

"Boyle's gone," she whispered. "How's the child?"

"She's fine, the woman and the non-magickal male are also okay, if a little beat up and upset."

Movement caught her eye on her right side. "Hey, champ," said Adam, limping toward them. "Just can't manage to keep your shirt on, can you?"

She raised her right hand. She hadn't lost her death grip on the knife's handle even in unconsciousness. The blade was bloody and rusted in places and the material of the shirt she'd used as a hand guard was crispy and eaten away.

"I don't think it likes copper," she said, a wide smile spreading over her mouth despite the pain burning like bonfire in the center of her chest.

They were going to make that demon pay.

"COPPER," MUTTERED MICAH, FROWNING AS HE RAN his finger down a page of printed text. "Copper . . . Oh, yeah, here it is." He mumbled to himself for a moment while Thomas shifted impatiently.

"Demons are greatly injured by copper weaponry and have difficulty healing wounds inflicted thusly," Micah read. "Copper is also known to cause a weakening of the beast's overall magickal structure and an allergic reaction in the physical structure." He looked up from the text with raised eyebrows. "Huh."

"Huh?" Thomas glowered. "We were nearly killed out there. That information would have been useful, Micah."

His cousin spread his hands, indicating the pages and pages of paper strewn across his desk. "I'm going as quickly as I can here, boss. You rushed off so fast after that lead on Alexander I hadn't even had a chance to download all the documents yet." He passed a hand over his tired-looking face. Thomas noted Micah's eyes were bloodshot and he had five o'clock shadow.

"So no other metals, just copper?"

Micah nodded. "Apparently. I'll keep looking for more information, but you have to know that some of it was corrupted. There are pages missing and—"

"Tell me what else you've found out."

His face instantly lit up. "There's lots of information here about their world. They reign supreme in their reality, having exterminated all other races. They're cannibalistic, too."

"Lovely."

"It looks like there might be different breeds of demon, but the information concerning that is unclear. It seems like there are four genetic groups, each possessing unique personality traits. Their culture appears rooted in some way by how these different breeds operate. Did you know that they actually call themselves *daaeman*? That's the name of their race. They call their world *Eudae*." He paused with an expectant air.

After a moment Thomas ground out, "Is that supposed to mean something to me?"

Micah rolled his eyes. "The Greeks called demons *daemon*, but with a different spelling. That Latinized spelling of *d-a-e-m-o-n* is very close to how the daaeman spell the word as *d-a-a-e-m-a-n*." He pronounced the words differently. *Dae-*

mon, Micah pronounced *demon*. *Daaeman*, he pronounced *day-man*.

"The Greeks also classified them into benevolent and evil categories, or races." He frowned. "Maybe even breeds, I'm not sure. The benevolent demons were called *eudaemons*, like the name for their world."

"Benevolent demons? The Greeks got that one wrong."

Micah shook his head. "No. They didn't get it wrong. Their race is like ours, some of us do horrific things, but that doesn't make all humans bad. They're a complicated species."

His lips twisted. "Please excuse my unfair comment."

Micah spread his hands. "You're missing the larger picture, Thomas. Don't you see? This suggests demons had contact with humans long ago. And, in fact, it says they did right here." He brandished a sheaf of papers in his fist. "It says once there was a bridge between the worlds that *daaeman* could traverse. That they came to"—he squinted, reading text—"hunt, frolic, and fall in love."

Thomas raised an eyebrow. "Frolic? Demons frolic? They fall in love? Wait a minute, they frolicked and fell in love with *humans?*"

"Yes, and here's where it gets really interesting. Apparently, long ago demons mated with humans and it looks like maybe, just maybe . . . their spawn were witches."

Silence.

"Not possible," answered Thomas in a controlled voice. His whole body had gone tight.

"According to these records, it's very possible. There are legends of a sort of Adam and Eve couple, the first human woman and a demon male who fell in love and risked everything to have children together."

Thomas instantly thought of the acidic blood that ran through a demon's veins. "Demons and humans can mate?"

"No, actually. It's not physically possible for a human woman to carry a demon's child. They cooked up a spell to make it happen, a spell based on the elements."

Shock rippled through Thomas as mysteries aligned. For so long they'd known nothing of their origins, even though the Coven philosophers debated different theories endlessly. As much as Thomas was loath to admit it, this had a ring of plausibility.

"This first couple had quadruplets," Micah continued. "Each of those children inherited a propensity for one of the elements. They were the first witches—earth, air, water, and fire. Other demon/human unions followed, and additional offspring were born through the use of the elements spell. This is the gene pool we're descended from."

It made an irritating amount of sense. Matings between witches and non-magickals almost never produced a child. The reason had never been determined, since biologically witches seemed completely human.

Micah continued. "The *daaeman* call witches and warlocks *aeamon*, their word for half-breed."

Thomas jolted, remembering what Boyle had called them right before he'd hit them with that thunderclap of magick. "So let's say, hypothetically, witch magick was born of demon magick. Do you think that witch magick would be powerless against demon magick because of that?"

Micah sat back in his leather chair, making it squeak, and placed his hands behind his head. He contemplated the question a moment before answering. "Witch magick is probably about half as powerful as demon magick. Plus, it's fundamentally different in nature, having been warped by the element spell cast originally to allow the first pregnancies."

"So?" Micah could pontificate for hours. Thomas just wanted a yes or a no.

He paused, lost in thought, then shrugged. "I think all bets are off. There's no way to know why our magick is powerless against them."

"So, the age-old question has been answered. Witches aren't really human after all. The Coven philosophers will have fun with this information."

"We have a foot in both worlds, but it seems we may be an amalgamation of human and demon."

Thomas suppressed a shudder and changed the subject. "Have you found any other weaknesses besides metal?"

He shook his head. "If I had, you would've been the first I'd told."

"I know."

Micah leaned back over the scattered papers. "How are Adam, Isabelle, and the others?"

Thomas pushed a hand through his hair. "Adam and Isabelle have gone to see the doctor, but they're mostly fine. The non-magickal, Simon Alexander, we sent home. Katie and her mother, Melanie, are here at the Coven, under guard. It's the most we can do for them right now."

"So what was Alexander's connection to the demon?"

"The demon never had any direct interest in him. Boyle was using him as a way to get to the little girl, Katie. The demon had come into contact with Alexander through the motorcycle shop where Alexander works. Boyle rides a vintage Harley, apparently. That's how Boyle became aware of the little girl. We're not sure why he wanted her. We're also not sure if the demon deliberately blew the intelligence to Mira, but I don't see where that would have benefited him. Right now it looks like she picked it up by pure chance."

"Sounds like Isabelle did a fantastic job out there."

"We might all be dead if it weren't for her."

Micah smiled. "I hear admiration in your voice."

Thomas grinned back at him. "I think she's pretty damn hot, too."

"Knew you did."

STEFAN SAT ON THE EDGE OF HIS BUNK, HIS BLOND head—hair perfect even in captivity—bowed. Thomas had come to Gribben immediately following his disturbing conversation with Micah. Stefan held answers and Thomas hated that. It shifted the power into Stefan's hands.

He hadn't felt the need to bring Isabelle with him for this because Isabelle had specified she wanted to be included in any official Coven communication with Stefan. This was personal.

Thomas stopped pacing in front of Stefan.

The warlock raised his head, a smug smile spreading over his lips. "I touched her, you know. Isabelle. She let me feel her up before she attacked me. Her breasts are beautiful. They feel nice against a man's lips, smooth and soft. Have you kissed them yet?"

Thomas stared down at him, teeth gritted as he tried not to react to the obvious bait.

His voice changed from honey-sweet to barbed. "I see how you look at her, that witch bitch. Was it *coup de foudre?* Was it love at first sight, Thomas? Or do you just want to fuck her? Either way, I hope you always remember I was there first."

"You didn't fuck her." Tightly leashed rage laced the words. The warlock seemed to know what buttons to push.

Stefan smiled. "How do you know for certain?"

Thomas turned on his heel and paced away, trying very hard to keep his anger in check. Doing that around Stefan was difficult in the best of times; now it was nearly impossible. He wouldn't lose his temper with Stefan again. It made him look weak, uncontrolled.

Stefan gave a soft laugh and leaned against the wall behind him.

Thomas turned toward the warlock. "I just spoke to Micah, who has finished examining some of the documents you provided. They point to a genetic and magickal link between demons and witches. Why didn't the Duskoff share this information with the Coven?"

Stefan leaned forward, resting his elbows on his knees and spreading his hands wide. "It is not like we're friendly organizations, Thomas. This naïveté is irritating. Why would the warlocks share anything with the witches? What possible advantage would the Duskoff gain?"

"We're enemies, but we still share a race," Thomas replied through gritted teeth. "Unfortunately."

Stefan gave him a slow smile. "And that is the core of what bothers you, is it not? Sharing a race? You worry that witches might be demon spawn. You are concerned that you and your Coven fight so hard to be a force for good, yet your magick may come from a dark and violent alien people. Has it occurred to you, Thomas, that warlocks may be truer to their parental nature than witches? Does it concern you that all witches have this propensity for chaos and mayhem because of our genetics?"

That's exactly what had occurred to him, though he didn't want to admit that to Stefan. So he got back to his reason for forcing himself into the same room with Stefan in the first place. "What more do you know about this?"

Stefan met his gaze. "I know it to be true. I can feel it in the center of my being. I feel it every time I take a life because the act fills me with such a sense of power. We are superior over the non-magickals, Thomas. Don't you see? Embrace what you are and realize this truth."

He had a wild glint in his eye and Thomas wondered for a moment if incarceration in Gribben might be stripping Stefan of his sanity. Of course, more than likely Stefan's sanity had been shaky before they'd caught him.

Stefan leaned forward, his voice becoming impassioned. "The witches and warlocks could rule the non-magickals if we combined our efforts. Have you never considered the power we wield, Thomas? We could take over the world. Do you never think of the possibilities?"

Thomas regarded him for a long moment before replying, expression grim, jaw locked. "No, I don't think about that. But I do think you have a complex about the size of your dick."

Stefan's face fell and he blinked slowly. His expression as he glanced away could only be described as vulnerable. "Control, Thomas. I have a complex about control. That's something a warlock has a lot of." His voice trembled.

For a moment, Thomas almost thought he understood Stefan. That scary second burned itself into his psyche. He knew Stefan's history, knew the abuse he'd suffered at the hands of his biological parents, knew he'd suffered even more when he'd run away from France's child protective services and survived on the streets. Knew he'd been shaped like hot glass in an artisan's hands by his adoptive father, William Crane.

Control? Yes, he just bet Stefan had issues about control. So would anyone who had been so completely under the thumb of another his entire life. Bitterness stung the back of Thomas's tongue. The last thing he wanted to have for Stefan was empathy.

"A warlock has control, you say?" Thomas narrowed his eyes. "Not here in Gribben."

Unable to take the sight of him any longer, Thomas turned on his heel headed for the exit. Stefan's crazy laughter followed him out the door and down the corridor.

Thomas could still hear it echoing in his head even when he'd left Gribben—with utter relief—and found sanctuary in the Coven library.

He sank down in the leather chair facing his desk, propped his elbows on the armrests and stared out the huge window at the end of the room, willing the sound of that laughter away. Stefan's voice, his laughter, the edge of sympathy he'd felt for him back in the cell, all of it infected him. It made him wish for a shot glass and something hard and wet to fill it.

"Thomas?" A warm hand touched his upper arm. He turned his head to see Isabelle's concerned face. He hadn't heard her enter the library—a thing that no other witch would have dared do without permission, no other witch but Isabelle.

Thomas found he didn't mind.

She'd changed out of her ruined clothes, into an ankle-length blue-patterned peasant skirt and a white blouse. Her hair hung long and loose over her shoulders. She looked beautiful, but then she always looked beautiful.

He stood, resisting the urge to catch her up and bury his face in her hair. He wanted to take her upstairs to his room and drown himself in her softness, scent, and curves. Sinking into her would drive off Stefan's laughter. Her body, breath, and spirit could chase everything else away and leave only pleasure. She'd let him. Thomas knew she was his for the taking . . . but she'd been injured in the fight. "Are you okay?"

She nodded and touched her ribs. "It wasn't a bad injury, just painful. Doctor Oliver fixed me up with the help of a few fire witches. But what about you? They told me you haven't been in to see the doctor yet." She glanced at his ripped and dirty clothes. "You haven't even changed."

"I'm okay. Just working."

She forced him to turn toward her and pushed his hair away from his face. "You don't look okay and you feel tired and troubled to me. Your emotions are . . . twisted. Why haven't you been to the doc?"

"I'm not injured, Isabelle."

"Then why do you feel so beaten up to me?"

He smiled. "I didn't know you cared."

She grinned, glanced down the length of his body and gave him a slow wink. "Maybe I'm just worried you won't feel like picking up where we left off in the apartment."

Ah. He traced the curve of her jaw with the pad of his thumb. "I meant what I said back there. I want you, Isabelle, but maybe this isn't the—"

She reached between their bodies and cupped his groin. "I need to have it all wiped away, Thomas." Her voice trembled. "Clean. Can you do that for me? Make it all go away for a while? The demon, the memories. Make me drown in you?"

Whoa. Warning bells sounded in his head. She wanted what he wanted. Maybe they could help each other. Still, this was going too fast, happening too soon, feeling too reckless.

Need overrode reason in two seconds flat.

He couldn't wait to feel her smooth skin against his, to slide his cock into her slick sex and to feel her come around him. Thomas wanted to hear all the sweet little sounds she made while she climaxed. Like a man who hadn't had anything to eat or drink in weeks, he caught her around her waist and kissed her.

No hesitation. Nothing to say. Just action.

TEN

His hands found her hair and fisted gently, controlling her head as he explored the depths of her mouth.

Isabelle's breath hitched and a shudder of pleasure ran through her at the press of his lips and the long, thorough swipes of his tongue against her tongue. The man could probably make her come just with his kiss alone. The sheer sense of being lost in all that masculinity and magick, the taste of his mouth on hers, all of it had literally taken her breath away, made her unsteady on her feet.

Now she drowned in him. That's what she'd wanted.

He kissed her hard and deep, driving his tongue past her lips and forcing her tongue to spar with his. His powerful chest rubbed her taut nipples through the fabric of her shirt and his hard cock jabbed her stomach through his pants. She ached to stroke that impressive erection, wanted nothing more than to have his bare chest against hers while his cock tunneled deep inside her.

As soon as she'd walked into the library, Thomas's mood had closed over her in a shroud of anger, grief, and confusion. Outwardly the world saw him as cold and controlled. Inwardly, hot passion flourished. It was a contradiction Isabelle found incredibly attractive. Wildness strained at the end of the tight leash Thomas kept on his behavior.

Isabelle intended to yank it free.

Once she'd touched his shoulder and he'd turned to see her face, all that complex, brimming emotion had transmuted to pure sexual hunger. Hunger for her. Even though he'd tried to downplay it, it had been there, beckoning.

She'd seen no purpose in letting all that lovely male need go unanswered. She needed him, too.

Lady, she needed him right now so very much. Her hands tightened on his upper arms, where his hard muscles bunched and flexed.

"The door isn't locked," she pointed out breathlessly when they finally came up for air.

"I don't care. Doesn't matter anyway. No one comes in here without knocking . . . except you," he answered before attacking her mouth again. Then he lifted his head. "Condom, damn it."

She shook her head and smiled. "I'm protected."

"What do you mean?"

"I can't have babies. My female plumbing is irregular."

He blinked. "I'm sorry."

"That's life, isn't it? She's such a bitch sometimes."

The familiar tang of loss welled up over never being able to have children, but she tamped it down. Her life wasn't made for babies, anyway.

She forced his mouth back down on hers for a moment before murmuring, "Make it sweeter for me for a while, Thomas."

He gathered her skirt in one hand, fisting it and dragging it upward, while he used his other hand to press her against him by the small of her back. Her spine curved, forcing her body into his, as his mouth dropped to her throat to lick and nibble. Goosebumps erupted over her body and a low moan escaped her throat.

Her hands found the buttons of his battle-bedraggled shirt and began working them free. She couldn't wait to explore that gorgeous chest and the six-pack abs he'd revealed earlier that day. She wanted to lick every inch of his tattoo. So much to do.

If any witch interrupted them now, she'd freeze them where they stood.

He finished yanking her skirt up to her waist and slipped his hand down her panties, finding her hot, wet, and very anticipatory.

If he wanted her ready, *well*. . . .

Isabelle had become aroused the moment she'd entered the library and found him sitting there looking so brooding. The man did brooding like nobody's business.

She spread her thighs, giving him better access. His fingers stroked her folds and found her clit. Her breath hissed out of her. He rubbed it with the pad of his index finger until he'd tripped her trigger.

"Does that feel good?" he murmured into her ear.

She did her level best not to pant. "If you're not inside me soon, I'm going to come against your hand."

He smiled against her earlobe. "I guess that's a yes."

"*Yes*."

He forcibly yanked her head to the side and nibbled his way down her throat, making her shiver, making her hotter and wetter between her thighs. Thomas made love the way she'd assumed he would—commanding her and overwhelming her.

He made a low sound in his throat when she ran her hands over his chest, tangling her fingers through the smattering of dark hair. She had an empathic flash of just how much he enjoyed being touched. He ached for it, craved her hands and lips on him. Perhaps, because of his position at the Coven, he wasn't touched that often.

She could definitely make up for some of that now. With pleasure.

Isabelle dropped to her knees in front of him, giving him a coy upward glance as she undid his belt and the buttons of his ripped and dirty trousers. Hell, they needed to come off anyway. Keeping her gaze on his, she pulled his pants and boxers down, and then allowed him to kick them off along with his shoes. She rocked back on her heels and stared.

Gah. The man was a God.

Her mouth went dry at the sight of him standing there in only his unbuttoned shirt. He had the body of a man who worked out on a regular basis, someone who really took care of himself. Strong legs met narrow hips melding into washboard abs and then into that wonderful drool-inducing expanse of muscled chest.

And his cock.

Nope, this guy had never been ashamed in the locker room a day in his life. She grasped the wide base and let her gaze eat up the ropy veins that traversed it, the swollen, velvet-soft head.

"Mmm," she murmured right before she licked it.

Thomas swore under his breath and fisted his hands in her hair.

She glanced up at him. "I have a feeling this lovely cock has been neglected, Thomas. What's wrong with the women in this Coven, anyway?"

He opened his mouth to reply but she lowered her lips around his shaft, relaxing her throat muscles so she could take him deep. A strangled groan of pleasure came from his mouth. He tipped his head back and closed his eyes.

Isabelle closed her eyes, too, enjoying the musky scent and taste of him, and the way his body tensed in pleasure. She petted his taut balls as she ran her tongue and lips over him, loving the way she could bring this powerful witch to heel, render him senseless, with only the stroke of her mouth.

It was better than magick.

Strong fingers dug into her upper arms, dragging her upward. "You do that well," he murmured with half-lidded eyes, "but now I want a turn."

"I'm not one to object."

He guided her to sit on the edge of his desk, pushed her skirt up to her waist and pulled her panties down and off her legs. The silk whispered over her skin and then was gone.

He held her gaze as he slid his hands up her thighs and slowly parted them. Cool air bathed her already throbbing, needful sex.

Holding her knees well apart, Thomas leaned in and dragged his lips from her inner knee upward, flicking his tongue occasionally to taste her skin. When he reached the apex, he yanked her to the extreme edge of the desk and buried his face in her heat, making her gasp and moan. The sight of his dark head moving between her thighs almost undid her.

His skillful tongue found her clit and licked as he braced her thighs open with strong hands. Isabelle arched her back and sought the opposite edge of the desk, papers, pens, and office paraphernalia be damned. It all slid off, clattered to the floor.

He found the opening of her sex, slick and warm with honey, and rubbed the sensitive area until she threw her head back on a moan. Then he slid two fingers inside, the way she wanted his cock, and thrust in and out while he tongued her swollen, aroused clit.

Her fingers were white where she gripped the desk. The rest of the world fell away as she rode the edge of a swiftly cresting climax. He found her G-spot with unerring accuracy and dragged his fingertips over it. She bucked, sighed, and moved her hips in time to his thrusts, completely swamped and overtaken by sensation.

Her climax tingled through the base of her spine and then exploded upward, engulfing her body in a sweet wash of pleasure that had his name spilling from her lips over and over. He rode her through it, unrelenting in his attention to her already climaxing sex, driving her orgasm harder and faster until she had to stifle her cries so she didn't bring the whole Coven running.

While the waves of her powerful orgasm still gripped her and her muscles had the consistency of warmed butter, Thomas flipped her to lay facedown across the desk. The papers, folders, and pens she hadn't cleared the first time showered to the floor. Neither of them cared.

He pressed the head of his cock against her opening and she spread her thighs wider for him, caught in a haze of decadent pleasure and physical need. The heels she wore made up the difference in their heights, making this position perfect and highly erotic.

She laid her flushed cheek against the top of the cool, smooth desktop and curled her fingers around the edge. "Yes," she breathed, closing her eyes.

Thomas grabbed her hips and, inch by incredible inch, impaled her on his cock. Her thighs hit the edge of the desk and her rear made contact with Thomas as he hilted within her. He stilled, allowing her body to stretch to accommodate his width and length.

"That's good, Thomas," she managed breathlessly. He filled her so deliciously it brought tears of pleasure to her eyes. She was no angel, but it had been a while since she'd been with a man.

"Not as good as this." He pulled out slowly and pushed back in. They both groaned. He set up a slow pace that allowed her to feel every luscious inch of his cock as it tunneled in and out of her.

Every inward thrust made her mind stutter and her breath come quick as he pushed her closer and closer to climax. He overwhelmed her body with pleasure, by the slow glide of his cock and how the head of it rubbed her G-spot in this position.

By the time she'd lost the ability to think at all, trading cognition for pure sexual sensation, he'd increased the pace of his thrusts, taking her harder and faster.

She hung on, her thighs hitting the desk on every primal, animalistic push of his cock into her body. Isabelle loved it when a man who knew what he was doing took control during sex—and Thomas knew what he was doing.

Another powerful climax overtook her, shaking her to the core. The muscles of her sex pulsed and contracted around his still-thrusting cock, pleasure exploding through her body. She clawed the top of his desk.

His big body shuddered and tensed against her. He let out a low groan that made the hair on her body stand on end, and then whispered her name.

Once the tremors had eased for both of them, they found themselves draped inelegantly across his desk and breathing heavily. "Uh," was all Isabelle could utter.

Thomas helped her up, turned her to face him and kissed her. The kiss was long and slow, all caressing lips and gentle nips of his teeth. She sighed contentedly into his mouth and allowed him to hold her close. His fingers played with the buttons on her shirt, slowly undoing them one by one.

"I'll never be able to look at your desk the same way again," she murmured.

He nuzzled her breast, where it swelled above her bra. "Come to my bed and let me change your perspective on that piece of furniture, too."

She gave a low, throaty, satisfied laugh. "Trust me; I never would've regarded your bed with anything but plans for how to get into it."

His long hair brushed her bare skin and she shivered. He cupped her breast and rubbed the pad of his thumb over her nipple through the silk of her bra.

"Consider your plan successful." He motioned to the door. "Come on, it's late. I bet we can make it all the way to my room half naked and not be seen."

She laughed and bit her lower lip in consideration. Isabelle wanted to feel his body bare and moving against hers, wanted to feel the luscious lick of all that hair against her skin.

"I'll bet you one sexual favor, winner's choice, that we run into someone on the way to your room. The odds are with me. It's Murphy's Law."

He shrugged. "It's a win-win situation for me. Either way you end up in my room tonight."

"Then let's go."

Thomas pulled his pants on, but left his shirt open and his hair mussed. Isabelle let her skirt fall into place and buttoned her shirt.

They left the library and made their way through the foyer and up the stairs. Whispering softly to one another, they passed through the darkened hallways of the Coven, the place seeming warm and intimate to Isabelle this late into the night.

When they were close to Thomas's room, they turned a corner and came face-to-face with Adam. He stood staring at them for moment and then broke into a grin. "Go on, boss, you bad, bad boy," he drawled with a wink before he continued on his way.

Isabelle grinned. "I win."

Adam's surprised reaction both times he'd seen her and Thomas together confirmed Isabelle's hunch. Despite Thomas's hotness, he wasn't exactly known for his sexual exploits around the Coven. Thomas Monahan was, for all intents and purposes, the king of witchdom. Maybe women avoided him because of his title.

Watching him open the door to his room, that seemed hard to believe. She knew that he was considered the ultimate leader of the Coven, but he was a man, too. Not only was he a man, he was the most striking one Isabelle had seen in a very long time—physically beautiful, intelligent, and possessing a lovely, tempting juxtaposition of passion and control.

Although as he stared at her in the middle of his dimly lit living room, he didn't look all that controlled. He looked like he hadn't had enough of her yet, not by a long shot. For a moment, it made her want to bolt.

It's just about sex, she reminded herself.

Instead of giving in to the urge to flee, she forced herself to stroll around his posh setup. Under her feet lay a polished wood floor, covered in places with plush throw rugs in dark primary colors. An overstuffed beige couch sat at an angle in the living room across from a plasma television Isabelle doubted Thomas ever turned on.

In the opposite corner stood a desk stocked with a state-of-the-art computer. Packed bookshelves ran all along the room. A darkened kitchen, separated from the living room by a breakfast bar, lay to her right. She could just make out a scattering of pots, vials, and other containers on the counters, probably for spellcasting.

This was a nice place. More like Angela's condo than the standard digs in the Coven, which were a little like hotel suites.

He took a step toward her and her gaze rushed to meet his. She took an involuntary step backward, away from his natural intensity. Sometimes it could be overwhelming.

Thomas studied for her a moment. "What's wrong, Isabelle?"

She took a deep breath, scenting his faint cologne. Something deep within her stirred and chased away her sudden unease. Her gaze drifted down over the half-bared expanse of his chest. The sight made her brow lift speculatively.

A chuckle rumbled through him. "I guess nothing's wrong." He turned, pulled his shirt off and threw it onto the couch. Then he walked down a hallway and disappeared into one of the rooms.

She followed, noting a spacious bathroom and a guest bedroom before she reached the master suite. Thomas stood near a king-size four-poster bed. A fireplace was set into the wall directly opposite it. A bathroom door stood to her right. She walked over and took a peek. Just as she'd expected, he could throw a party in his bathtub.

She walked toward him grousing, "My room isn't anything like this one."

"I live here year-round. Most of the rooms are for people who don't." He stepped toward her and lowered his voice. "I owe you a sexual favor. Take off those clothes and get on the bed."

Isabelle shivered at the command in his voice. "Aren't I the one who should be ordering you around?"

"I think you like it better when I do it."

Yep, he had her number. "What if I refuse?"

He gave her wicked grin. "I'll remove them for you, so, please, do."

"Hmm, tempting, but I think I'd rather tease you a little."

She kicked off her shoes and unbuttoned her shirt slowly, letting him have minute peeks of her cleavage in the silky demi-bra she wore before tossing her top to the floor. Next went her skirt, which slithered to the carpet with a whisper, leaving her in just her bra. Her panties were still somewhere in Thomas's office, waiting to give the cleaning lady a bad moment. Last, she turned and took off her bra, then held it out to the side between two fingers before letting it drop to the carpet.

Isabelle turned and walked across the carpet toward Thomas. His gaze ate up every inch of her skin as she approached. When she reached him, she hooked her hand into the waistband of his pants and yanked him toward her. "I'll take my sexual favor now."

His eyes were fathomless, black and intense. Focusing that deep gaze on her, he dipped his head and kissed the tender place just under her earlobe. His voice rumbled out of him and smoothed over her like heated chocolate. "Get on the bed." He didn't give her a chance to comply, instead pressing her down onto the mattress. Her knees already weak, she went easily.

Thomas's hair made a dark curtain around them, creating

their own private room, as he lowered his head and brushed his lips across hers, and then nipped her top and bottom lips in succession before sliding his tongue into her mouth to stroke languidly within. The kiss was sweet and slow as molasses and it heated her blood.

Isabelle lifted her hips and ground against him through the fabric of his pants. He broke the kiss with a groan and slid one hand under her rear, pressing his pelvis down on her sex so she could feel the hard ridge of his cock.

Lady, he was going to make her crazy.

She pulled at the waistband of his pants and whispered, "Let's get these off you, shall we?" Her fingers made quick work of his belt and buttons. Soon the rest of his clothing had been tugged off by both of them.

Thomas moved down her body, leaving little nips and kisses across her abdomen. "Not only are you gorgeous, you taste good, too." His dark head disappeared between her legs and she squealed in surprise. Then all the noise she could make were moans as he thoroughly tongued her clit to swollen and exquisite sensitivity.

Once he'd succeeded in arousing her to a fever pitch, he worked his way back up her body—tasting her skin at the curve of her waist here, nipping the swell of her stomach there.

His hair brushed her whenever he moved, silky and smooth, raising gooseflesh all over her. He paid special attention to each of her nipples, licking every pucker and crevice more fastidiously than a cat. All the while he stroked her between her thighs, bringing her to that blessed place where she couldn't form any coherent thought.

By the time he slid inside her she writhed on the mattress beneath him as if in heat, arching her back and thrusting her hips to push his cock as deep as possible into her body.

She couldn't remember the last time it had been this good, couldn't remember the last time she'd had multiple orgasms this way. Isabelle was no angel. She'd lost her virginity young and had plenty of lovers in her life, but the chemistry between her and Thomas was something different altogether, *better*.

"Are you using a spell on me?" she asked thickly in the

semidarkness, with Thomas staring down into her face. His hips rocked back and forth as he slid in and out of her. "Some kind of earth charm to enthrall me?"

"I would never do that, Isabelle. This is just you and me."

"Maybe it's the water-earth attraction."

"Why are you trying to find an explanation? Just let it be what it is." He shifted his hips and drove into her from another angle, hitting her G-spot and pumping harder and faster.

Her orgasm hit her then. She arched her back and sunk her teeth into her lower lip to hold back her cries. He came down on top of her and gently bit her throat as her climax tore through her. Her orgasm triggered his and they both spiraled into ecstasy together.

Later, after Thomas had tucked her against him and his hair covered her upper arm and shoulder like a blanket, he lay sleeping but she remained wide awake. She couldn't catch her breath or keep her eyes closed long enough for sleep to snag her.

Carefully, she pulled from beneath him and sat watching him sleep for several minutes. Light from the night beyond the window caught in the black strands of his hair, bleeding it to silver, and spilled over his chest and arms. The sheet had wrapped itself around his waist, leaving the air free to kiss his muscled stomach, chest, and arms.

Isabelle reached for him and then curled her fingers, drawing her hand back. If she woke him, they'd make love again.

Sexually, she and Thomas were an excellent fit. He was commanding both in and out of the bedroom and, while Isabelle was an assertive woman in general, in bed she wanted her partner to take change.

Thomas hit all her buttons exactly right.

Watching him now, with all that luscious hair spread out like the wing of a crow and his chest rising and falling with his breath, she wanted him again. And again. Normally once she had a man she was ready to move on, move out, move away.

She shuddered in pleasure, remembering his hands on her. Sex with this man could be addictive and that's exactly why it had to stop here and now. The last thing she needed was any entanglements.

Isa, you have to learn to invest yourself in other people . . .

Isabelle closed her eyes at the sudden prick of tears. Her sister had said that to her over the phone right before she'd traveled to Chicago.

And so maybe it was true.

Still, the impetus to get away from Thomas was far too strong to resist. Every breath the man took, every word he spoke, every brush of his hand against her body was a trap. Isabelle abhorred traps.

She slipped from the bed, dressed in the dark, and left the room.

ELEVEN

⤜

THOMAS TRIED TO IGNORE ISABELLE'S PROXIMITY IN the passenger seat of his car, and especially the way her light musky scent filled the interior. He wanted to reach over and touch her jean-clad thigh, but she'd made it clear she didn't want that from him.

It was almost as if last night had never happened, as if they hadn't spent hours, first in his office and then in his bed, exploring every part of each other's bodies intimately.

This morning when she'd come downstairs, face bright and cheerful, eyes empty of memory, acting as though nothing had happened at all, Thomas had felt more removed from Isabelle than he had since they'd first met.

Damn it, he'd been a one-night stand to her. He had to admit it pricked his pride a little.

He downshifted too hard in his agitation and the car jerked.

Isabelle braced a hand flat on the dash and glanced at him. "Be nice to your car, Thomas. It's a Mercedes, a fine piece of machinery."

"We're almost there." His voice sounded tight. "Tell me if you see a parking place."

A moment later she pointed to a spot near their destination—Boyle's only known residence—and he guided his car into the space. No Harley was parked outside, but that didn't mean the demon wasn't home.

They peered out the window at the building. It was a nice place in an upscale area. Still, it looked like any other apartment building in this part of Chicago. It just went to show you how little you knew your neighbors. These people had no idea they lived near a demon. Thomas hoped no one had tried to borrow a cup of sugar.

That morning they'd gone to Thompson's Motorcycles, where Simon Alexander worked. Posing as detectives, he and Isabelle had managed to persuade the manager that their loyal client, Erasmus Boyle, was a suspect in the attack on their accountant.

The manager had given up all the information on Boyle he possessed—license plate number, credit card numbers, home address, and phone number. He'd also told them that Boyle was a quiet, yet disturbing man. Boyle frequented the business often, having work done on his vintage 1977 Harley Davidson Low Rider, and buying and trading other cycles.

According to the manager he rarely said much to anyone that wasn't related to his hobby. No one at the shop knew a whole lot about his personal life and the consensus was that the man was creepy. The manager and employees could've had no way to know that Boyle was a demon, but apparently they'd sensed the monster in him on some level.

The manager was able to give them a few helpful tidbits. For example, a bar that Boyle liked to frequent. A bar that, not so coincidently, was a hangout for many witches. Since Boyle could mask his demoness when he wanted, none of the witches in the establishment would be clued in to his true nature. Hunting was probably easy for him.

The trip that morning had yielded a few tools to track Boyle down, if the demon *could* be tracked down. Thomas had sent Jack, Micah, Theo, Ingrid, and Adam out on leads he wasn't following up on with Isabelle—places where witches congregated and might draw Boyle.

They needed to work up an area where Boyle was known to frequent, places where they could patrol in hopes of finding him. That was their only hope of locating the demon. After all, they couldn't wait around for Mira to get another lucky break, although the powerful air witch was on constant surveillance for any other hint of Boyle.

He and Isabelle sat with the engine running while Isabelle

sent her magick through the water in the building, right into Boyle's apartment. All she needed to tap into the water in a building was close proximity and a little dampness between herself and her target. Fortunately, it had recently rained.

"There's no one there that I can feel," she said finally. "Either the place is empty, or he's masking somehow. But I don't think he's masking because I can't sense any sort of barrier anywhere."

"He likely feels he has nothing to fear from us, so no barrier."

She snorted. "We're gnats to him."

He shut off the engine. "Okay, let's go in while we can."

Isabelle opened her door. He put a hand on her leg to stop her and she turned to glare at him. "No, you're not getting all macho and protective on me, Thomas."

He sighed. "We need to make sure we do this carefully. That's all."

"We will. We'll do it like we discussed."

"First sign of trouble and I want you out of there, Isabelle. Understand?"

She stared at him for a long moment, then leaned in and kissed him. He had to stop himself from threading his fingers through her hair and crushing his mouth to hers. A groan rose in his throat from the pure pleasure of the taste of her, but he stifled it. He settled for the swipe of her lips on his and the light brush of her tongue into his mouth. Right now pushing for more was not a smart move.

Isabelle broke the kiss and set her forehead to his. Her sigh bathed his lips in her warm, sweet breath. "Maybe I like it a little bit when you're macho and protective." And then she was gone, striding toward the door of the building.

Thomas had to hurry to keep up.

The building was located in a swanky part of Chicago, but Thomas was glad to find the absence of a doorman or any added security in the sterile, polished lobby.

Isabelle called the elevator, and they traveled up to the fifth floor. When they reached Boyle's place, Thomas set his ear to the door, just to double-check for sounds within, while Isabelle did one last check via the water through the condo.

They both came back with nothing, and Thomas pulled his magickal ace, one of the earth charms he'd brewed and stored before they'd left the Coven on this errand. He took a black pen out of his back pocket and, muttering another incantation, basically words that he'd imbued with his own power, wrote a symbol of his own devising on the door. Earth magick was all about intention and the ability to channel magick though words and symbols of the witch's choosing. This spell was designed to muffle sound. Immediately after he'd finished marking the powerful charm, the release of the stored magick immediately diminished his strength, straining his body.

Once he was happy with his handiwork, he stepped back and drove his boot into the door until the lock broke through the jamb and swung open. Thanks to the charm, no sound alerted the neighbors.

The subtle scent of demon wafted out from the condo. Both of them flattened their backs against either side of the door at the same time in response. That smell brought back the horror of the previous night.

He glanced at Isabelle and saw her face had taken on a greenish cast. He wasn't much better off.

When no demon roared through the doorway at them, they entered cautiously, Thomas making sure he went first. The interior, despite the odor, looked like a model home. The furniture, artwork, and area rugs all looked like they'd been selected by an interior designer. The place was spotless, too. Thomas could see not one thing misplaced, not a smear on the glass table or any of the mirrors, nothing.

"It's almost like he doesn't live here," said Isabelle, taking the words from his mouth. "Where does he get his money anyway? I doubt he holds down a job, right?"

Thomas shrugged. "He's a demon. I'm sure he's got lots of ways. He can manipulate this dimension in ways we can't. That's why the Duskoff covet them."

Thomas went into the kitchen and opened the refrigerator door. Inside laid package after package of hamburger and steak, all past expiration. According to Micah, that was a demon's favorite meal, slightly spoiled raw meat. "Well, he's eating here. The refrigerator is filled with demon snacks."

"Yuck!" called Isabelle from somewhere else in the condo. "I know Micah said that a human woman fell in love with a demon way back then . . . but how could she stand to watch him eat?"

"Or stand his breath," he answered. "Or just the simple everyday scent of him when he's not masking."

"Bleh. No kidding," Isabelle called from the bedroom. He could hear her opening and slamming shut drawers. "Of course way back then everyone smelled bad."

"True." Thomas sifted through a pile of junk mail on a small table near the front door. "At least we can tell he's been here since the fridge is full and the place reeks of demon magick."

"But there's nothing here! Nothing at all. All the dressers are empty. The bathroom's empty. The closet's empty."

Thomas pivoted and opened a cupboard. Empty. As were all the drawers. A further thorough exploration of the apartment yielded more of the same—empty, empty, empty.

"Damn it!"

Isabelle walked down the hallway toward him. "What were we expecting to find? A diary detailing his nefarious plans? A map leading to the person he plans to attack next? I doubt it will be so easy."

He turned toward her and pushed a hand through his hair. "I was expecting to find something more than rotting meat. I hoped to find a book, magickical paraphernalia, something that might give us a handle on Boyle's intentions."

She sighed. "It's like he doesn't stay here. Like this place is only for show. Like he stores food here, but that's it."

Thomas nodded. "I wonder who the show is for. Us?" He rubbed his chin. "Maybe we're not gnats after all."

She turned in a slow circle in the center of the living room, surveying the place. "Maybe." She shivered. "Let's get out of here. It gives me the willies and I think we're done anyhow. We've got other places to check, right?"

Thomas nodded. "One more. The store manager said he'd seen Boyle at a bar lots of the bikers hang out at." He checked his watch. "It's late afternoon. We can check it out now."

Isabelle headed to the door. "Thank the Lady, a bar. I need a drink."

THE BAR WAS A BUST.

Isabelle mumbled her good night to Thomas as soon as they were through the doorway of the Coven.

Thomas stopped her dead with two words spoken in his low, mesmerizing voice. "Going somewhere?" She should've known she'd never get away so easily.

He crowded her back against the wall and pinned her there with both arms on either side of her body. Unease at being trapped against the wall licked through her and she drew a deep, steadying breath, reminding herself that she wasn't back in that closet. She was safe. She was free and no longer dependent on anyone else. At any time she could push away from Thomas and leave. Her fear abated with her reasoning.

His black pupils nearly swallowed up the dark-colored rims of his eyes. She watched in fascination as his jaw locked for a moment and his gaze dropped to her lips.

"What is wrong with you today?" he asked as he lazily dragged his gaze back up to meet her eyes.

She suppressed a shiver. Wrong with her? Did he mean other than the fact that all she wanted was to fuck him now, this very second? That kind of desire was dangerous.

Everything about Thomas Monahan was dangerous.

She tried to sound flip. "Nothing's wrong."

His jaw locked again and his eyebrows rose. "Then explain to me why you left my room last night like a thief?"

"I don't sleep well in other people's beds."

He cocked his head to the side. "That sounds like such a practiced line."

She glared at him. "I'm not lying."

"And you're not telling the whole truth either."

"Look, I don't owe—"

"Did you dislike it that much?"

Lady, no. She gave him a slow smile. "Dislike is not the word I would have chosen."

"Then why the coldness?"

She chewed her lip for a moment before speaking. "Well, it's not like I want to get married or anything."

"Never thought you did," he murmured, staring at her mouth. "So what's the problem?"

His head drifted closer to hers with the clear intention of kissing her while Isabelle tried desperately to remember what the problem actually was. . . .

"Thomas?"

They both jerked, startled by Micah's voice. Thomas swore long and fervently under his breath and turned toward him. "What is it?"

Micah looked surprised once he saw whose body Thomas's had been blocking, the one pressed up intimately against the wall. Isabelle colored, the curse of the fair-skinned.

Micah blushed, too. "I'm, uh, sorry."

"Don't be," answered Thomas. "What is it?"

"Just thought you'd like to know that Stefan tried to commit suicide today."

"What?" asked both Thomas and Isabelle in unison.

"He ripped his sheets into long thin strips and tried to hang himself. He only managed to knock himself unconscious, though. We put him in an empty padded cell."

Thomas looked thoughtful for a moment. "Gribben is getting to him a lot faster than I thought it would."

Micah snorted. "Do we care?"

"I don't know." Thomas passed a hand over his face, looking weary for a moment. "Any other news from today?"

"No. You?"

Thomas gave his head a short shake. "Nothing from Jack, Ingrid, or the others either."

"Then we wait." Micah sighed and turned away, waving a dismissive hand. "Carry on."

Thomas turned back to her, his eyes stormy and troubled. The sexual mood had been broken. Good thing since she'd been about to succumb. The reality of their situation had been asserted by the exchange with Micah. They were nowhere

closer to finding this thing and they had no idea when it would
kill again.

Gods.

Sobered, she turned to walk up the stairs. "I'm going to hit
the—"

"You haven't eaten."

She turned back around. "Excuse me?"

"I've been with you all day and you haven't eaten anything." He paused, considering. "Well, unless you count the
Snickers bar and Coke you had for breakfast."

"I'm not hungry."

"Nonsense. You need to eat something."

"Nonsense?" She crossed her arms over her chest, gave
him a slow smile, and glanced pointedly around at the dark,
quiet house. It was late. Maybe they should have stopped for
pizza. "Well then, *Daddy*," she drawled, "what did you have in
mind? There's no food around here I can see."

"The kitchen is closed, but we can still find something to
make a meal. They know me around here. I'm sure I can get
us a table."

"Ah. Humor." She nodded. "All right. Lead the way."

Isabelle followed him down one of the darkened corridors
of the house, past the carefully hung artwork, the small, intimate sitting areas and the lovely carved wood tables upon
which sat vases filled to bursting with fresh flowers until finally they reached the huge Coven kitchen.

He opened the swinging doors, allowing her to step through.
By the small amount of light, she saw it was all stainless steel
and spotless. A large middle island stood amidst the stoves,
refrigerators, and countertops.

"Wow."

Thomas went for the bank of refrigerators. "There's a wine
cave, too."

She wandered over to sit at the island, sliding onto one of
the cushioned chairs, and watched Thomas pull random items
out of the fridge and set them on the counter—strawberries, a
platter of leftover chicken swimming in some sort of yummy-
looking sauce and a plate of steamed asparagus.

She caught sight of a bowl of ripe avocados on a nearby counter, grabbed one of the pieces of fruit along with a salt shaker, a knife, and a cutting board, and sat back down to peel it.

"Aha!"

She jerked her head up from her work on the avocado to see Thomas take a plate of something from the fridge. She leaned over to take a closer look while he pulled off the plastic covering it. "Oh, no. I'm not eating that."

He glanced up at her. "What? You don't like oysters? What's wrong with you?"

She shuddered. "They're slimy and hideous."

"You've never tasted one."

She peeled the last bit of the avocado, extracted the seed and cut a bit of the ripe fruit. "I don't need to." She popped a thin slice of the avocado into her mouth and let the creaminess of it spread over her tongue.

He turned to the oven with the plate of chicken in hand. He put both the meat and the asparagus over a low flame in a wide skillet. Soon the gentle scent of basil chicken wafted to her nostrils and made her mouth water. As the chicken and asparagus warmed, Thomas found a bottle of champagne in the fridge and popped it.

She bit into another slice of avocado and watched him. "Are we celebrating?" She didn't see anything worthy of such at the moment.

Thomas only lifted a brow, theatrically shot his cuffs and then poured a few drops of the *Veuve Clicquot* into an oyster.

Isabelle curled her lip and tossed the half-eaten slice of avocado to her plate. "Ugh. That is such a waste of good champagne."

He rested his elbow on the counter, oyster in hand, and leaned toward her. "You don't know what you're missing." His voice rolled over her, satiny smooth and low.

Her gaze found his mouth when he lifted the oyster to his lips, lingered on the curve of his lips. As he tipped the small shell to partake of the dubious delicacy, she wished for a moment *she* were the oyster. Then the slimy bit was gone and he wore a rapturous expression on his face, head thrown back, eyes closed, dark hair cascading down his back.

Oh, yeah.

She closed her mouth and managed to stop drooling before he opened his eyes and looked at her. "I never thought you were afraid of trying new things. Are you sure you don't want one?"

She bit her lip for a moment. "Hand one over, but if I puke on your five-hundred dollar shoes, I was coerced, so don't sue me."

He laughed low as he prepared one for her. That laugh was a silky, dangerous thing and it made her shiver. She barely noticed when he handed her the half shell and came to stand beside her.

"How should I eat it?"

"Let it lie on your tongue for a moment, just a moment, then allow it to slide down your throat."

She studied it for a moment, and then decided staring at it was a bad idea. Pretty, it was not. "Down the hatch." She tipped her head back and slurped it between her lips.

It filled her mouth, cool, champagne-laced and mildly fishy, before she allowed it to ease down her throat. Like him, she found her head falling back on a *mmmmm* of surprised culinary delight.

She opened her eyes to find him studying her intently. "Good?"

Isabelle pursed her lips and chose her words. "Unique. Interesting. Complex. Definitely unforgettable."

His eyes went heavy-lidded and he reached out to wipe a bit of juice from the corner of her mouth. "Sounds like someone I know."

Before she'd even known she'd done it, she'd taken his hand and licked his finger. His eyes went darker immediately, the pupils growing larger, and his luscious lips parting. They stood there for a moment in the semidarkness of the kitchen and held each other's gazes.

The chicken on the stove popped and sizzled.

She blinked, breaking herself away from the intimate moment. "Dinner's burning."

He made a low, frustrated sound and backed away.

Thankful for the chance to catch her breath and snap herself out the second spell he'd put her under that evening, she rested her chin on her palm and watched him prepare two plates. He poured them both champagne from the open bottle and sat beside her to eat.

Her stomach rumbling, she picked up her fork and took a bite. Spices and tender chicken caressed her taste buds. "God, that's good," she said around a mouthful. "You have excellent chefs here."

He swallowed his bite and studied her as she dug in with relish. "To a woman who lives on Twinkies and Coke, I'm sure it does taste good."

"I don't live on Twinkies and Coke!"

His lips twisted. "That's true, sometimes you throw a bag of Doritos in there, or a peanut butter sandwich. Is that for protein?"

She shrugged, knowing full well her diet was less than exemplary. "I'm used to eating on the road. I never learned to cook for myself."

"Maybe while you're here, I could help you learn."

She gave him a lingering glance, from the tips of his Ferragamo shoes to the cuff of his Armani shirt. Nothing about Thomas Monahan was prêt-à-porter. "You cook?"

"Why wouldn't I? Most earth witches do. Something about cooking up spells translates to cooking up meals." He took a bite of chicken.

She picked up an asparagus stalk and studied him as she licked the tip. His chewing abruptly stopped and his gaze locked on her mouth. Isabelle suppressed a smile and puckered her lips as she slid the stalk within slowly and took a bite. Once she'd swallowed, she asked, "What would we make together?"

"Whatever you wanted. Vegetable stir-fry or miso chicken for example. Anything you can think of."

"Miso chicken? What the hell is that? How about something practical, like tuna fish casserole. That's the stuff I really need to learn how to make."

"How about meatloaf, then?"

A memory swelled. She closed her eyes for a moment, remembering. "I haven't had meatloaf in forever. Angela and I lived with a woman named Maggie Price for a while who would cook and bake for us. She used to make the best meatloaf. On rainy days when we couldn't go outside to play, we'd stay in and bake chocolate chip cookies. Staying with her was one of the few times"—she glanced at Thomas, realizing how much she'd disclosed and how easily she'd disclosed it—"I felt . . . safe." She ducked her head and nibbled another asparagus stalk.

Thomas took a bite, carefully chewed, and swallowed before he asked, "You didn't feel safe when you were a child?"

She tossed the half-eaten asparagus stalk to the plate and sighed. "Stop pretending you don't know. I'm certain you looked up my Coven records after I tried to off Stefan. You know what our mother is like, how she shuffled me and Angela around to her friends and lovers all through our childhood."

"Yes, I know all that. I did check out your records, but they didn't reveal how you feel about it."

"It was kind of rough sometimes, but I don't go there. It's in the past, can't change the past. It's useless to look backward."

"Sometimes the past echoes into the present. That means sometimes you have to deal with those events in the present, so they don't echo as much."

She picked up her fork and toyed with the chicken, not feeling very hungry anymore. "No echoes over here." Much. "How about you, Mr. Pop Psychology? How was your childhood?"

Thoughtfully, he chewed and swallowed. "Fine."

"Fine?"

He lifted a shoulder in a shrug. "I had siblings, a caring mother, an attentive father. You can't ask for much more than that."

She had a flash of jealousy she quickly squashed. It would have been nice to have even one of those things, a caring mother or an attentive father, but she was happy Thomas had had both.

"I had my sister."

Thomas didn't say anything for several moments. "We'll get the demon, Isabelle. We have to."

"I know." She spoke with the certainty of the obsessed.

TWELVE

◄══

ON THE WAY BACK TO HER ROOM LATER, SHE COULDN'T get the scent and feel of Thomas out of her memory. After they'd finished eating and cleaned up, he'd pulled her against him and kissed her. She'd meant to leave the kitchen before that happened simply because of the power coursing between them in the entryway earlier. Resisting Thomas was nearly impossible.

And then, there, in the kitchen, he'd pulled her up against him, settled his mouth over hers and kissed her so long and hard she'd practically forgotten her own name.

Her body still tingled from it. Her lips were still swollen and marked by his.

Then, he'd said, "Good night, Isabelle," with a little regret on his face . . . and had left her.

She'd slumped in relief back against the counter to catch her breath before she'd headed up to her room. If he'd taken her by the hand and led her upstairs, into his bed, she wouldn't have raised a word in protest. Thomas made her weak. He was like kryptonite to her.

Isabelle stopped in the hallway a short distance from her room and breathed quickly in the semidarkness, just on the edge of a panic attack. As the familiar anxiety ratcheted her heart rate up, she turned and fled for the exit. She needed air, open spaces.

Her feet pounded on the stairs as she descended and went

out the front door of the Coven. Once down the front steps, she leaned over and braced her hands on her knees, trying desperately to regulate her breathing.

For a moment she'd felt trapped, claustrophobic. Physically, she hadn't been in a tight place. However, for a minute, in her mind, she'd been in the closest space she could imagine. *That's* the danger Thomas presented.

Dragging the moist early morning air into her lungs, she straightened and stared down the twisting, tree-lined road that led away from the Coven.

Coming here had been a mistake. Maybe thinking she could settle anywhere, even her sister's apartment, had been a mistake. It just wasn't in her blood the way it had been in her sister's. Maybe Angela had been a changeling.

Even now she felt the pull of the busy airports and their crush of anonymous, self-concerned strangers, the embrace of foreign cities where no one knew her name, where fresh starts occurred every day.

No ties. No entanglements. No messy relationships for her to fuck up. Just nonjudgmental, impersonal hotel rooms and rented villas.

The thought comforted her and her breathing returned to normal as she stood in the darkness, staring down the road.

THOMAS STOOD IN THE MIDDLE OF THE FOYER, EXAMining the wicked copper blade of the sword he held. They'd ordered them forged as soon as Isabelle had discovered the demon's weakness, enough for all the witches in the Coven. The metal was soft, not practical for a weapon meant to be used in serious combat.

The first thing they'd thought of had been bullets, which would have been far more useful, but copper bullets were proving difficult to have made. Micah was looking in to having various weapons made using copper, bullets included, but swords and knives had been the easiest to procure right away. Pretty, but not practical. Unfortunately, it was all they had.

Movement on the stairs drew his eye. Isabelle descended,

barefoot, her hair long and loose. She wore a pair of worn blue jeans and an old burgundy T-shirt with the faded letters of some college across her breasts. The T-shirt was tight and the way she walked—all rolling hips and long-legged grace—made his mouth go dry.

She looked up, hesitated on a stair, then continued to descend. "Off to slay a dragon, milord?"

"Maybe a demon."

"Ah." She walked to him and he handed her the sword. She wrapped her fingers around the grip and examined it from tang to the tip. "Nice."

"Know something about swords?"

She shrugged and handed it back to him. "Not a thing, other than the pointy end goes into people. Clever, though, thinking about this as a weapon to use against the demon. Only one thing, how the hell are we supposed to walk around on the streets with these unnoticed?"

"I figure they can be sheathed to our backs and hidden under our coats. We intentionally had them made short for that. It's still spring, not that warm yet, so the jackets won't seem odd. I ordered some regular knives, too, but I think most will prefer these."

She nodded. "Gives you a little distance."

"Exactly."

"Would be better to have some copper bullets or something. That would give us even more distance."

As she spoke, Theo and Ingrid entered the foyer from the direction of the conservatory, both talking to each other.

"We're working on that," added Thomas. "Isabelle, I'd like you to meet Ingrid. She's Jack's counterpart and shares a lot of responsibility here at the Coven."

Ingrid was a short, thin, blonde. She always wore a suit, had her hair in a bun and glasses perched on her narrow nose. Ingrid was a fire witch with a temper to match, despite her innocuous appearance. She stuck out her hand. "I've heard a lot about you, Isabelle. I'm happy to meet you."

Isabelle shook her hand. "Same thing here. It's an honor."

Theo, a severe-looking man with longish black hair, a goatee and dark olive skin, stood very close to Ingrid. Thomas got an intuitive hit they were sleeping together. *Good*. Theo needed a little sex to bleed off his natural intensity.

Tattoos peeked from under the tight blue shirt Theo wore. What few people knew was that the tattoos complemented a large amount of scarring on his body, inked to show off what Theo considered his battle scars. When Theo had been a teenager, the Duskoff had captured him, lured to him by the massive amounts of earth magick he could wield. The warlocks had tried to crush his will for their own uses and had tortured him mercilessly, breaking bones and scarring his body. He'd been with the Duskoff a hellish two months before the Coven had broken him out.

Thomas, just barely in college at the time, had been with those who'd gone in after him. He could remember finding Theo, bloody and beaten, but still defiant and pissed off. Ever since, Theo had channeled his energies toward hunting down warlocks and rogue witches.

"And this is Theodosius, otherwise known as Theo—"

Isabelle grabbed his hand in both of hers with enthusiasm. "The artist. You did Thomas's tattoo."

Theo nodded. "I do work for many of the earth witches in the Coven."

"Ever do any for water witches?"

A flicker of unwelcome jealousy ran through Thomas at the thought of Theo putting his hands on intimate parts of Isabelle's body . . . any part at all, actually. He frowned at their clasped hands. *Gods*. He shook it off. He felt possessive of Isabelle, but he had no right.

"Come see me sometime and we can talk about it," answered Theo with a smile a little warmer than Thomas liked.

"Jack told me the swords came in," said Ingrid. "We came by to take a look." Thomas handed her the weapon and she looked it over. "Nice."

"Metal's too soft to use for a sword," Theo put in, catching the blade and examining it.

"I know, but it's all we've got," answered Thomas. "This is our only known weapon in fighting the demon."

"And training?" asked Isabelle. "I don't know about you but I skipped fencing class in college. In fact, I skipped college."

"You and I start as soon as you're ready." He glanced at Theo and Ingrid. "Theo, I know you're familiar with swords. I thought you could take over training some of the others."

Theo nodded. "Micah's got the rest of the weapons?"

"Yes. He's got training swords, too. I think Jack and Adam are with him now."

Ingrid handed the sword back to him. They said their good-byes and went in search of swords to practice with.

After they'd gone, Isabelle looked directly at him, something she hadn't done yet that morning, and he saw shadows in her eyes—trouble. "Do *you* know something about sword fighting?"

"More than the average person."

She grinned at him. "So you want to be the one to train me, huh? Don't trust me to Theo?"

"Never."

She shrugged. "Let me get a cup of coffee and let's go."

Twenty minutes later they went to the ballroom of the Coven, a place big enough for them to move. Mirrors lined one wall and an area of hardwood flooring lay like an island in the middle of the plush red carpeting. Thomas and Isabelle stood on the hardwood, each holding a sword and facing each other. They had traded the viciously sharp swords for blunted training blades.

"We're not going to train like fencers," said Thomas, "since the demon's not going to have a sword and, if he did, he wouldn't be playing by any kind of rules anyway. I just want everyone to get a good feel for the weapon, learn to move with it in the most effective way."

"Makes sense."

"So the first thing to remember is to breathe."

Her eyebrows rose. "Breathe? I'm doing that already. I intend to keep doing it for many more years."

"I mean breathe in a regulated, focused way."

"Be one with the sword?"

"Exactly. Breathe like you're meditating, deep and regular. It will keep you calm and give you enough oxygen to fight."

She tried it, turning around a circle with the sword in hand and breathing deeply as she moved. Closing her eyes, she rotated on the balls of her bare feet with the natural grace of a dancer or a warrior. Just by looking at her Thomas could tell that he didn't need to discuss the second basic with her—balance.

Isabelle finally came to a stop and opened her eyes. "That was a lot more relaxing than fighting the demon will be."

"Undoubtedly. All right, now we spar in order to familiarize ourselves with the other basic concepts, as well as to get a feel for the weapon."

She swung the blade experimentally. "And the other basic concepts are?"

"Tactics and timing."

She jumped and pointed the blunted training sword in his general direction. "*En guard*! But take your shirt off first, champ. Because, you know"—she shot him a salacious grin that made him chuckle—"you'll get warm dressed like that. Yeah, that's it. I'm worried about your comfort."

They sparred into the late afternoon. Isabelle was good with the weapon and he found himself on the defensive many times in the face of her surprising aggression.

The way she looked—her face and neck shining with perspiration, pupils wide and dark, lips pursed in absolute concentration—made it seem like the workout was therapy for her. Her movements were quick and self-possessed, too. What Isabelle lacked in terms of upper body strength, she made up for in speed and flexibility.

In the end, they were evenly matched, despite the fact that he was stronger physically.

Isabelle turned and brought her training blade down against his in a wide arc. He threw down his weapon, intercepted her and pulled her back against him. Thomas needed to touch her, just for a moment.

She thumped against his chest and went still, breathing heavy. Then she tossed her training sword to the floor and turned in his arms, rising onto her tiptoes to devour his mouth in a deep kiss.

He took a step back at the passion pouring through her, but she stepped with him, winding her arms around him and nipping at his lower lip. She tasted like hot magick and urgency, and acted like she might die if he didn't return her ardor.

Not breaking contact with her mouth, Thomas scooped her into his arms, knelt, and laid her on the floor. Isabelle wrapped her legs around his waist. He balanced over her, covering her body and slanting his mouth over hers to take control of the wild kiss.

Thomas's body tingled with the awareness of her, as if every molecule had been tuned to the frequency of *Isabelle*.

That's how he knew, despite the hardness of his body and his intense desire to strip her clothes off and take her right on the floor, despite the passion with which she tangled both tongue and lips with his . . . something was wrong.

It had been in her eyes that morning, in the way she'd thrown herself body and soul into the sparring, and the way she threw herself at him now.

Escape. Distraction.

That's what it seemed like to him. Like she tried to drown herself in stimulus to order to avoid thinking about whatever was bothering her. That's what she'd wanted him for the first time, too. *Make it all go away for a while.* That's what she'd said to him in the library.

"What's wrong?" he murmured against her lips.

"Nothing." She renewed the assault on his lips and grazed his bare back with her fingernails. He shuddered against her, desire flaring in his groin and swamping his mind.

"Isabelle," he whispered between kisses, "I know something's bothering you."

"You're wrong." She ground up against him. The delicious heat of her sex rubbed the length of his cock through the fabric of their clothing.

Thomas lost his train of thought.

It took a monumental act of strength to catch her wrists and pin them to the floor on either side of her. She stilled instantly, staring up into his eyes. It wasn't lust that colored them dark now, but the edge of panic.

Why panic?

"Isabelle, don't lie."

The glimmer of panic receded and her expression relaxed. "You worry way too much, Thomas."

"I can tell there's something bothering you."

She sighed. "Maybe. So what if there is?"

He released her wrists and collapsed on his back, breathing heavily. His rapid heart rate had nothing to do with their sparring. Neither did his rock hard cock. The absolute male of him wanted to just *take her*, curse the reason she was willing to throw herself into gritty, urgent sex here on the floor.

He wanted her, wanted her so much his cock had gone rigid at the first touch of her body against his. The thought of yanking off her clothes and rolling her beneath him now, spreading her thighs and sinking his cock into all that soft, warm, and willing heat was hard to resist.

But his yearning for Isabelle went past the physical.

Isabelle rolled away and sat up, pulling her knees to her chest in one lithe movement. "Maybe something *is* bothering me, but I'd prefer to keep it to myself if you don't mind."

He sat up, his hair trailing over his shoulder. "You want to use sex with me as a way to escape. Fine. But you have to level with me about it first." His voice came out harsh and cold.

"Thomas, I—"

The ballroom doors burst open and Mira rushed into the room, her face pale and drawn. Jack and Micah followed her.

Thomas leapt to his feet. Coldness curled through his stomach at the expression on their faces and at the psychic hit he got off Mira. It was something really bad. The demon had killed again.

Mira didn't bother with the preliminaries, probably reading in Thomas's expression that he already knew. "It's worse than you're imagining. I know because I heard it all."

Jack stepped up behind her and encircled her in his arms, his hands coming to rest on the small bulge of her belly.

Isabelle got to her feet, her gaze fixed on Mira's face. She hugged herself. "Boyle murdered another witch, didn't he?"

Mira shook her head and licked her lips. "He murdered *two*."

For a long moment the room was completely silent. Mira's mouth opened and closed. Perhaps she was stalling before she expressed her thought, hoping it would somehow disappear.

Thomas tried to make his voice as gentle and warm as possible. "Please just say it, Mira."

Silence dominated for another moment before Isabelle pushed out the words, *"Who were they?"*

The sentence exploded from Mira in a rush, "A twenty-one-year-old water witch named Brandon Michaels and an elderly fire witch named Mary Hatt."

Mira turned in Jack's arms for comfort and showed them her back while she continued, her words muffled against Jack's chest. "I was so tuned in to anything having to do with Boyle that I heard the entire murder. I became locked in it, mired down in a kind of psychic quicksand. It was . . ." Her voice broke and she trailed off.

Mira didn't have to explain. He understood what she'd just vicariously lived through. Her words punched him in the solar plexus. He closed his eyes and bowed his head. Beside him, Isabelle took a shuddering breath.

Focus. He had to focus on what they could do.

"What else do we know?" Thomas's voice sounded forced to his own ears.

For the first time, Jack spoke. "Since Mira was able to glean their full names, I took the liberty of having Ingrid organize the witches in the area of the killing to go to the scene immediately. I understand Adam and Theo are on their way there now. She's going to start the process of notifying next of kin, too."

"How long ago did you learn of this?"

"Minutes ago."

He glanced at Isabelle, who stared at a fixed spot on the floor. She'd tightened her arms around herself and her face had gone white. Was she fighting memories of finding her sister? Thomas wanted to go to her, to slip his arms around her, but his intuition told him that was the last thing she wanted right now.

He moved to her anyway. There was a difference between what she wanted and what she needed. Thomas wasn't sure if Isabelle had any comprehension at all about what was best for her.

He slid his arms around her. She stiffened against him and Thomas thought for a moment she might push him away, but she relaxed, melting against him and resting her head against his shoulder.

"I tried so hard to save that little girl and he just chose other witches to take her place." Her whisper sounded like silk and sand at the same time. "Lady, *two* instead of one."

Thomas closed his eyes and kissed the top of her head. "I know." Then louder, "Where's the scene?"

Micah answered. "A warehouse on the corner of Thurston and Maple."

"Jack, take Mira to see Doctor Oliver." He worried about her experiencing something so stressful while she was pregnant.

"Already on my immediate to do list," answered Jack.

Isabelle instantly stepped from Thomas's embrace. "Let's go."

Thomas took a moment to reply. "I don't think that's a good idea . . . not for you, anyway."

She shot a look at him that froze his balls. "Oh, no, you don't. See? This is where macho and protective stops being sexy and gets irritating. Anyway, I'm the only one who can access the moisture memory. That's one of the reasons you hired me, right?" Without waiting for his response, she turned on her heel and walked out the door.

THIRTEEN

⟜

BY THE TIME THEY REACHED THE WAREHOUSE, IT WAS past twilight and stars twinkled in the clear black sky. A few hours prior it had showered, leaving the air a little damp. Now Isabelle pulled that soothing dampness around her body like a cloak.

It was far too pretty a night for the job they were on.

Adam was the first to meet them when Isabelle and Thomas entered the large, brightly lit warehouse. Inside two witches had been killed in tandem, the magick sucked from the center of their souls and their bones picked clean.

Isabelle had a flash of a memory—blood, unnaturally tangled limbs—but she stopped short, squeezed her eyes shut, and willed it away.

Thomas's warm hand touched her arm. "Are you all right?"

She opened her eyes and glanced at him. He parted his lips but before he could utter the words—undoubtedly about her sister—she stepped past him. "I'm fine."

"Welcome," Adam greeted them in a flat voice.

She nodded. "Adam."

Adam leaned against the doorway of the warehouse, watching them approach. His handsome face was drawn in grim lines, his customary grin absent and shadows present in his dark blue eyes. "Isabelle, a beautiful woman on a beautiful night." He paused and glanced back toward the center of the building. "On not such a beautiful errand."

"How clean is the scene?" Thomas asked, coming up next to her.

Isabelle glared at him and did a quick translation in her head. *Have you removed the bodies so Isabelle doesn't have a meltdown?*

Damn it, Thomas. She could take care of herself.

Adam rubbed his chin and looked for a moment about twenty years older than his thirty-five years. "It's clean."

Even though Isabelle was annoyed by Thomas's high-handed protectiveness of her, she couldn't help but feel a little relieved. Adam moved out of their way and allowed them to enter the building.

A handful of witches who had reached the warehouse before them labored within the cleared interior, some working earth magick. That power rubbed against Isabelle's skin like rich planting soil—deep magicks meant to bury and conceal. They worked to cover up the scene of the crime from non-witches, just as they'd done at the scene of her sister's murder.

At the far end of the building, she noted two large open doors big enough to drive a truck through. She wondered if they'd been open when Boyle had killed the witches. It would make it easier for her to work if the water from the brief rain shower had been lingering in the air during the killings. Since Boyle didn't seem all that concerned with his murders being discovered and because this part of town was devoid of humanity at this time of night, it was possible he'd left the doors open.

A flash of white caught her eye and she glimpsed two sheets covering a section of the cracked concrete floor. The bodies had been removed, but those sheets marked the location of where they had lain. They'd done that with her sister, too.

The world lurched a little and Thomas took her by the upper arm to steady her. She straightened, calmly pulling from his grasp.

Adam walked over to them. The man always had a five o'clock shadow, but Isabelle didn't think it was so much a fashion statement as it was simple forgetfulness to shave. Right now it made him look weary. "The warehouse is owned by Erasmus Boyle."

Isabelle let out a small laugh. "Color me surprised."

Thomas glanced around. "I wonder what a demon wants with a warehouse?"

"Maybe he's planning to start a shipping business, specializing in sending packages to hell," she commented.

She knelt and put her palm flat to the cold concrete floor, sending out tendrils of her magick to search for any moisture that might have a story to tell. Water held emotion like none of the other elements. When something violent happened in a place, the moisture picked up and retained a record of it, burned there by the intense feelings of the participants. Accessing that emotional echo was not a skill all water witches possessed, but Isabelle had been lucky enough to inherit it.

Or unlucky, as the case may be. Reliving all that emotion was rarely pleasant.

She drew a breath. Damn it. No moisture to note along the floor. Maybe in the air. There was always a little bit of moisture in the air, and her magick was usually strong enough to pull it.

She stood. "But I might wager a guess he needs a large open area that is also concealed in order to . . . *work*."

Thomas pushed a hand through his hair, freeing it partially from the queue at his nape. "Toward what goal?"

"And," Adam added, "if he needs a place like this, why kill a witch here and blow his cover? He killed the first two witches in their own"—he hesitated and winced, probably realizing he spoke of her sister—"environment. Sorry, Isabelle."

"It's okay." Isabelle shrugged. "It was just a theory."

"And not a bad one."

"Well, at least we can rule out that he's targeting young female witches now that he's taken a man and an elderly lady," Thomas put in.

"He's selecting them on other criteria," Theo jumped in, striding to the three of them. He wore rubber gloves over his broad hands. Isabelle didn't want to think about why.

"Well, I'm leaving you three to hash that out," Isabelle put in. "I need to search for water molecules."

Isabelle left them talking and circled the sheets, examining the floors. Reaching out with her magick, she explored the area for any residual moisture that might have retained memories of the murder. She halted in the center of the warehouse and drew the water droplets to her, petting them and purring at them with her magick until they coalesced and began to give up their recollections of what had happened that night. Warm magick rippled from the center of her chest to complete the task.

"Come on. What secrets are you keeping?" she murmured.

Isabelle grimaced as the hazy, watered down images began to flicker through her mind's eye. She put herself through this torture for one reason and one reason only—to discover something new and different, some puzzle piece that would fit to make the picture clearer.

Now that she had her magick on the moisture, she doubted the doors had been open during the killings. Sifting through, it was difficult to find much memory.

As she gathered more moisture from the air, she felt the strain on her body from the expenditure of her magick. At the same time, the images grew more frequent and came to her a little less hazy, although fragmented, like a horror movie being played, fast forwarded, and then played again.

And then it slammed into her in one short blast of hell.

She tasted the fear of the victims on the back of her tongue—sharp and metallic. She heard their screams echoing in the cavernous building . . . until they didn't echo any longer.

Isabelle didn't know how long Thomas had had his arms around her, or how long she'd been crouching on the floor of the warehouse, both hands flat on the gritty concrete floor. Her vision had gone black and she'd lost her hearing, though she hadn't passed out. Her body shuddered as if she were outside naked in the middle of January.

Her mouth opened and a puff of air came out as she tried to answer Thomas's frantic questions of *Are you all right?* He held her close, rubbing her arms, trying to warm her up.

No.

No, she'd never be all right again. Not ever totally all right for having subjected herself to that. Worse, she'd gained nothing. There'd been no new puzzle piece. Nothing but a nightmare. Lady, and she'd just had flashes of moisture memory. How had Mira endured hearing the whole thing in real time?

She almost turned into Thomas's chest, almost wrapped her arms around him to draw comfort. Isabelle knew without a doubt she'd find it there.

Warmth. Strength. Protectiveness. Comfort.

She stopped herself just in time.

Gathering every ounce of strength she had left and pulling the tattered remnants of her magick around her like a cloak, she pushed to her feet. "I'm fine." The words came out without a quaver. Amazing.

Thomas rose and stared at her, unspeaking.

She turned her head and met his eyes. Isabelle could only hold the dark warmth of that gaze for a moment before glancing away.

"You won't ever ask for help, will you, Isabelle? You think you can do it all on your own, don't you?" His voice sounded brittle. "You think you're so tough, but you're not tough enough to let another person in, are you?"

Isabelle stared at the ground, completely unable to look up and meet Thomas's eyes. The truth of his words twisted in her stomach. "I don't need you to try and understand me, Thomas."

His response was swift. "I think you do."

"*Whoa.* What the hell?" Adam's voice saved Isabelle from responding.

She and Thomas turned to see him standing about seven feet away from them. He'd gone stock still as he waved his hand in the air front of him.

Isabelle blinked. "Um, Adam?"

"There's something strange about the air here. It feels . . . sticky."

"Sticky?" She walked to him, followed by Thomas.

"Yeah. Like the air here has something in it, some kind of—"

"Magick?" Thomas asked.

Adam stepped back. "Feel it."

Thomas stepped through the area that Adam had indicated. It was, Isabelle noted, very near where she'd seen the victims killed in the moisture memory. It may have been *exactly* where the two witches died, but she couldn't be sure.

Thomas stopped and waved his arm. "Hmmm. It's almost like this space is out of sync with the rest of the air around it." He stepped to the side. "Isabelle?"

She stepped through. It was like walking through thick cobwebs. "It's as if the molecules are vibrating slower than they should be. It feels like a warding, but not quite. More like a—"

"More like how a doorway to the demon dimension might open?"

"Maybe." Isabelle licked her lips, her thoughts whirling. "In the moisture memory the demon said something . . . something about his victims having certain qualities he needed. I think he meant magickally."

All three of them went silent.

"Are either of you thinking what I'm thinking?" asked Adam finally. "Maybe this demon is trying to get back over the rainbow?"

Thomas rubbed his chin and sighed. "There's no way to know for sure, but I'd say this is a decent find and a powerful clue. Maybe this demon is trying to go home. Maybe there's some spell we don't know about that will allow him to open a portal on this side."

Isabelle glanced at the white sheets and tried to not go where her memories wanted to take her. Seemed she just kept collecting bad ones. "Some spell that requires a lot of blood magick."

THEY ARRIVED BACK AT THE COVEN AT TWELVE PAST three in the morning after scouring the warehouse for every clue they could. There hadn't been much. Isabelle leaned against the wall by the side of the door in the Coven's dimly lit foyer and watched Adam and Thomas enter after her.

Both men looked tired and unkempt. So did she, but tired and unkempt looked a hell of a lot better on them than her. Adam's hair was an inch too long and stuck up all over his head in spikes, and his jeans were worn tantalizingly thin in some places.

Thomas's hair hung loose over his shoulders and dark

stubble marked his jaw. He looked bed-mussed. He'd looked a lot like that after they'd made love, his eyes hooded and dark with lust. Remembering made her shiver.

"I'm going to bed. I'm so damned tired I can't even think anymore," mumbled Adam as he walked past.

"Night, Adam," she mumbled back.

Thomas started to walk past her, toward the stairs. She reached out and touched his upper arm. He turned to look at her and she said, "You were right. Right about me not being as strong as I would like to think. Right about not being able to ask for help or let people in." She shrugged. "I hate it, but you're right."

In response, Thomas only swept his arm around her waist and crushed her to his chest. His mouth came down on hers. Stubble rubbed the skin around her mouth, playing contrast to his warm exploring lips.

Isabelle didn't have time to breathe, let alone object to the impulsive action. She wanted to, she really did, but the ability to push him away had died with a whimper as soon as he'd touched her.

She responded to his hot, urgent mouth without a flicker of hesitation. He demanded she part her lips to admit his tongue, but she was there first. She slanted her mouth across his and slid her tongue within to spar and stroke. His hand found the hem of her shirt and pushed beneath it, where he used skillful fingers to massage the tense muscles of her back. Her body let go of a degree of her tension with a shudder.

Brushing his lips languorously against hers for several moments, he broke the kiss and cupped her cheek. "Maybe you can practice on me."

Isabelle stumbled back, feeling a little breathless. No man but Thomas had ever made Isabelle Novak feel breathless.

She swallowed hard and tried not to let uncertainty show in her eyes as she remembered the panic attack she'd had in front of the Coven the other night and the inviting length of the driveway leading away from the building.

But she didn't want that anymore. That fear. That loneliness and self-reliance that she'd been wearing like a protective coat of armor for as long as she could remember.

Gazing up into Thomas's eyes, she realized just how much she wanted *him*. Not just for the sex, but wanted his strength and caring, his protectiveness and intelligence.

She smiled, letting the uncertainty bleed away from her eyes. "I want to try, Thomas."

He leaned in again and kissed her senseless. She hung on to his shirt, fingers fisted, as his lips worked over hers—teeth nipping at her lower lip, tongue exploring her mouth. Warmth bloomed through her chest, comfortable and nice.

When he stepped away from her, Isabelle could hardly focus her gaze, but Thomas had a distracted look on his face.

"He's collecting them," Thomas said, rubbing his chin the way he did when he mulled something over. "That has to be it. He's going after certain witches with certain qualities and absorbing their magick. Once he has the right combination, the right balance, something happens."

Isabelle took a moment to yank herself from the Hormonal Happy Land where Thomas's kiss had sent her and focus on the important issue at hand. "A doorway opens and he gets to go home."

"Exactly."

"He trades the lives of at least four witches just so he can go home." Anger vanquished the last of the passion Thomas had kindled in her moments ago.

"I'm sure we're nothing but cattle to him."

She chewed the side of her thumb, thinking. "When we foiled Boyle's attempt to take the little girl yesterday, he simply found other witches to fulfill what he would've gotten from the child. Like ingredients for a stew." Her voice broke on the words. "So there's no way for us to protect anyone."

"You did protect someone."

"But in the long run—"

He cupped her chin and guided her gaze to his. "No. Isabelle, this was not your fault in any way. Don't even go there. I know it's hard. I'm trying not to go there either. I keep thinking there should've been some way to stop this from happening and I feel guilty I didn't—"

"There was nothing you could've done—"

"*Exactly*, Isabelle. There was nothing either of us could've done." He stared into her eyes for several heartbeats, his vehement words echoing through her mind.

Isabelle pulled from him and walked away a few paces. He was right. Plus, they didn't have the luxury of wallowing, not if they had any chance of finding Boyle and protecting future victims.

"I know," she answered. "We need to concentrate on the task at hand and not dwell on might-have-beens. Boyle will kill again and this needs to be about those targeted witches, not us." Sorrow for Brandon and Mary clogged her throat and made the words come out husky. Because of the moisture memory, she almost felt like she'd known them.

"Yeah. That means sleep so that we can function at our best. We both need to get some of it. It's late and we have a long day ahead of us."

She snorted and turned toward him. "Sleep? That's not something I'll be getting much of tonight."

He sighed in defeat. "Yeah, me neither. Drink?"

"Definitely." She considered the options. "I have some great peppermint tea in my room."

"Tea? I was thinking bourbon, whisky, or scotch. Hell, maybe tonight all three at once."

"Are you afraid drinking peppermint tea will hurt your manly image?"

His lips twisted. "Only if you serve it in tiny china teacups and make me raise my pinky when I sip it."

"I won't do that, but I will put lemon in it."

"I can hardly wait," he answered in a dry tone. He motioned toward the stairs. "Lead the way."

Once in her room, she poured two mugs of steaming hot water from the purified water dispenser, plunked a couple of peppermint tea bags in each one, and then finished them off with the highly anticipated lemon wedges.

Thomas sat sprawled on the couch in the sitting room, looking too big for the small area. He had one long leg extended and one arm thrown up on the couch back. His silky hair cascaded down one shoulder and he'd unbuttoned the first few buttons of his shirt. She could see a bit of smooth, fine muscled chest beneath. Even though she tried to suppress her reaction to him, her mouth watered.

He glanced at the pieces of clothing she had lying around with a raised eyebrow. A blue shirt was draped over the back of a chair. A pair of jeans lay wadded up in the corner. She remembered how spotless his room was. Though from Thomas she'd expect no less. At least she hadn't left any of her underwear wadded up on the floor.

"No one ever said I was tidy." She shrugged and handed him a cup. "Voilà."

He took a sip, grimaced and set the cup on the table.

Isabelle sank into a chair across from him. "Mmmm . . . I love a man secure enough in his masculinity to drink a cup of tea. It's so sexy."

Thomas picked the cup back up again and leaned against the couch. Isabelle hid a smile.

"You did a fantastic job at the warehouse, Isabelle. It took a lot of courage to tap the moisture in the room. I know what it cost you. I don't regret asking you in to help out the Coven."

"Well, I'm glad you think I did a good job, but my agenda isn't the Coven's agenda, it's my own. They just happen to coincide in this case." She took a sip of the tea. "So don't go offering me a job or anything. I won't accept."

He held up a hand. "Wasn't going to. You've got a career already. You're a travel writer, right?"

"Yes. Although I wouldn't call it a career, more like just an excuse to take trips."

She didn't have to work for money. It was the one way Catalina seemed to show she cared about her daughters, though dollar bills were a cold substitute for motherly love.

"I never travel unless it's on Coven business."

"What? You never get vacations?"

Thomas shrugged.

"Oh, I get it. You just don't *take* vacations."

"Not usually."

He rested his feet on the coffee table in front of him, slumped in his chair and let out a deep groan of relaxation that

Isabelle felt all through her body. Thomas rolled his head lazily. "So, tell me about some of the places you've been."

She shrugged a shoulder. "Eqypt, Tibet, India, Australia, Russia. I've been just about everywhere."

"What country do you like best?"

"That's like asking a parent to pick their favorite child. All countries have different good points, depending on what time of the year it is." She paused, thinking. "I don't know. I would have a different answer to this question every single day."

"So what's your answer today?"

Smiling a little, she reflected on some of her favored places before answering. "I love Naples, Italy, in the spring. I love the smell of the city and the yowling of stray cats everyone feeds at the water's edge. I love waking up and down the cobblestone streets to buy a loaf of fresh bread. I love sitting in an outdoor cafe and drinking small, strong cups of coffee while I eat the warm bread straight out of its white bakery bag."

He took a sip of the tea, grimaced again and set it on the table. "So you do that alone?"

Isabelle fought the urge to defend herself. The comment pricked and she knew why. *Yes, alone*. She was always alone. Only until recently had that become tedious.

"I like being alone," she answered simply.

He nodded, but his eyes said clearly that he didn't believe her. He was right not to.

"So what about you? Why no vacations? Why no traveling?"

"My work has kept me in the States for the most part. I started working for my father when I was fifteen. When he died, the Coven appointed me head. This job has taken all my time and energy."

Isabelle *tched*. "All work and no play."

He gazed at her through hooded eyes. "Do you think I'm a dull boy, Isabelle?"

She smiled. "I wouldn't say *that*. I would say that I might be a loner, but you're a workaholic."

"We're the perfect pair."

"A match made in hell."

A speculative look enveloped his face. "All opposites, you

and I. You can't stay still and all I've ever done is stay still. I'm patient and a planner and you're impulsive."

"You drink champagne and eat gourmet food and I like Ho Hos and Diet Coke." She rested her head on the couch back and dropped her eyelids to half-mast. "Like I said, a match made in hell."

"Or somewhere."

They sat for a while in companionable silence, Isabelle with her feet tucked beneath her. She closed her eyes for a moment, but opened them when she felt Thomas take the cup from her hand and set it on the coffee table.

"It's time to sleep," he murmured. "We have a demon to catch tomorrow."

She nodded and stood, wavering on her feet. He caught her around the waist and she leaned into him, enjoying for a moment that he could take her full weight and not even notice it. Thomas guided her to the bed and undid the buttons of her shirt with deft fingers.

She gave him a heavy-lidded leer. "What exactly do you think you're doing, Mr. Monahan?"

She'd been going for playful, but his expression was serious. "I'm getting you ready to sleep." He dragged his gaze to her eyes. "It's not like I haven't seen you naked before." He eased her shirt down and off her shoulders, then unbuttoned her pants.

She had mixed feelings about his response and the businesslike way he undressed her. On the one hand, she'd wanted to avoid any more intimate contact with the dangerous Thomas Monahan. On the other hand, now that he was here with his hands on her and the scent of him teasing her . . .

"You're such a gentleman," she murmured.

He sent her pants sliding down her legs and glanced at her face. "Trust me when I say I really don't want to be a gentleman right now. Where are your pajamas?"

She reached around and undid her bra. The bit of fabric fell to the floor between them. "I don't own any."

A muscle in his jaw twitched.

Grabbing fistfuls of his shirt, she went up on her tiptoes and pressed her lips to his. He slanted his mouth over hers and parted her lips, spearing his tongue into her mouth hungrily. He tasted like peppermint tea and lemon.

Thomas wrapped his hands around her waist and slid them up her bare back. One hand pressed her against him, the other found her nape and controlled the movements of her head while he kissed her.

When they finally pulled apart, she breathed heavily. "I think I just decided I don't want you to be a gentleman."

"Isabelle," he murmured, "you're a confusing woman." Then he pushed her backward onto the bed and came down on top of her.

This was wrong, so very wrong, but damned if she cared right now.

FOURTEEN

She curled her legs around his waist, feeling the ridge of his hard cock rub against her tender flesh. The scent of him—part cologne, all man—teased her senses, and the brush of his hair over her skin raised goose bumps along her flesh. She loved the weight and heat of him on top of her; lying flush up against Thomas Monahan was fast becoming one of her favorite places to be.

"Being confusing is part of my charm," she sighed as she slid her hands between them and impatiently undid the rest of the buttons on his shirt. "Keeps a man on his toes."

Thomas only grunted in response and slid his palm down her outer thigh and under her to cup her bottom and grind himself gently against her. They both groaned. Isabelle's clit plumped with need, becoming sensitive and yearning to be stroked.

Lady, she had to get his clothes off a lot faster than this.

She finished with the buttons of his shirt and ran her hands over his chest, feeling the smooth, hard muscle that lay beneath his satiny skin and the rough rub of his chest hair.

"Off," she ordered softly and he shrugged his shirt down his shoulders and threw it to the floor. "Mmmm . . . much better. You have an exceptional upper body, Thomas."

He dropped his head to a breast and murmured, "So do you. Can't keep my mouth off it," right before he took a nipple between his lips.

Isabelle arched her back at the erotic, punishing scrape of

his teeth, followed by the soft swipe of his tongue. The combination caused lust to flare low in her body and made her want much, much more.

Rolling to the side, he reached down between them and yanked her panties to her knees, then dragged his hand between her thighs. His fingers found her swollen, aroused clit and petted it while his lips worked over one nipple and then the other with exquisite care.

"You have an exceptional lower body, too," she breathed, running her palms up his biceps and over his shoulders to enjoy the satiny hardness of him—like silk poured over steel.

He chuckled low, sending vibrations through her breast. He raised his head for a moment and murmured, "Is that a hint?"

Isabelle threaded her fingers through his long, silky hair that spread over her chest and stomach as he moved, and closed her eyes. "Uh, maybe. Not sure I'm capable of something as complex as a hint right now, though."

In an impatient, almost rough gesture, he pulled her panties all the way off. Pleasure warmed her sex and tingled through her body, making her half-crazy with the need to feel him thrusting deep inside her. She moved her hips toward him in an unconscious way, seeking his cock to ease the throbbing ache he'd kindled in her.

He dragged his hands up her legs, and parted her thighs. For a moment, he just looked down at her, taking in the view of her aroused sex. Then he dragged his skillful fingers over her folds, rubbing between her labia until she moaned, and slid them inside her.

She felt the walls of her sex clamp down as he moved them in and out. Isabelle rode his fingers, fisting the blankets on either side of her, and tossing her head.

"Hint or no hint, I need to taste you," he murmured, dropping his mouth to kiss between her breasts. He trailed his tongue down, over her abdomen, into her belly button and lower, all the way to her clit. There he teased her with his tongue and lips until she felt herself break apart beneath him.

Pleasure burst over her body, swamping her mind and forcing her to arch her back. Thomas rode her through it, petting her sex and tonguing her clit when her climax stuttered nearly to a halt. Her clit became sensitive almost to the point of pain, and then her orgasm flared again, engulfing her body once more and making her cry his name.

Once the ripples of pleasure had subsided, she yanked him up and kissed him, her tongue skating between his lips to mate with his. She dropped her hand to the waistband of his pants between them and undid the button and zipper as fast as she could. Not wanting to take the time to pull his pants off, she simply pushed them down far enough to pull his cock out and stroked it in her palm until he groaned into her mouth and shuddered against her.

"Isabelle, I want you," he rasped.

She smiled against his lips at the need in his voice. "I'm right here. Not going anywhere."

He pulled away from her and nearly ripped his pants and shoes off. Thomas stood for a moment, watching her. His hair had fallen across his face, shadowing his eyes. She let her gaze travel over his gorgeous body and long, wide erect cock for a moment. The man's beauty was breathtaking.

Then he stepped forward, grabbed her by the back of the knees and pulled her so her ass was nearly off the edge of the bed. She gave a squeal of surprise.

Thomas grabbed her wrists and pressed them to the mattress above her head. She had a flicker of unease that made her breath catch, but then Thomas kneed her thighs apart roughly, and guided his cock into her and she forgot her fear, forgot everything.

He held her hands above her head and pushed into her wet heat slowly until he'd seated himself to the base. He stayed that way, staring down into her eyes. Isabelle's heart beat faster. With her wrists restrained, his cock buried deep inside her and his dominant, almost challenging, gaze on her, she felt trapped, possessed. It edged her pleasure with the slightest bit of panic that she fought to control.

Thomas withdrew and thrust back in, steadily increasing the pace of his thrusts, setting up a rhythm that would soon send them rushing headlong into ecstasy.

She dug her heels into the mattress and curled her fingers around his wrists as he held her captive. Pleasure skittered through her sex and up her spine, signaling her oncoming climax.

Thomas rotated his hips a little, driving into her by another angle, one that brushed the head of his cock against her G-spot with every thrust. Isabelle sank her teeth into her bottom lip and came. It slammed into her body with the force of a train, stealing all her thought and her breath momentarily along with it. She felt the muscles of her sex pulse and ripple along Thomas's thrusting length.

"Isabelle," he breathed a moment before he released himself inside her with a long, rumbling groan of pleasure.

They lay tangled together, breathing hard. She'd thrown one leg around his waist and the other now hung off the side of the bed. Thomas released her wrists after a moment and she rotated them. He'd held her firmly, but he hadn't hurt her. Oddly, she felt a bit sad that their contact was now broken.

"Isabelle," he murmured again as he moved to her left with a groan of exhausted satisfaction. "You kill me, woman." He crawled onto the mattress and collapsed. After a moment she followed him.

Thomas rolled onto his side, tucking up against her body and propping himself up on one elbow, and stared down at her with an unsettling intensity. He said nothing. He didn't need to say anything; his emotions lay in his gaze.

Thomas cared for her a great deal.

That knowledge made a wisp of fear curl through her stomach, brought images of long, dark winding roads and airport terminals flickering through her mind. Instead of giving in to her fears, she reached up and cupped his face, feeling the rough stubble that he hadn't shaved since that morning.

She'd meant what she'd said about *trying*. For the first time in her life, she'd found a place and a person she just might want to hang around for. Maybe. Thomas Monahan was worth a closer look, at least. There was no doubt about that.

Idly, he stroked her breast, playing with the nipple until it hardened and she squirmed on the bed from the heat it kindled in her sex. "Never thought I'd fall for a high-maintenance woman."

Her eyes widened. "First of all, who's *falling* for anyone?

This is all about the sex, bub. Second of all, who's high-maintenance?"

He chuckled. "Funny." Then he lowered his head, closed his lips around her nipple and she forgot the flare of panic she'd felt when he used the words *falling*, as in *falling in love*, in reference to her.

His hand slipped between her thighs to stroke as he paid careful and thorough attention to each of her nipples in turn. Her breath came sharper and her body tingled. He could play her like an instrument, make the sounds of pleading fall from her lips like music.

Dangerous was the man who could make her beg for him. . . .

"Thomas." One word. His name. But it was spoken like a prayer and an entreaty all at once.

He kneed her thighs apart and slid between them, slipping his cock into her body as though it were a part of her. His hand followed the curve of her waist and hip until it slid under her buttocks to cup her against him as he rode her so slowly the pleasure made tears sting her eyes.

Yes. This was a man she could stay for. Here was a man who could be her home. The thoughts came into her mind like leaves falling from a tree, so naturally. In a haze of pleasure, she felt warmed by them.

Her climax rose slowly this time, teasing her with the edge for many moments until it stole over her and then exploded. It rolled up her spine and through her body, thieving everything in her world for a moment that wasn't directly related to the sensation.

Thomas responded to her climax only a moment after hers had ended. He groaned her name low, while she scattered kisses along his throat and gently dragged his skin between her teeth.

After it was over, he pulled her to the side with him, burying his face in the curve of her throat and breathing heavily.

"Orgasm blindness," she murmured.

His breathing paused for a moment and he lifted his head. "What?"

"Orgasm blindness. When I climax, for those few moments, I can't think at all. Can't focus on anything but the pleasure. It's like I'm blind and deaf to everything else." She adjusted so she lay on her side and propped her chin in her palm. "Is it like that with men?"

"Yes." He pursed his lips. "Although you seem to have that effect on me all the time."

She buried her face in the curve of his neck, breathing in the scent of him and hiding the pleasure his words gave her.

Eventually Thomas's breathing evened out and relaxed into that of deep slumber. Her thoughts were heavy tonight, and complex, just as complex as the emotions that Thomas engendered in her.

She might be falling in love with him.

That realization came with equal parts terror and joy. Joy that she might actually be capable of a deeper relationship, a tie with another human being. The terror came from the same thought.

Unable to sleep, she slipped from under the blankets, dressed in a pair of sweatpants and a light white sweater, and left the room. Wandering the halls of the Coven in the dark was actually relaxing. The gentle magickal hum of the building's wards warmed through her, soothing her. Just the very leading edge of morning filtered in through the windows. The world outside was still hours from truly stirring.

Finally, she reached the library and slipped inside. She knew why she'd been drawn there; within, it smelled like Thomas. This was his favorite room in the Coven, the one that doubled as his office. The place was steeped in the energy of *Thomas* and she felt comforted here.

She hesitated at the doorway, suddenly torn between wanting to enter and wanting to go back to Thomas. The desire jarred her. She'd never wanted to return to a man's bed before. Moving by only the light that filtered through the big window, she felt her way to Thomas's desk and flipped on the lamp.

Then she turned around and came face-to-face with Boyle.

Isabelle stared into the demon's eyes for a moment, unblinking. Adrenaline zinged through her body. His eyes were flat gunmetal gray. She'd expected them to be empty, but they weren't. The demon's eyes were full of emotion, of personality. Like a human's.

One would have to have emotion to want to chew on the bones of a child, wouldn't one? One would have to have a force of personality to lie in wait within an attorney's office for an innocent witch and then suck the life from her body and the magick from her soul.

Isabelle lunged backward, skidding over the top of Thomas's desk, knocking everything off and grabbing a letter opener she'd seen as she went. The demon didn't move as she put the heavy piece of furniture between them and brandished the weapon in her hand.

"You killed my sister." She didn't even realize the words had come from her throat until they were out. They didn't even sound like they'd come from her, so low, so sinister, so gravelly. "You killed those four innocent witches. You tried to kill that little girl!"

The demon remained disconcertingly motionless, his eyes unblinking as his gaze bored into her. "It was necessary. I needed them."

The answer was far from satisfactory. Pure rage blossomed in her chest. She moved from behind the desk. Taking her eyes from the demon fleetingly, she glanced to note Thomas's sheathed sword lying against one of the floor-to-ceiling bookshelves. That would be so much nicer to have between herself and the demon than a tiny letter opener. As it was . . .

She hurled herself at the thing in front of her and plunged the letter opener straight into where she assumed the demon's heart would be, if he had a heart.

Blood dripped from Boyle's wound, but he didn't move, didn't react. It was like stabbing a living statue. She backed away, the letter opener still embedded to the hilt in his chest. Blinking away the sting of tears, she fought to comprehend that she hadn't hurt him, not even a little.

She wanted so much to hurt him.

"I need you, too, Isabelle Novak."

She blinked. Why wasn't he fighting her, trying to kill her then? "What does that mean?"

"You have the right combination I need for my spell. You are perfect in your magickcal balances and fit the puzzle I am trying to piece together."

"You mean you want to chop me up and stir me into your magickal stew?"

Boyle thought about that for a moment. "Yes."

"You know what, Boyle? Fuck you."

She lunged to the right and caught up the sword. By the time she'd unsheathed it, he was on her.

He grabbed her around the throat and squeezed. Isabelle felt her eyes bulge and her larynx begin to crush. He lifted her and the sword dangled impotently at her side. The handle of the letter opener still embedded in him poked her chest.

Even though it was a violent action and it made panic race through her veins like drinking ice water on a hot summer's day, the demon was being gentle with her. He could crush her throat as easily as she could break an egg in her fist. He wasn't killing her because he needed her alive for some reason . . . at least for now.

Isabelle brought her knee up hard and fast, right between his legs. The demon yowled and dropped her. Isabelle crashed to the floor and landed on her ass, still holding tight to the sword and gasping for air. Well, that was one part of the demon's anatomy he had in common with a human.

When she could, she looked up to see Boyle doubled over. She took the opportunity to bolt to her feet and swing the sword at him. With lightning fast reflexes, he blocked her stroke and grabbed the blade with his bare hand.

He pushed it away and she yanked it from him, demon blood dripping from his palm and sizzling to the floor where the sword had bit into flesh.

Isabelle went into a half-crouching position and circled him, waiting for a better opportunity.

He opened his hand and showed the cut made by the copper sword. It wasn't smoking, not peeling away. Nothing. Why hadn't it worked? Why wasn't he screaming and writhing in agony like he had before?

"I can see the questions on your face, little witch. You're wondering why the copper isn't making me sick. I have treated myself since we last met. I've given myself allergy shots, so to speak. Such a superficial exposure to copper will not harm me now, though the swords are clever."

Then she'd have to make sure the exposure wasn't *superficial* then. "Whatever. Swords still maim. They're still capable of hacking off limbs. I guess you can't grow limbs back, right? No allergy shot for that." She feinted to the left, then turned and brought the blade down toward him.

Boyle moved at the last moment, but he wasn't quick enough to avoid the satisfying bite of the blade into demon meat. He bellowed, grabbed the blade with both of his massive hands and threw it across the room. It shattered the window at the far end.

Isabelle cringed at the sound of breaking glass and the noises of an animal in pain. She'd wounded him with the blade, but he still hadn't had the allergic reaction he'd had in the parking lot, damn it.

Blood coursed from the demon's side, soaking his jeans and the black T-shirt and leather jacket he wore. With one mighty sweep of his arm, he smashed the liquor cart near him, sending the bottles and glasses crashing to the polished wood floor.

"You have the blend I need, Isabelle Novak, but there are others. You have time to think on my proposal. I'm doing this only because I felt how distraught you were over the most recent deaths. Ah. I see your face. Yes, little witch, I'm empathic. I will come for you when I am ready. I have work to do before you. Sacrifice yourself and you save another witch, or save yourself and doom another to death. The choice is yours."

She stared up at him. Boy, she didn't like the options.

"The head mage has grown fond of you," Boyle added. "The one ridden by the angel. Do not let him know of my offer. His interference will mean his death. You have been warned." Boyle turned, threw open a doorway, and exited. *Poof* and he was gone.

Shock numbing her body and stealing her thought, Isabelle sank to the floor amid the jagged edges of broken bottle and glass. Amber-colored liquid mixed with clear on the dark wood floor. From the opening of the shattered window at the far end of the room, early morning air drifted in and made her shiver.

Lady . . .

Soon the numbness let go and pain registered. Her throat

ached and burned at the same time. Now that the demon was gone the adrenaline slowly leaked from her system, leaving her feeling like she'd just been hit by a freight train.

Her life for another witch's.

Would she have traded her life for Brandon's or Mary's? Her mind balked at the choice, riffled through scenarios. Selfishness screamed *no*. How could she sacrifice her life for a stranger's? She liked life. She liked *her* life. Dying wasn't on her agenda for a good sixty or more years. Isabelle was no martyr and she'd never been particularly self-sacrificing.

But would she have traded her life for her sister's? Nausea roiled through her stomach. The answer, of course, was *yes*. Would she have given her life to protect that little girl from the demon? She'd done her level best, hadn't she?

Mary had been a mother, a grandmother, a sister, and a freaking retired kindergarten teacher, for the sake of the Lady. Brandon had been a son, a brother, and a devoted uncle. They each had had strong familial ties. Many people now grieved them. They each had left large holes in the world.

Isabelle closed her eyes. If she died few people would even notice. She wouldn't leave a large hole, just a pinprick. These thoughts didn't come from a place of self-loathing; they were simple facts.

In the face of that realization, her choice became sickeningly, stomach-lurchingly clear.

She closed her eyes for a moment and just concentrated on breathing—in through her nose and out her mouth. Breath by breath, moment by moment, that's how she had to take this.

How long did she have until Boyle came for her?

Once her heartbeat returned to something resembling normal, she opened her eyes and surveyed the damage to Thomas's office. The breeze that shouldn't be there buffeted the papers that had been knocked off his desk. Alcohol soaked through files and made ink run. She hoped it was nothing too important.

She doubted anyone would have heard the ruckus. The library was far from the residential portion of the Coven and it was the middle of the night. The wards were set to register magickal disturbances, not swords thrown through windows.

Isabelle wondered how Boyle had gotten into the Coven,

though she suspected she knew. Witch magick didn't work on demons, so it went to follow that neither did wardings. The reason was moot; obviously, he'd gotten through. She would have the bruises on her throat to show for it, not to mention a lovely decision to make.

Not that it was much of a decision.

She wouldn't go out without a fight, though. Already her mind worked through the possibilities. Maybe there was a way she could defeat Boyle, keep her life and that of the witch of the equivalent magickal consistency who would serve in her place. Maybe she could.

Or maybe not.

FIFTEEN

THOMAS STOOD ON HIS SCATTERED, SOAKED PAPER-work in the middle of his office, morning light shining through his shattered window, wondering what the hell had happened. It looked like a bomb had hit.

"Thomas?"

Isabelle appeared in the doorway, looking somehow pale and fragile. What the hell could make *Isabelle* look pale and fragile?

Alarmed, he walked toward her. "Are you all right? What happened in here? Fuck," he breathed as he got closer and glimpsed the bruising around her throat. He took her by the shoulders. "Isabelle, what's going on?"

"I'm fine." Her voice, gravelly and tired-sounding, revealed the lie. "But we have a problem."

"Just one?"

She smiled faintly. "I found out last night the demon can breach the Coven's wards."

Everything became clear. A cold jolt of terror for Isabelle's safety replaced the blood in his veins for a moment. "You fought the demon here, in the library?"

"Yes, and another thing, he's not allergic to copper any-more."

He considered her words. "You're telling me that the demon has no weaknesses and you still defeated it?"

She nodded. "He almost choked me to death, but I managed to beat him off. Then I wounded him with your sword. It didn't cause the reaction in him, but it did injure him enough to cause him to retreat and leave me alive."

The coldness in his veins transformed to hot rage at the thought of Boyle putting his hands around her throat. He had to force his vocal cords into action and his hands to unclench. "Why did he come after you?"

She shrugged. "I don't know. All I know is I went for a walk last night and decided to come to the library. When I flipped on the light, there he was."

"Did he say anything? Did he give you any kind of a clue about why he came here?"

She shook her head.

His intuition niggled. "Are you sure?"

She stared straight up into his eyes. Isabelle had such pretty eyes, too bad there was a lie in them. "I'm sure."

"What are you hiding from me, Isabelle?" he pressed. "Tell me."

She blinked and licked her lips. "I think he's taken a liking to me."

Fear fisted cold in his stomach. His hands on her shoulders tightened. "What makes you think that?"

"His way with me, asking me personal questions. Didn't Micah say demons could become infatuated with their prey?"

"Yes." He compressed his lips into a thin line. "Do you think you're prey to him?" His desire to protect Isabelle was overwhelming. All he wanted at this moment was to lock her away in some steel room and put fifty guards on her, then go out and kill the demon with his own bare hands.

"Aren't we all? Why do you think Boyle was able to get into the Coven?"

"I'm not surprised he could penetrate our wards," he replied. "I always suspected he could since his magick isn't anything we can tool our security system for."

"Alien magick. So he can just come and go as he pleases."

"It appears that way."

"Lovely."

"That means, first, you go see Doctor Oliver and, second,

you stay in my room with me every night." He felt his expression harden. "I don't want you out alone in the Coven after hours when there's no one around."

Indignation overtook her face in a millisecond. Her shoulders and spine straightened. "I'm not hiding from Boyle under your covers every night."

"The hell you're not. You just lied to me. That demon came gunning *for you* for some reason and you're not telling me why. I'm not leaving you alone so he can pick you off. This is not a discussion. You're staying with me, Isabelle. I want you protected."

Cold fury lit her eyes and set her mouth into a thin, dangerous line. Her voice shook when she replied. "I won't do it. You're going to have to drag me in there and lock the door."

"I'll do what I have to do."

She turned on her heel and walked away from him.

"Go find Doctor Oliver!" he called after her as he followed her out the door.

"Go to hell, Thomas!" she called back.

Thomas watched her climb the stairs to the second floor and disappear from view without looking back at him. He didn't care how she felt about it, didn't care at this point how she felt about him. His only goal was to keep her safe. If that meant pissing her off, so be it. He really would throw her over his shoulder and lock her in his room if it was necessary. The tattoo on his back tingled. He knew just the spell to keep her from leaving.

Some primitive male portion of his psyche had declared Isabelle *his*. Some leftover caveman part of his brain had decided he needed to protect her, destroy anyone—or any demon—who wanted to hurt her, challenge any other man who dared try to take her away from him.

He wasn't sure when that possessive tendency over Isabelle had kicked in; maybe it had happened when he realized his feelings for her went further than just the physical. Maybe it was the maddening vulnerability that Isabelle possessed underneath all her bravado. In any case, knowing Isabelle had battled the demon alone made the part of him that had marked her as *his* go crazy.

The thought of finding Isabelle like her sister had been found was incomprehensible. His mind couldn't even go there. So Isabelle would be spending her nights with him from now on. He would protect her. If she hated him for it, so be it.

"SO... YOU AND THE BOSS MAN, HUH?"

Isabelle glanced at Adam. "It's just sex." *It wasn't. Not anymore.* But that wasn't Adam's business.

They were headed back to the Coven after another day of fruitless searching for Boyle. Every day they checked and rechecked all the places where they knew he hung out and had the warehouse under constant surveillance, but they kept coming up empty.

"That's cool. I'm not judging. I think it's pretty healthy, actually. Monahan is one guy who could really benefit from a little no-strings-attached shagging."

"Yeah, he seems a little . . . immersed in his job."

"Immersed, yeah. Try: That man's ass is so tight if you shoved a lump of coal up there you'd have a diamond in no time."

She grinned. "Kinky."

"He's chilled out some since you came along. Thank you for that."

"Anything I can do to help." She paused. "Or anyone, in this case."

"If that's the truth, I've been a little tense lately, too—"

She punched him in the shoulder and laughed. "That's your current flavor-of-the-month's responsibility, you man-whore."

"Man-whore?" He cast her a look of mock indignation. "I am not a *man-whore*. How can I help it if I'm beloved by all the ladies? I would be doing them a disservice if I didn't oblige."

"Yes, I shudder to think." She laughed. "The world without your willing body in it would definitely be less bright for womankind."

Adam turned his SUV past the security gates of the Coven and guided it down the winding road toward the house.

"So what's Micah's story anyway?" she asked him when

the conversation had lulled. "I heard he's got some serious issues with the Duskoff?"

"Don't we all?" he muttered.

She stared out the window at the dark, winding road and
tried not to think of Angela. "Yes."

Adam's hands tightened noticeably on the steering wheel.
"Micah's mom was killed by a warlock when he was just a
kid. Ever since then he's been jonesing for some revenge. But
Micah's skills are more in the realm of the brain than the
body. Guy graduated top in his class at MIT and he's got ma-
jor mojo, too. Serious ass amounts of magick. Anyway, after
he got his degree he could have done anything, made lots of
cash working in the non-magickal world. Instead, he came to
work for the Coven and he's been here ever since, doing research and fetching and carrying for Monahan."

"Sounds like he's hiding," she commented.

Adam laughed. "Micah? Nah. Micah is deceptive as all
hell. He's just looking for the right opportunity to kick their
collective asses, you'll see."

She nodded. All of them had really been touched in some
way by the Duskoff. "So what's Theo's story?"

"Theodosius? Oh, man, he's got a story all right. The
Duskoff got him for a while when he was a teenager, tried to
break him because he has all this earth magick to call. The
warlocks thought they could get him young and twist him for
their own purposes. They tortured him and nearly killed him
in the process, but the Coven broke him out. Got scars all over
his body to show for his little stay with the warlocks. The second he could, Theo joined the Coven. He's one of our top
hunters."

She chewed her lower lip. That's why she'd felt a strange
sort of kindredness with Theo. Their histories were dissimilar,
but they shared one past incident—abuse, though it sounded
like Theo's had been far more traumatic than hers.

"And your story?" she asked him.

Adam went silent for several heartbeats, then laughed
harshly. "Sorry, baby girl. That one's not up for discussion."

"Sorry, Adam. Didn't mean to touch a nerve."

"No sweat, but it's just not something I want to talk about."

He parked the SUV in front of the house and put it into park. She climbed out and looked up into the night sky to admire the scattering of bright stars.

Where was Boyle tonight?

She hadn't told Thomas about the demon's ultimatum . . . and she never would. *His interference will mean his death.* That's what Boyle had said.

Her life wasn't worth Thomas's life. It just wasn't.

Thomas strode from the front door of the Coven, drawing her eye. He wore a pair of close-fitting jeans, a black sweater, and black boots. His shoulders were hunched, his eyes hooded, and his jaw locked, and his long, loose hair streamed around him as he walked toward her with purpose.

"Thomas—" She only had time to get the one word out before he grabbed her around the waist and hefted her over his shoulder. "Thomas!" she yelled at him as he turned without a word and walked back up the stairs and into the Coven.

Lady, she never thought he'd literally do this!

Adam's laughter rang behind her as Thomas carried her off.

Despite her outrage and despite the looks they got from the Coven's inhabitants, he carried her through the building. Thomas was single-minded in his focus and nothing she said or did stopped his slow, purposeful stalk to his room.

Once inside, he slammed the door closed with his foot and Isabelle felt the *hiss snap* along her nerve endings as a warding spell seal his apartment.

Her throat closed and the familiar panic tingled through her limbs. Her breath came quick, her heart started to pound, and she felt her eyes grow wide. She dragged in a harsh, ragged-sounding lungful of air.

Thomas sat her on the couch. Looking down at her, he frowned. "What's wrong?"

She raised a hand and shook her head, trying to ease her panic enough to speak. Closing her eyes, she fought to regulate her breathing and talk to herself rationally. Thomas didn't know about her problem with locked rooms and small places. She was safe here, safe. She was always safe with Thomas.

His hands closed over her shoulders. "Isabelle?"

She opened her mouth to tell him she was okay, then shook her head again. Even though she knew she was safe here with him, she couldn't tamp down her primal reaction to being locked in a room. Isabelle bolted from the couch, pushed past Thomas and ran to the door.

The warding spell felt heavy, viscous, as she slid her hand into it to try the knob. Thomas's magick was strong. She could taste it on the back of her tongue like dark, fertile soil.

The door knob wouldn't budge, of course. Thomas had keyed the spell to prevent her from turning or manipulating the door in any way. Her mind sought ways her water magick could counter it and came up empty.

"Thomas, don't do this." Her voice sounded shaky.

"Already done."

She couldn't spend the night locked in this room. She couldn't. "What if"—her mind cast about for arguments— "what if Boyle shows up tonight and I'm locked in here with no escape? This could be dangerous."

"The warding is set to register your emotions. If you're fleeing for your life in absolute terror, the magick will know and allow you through."

A key to the warding. Maybe she could turn it.

Isabelle opened the floodgate to her fears, allowing all her terror to come pouring forth. She remembered . . . a tiny, dark closet.

Sand washed mouth, or so it felt like. Pressing her tongue to the floor where Angela poured water under the door's crack. Never enough, never enough. Stomach gnawing on itself from the inside. Searching jacket pockets for crumbs. Curling up in a corner with only two tattered coats and the smell of mothballs for company.

She remembered imagining she was one of those cave-dwelling insects she'd read about at school. They'd evolved without eyes since their world was constantly dark. Would she eventually lose her eyes, too?

But most of all, Isabelle remembered her sister's tiny, child's voice on the other side of the door. *I can't find the key, Isa, I can't find it.*

Her heart beat faster. Her breath came in short, hard little pants that stabbed her chest. Isabelle tried the door again and it opened a crack.

Thomas placed his hand near her head, palm flat against the door. He pushed it closed. "Is staying here tonight with me so frightening, Isabelle?" His voice was a low, silken murmur.

She closed her eyes and felt the prick of tears. Again she reminded herself that she wasn't in that closet anymore. Now she was an adult, empowered, able to take care of herself. She was with a man who had never hurt her, would never hurt her. Indeed, he only wanted to protect her, would probably give his life to do so.

Thomas cared about her. He was one of the few in this world who did.

Her panic receded and she wrestled her breathing and heart rate under control once more. Her breath shuddered out of her in relief as she gave up the last of her terror. A tear plopped onto the carpet at her feet.

Thomas turned her to face him. Concern for her marked his handsome face and for a moment she loved him for it.

Maybe for even more than a moment.

He brushed the pad of his thumb down her cheek, catching a second stray teardrop. "Please talk to me for once, Isabelle. It's clear this is about more than me locking you in this room for your protection."

She stared at him, her lips parting a little. Finally she nodded. "It is. I have claustrophobia, and I tend to panic when I'm locked in rooms."

"Shit, Isabelle. I'm sorry. I—"

She put her fingers to his lips and gave him a shaky smile. "It's all right. I'm okay and you didn't know." She dragged her fingers from his mouth, up his jawline to cup his cheek. "I think I'm all right now."

He opened his mouth to say something, but she went up on her toes and kissed him before it came out.

Thomas reacted instantly, threading his arms around her waist and lifting her away from the door. His hands were on her everywhere at once, working the button and zipper of her jeans, and then pulling her shirt over her head.

She went to her knees and dragged the hem of his sweater

upward, licking her tongue over his hard abs as they were revealed. Having risen to meet his mouth, she pulled the sweater over his head and quickly divested him of the rest of his clothing between kisses. Soon she slid against him skin-on-skin.

Mouth and tongue working, Thomas muscled her up against a nearby wall and turned her to face it. He'd left her shoes on and now she saw why. They had a thick heel and elevated her, lessening the difference in their height so they could make love in a standing position.

Panting with anticipation, she spread her palms flat against the wall in front of her as he ran his hands down her body lovingly, over her breasts, across her stomach. He delved between her buttocks, planing the curves, and then dipped between her thighs to drag his fingers over her intimate flesh.

Her breath hissed out of her and she felt herself cream. Thomas slid two fingers deep inside her and at the same time pressed his body against hers. His teeth nipped at the nape of her neck, raising gooseflesh along her body.

Maybe being locked in Thomas's room for the night wouldn't be so bad.

"Isabelle," he murmured, his lips giving butterfly kisses to her skin as he spoke. "Forgive me. I don't want to lose you, and I never want to hurt you. You're becoming very important to me."

As he was to her.

Every moment brought that truth more firmly to bear within her heart and mind. Thomas was a man to *stay* for. At this point all of that was lovely, but moot, wasn't it? How could she admit her feelings for Thomas now, when the demon had designs on her body and soul?

The time for that was long past, gone with a visit from a demon in the silent dead of night.

"Stop thinking," Thomas growled and then sank his teeth into her shoulder just hard enough to get her attention.

She gasped in surprise and intense pleasure at the possessive bite. Her fingers fisted against the wall in front of her and her body reacted, her sex becoming slick and warm.

Still biting her shoulder, he slid his knee between her thighs and forced her to spread them. Then he shoved his cock against her opening and thrust the head slowly within. His hands found her breasts and cupped them as he eased himself deep inside her inch by delicious inch.

Isabelle's breath came in short, hard pants as her body stretched to accommodate him. The pleasure of having him inside suffused her. Then he began to thrust and the pleasure became sharper. He teased her nipples, pinching and rolling them between the pads of his fingers as his cock tunneled in and out of her sex.

Just the thought of how they must look excited her to the point of orgasm—her pressed face-first against the wall, Thomas's hard, fine body working behind her, his buttocks flexing as he thrust deep within her and his big hands possessively controlling her breasts.

The first skitterings of climax rose along her spine and nerve endings. Thomas sensed it rising, slipped his hand down her abdomen and between her thighs to stroke her clit. Her orgasm exploded, heady and overwhelming. Her back arched as it washed through her, making her sex pulse around his thrusting cock.

While the last remnants of ecstasy still clung to her, Thomas turned her to face him. Her expression was lusty and satisfied, she knew—parted lips, eyelids at half mast. She wanted more of him. Thomas's expression was serious, almost severe.

He cupped her cheek and stared into her eyes. "Isabelle." It was just one word, but there seemed to be a world of emotion in it.

She covered his hand with her own and fought to divest herself of her initial desire to reject that emotion, to run away. *You care about him, too. Let it be.*

At least for now, she could let it be.

Thomas slid his palm from her waist, down her thigh and hooked her leg over his hip. Then he pushed within her again. Isabelle's eyes widened as he thrust slow enough that every inch of his cock registered a ten on the pleasure scale. Then he slowed the pace of his thrusts even more. The entire time his gaze held hers intimately, until he finally came deep inside her.

After it was over, they stood motionless, breathing heavily, still coupled at the pelvis, their gazes locked on each other. To Isabelle the connection felt much deeper. That soul-deep union terrified her to the bone. This time her fear was not because of the connection itself . . . but because she might lose it.

She had a demon gunning for her.

Thomas gathered her against him after a moment and they went to bed. He held her close, stroking her arms and back for a long time until, even as disturbed as she was, sleep caught her.

WHEN ISABELLE AWOKE, IT TOOK HER A MOMENT TO remember where she was. She opened her eyes to the morning sunshine filtering in through the sheer curtains covering the window in Thomas's bedroom. Her body felt tired and achy in a way that signaled she'd been well-loved the night before. It was a lovely sensation. She stretched like a cat, feeling Thomas move on her other side.

His arm came around her waist and he pulled her against him, burying his face in her hair and inhaling. "Mmmm, it's better waking up with you in my bed. I've wanted this."

She snuggled back against him and smiled. For a moment she pretended that nothing lay between them. No demon. No responsibilities to anyone else. No slavery to her own fears. For a moment she pretended she could remain with him, that he loved her and she loved him . . . and she could *stay*.

Isabelle turned over and pressed her nude body flush against his, wrapping her arms around his waist. He did the same, locking her against him. She liked to be locked against Thomas Monahan.

After a while, unable to resist, she ran her palms over his body, enjoying the powerful flex of his muscles, the hum of his magick and the feel of his long silken hair. With a groan, he rolled her beneath him, parted her thighs, and slipped the head of his cock inside her.

Her breath caught at the natural, easy way he'd done it. Like they were meant to fit together. He dropped his mouth to hers and kissed her softly. At some point they'd gone from fucking to having sex to making love. The change had been seamless. Isabelle's breath left her in a long, slow sigh when they finally broke the kiss.

He held her gaze and rolled his hips forward, sliding within her another delicious inch. The head of his cock hit her somewhere sweet inside, somewhere that made passion rush through her veins and that curious lust-haze begin to settle over her mind.

"Are you sure you never use magick on your women, Thomas?" Her words came out laced with sexual need, heavy and halting.

"I haven't with you. Not once. I wouldn't unless it was agreed upon beforehand."

She'd heard that some of the more powerful earth witches could use magick during sex, though the skill was rare. The earth witches who possessed this ability were sought after as lovers. There were some people who became addicted to the power of it. "So you can, then?"

His hips rocked back and forth, in tantalizing, pleasurable little jabs into her sex. "Of course. Want me to show you?"

"I'm curious."

"Put your hand on my tattoo."

Feeling like her bones were made of warm honey, she slid a hand to his tattoo and splayed her palm against it. It pulsed with his magick and her skin tingled in response. The magick intensified, rippling up her arm and through her body. A drugged-like haze settled over her mind and her hand fell away.

Thomas rolled his hips so his cock penetrated her as deeply as possible. A long, slow easy climax flirted with her body instantly. It tickled her and teased her as Thomas rode her. Then it burst over her and lingered, racking her body with spasm after spasm of pleasure. It was enough to make her near insane, enough to make her cry with the intensity of it. On and on it went.

He spilled inside her with a low groan followed by her name on his lips.

"Holy . . ." Isabelle breathed into the curve of his neck. "You completely overpowered me with your magick."

He raised his head to look at her. "Did you like it?"

"One continuous unbroken orgasm?" She snorted. "I hated it." Her body still hummed from it, her nerve endings tingling. She felt almost drunk, sex drunk. "I could see how someone could become addicted to that and yet . . ."

"What?"

"It was too much, too intense. It was delicious, but I want to focus on you, not only on my own pleasure. I want to feel your cock moving inside me, the scent of you, the slip of your skin against mine. When you're giving me one long, unbroken orgasm, as nice as that is, I can't enjoy the rest of it, all the parts I like most."

He laughed, a low, silken sound she loved, and rolled to the side, bringing her with him and tucking her against his body. "You're incredible, Isabelle."

She sighed and murmured with mock arrogance, "So everyone tells me."

"I'm glad you stayed the night with me. I've wanted to wake up next to you for a long time."

She nuzzled his throat and gave a kiss to the sleep-warmed skin. "It's not like I had a lot of choice."

"True."

"But I'm glad I'm here, too." She sighed and tried not to think about the demon and failed. "So what's the plan for to-day?"

"The usual. Later, once the sun goes down, we'll hunt him. Take all our collective leads and search the locations where he's known to hang out. At this point it's the only thing we can do."

"I hate just waiting around."

"We're doing all we can. I've got the few air witches in the Coven scanning for any whisper of his presence, all the water witches and earth witches using their skills to locate him. Until we get a break, that's our best plan of action since we have no way to predict which witch he might target next."

"Did Micah find anything else in the texts?"

Thomas sat up abruptly.

Isabelle pushed up onto her elbows. "What is it?"

He pushed a hand through his hair, his bicep flexing. Dark strands caught between his fingers. Thomas turned toward her. "I forgot to tell you last night. Once we got to my room—"

"We were occupied. What did he find?"

"Micah's been scouring the texts for any hint of demon spells that open doorways. While you were out with Adam, he finally found something. There are several ways to do it, all requiring the type of blood magick Boyle is using. The spells work like combination locks. The demon consumes and stores the energetic magicks of the witches, much in the same way an earth witch consumes and stores spells. Each witch must have a certain magickal makeup and they must be killed in a certain order and at certain times. If the demon takes the right witches at the right times, it unlocks a doorway."

Isabelle sat up straighter, pulling the sheet around her. "Magickal makeup?"

"As far as Micah can tell that means the witches must possess a certain kind of magick and a certain level of power. The power patterns of all the witches registered with the Coven have been documented."

She pushed a hand through her sleep-tangled hair, thinking. "Can you get all the files on the witches the demon has killed?"

"Yes . . . why?"

I have work to do before you. That's what Boyle had said in the library. Did that mean other witches to kill before he came for her?

"I want to see if there's a pattern."

He shook his head. "Even if we could find a pattern, I doubt we could predict the next witch he might go after. There are too many witches with similar power patterns for the information to be relevant. Micah has already thought about this. We wouldn't be able to narrow it down enough for it to be useful."

"Maybe not, but I still want to check. The more information we have, the better."

"I agree." He kissed her shoulder. "I'll have Micah look into it."

"Thank you."

He gave her another lingering kiss while running his palm down her arm and over her exposed breast where she'd pushed the blankets away. Isabelle closed her eyes. Her body, even after so much recent erotic attention, reacted to him.

He dragged her lower lip between his teeth. "Now, shower time."

She grinned. "What if I want to take a shower in my own bathroom?"

"You can't leave here until I lick the water rivulets running down this gorgeous body. After that I'll release you."

Isabelle couldn't for the life of her find a flaw in that plan.

SIXTEEN

THOMAS WATCHED ISABELLE GO OVER THE RECORDS of the demon's four victims, her hair a strawberry-blond curtain around her bent head and her tongue tucked firmly between her teeth as she concentrated. Thus far she'd been businesslike about the whole thing, even though her sister's records were in the batch she studied.

Along with Micah, he and Isabelle had spent the morning examining every piece of information they had on the flow of power of the four victims. Luckily, all the victims had detailed Coven records. Otherwise no type of analysis would have been possible.

Micah had entered the data into a software program he'd developed to look for patterns, but analysis would take some time. He was fussy with his numbers and had to tweak the recently created software to run the info through various sets of algorithms or whatever it was he'd been mumbling to himself about. His cousin had thrown himself into the project, heart and soul.

Someone knocked on the door. Thomas called *enter* and Adam stuck his head in. "You're not going to believe this." His gaze went to Isabelle.

She looked up at Adam and frowned. "What?"

Micah seemed oblivious to everyone and everything except the keyboard and the flickering computer screen in front of him. He never stopped typing.

"Your mother is named Catalina, right?" Adam asked.

Her frown deepened. "Yes . . . why?"

"She's here."

Isabelle blinked once and went very still. "As in at the Coven?"

"Yes. She's asking for you."

"Great. Just when you think things can't get any worse, Catalina shows up." She pushed her chair away from the desk, stood and gave a heavy sigh. "Where is she?"

"We put her in the second-floor receiving room."

"Thanks, Adam."

"She's, uh, interesting."

"Interesting, yeah. That's one word of about five hundred you could use to describe my mother. All bad."

"I'll come with you," Thomas broke in.

She glanced at him. "Please. You can play wrestling referee if she pisses me off."

"Sure thing."

They headed out the door, leaving Micah crown deep in his analysis. If Thomas knew his cousin, he'd be awake all night running numbers and rearranging the input. He probably wouldn't even notice they'd left for a good hour.

Adam walked through the foyer and opened the front door. "Later. I'm off to meet Amy."

"Amy! What happened to Elizabeth?" She waved a hand, cutting off Adam's answer. "Whatever. I don't want to know."

Adam just grinned, shook his head and closed the door behind him.

"Oh, Lady, I don't want to do this," she muttered as they climbed the stairs to the second floor. "What the hell is she doing here?"

Thomas let his hand glide along the banister. "Maybe she's here for you."

Isabelle snorted. "That's optimistic. Clearly, you've never met my mother."

They walked down the corridor to the formal room they used to receive visiting witches from other Covens or members of the Council. She stood for a moment outside the door as if gathering her strength, then entered the room, Thomas behind her.

A thin, polished blonde with a ram-rod straight spine rose from where she'd been sitting on a wine-colored couch. She turned toward them, her gaze going from him and fixing on her daughter. Apprehension showed on her strikingly beautiful face for a moment before haughty pride took over.

He'd met Catalina Novak once before, years ago, at a Coven dinner. She still looked the same, five foot seven inches of woman who would have looked her age but for the wonders of modern plastic surgery. Catalina had spent a bundle on it, too. She passed for forty when her records put her age closer to fifty-five. Expensively dyed honey blond hair hung to her shoulders, framing a face with hardly a wrinkle or laugh line to be seen. It was a face that most men would fall for. It was a face most men *had* fallen for. Catalina Novak had made a fortune snaring wealthy men. She'd been widowed twice by rich elderly men and divorced once from an oil baron who should have insisted on a prenup.

It jarred him to see Isabelle's eyes staring from that face, with its collagen-enhanced lips and artificially sculpted eyebrows.

Were Catalina's eyes the only original part of her chassis?

"Mother." Isabelle's voice could have frozen the balls off a snowman.

"Isabelle." She took a step forward and then stopped near the edge of a glass coffee table. "I came as soon as I heard."

"You missed her funeral."

Catalina looked at the floor. "A man named Micah tracked me down in Rome and got a message to me. I came as soon as I could."

Isabelle pursed her lips. "I'm glad someone was able to locate you. I had no idea where to start looking. I left messages with all the men I could remember you having . . . *congress* with."

"I'm sorry I didn't come sooner." Catalina glanced up at Isabelle, but seemed unable to hold her gaze.

"Are you? Are you really, Mother? You not only missed her funeral, you missed her entire life. I'm surprised you even bothered to come now."

"Do you think so little of me?"

Isabelle considered that for a moment. "Yes."

She turned and gave Thomas a withering look. "Mr. Monahan, please excuse my daughter and the massive chip she has on her shoulder. This is an old issue between us. She hates me because I wasn't your regular *Leave It to Beaver* kind of mother. I gave her everything she needed but—"

Isabelle snorted.

Catalina turned that withering gaze back to her daughter. "*Everything* she needed, and yet—"

Thomas broke in, even while he knew he shouldn't. "Maybe children need more than just material things, Catalina. Maybe sometimes they need parenting, sometimes they need affection and love." This was not his affair, but he cared too much about Isabelle to keep his mouth shut.

Isabelle's gaze shot to his face and locked for a moment. Then she gave him a smile that made his heart clench and warm at the same time.

Catalina blanched and looked away. She probably didn't like being reproved by the head of the Coven. Catalina was an extremely class-conscious type of person and he represented the head of the class itself.

"Why have you come, Mother?" Isabelle asked.

Catalina finally looked up into Isabelle's face. "I came to see you, Isabelle. I wanted to find out if you were holding up all right."

Isabelle took a step toward her mother and then halted. "Really?" Hope and wariness warred in that one word.

"Don't sound so surprised. I do care about you, you know." The words sounded genuine but were spoken awkwardly.

Thomas watched Isabelle shift her weight and frown, unsure how to react to her mother's admission.

"I know I've made mistakes, Isabelle." Catalina took a couple steps toward her daughter. "Maybe I've *only* made mistakes. One of the reasons I came was to find out if there's a way we might be able to mend things between us."

Isabelle shook her head. "I think I'm getting a headache. Did hell just freeze over?"

"Isabelle—" Catalina started.

She held up a hand. "We can deal with all that in a minute. What was the other reason you came?"

"To see if there was anything I was supposed to do as a result of Angela's death." The older woman glanced away.

"I don't know what you're talking about. The funeral was months ago. Angela, what's left of her, is in the ground. I've met with the attorney and all her affairs have been dealt with."

Catalina looked up from her shoes.

Isabelle sucked a sharp breath. "Oh. You're here about the will, aren't you?" She nodded. "Of course that's why you're here. I'm so stupid."

Catalina lifted her chin. "It's not the primary reason I came. I wanted to see you, see how you were doing with everything. I came for you, Isabelle."

Before Catalina had even finished her last sentence, Isabelle had turned away and wrapped her arms across her chest. "The will has been read, Mother. You weren't in it. There's nothing for you."

Catalina shook her head. "That's not possible. Angela had some jewelry, diamonds. She said once that if she—"

Isabelle rounded on Catalina. "There was *nothing* in Angela's will for you. She left everything to me, even the diamond jewelry. I don't wear jewelry, so I plan to give it all to charity. You see, Mother, you came all this way for nothing."

"Isabelle, you keep those diamonds in the family! Do you hear me? I will not allow you to give those Harry Winstons to charity!"

"What family, Mother? What we have is not family! Don't even use that word when you're talking about our relationship." She narrowed her eyes. "And don't say another word to me about those diamonds." Isabelle whirled, left the room, and slammed the door behind her.

Catalina stood frozen, staring at the door. "My daughter has always been a handful, Mr. Monahan. She's always been . . . volatile."

Thomas took a moment to answer. "I like her that way."

"That didn't go as well as I'd hoped. I don't know what's wrong with me." Catalina's perfect face crumpled for a moment before she regained her composure. "I do want a relationship with her. I do love her, you know."

"That's not something you should tell *me*, Catalina."

She turned her gaze to his and he was jarred once again by Isabelle's eyes staring from her face. "You're with her romantically, aren't you?"

"Yes."

"She won't stay with you, you know. She never stays. Isabelle is like me that way. She's a traveler, a mover. Isabelle might hate me, but she's a kindred spirit in that regard. Even when she was a child she liked it when I moved them between caregivers and countries."

"Are you so sure about that?"

She licked her lips and glanced away. "I was not cut out for motherhood."

"Then why have children?"

She shrugged. "It happens. You know Angela has"—she swallowed hard—"*had* a different father than Isabelle?"

"I suspected, yes."

"They were both accidents. I never meant to have kids at all. It probably would have been better if I hadn't."

"I strongly disagree. The world would have suffered for the lack of Isabelle and Angela."

A smile flickered over her lips. "Through no help from me they both turned out well. Especially Angela. I still don't know how that happened. Must have been her father's genes. Isabelle is—"

"Perfect. Isabelle is perfect in every way."

Catalina tilted her flawless face toward him. Vulnerability engulfed her expression for a moment. "Does she still have claustrophobia?"

Guilt filled his stomach with lead. When Isabelle had revealed her phobia of locked rooms right after he'd locked her in one, he'd felt so bad he would have done anything in the world to make it up to her. "Yes."

"She has that fear because of me, because I left her with someone who mistreated them."

"What?" Anger simmered. "Mistreated them? What are you talking about?"

She turned away from him, showed him her rigid back, and took a couple steps away. "They spent time with some people they shouldn't have once or twice." She shrugged a shoulder. "Maybe more often than that. Isabelle was a handful, always misbehaving. Once, when she was six, one of her caretakers locked her in a closet for four days. No food, no water, no light. She ended up in the hospital, would have died of dehydration if Angela hadn't spilled water under the door's crack. That's why Isabelle is claustrophobic. She used to have recurring nightmares, too."

Four days. She'd only been six years old.

The anger simmering in his blood came to a boil. He took a step toward the woman in front of him and clenched his fists so hard he probably drew blood from his palms with his fingernails. "Why are you telling me this?"

She turned toward him with sorrow in her eyes. "Because someone who cares about Isabelle needs to know."

Thomas closed his eyes so he wouldn't have to look at the woman who had caused Isabelle so much pain. "I'm going to ask you to leave now, Catalina." The words came out steadier than he'd expected.

"Yes, it's past time. I'm more than happy to since I failed so miserably with Isabelle." She paused. "Where is Angela buried?" The words came out barely a whisper.

"Groveland Cemetery."

"Thank you."

Thomas listened to the click of Catalina's shoes on the floor and the door gently close behind her. He stayed that way for a moment, confused.

Catalina did love Isabelle, though in a mystifying way that he couldn't wrap his mind around. Catalina was far too self-serving and egotistical to be a decent mother, yet she knew it and felt guilty about it. It was clear she regretted how she allowed her daughters to be raised and what had happened to them in the care of others. . . .

One of her caretakers had locked Isabelle in a closet for four days.

Thomas tried to find some pity in his heart for Catalina, some way to help her make the connection with her surviving daughter that she was too clumsy to make herself . . . and came up short. He only felt searing rage for Catalina right now. Maybe sometime later he'd feel something else.

All Thomas wanted now was Isabelle in his arms. All he wanted was the impossible—to turn back the clock and make the pain go away for her, to give her a childhood like he'd had. One in which she'd been safe, loved, and protected.

He turned on his heel, sought the door and the woman he was falling in love with.

ISABELLE STOOD ON ONE OF THE MANY BRIDGES IN THE Coven conservatory, watching gardeners tend the plants and flowers that grew in profusion. This was the first place she'd thought of when she'd left her mother, a quiet, serene place where she could be alone with her thoughts.

And there was water here. The sound of the small stream burbling happily underneath the bridge upon which she stood calmed her. She focused on the current, the flow of the water around rocks and over pebbles, sluicing by the koi that swam in it. Isabelle joined her consciousness with it for a moment and all her residual tension leaked away.

Water took the path of least resistance.

For just a flicker of time when she'd first seen Catalina, she'd seriously wondered if her mother had come because she was grieving Angela. Perhaps her mother had made the trip to Chicago because she cared that one of her daughters had died. Maybe Catalina had even come for her remaining daughter, Isabelle. The little girl inside her who still yearned for her mother's affection had experienced a flash of guarded happiness. That one instant of hope had made the realization Catalina had come only for the will that much more devastating.

Isabelle closed her eyes. She couldn't deny there was still a part of her that longed for her mother to be a mother. Clearly, that would never happen. She needed to stop wishing for it.

Isabelle sensed Thomas behind her long before she heard his step on the bridge or felt his broad, warm hand on her shoulder. She closed her eyes and sighed. How could it be that his presence made everything seem better?

She wasn't some stupid woman whose problems were solved by the touch of a man, but maybe this was what everyone talked about, sang about, and wrote books about—love? At the very least perhaps it was the magic of a close relationship.

Thomas massaged her shoulders, his strong fingers seeking out and easing away all the knots and tension that existed there. Isabelle opened her eyes and let a smile play on her lips. Whatever it was, it was good.

He leaned down and whispered in her ear, "You okay?"

She shook her head. "Not really, but I'm better now."

"Your mom is fascinating. I think a shrink would have a good time with her."

She snorted. "She's not really my mom. She's just the woman who gave birth to me." Isabelle didn't want to believe that, though. The words felt too harsh in her mouth.

Thomas pulled her back against him and enveloped her in his arms. She nestled into his chest, inhaling the scent of him and enjoying the warmth of his body. "I think Catalina is starting to understand what she missed in you and Angela."

Tears pricked her eyes. "Do you think she's capable of that? Truly?"

Thomas went silent for a long moment. "Yes."

A sob of grief bubbled up from somewhere deep inside her, like a pocket of sorrow that had been stored in the depths of her soul had suddenly been popped. "I miss my sister, Thomas."

She hadn't cried once since she'd found Angela, not really, but now it seemed like all the tears she'd stored up rushed forth in a torrent.

Thomas eased her down to the bridge and sat, holding her in his lap, and let it happen. He made soft sounds at her and brushed his fingers through her hair, seeming to understand as well as she did that she needed this release.

Memories flooded her mind. Playing jacks with Angela on the front steps of the brownstone where they'd lived for a time in Chicago. Running down to the pond in France where they'd watched the other kids race toy sailboats. Isabelle remembered her first date and how her older sister had given her a small amount of advice based on her own limited experience. She'd helped her do her hair and then sat up with her when she'd returned home crying because the boy hadn't been all she'd hoped.

Lord and Lady, she missed Angela.

Isabelle cried until her eyes were dry, her makeup was non-existent, her nose ran, and her head pounded. Despite all that, at the end, she felt better than she had in a long time. She felt emptied of the heaviness she'd been carrying around since her sister's death.

As the afternoon faded into twilight and the small lights illuminating the pathways in the conservatory gradually grew brighter, Isabelle rested her head against Thomas's shoulder and sighed. "I ruined your shirt. My mascara ran all over it."

"I didn't like this one anyway." His low voice rumbled through her, rough and silken at the same time.

All of a sudden Isabelle wanted to be in bed with him, craved the slide of his skin across hers, the slip of his lips over her mouth and all that wonderful dark hair brushing over her body.

But it would have to wait. Twilight had fallen and they had a demon to hunt.

"Do you really think it's possible my mother could regret?"

He stroked her hair. "I believe she is regretting now, Isabelle. It's just that she doesn't have the first clue how to make amends."

"And maybe it's too late."

"Yes, and maybe it's too late. That's for you and her to work through." He paused. "She mentioned that sometimes she left you and your sister with people who didn't treat you well. Is that true?"

Isabelle stiffened against him. "It didn't happen that often. There were two times . . . Neither was very long. But once she paid this woman, Marie, to keep us for a while. She lived in Marseilles. Anyway, I was a little kid, always getting into trouble. Smacks never really bothered me as far as discipline went. So one day . . . I don't even remember what I did anymore . . . Marie got fed up with me and locked me in a closet."

She swallowed hard, still able to feel the press of the darkness like a physical presence and her throat working dry from a lack of water. "And there I stayed for four days."

Thomas tightened his arms around her.

"Angela tried and tried to open it, but couldn't. She stayed with me the whole time, tried to push food and water under the tiny crack beneath the door."

"Catalina said that's why you're claustrophobic and that you used to have recurring nightmares."

"Yes, that's right."

"What did your mother do when she found out what happened?"

She shrugged. "She moved us somewhere else. That time we went to live with her and her flavor-of-the-month, Fredrick, in Switzerland for a while." She sighed. "Anyway, all that's ancient history. You can't change the past. I rarely have nightmares anymore and the claustrophobia is much better than it used to be."

Isabelle lifted her head, aware that she probably looked horrible—no makeup, tear-stained face—and was happy for the dim light in the conservatory, though she felt comfortable with Thomas, even looking like shit. "So when do we go?"

"Go?"

She wiped at her cheeks. "When do we leave to make the rounds for Boyle?"

His face tightened. "I don't want you going tonight."

Damn it. Pleasant mood shattered, Isabelle pushed away from him and stood. "I really don't care, Thomas, what you want."

Thomas rose. "I'm going with Adam and Micah. I want you to stay here with Jack McAllister. He's been instructed to guard you against Boyle if he shows up here again."

Isabelle stared at him for a moment, her teeth clenched. She had to force words through her locked jaw. "I can take care of myself. Just because you're fucking me doesn't give you the right to tell me what to do." She turned on her heel and stalked away.

She got five steps away before his commanding voice filled

the air. "As the head of the Coven, under which you are subject at this time, I *order* you to stay behind tonight. This has
nothing to do with the fact I'm fucking you."

"Bullshit, Thomas."

Isabelle summoned her magick, feeling it flicker warmly in
the center of her chest and spread down her arms. She reached
out to the nearby stream and manipulated the molecules to do
her bidding. A splash and a series of curses met her ears. Isabelle didn't even break stride.

SEVENTEEN

❦

THOMAS HAD CHANGED INTO DRY CLOTHES. NOW HE wore a pair of jeans broken in enough he could move in them, leather boots, and a dark sweater. Sheathed to his back was a short sword, a long black coat covering it. It was warm outside and he felt stupid wearing the thing, but it was the only way to keep the blade concealed.

Worse, based on the experience Isabelle had had with the demon in the library, it was possible the blades wouldn't even work. However, copper was still their best—and only—weapon against Boyle.

Isabelle descended the stairs. She wore a pair of well-worn jeans, black boots, a black sweater . . . and a stubborn set to her jaw. Clearly, she had every intention of accompanying them.

Clearly, she was mistaken.

Thomas knew logically that if the demon desired it, he could find Isabelle anywhere and at any time. The Coven walls were no defense. However, the likelihood of surprising the demon at some point during their nightly canvasses of the area was higher than the demon returning to the Coven.

So Thomas presumed anyway.

He just wanted—*needed*—to do all he could to keep Isabelle safe and this was the best way he knew how.

"You're not coming," he said flatly as she reached the bottom of the stairs. Micah and Adam hadn't shown up yet.

Isabelle opened her mouth to reply, but someone rang at

the Coven's guard gate, cutting her off. Douglas, the witch who managed the house, emerged through a door, but Thomas waved him off and walked to the entryway console and pressed Talk.

On the front gate's video monitor, an image of Catalina appeared. She was seated in a black convertible. "Mr. Monahan? I'm here to see Isabelle."

Thomas looked over at Isabelle who had gone from looking stubborn badass to vulnerable in about two seconds flat.

She hugged herself. "If it's about jewelry, don't let her in."

"It's not about jewelry," answered Catalina right away. "It's about me and Isabelle." She pursed her lips. "It's private."

Thomas looked at Isabelle again. She only nodded once, slowly.

"Are you sure?" Thomas asked.

She nodded again. "Goddamn it, yes."

Thomas pressed the button to open the Coven gates and watched Catalina drive through. Then he took a couple steps toward Isabelle, holding her now uncertain gaze, as Adam walked through one of the doors leading off the entranceway. Thomas halted.

"I have a feeling about tonight," Adam announced, walking toward them as he rolled up the sleeves of his dark blue shirt. "I think tonight—" He stopped short. "What's wrong?"

"Nothing," Isabelle answered, breaking Thomas's gaze to look at Adam. "Everything is fine. Thomas didn't want me to come and, now, conveniently, I can't go."

She turned and walked upstairs. "Can you please tell Catalina to meet me upstairs?" She stopped and looked at Thomas, her face grim. "And please be careful. I have a feeling about tonight, too."

THE RED ROCK WAS A BAR ON THE FRINGES OF Chicago owned by a witch and patronized by the same. It was also one of three witch-frequented watering holes where Boyle was known to hang out. Thomas had a hard time picturing the demon slamming back a cold brew, but apparently he enjoyed one now and again.

Or maybe it was the witches he enjoyed.

Adam entered the bar after Thomas and headed straight over to order a tall glass of Absolut. He couldn't blame him. This was the last stop after a long evening of dead ends.

Thomas was sick of dead ends, sick of flying blind. If there was one thing in this life that made him insane, it was his inability to control situations. Especially situations that put people he cared about at risk.

The tattoo on his back twitched with the extra large store of magick he'd infused it with. Thomas wanted a fight, wanted something, *anything*, with Boyle. The entirety of his magickical body trembled with the urge to engage.

He scanned the room, resting his gaze on each of the patrons in the smoky, dimly lit space in turn. There were a few witches in the place, but it was mostly filled with non-magickicals tonight. Again, he didn't see Boyle.

"Fuck," he muttered under his breath.

Every night they didn't find the demon was another night a witch could be killed.

Micah laid a hand on his shoulder. "Let's get a drink."

He passed a hand over his tired face. "Sounds good to me."

At the bar Adam chatted up an attractive brunette whose date Thomas had seen disappear into the bathroom a few moments prior. She was an earth witch of low ability, if Thomas judged correctly.

Thomas slid onto the stool beside him—the swords they wore weren't long enough to impede sitting—ordered a bourbon, and tried to ignore the low sultry laugh of the woman Adam was busy flattering.

Thomas pulled his cell phone from his pocket and stared at it for a moment, deliberating over whether he should call Isabelle or not. He wondered how it had gone with her mother. His gut reaction had been to lock Catalina out of the Coven grounds when he'd seen her face come on the monitor, but as protective as he felt over Isabelle, it was not his place to interfere in her family life.

He stared at his cell phone for another moment and then snapped it closed. It was two in the morning. Isabelle was probably in bed right now. Jack had been instructed to stay in the living room until he returned. Thomas could only imagine how pleased Isabelle must have been to hear about those orders.

Even though it wasn't his place to interfere with Isabelle's family life, as head of the Coven it most definitely *was* his place to interfere in matters concerning her safety. Isabelle would simply have to get used to that.

If he was fucking her, that only made it more his concern.

If he loved her, that made it an imperative.

And he *was* coming to love Isabelle. Her chaos played a nice counter note to his control. He'd never realized how much he'd need a force like her in his life until she'd landed in the middle of it.

The bartender sat his bourbon and Micah's drink down in front of them. Thomas picked up his glass and took a long swallow of the second-rate alcohol, enjoying the satisfying burn of it down his throat.

"You look tired, boss," said Micah.

"Not sleeping well. I can't rest for wondering when we'll get the next phone call about a witch slaughter."

Micah grunted. "I would've thought you weren't sleeping for other reasons. Isabelle reasons."

"There's that, too." Thomas shrugged a shoulder. "It's just a thing. Isabelle will move on once this is over." Whether he wanted her to or not.

"Think so?"

He swirled the amber alcohol in his glass. "Know so. All you have to do is look at her records to see that much. She's a traveler. She doesn't form attachments."

No matter how much he might wish her capable of it, Thomas preferred the truth. And the truth was that Isabelle had been damaged long ago. Maybe she was too damaged for the love he was beginning to feel for her.

Micah went silent for a heartbeat before replying, "People change."

The brunette's date returned from the bathroom. He was also an earth witch of relatively limited power. Thomas listened to the ensuing brief jealousy-fueled altercation between him, the brunette, and Adam, and then watched the man drag the woman from the bar.

"Not most people," Thomas replied.

Adam turned toward them with a satisfied look on his face. He grinned. "Got her phone number."

"Case in point." Thomas stared at the row of bottles in front of them and took another drink.

Micah snorted. "Don't you get sick of breaking up relationships, Adam?"

"I don't think of it like that. I can't break up a relationship that's not destined to be broken up anyway." Adam wiped a bead of moisture off his glass. "Which is pretty much all of them, in my opinion."

Micah pushed his glass away. "Damn, you're both depressing the hell out of me tonight."

Thomas glanced at him. "That's because it's a fucking depressing night."

"I'll drink to that." Adam hoisted his glass.

Thomas fished some bills out of his wallet and tossed them on the bar. "Finish up, guys. I want to get back to the Coven."

"Back to Isabelle, you mean," said Adam, right before he drained his glass.

"Yeah, back to Isabelle."

He and Micah finished their drinks. They settled their bill and headed outside to the car, parked in a lonely part of the nearly empty lot. Above their heads, the full moon lit their path across the parking lot. Gravel crunched beneath their shoes.

As Thomas hit the remote locks on the door, he heard a low moan coming from around the side of the building.

"What the hell?" whispered Adam.

Furrowing his brow, Thomas pocketed his keys and edged his way around the side of the building, trampling weeds and tripping over litter as he followed the low sound. Adam and Micah stayed behind him.

At the back of the bar lay an employee parking lot. Three cars were parked there and a Dumpster stood near the rear exit. Weeds sprouted through the cracked pavement. Shrubs and small trees grew around the periphery.

They stopped at the corner of the building and waited until another low moan resonated in the night air. It came from behind the Dumpster.

Thomas turned and motioned for Micah and Adam to go around the opposite side of the Dumpster. The three of them moved in close. Thomas didn't pull his sword yet. It could be anything from a prostitute or some other illicit liaison to a mugging to—

"Demon," he murmured.

He could smell him—that distinct dry, earthy smell that wasn't quite of *this* earth. Perhaps it wasn't Earth, but Eudae. Catching Adam's eye, Thomas reached over his head, grasped the handle of the sword and drew it slowly.

The moan came again. Thomas and Adam rounded the corners of the Dumpster at the same time, cautiously, swords held ready to swing. The brunette from the bar lay crumpled on the ground in fetal position. The demon was nowhere in sight, but his scent lingered in the air. The man who'd been with the woman in the bar was also missing.

Adam ran to the woman, knelt, and laid his sword on the pavement beside her shoulder. "Susan? Can you hear me?"

The woman moaned again and put a hand to her head.

Thomas sank to the ground on her other side. Blood marked her cheek and spattered her shirt. Thomas suspected her nose might be broken. "Susan, where is your date? Where is the man you were here with?"

She rolled to her back, wincing. "Jake?"

"Yes, Jake. Where is he?"

She moaned again and Adam pulled her onto his lap. "There was a . . . man . . . a big man. At least I think he was a man. He didn't seem human, but didn't feel like a witch. He punched me and fought with Jake." She swallowed hard. "Jake lost. The man dragged him off."

"In what direction did the man take Jake?"

Susan raised a trembling arm. She pointed to the scrubby line of vegetation that edged a small stand of trees around the employee parking lot. "There. He dragged him in there."

Thomas stood and grabbed his sword. "Micah, get this woman medical attention. Adam, come with me."

He and Adam took off in the direction she'd pointed, wading cautiously into the weed-choked area. Brambles pulled at his clothing and vines tried to trip him. Thomas could detect no scent of the demon now and could hear nothing—no struggle. Were they too late?

They made their way through the clearing and found themselves behind a factory. The gentle *whirr* of a ventilation system met their ears.

A short distance away they could see a vintage Harley parked in another lot, metal and chrome gleaming in the moonlight. Glimpsing it at the same time, he and Adam both walked toward it. Boyle had come to snatch a pretty big witch, but the demon wouldn't need physical means to transport Jake out of here. He might have come on his cycle but he likely planned to leave through a doorway with his captured prey. Micah had found an entry in the texts that said it was possible for Boyle to do that.

A blur of motion came toward them from Thomas's left. They both whirled toward it and something caught Adam in the face. Whatever it was moved too fast for Thomas to track. Adam grunted and collapsed.

Then nothing. Silence but for Adam's harsh breathing and soft curses uttered from where he lay sprawled on the ground.

"You okay?" Thomas said, making a wary circle with the sword in hand. The scent of demon now filled the small clearing they stood in.

"No, goddamn it. That's a dumb question," groaned Adam, but he struggled to his feet anyway.

The blur came again, this time straight at Thomas. He swung his sword, hit air. Then a heavy fist struck the side of his head and it was his turn to kiss the ground.

Thomas blacked out for a moment under the force of the punch, but then pushed quickly to his feet, knowing they didn't have much time. The demon was just playing with them now and it wouldn't take long before he got serious. Nausea rolled around in his stomach as he balanced unsteadily, pain throbbing through his head and shoulders.

Playing with demons was just no fun at all.

He and Adam exchanged a glance and stood ready in the moonlight, both swaying a little. Blood trickled into Thomas's eye and made it burn.

Silence.

Stillness.

From Thomas's right came another blur of motion. With all his might, he concentrated on the movement and calculated the swing of his sword. Blade bit into flesh and Boyle roared. The demon's fist came down again, backhanding Thomas. His sword flew from his grasp to land in the nearby brush.

As Boyle lifted his hand again, Thomas tapped his magick. Power coursed, channeled through his chest and down his arm. He concentrated it on the earth beneath Boyle's feet, causing it to rumble and shake.

Boyle, caught off balance, stumbled backward. Adam stepped in immediately, swinging his sword at the demon who dodged the blow at the last second. The blade whistled through the air an inch from the demon's throat.

Thomas lunged for his lost weapon. As his hand closed around the grip, he heard Adam's warning, "Watch out!" and rolled to the side to see Boyle had picked up a huge branch and was attempting to skewer him with the end like a marsh-mallow at a campfire. The end of the branch stuck in the ground where Thomas had been just a moment before.

Thomas took the opportunity to swing the blade in an arc toward Boyle's knees, but the demon managed to pull the branch free and block his swing. The blade stuck fast in the wood like Excalibur to stone. Boyle and Thomas both pulled to extract their weapons at the same time. Wood and blade separated. Thomas rolled away while the demon turned and engaged an attack from Adam.

He pulled himself to his feet and glimpsed a prone figure in the weeds. *Jake*. Thomas couldn't tell if he still lived or not.

Thomas turned and bellowed, *"What do you want with them?"* Rage and frustration made the words echo raw and bloody into the night air, pulled from his throat with savage intensity.

Just then Adam sank the sword into the demon's leg. Boyle yelled out in pain and punched Adam so hard he flew backward, hit the ground and lay still. Icy fear clenched in Thomas's stom-ach. He wanted to get to him but at the moment a very pissed off demon blocked his way.

Boyle turned, pulled the sword from his leg and tossed it to the side. "I want to go home!" He took several menacing steps toward Thomas. The demon's skin now had an unnatural reddish cast to it. His eyes had bled to obsidian and the demon's grimace revealed unnaturally sharp teeth.

According to Micah these bodily changes meant the demon had entered a killing rage. *Fun.*

"I just want to get home, *aeamon*," repeated Boyle.

"So you're using the witches to open a doorway between Earth and Eudae? Is that what you're doing?"

"I am amused by the tie you have with the water witch, but your ignorance annoys me."

Thomas circled the demon warily, sword tight in his grip. He really didn't like any words coming from the demon's mouth that concerned Isabelle. "Since I'm so ignorant, why don't you enlighten me?"

"Educating you is not my concern, *aeamon*. You're only delaying me."

"Really? Are you in a hurry?" He paused for a moment and then rasped, "Tell me how you're doing it, Boyle."

"It's almost done. I have only two more keys to make and I'm finished. This is nothing to you, and I have nothing to say. Leave me alone. Let me go home."

"This is everything to me! You're killing my people!" Thomas's throat felt raw more from shouting and rage than from the beating he'd taken. Rage at not being able to stop the demon filled every molecule of his body.

"Your people, my people. We are all one people. I want to go home. Stop trying to prevent me. Once I am gone, the killing will stop."

"Are we really related, Boyle?" he pressed. "Are witches the offspring of demons?"

"Yes. We are kin."

Thomas lunged for Boyle, bitter acid roiling through his stomach and burning his throat. The demon stepped to the left, but Thomas anticipated his move and twisted his blade to intercept. It caught the demon deeply in the side.

The wound smoked and the skin peeled away, just as the first time Isabelle had used her knife. Boyle keened in pain and the first drops of his acidic blood began to fall.

Thomas only had a moment to consider why this particular stroke of the copper blade had caused the reaction when the others had not, perhaps because the blade had bit so deeply. Screaming in agony, Boyle swung his heavy tree branch like a baseball bat and hit Thomas in the midsection.

Home run.

Thomas's breath woofed out of his lungs as pain exploded through his body. His feet left the earth and he landed heavily on his side, his head making hard contact with the ground. His vision blurred and his breath gone, he saw the demon there one moment and not the next.

Thomas thought of Isabelle, irrationally—her face, the feel of her breath on his throat, the scent of her skin. Lord and Lady, he wanted Isabelle now.

All he got was blackness.

EIGHTEEN

"WHAT THE HELL HAPPENED?" ISABELLE RACED DOWN
the steps of the Coven, her bare feet slapping on the pavement.

A blast of cool early morning air billowed under the T-shirt
and boxers she'd worn to bed since Jack McAllister had been
babysitting her . . . and because she didn't want to be sword
fighting in the nude if the demon showed up in the middle of
the night. That would be inconvenient.

Some of the stronger male Coven witches helped Adam
and Thomas, both clearly injured, into the house. Others carried a large unconscious man whom Isabelle didn't recognize.

Damn it, she wanted to be mad at Thomas for forcing Jack
on her, but instead she was terrified for him. Thomas and
Adam both had torn clothing. Blood and dirt streaked their
faces and shirt collars. Bruises bloomed all over both them
and Adam's lip was split. Thomas walked with a distinct limp,
aided on one side by his cousin Micah.

"What the hell happened?" she demanded to know again
once she reached the motley group.

"Isn't it obvious?" Micah answered her. "They met the demon and the demon won."

"Demon didn't win," slurred Adam. "Demon didn't kill us.
Demon left his prey. So . . . didn't win." He staggered forward
and almost planted his face on the steps—an extra injury he
didn't need—before the two witches helping him walk managed to catch him. "He did kick our asses though."

"Prey?" The word stopped her in her tracks.

Thomas held Isabelle's gaze. Now she saw his lip was also split. Blood covered the right side of his face. "The demon didn't get Jake, so he didn't win."

"What? Who the hell is Jake?"

Thomas motioned with his head to the unconscious man they were just getting through the front doors of the Coven. "Isabelle, meet Jake. Jake, Isabelle." The unsplit part of his mouth crooked upward in a smile before he winced and dropped it. "I don't think he'll say hi right now."

She frowned. "Cute. Did they give you painkillers or something?"

He grimaced, but Isabelle was pretty sure he meant it to be a grin. "I missed you."

She looked at Micah. "Seriously, did you give him painkillers?"

Thomas grimaced again. "I'll tell you everything, Isabelle. Stay with me while Doc Oliver patches me up."

Isabelle followed them into the house and down a corridor to Doctor Oliver's facilities. They entered the large waiting room after Adam. Doc Oliver and her nurses did a booming business at the Coven these days.

Jake, Boyle's almost-dinner, was being pushed into one of the private examination rooms on a gurney. "Is he going to be all right?" she asked Micah, watching the door close behind them.

Micah shrugged. "I think he's just been knocked out cold, but it's too early to say. The doctor needs to look at him."

Thomas rebuffed Micah's attempt to lead him to an examination room and sank down into one of the plush burgundy waiting room chairs. Adam had disappeared into one of the other rooms, probably to await the doctor like Thomas. Clearly, she needed to deal with Jake first. His injuries were the worst.

A nurse approached Thomas, but he waved her away. "I'm fine, see to Adam first." He sounded grouchy. The nurse nodded and moved away.

"Thomas—" Isabelle objected. He didn't look fine to her, covered in blood, wincing, bruised, and limping.

He held up a hand. "Really, Isabelle. I'm okay. I didn't break anything . . . I don't think."

"Great. You don't *think*. Stubborn," she muttered, shook her head and gave up. "Tell me about this guy Jake and how he came to be Boyle's prey."

Thomas adjusted his position for more comfort, trying not to jar his leg. Micah had taken a chair nearby. "We went to the Red Rock. It was our last stop for the night."

"We all thought the troll for Boyle was a wash . . . again," Micah added.

"But as we were leaving we heard sounds coming from behind the building. When we went around to investigate, a woman was there, beaten nearly unconscious. We recognized her from the bar, but she'd been with a man—"

Isabelle stopped chewing her thumbnail to ask, "Jake?"

"Yes. We could smell the demon had been there. That damned stink of turned, scorched other-Earth was in the air. So when she pointed to the stand of trees nearby, we went for it."

"I stayed behind to help the woman on Thomas's orders," Micah interjected. "Adam and Thomas went in."

Thomas shifted again and closed his eyes for a moment. Isabelle battled the urge to call for the nurse. "We fought the demon. He kicked our asses, but I managed to lay one good swipe into him with my sword—a swipe that gave him that allergic reaction, or whatever it is. It made him leave immediately . . . without Jake. Maybe I laid into him so deep whatever he did to give himself resistance to the copper couldn't work. I don't know."

Isabelle nodded. "So you think the demon was lying in wait for Jake as his next victim and you interrupted the abduction?"

Thomas nodded. "That's what I think."

She glanced at Micah. "So when you were finished helping the injured woman, you came back and found them?"

Micah nodded. "I called the Coven and they came out immediately."

Isabelle turned away, Boyle's words echoing in her head. *I will come for you when I am ready. I have work to do before you.* How many others were to come before her? When would Boyle come for her?

"Isabelle, are you all right?"

She turned to see Thomas's concerned expression. "I'm sick of this, sick of being one step behind Boyle."

He rubbed a hand over his face. Thomas looked weary and she knew it was from more than a simple lack of sleep or his current physical condition. "Me, too, Isabelle. If we hadn't found Boyle when we did, Jake would have been the next victim."

Isabelle wrapped her arms around herself and hugged. "And who knows if the demon hasn't already chosen a replacement." She swallowed. "Maybe two of them."

Thomas's jaw worked as he probably gritted his teeth. "I know. Takes the shine off stealing Boyle's prey tonight."

All three of them fell silent. In the other room they could hear the doctor and her assistants working on Jake. Urgent, raised voices, beeping machines, shuffling feet.

Apparently Jake was worse off than Micah thought.

"Damn it. I have to get out of here." Thomas pushed up from the chair onto his bad leg and winced. "I'm starving. Let's go get something to eat."

Isabelle gaped. "What? You need to be seen by the doctor."

Micah blew out a frustrated sounding breath. "Don't be dumb, boss. You're bleeding all over the place and your eye is almost swollen shut."

Thomas touched his forehead. "The bleeding has stopped and my injuries aren't as bad as Jake's or Adam's. Anyway, she's going to be a while. I can grab a bite and be back before she's ready for me."

"You stay here. Let me go get you something, Thomas." Isabelle moved toward the door, but he caught her wrist in his iron grip.

"We'll go together. I'm sick of seeing Micah's ugly mug. It's the first damn thing I saw when I came to. All that on nothing but bourbon in my stomach. It's enough to—"

"Hey, hey!" Micah objected with a raised hand. "All right already. Go on. I'll tell the doc you'll be back soon and to tend to Adam first."

"Thanks, cousin." Thomas answered with a grimace-trying-to-be-a-grin and moved toward the door. "You know I was only partially kidding, right?"

"Partially. Yeah, got it. I feel the love, I really do." He paused and glanced at Isabelle. "You know I have you to blame for this."

Isabelle lifted her eyebrows. "What do you mean?"

"He never used to give me shit before you came along."

"Come on." Thomas dragged her toward the door, limping. "I'm about ready to pass out from hunger."

"Or blood loss," she muttered as she followed him out.

They went to the kitchen where Thomas dragged his bad leg around, filling a plate with leftovers and pouring a glass of red wine. He put two forks down and sat in a chair beside Isabelle.

"So, how did it go with your mother?" Thomas picked up a fork and dug into some warmed-up mashed potatoes.

Isabelle shrugged. "It was weird. She wasn't cocky at all. She was . . ."

"Contrite?"

She shrugged again, smoothly took the fork from him, took a bite and handed it back. "I guess. Like I said, weird."

He took a sip of wine. "And so?"

She sighed. "I'm not ready to flat-out forgive her for passing us around like she didn't want us when Angela and I were kids. I'm not ready to forgive her for a lot of things."

"I wouldn't expect you to be."

She took the wineglass from his hand as he set it down on the table, their fingertips brushing, and took a drink. She studied him over the rim for a moment. "But there is part of me that wants to see where this goes."

"I'm glad, Isabelle." He slipped the wineglass from her fingers and took a sip.

"I'm having lunch with her next week. That's all I can commit to at this time. But I think you were right."

He served up a forkful of food for her and she ate it. "About what?"

Isabelle chewed and swallowed, then took the fork and offered Thomas a bite, which he accepted. "About her regretting. Anyway, we'll see what happens."

Thomas pulled her chair closer to him and kissed her temple.

She turned her head and kissed his lips—the side that was the least damaged. "You smell like mud, blood, and demon."

"I hurt just about everywhere, too."

"So tell me more about what happened before I drag your ass back to Doctor Oliver."

Thomas took a moment to reply. "Boyle told me all he wanted was to go home. There was longing in his voice when he talked about it."

She screwed her face up. "Longing? Do you really think demons *long*?"

He shook his head, passed a hand over his tired-looking face. "I don't know."

"Why would Boyle want to go home anyway? Wasn't he incarcerated as a criminal in his world? You'd think they'd just lock him up again if he went back. You'd think he'd know that."

"Yeah. Who can understand what Boyle might be thinking? Maybe he thinks he can escape that fate once he gets there. Or maybe he hates this place so much he's willing risk anything to get home."

She turned sober. "I wonder what he's doing right now."

His arm tightened around her and he set his fork down.

"Yeah, you're right," she muttered. "Let's not wonder."

"Let's not. Wondering just killed my appetite." He pushed his plate away. "I'm sorry about being a hard-ass about you staying at the Coven."

Her irritation, suppressed by recent events, flared. "You're sorry? Please, Thomas, you're a total control freak. Your need to protect those around you is admirable, but—"

He turned and cupped her cheek. "Those I care about."

"What?"

"You said I have a need to protect those around me. The category is actually a lot narrower, Isabelle. Also, it's not a need, it's an obsession."

She tried to hold on to her anger, she really did, but the look in his eyes—his one good eye, anyway—spoke such truth to what he said. Protecting people was Thomas's calling. Her mouth twitched as she forced away a smile of happiness.

She directed her gaze across the kitchen. "You should see someone for that."

He dropped his hand from her face. "Maybe."

Thomas picked up his wineglass and took a drink. Again Isabelle took it from his fingers without even thinking about it, raising the rim to her lips and sipping. The way they sat there so close, sharing food and wine, it was like they were a couple.

Like they were in love.

Lord and Lady, she couldn't do this. Boyle was coming for her. Unless she could find a way to stop the demon when her number came up, she was going to die. She couldn't allow herself to get any closer to Thomas than she already was, both for her own sake and for his. Anything else would be cruel.

She hesitated lowering the wineglass from her mouth, then set it aside and pushed away from Thomas a little. "I thought after all this was over I might try Asia for a couple of years." She tried to sound flippant, but her voice came out tight.

Something dark flickered through his eyes. He glanced away and when he looked back at her there was mild, polite interest on his face—feigned. She could feel displeasure and anger emanating from him. "Asia? Really? Where exactly? Asia is a big place."

She waved a hand dismissively. "Thought maybe I'd start in Japan and work my way through."

"And if I asked you to stay?"

Isabelle sighed and glanced at the door. "Haven't you learned anything about me, Thomas? I'm not the type to stay."

He pulled his arm from around her waist and stood. Grief bubbled up inside her from the loss of his body heat and the hurt look in his eyes. "I should get back. You coming? I don't want you here alone."

Isabelle watched him limp to the doorway and then through it. She gripped the edge of the table, forcing herself to not run after him and tell him that if there was any man in the world she would settle in one place for, it was him. Despite his stupid protectiveness. Despite his control issues.

She rose to follow him slowly, forcing herself not to run after him and tell him about Boyle and the position the demon

had put her in: her life for another witch's. Isabelle wanted—
needed—his support and advice. But she couldn't do that, no
matter how much she wanted it. Thomas would try and protect
her from Boyle at all costs, and the demon had already told
her he'd kill Thomas if he got in his way. Isabelle couldn't let
him risk his life, because she knew she was falling in love
with him.

This time she would be the one to protect him.

THOMAS AWOKE TO FINGERS RUFFLING THROUGH HIS
hair and the sweet scent and warmth of a woman's breath on
his cheek. His eyelids lifted a moment to see that Isabelle had
climbed into bed with him.

She had no intention of staying. He wanted to kick himself
for the moment he'd allowed himself to hope.

She'd shown up at his door only moments after he'd arrived home saying she wanted to sleep in the guest room. It
was lucky she'd come on her own. Physically, he hadn't felt
like dragging her over, even though he would have. Thomas
had opened the door and let her in, but hadn't said much because he was still hurt and pissed off that she'd made it pretty
clear she was just using him for sex.

He could give her sex, but Thomas suspected she wanted—
needed—the other things he had to give, too.

She was just too afraid to take them.

He moved, wrapping his arms around her and rolling to the
side. The sheets tangled between him and her long, slim—
nude—body as he pulled her underneath him. Isabelle was
only a temporary addition to his life, a fleeting whisper, tran-
sitory, and impossible to keep.

But damned if he wasn't going to try and hold on to her
anyway.

Thomas slid his good knee between her thighs and winced
when the other knee protested the weight he placed on it.

Her cool hand slid up his shoulder. "Doctor told me you
twisted your knee. I promise I'll be gentle with you." She bit
her lower lip. "I needed to touch you tonight."

He forcibly spread her thighs and pressed the length of his

cock against her heat, making her gasp. The only thing that separated them was the sheet and he'd soon make that disappear. "Gentle is the last thing I want from you."

She smiled and raised her leg to run her heel up his calf and the back of his thigh. "So you sleep in the nude."

He raised an eyebrow. "Would you prefer flannel?"

She licked her lower lip. "Only if I could take it off you. I like you much better without clothes." She reached up and traced the edge of the bandage that covered his forehead. "But maybe my coming in here wasn't a good idea."

"Why are you here, anyway? Just using me for sex again?"

She pursed her lips. "Got a problem with that?"

"I'm a man. Do you really think so?"

Isabelle laughed softly and pushed up at him. He allowed it, letting her force him onto his back so she could straddle him. The heat of her sex teased his cock.

Her gaze explored him for a moment. "I love that lazy look you get on your face right before we have sex. I love the flex of the muscles in your arms and chest when you touch me. I love—" She bit off the end of her sentence and stared at him a moment before glancing away.

"Are you getting shy? You?"

Isabelle ducked her head and brushed her lips across his. Thomas snaked his hand to the nape of her neck and pressed her mouth down on his so he could part her lips and lazily swipe his tongue against hers. She sighed and kissed him back, pushing her tongue into his mouth more aggressively.

I'm keeping you, Isabelle. You just don't know it yet.

NINETEEN

❧

ISABELLE BROKE THE KISS AND MOVED DOWN HIS throat, kissing, nipping, and licking. She worked her way down his chest, her warm, moist lips exploring every inch of his skin. When she reached his abdomen, she dragged her tongue down his flesh until she reached his cock. Isabelle gave him a single coy look and then engulfed the head of his shaft in her mouth. All his nerve endings shot to life. Thomas tipped his head back and groaned.

He threaded his fingers through her hair and fisted, stopping himself from thrusting gently into her mouth. Her ability to render him completely helpless with the swipe of her tongue always amazed him.

She moved over him while pulling the length of his cock into the warm, wet recesses of her mouth and skating her tongue up and down. Her hair brushed his thighs and made him jump. His balls felt ready to explode and pleasure tingled through his body, but when he went, he wanted to be buried deep inside her sex, not down her throat. He wanted to feel the evidence of her pleasure rippling around his cock before that happened.

"Isabelle." It came out in an agonized-sounding groan.

She ignored him, glancing up at him once and then sucking his length between her lips once more. Isabelle swirled her tongue around the sensitive underside of the crown on her outward mouth stroke. Clearly, she meant business.

Thomas forced himself up from Shangri-la to seek heaven.

He eased her off him and twisted, pinning her face down on his king size bed beneath him in one smooth movement.

Isabelle gasped into the blankets and mattress. "Your knee!"

He hovered over her and spread her thighs. "Hardly noticed it. You're the best kind of painkiller." He dragged his fingers over her sex and she wiggled beneath him.

Isabelle raised her hips, fitting her sweet ass against his groin and arching the smooth slope of her back. Placing a hand to the curve of her hip, he leaned over to lick and nibble his way down her spine. She turned her head to the side and he watched her tongue steal out to wet her lips, her eyes closed and her long, dark eyelashes swept down on her passion-rosy cheeks.

Her fingers fisted in the covers on either side of her and she moved her hips, looking for a way to slide his cock inside her. Thomas slipped his hand between the mattress and her stomach, seeking and finding that hot place where she wanted to be touched. Finding her clit, he rubbed it with his index finger. She gasped and moaned into the blankets.

She tried to push up, but he kept her pinned there as he caressed her into a thrashing frenzy, but stopped just short of making her come. Then he slipped two fingers into her warm, wet heat and pumped. Isabelle moved her hips in time to his thrusts, an action that almost made him lose his mind.

Embracing his sudden and feral need to claim her, Thomas forced her thighs apart and grasped her hips, pulling her upward to impale her on his cock. In one smooth move, he set the head of his shaft to her entrance and thrust inside, seating himself to the base in all that wet heat.

She arched her back, grabbing fistfuls of blanket. Her breath came out in a gasp, then a moan.

At the same time, Thomas dropped down over her back and sank his teeth into the nape of her neck as he began to ride her.

Isabelle exploded in climax beneath him, the muscles of her sex clenching and releasing around his cock. She panted and thrashed, moving on his thrusting shaft. Thomas fought not to come. He wanted this to last.

Thomas threw his head back, his hair falling around them

both as he pumped into her harder and faster. They probably had the appearance of one animal with no beginning or end as they moved together on the bed. She pressed up against him, gaining leverage with her knees and hands so she could push back against him, meeting his thrusts into her sweet body.

Thomas let his hand play around her now exposed front, running over her stomach, teasing her nipples and cupping her breasts.

"I'm coming again," she gasped. Isabelle shuddered beneath him as another climax drove through her. This time Thomas let go, too. Pleasure exploded from the depths of him and poured into her.

They collapsed in a tangle on the mattress, each wrapped up in the other. His cock pulled from her body as she moved and he felt the loss of that connection. He dragged her against him and she tucked her head under his chin.

"I'm not letting you go, Isabelle," he murmured into the top of her head.

She stiffened against him. "You're going to have to." Her voice sounded flat, expressionless.

Thomas lay still for a moment before speaking. "I want you and I always get what I want."

He'd expected her to get angry at the arrogance of his comment—even though he meant every word. Instead, she rolled to the side and laughed. Idly, she picked up a length of his hair and wound it around her finger. "The world has winds, Thomas. Sometimes they blow us where we don't want to go."

"What's that supposed to mean?"

She shrugged and unwound the tendril of his hair. "Whatever you want it to mean. How's your knee?"

"Hurts like a motherfucker. What we just did wasn't ordered in my physical therapy." His knee would be healed soon anyway. A few good sessions with the Coven fire witches would see it improved in a matter of days.

"A good soak in that massive bathtub would probably make it feel better."

"That's a hint, isn't it? I still smell like mud, blood, and demon, right?"

She propped herself up on her elbow and grinned. "Well, yes, but it's true that water makes everything feel better."

"Maybe, but I don't want to move."

She rolled off the bed and he got an excellent view of her lovely heart-shaped rear as she disappeared into the bathroom. A moment later he heard water filling his sunken spa tub.

He propped himself up on the pillows just in time to see one of Isabelle's lithe legs appear around the side of door frame. She slowly dragged her heel up the wood . . . and Thomas was up and out of bed in a flash, twisted knee bedamned.

As soon as she heard him coming, Isabelle scampered into the water, which she'd filled with bubble bath. He gaped at the lavender- and rose-scented mountain of foam. It smelled like a rainbow had puked. "Where the hell did you find that stuff?"

"It was hidden in the back of one of your cabinets."

She stood and Thomas raked his gaze over her—pink nipples peeking from the white froth, bubbles sliding down her legs.

Revising his opinion of the fragrant froth, he limped to the tub. "Thank the Lord and Lady."

ISABELLE ACCEPTED A SMALL VIAL OF A METALLIC substance from Micah and held it up to the light. The fluid within looked like liquid gold. "It's charmed copper, you said?"

Micah nodded and took the vial back from her. He gestured at Thomas who stood nearby, his arms crossed over his chest. "We had Thomas and a group of our best Coven earth witches work on a special blend of magick that will keep small amounts of copper in a liquefied form. We don't have much of it, unfortunately."

She turned to stare at Thomas. "How are you able to do this?"

He uncrossed his arms. "It wasn't easy. The only way we were able to do it all is because copper comes from copper ore and occasionally from crystal chunks, both a part of the Earth originally. That makes it much easier for us. It took a while but we were able to develop an earth charm that keeps it liquid in very limited quantities."

"So you're hoping that getting it into Boyle's bloodstream will cause a massive reaction and kill him?"

"That's the general plan," answered Micah. He paused and pursed his lips. "Of course it may be like a bee stinging a bull, too. We might just piss him off."

Isabelle gritted her teeth, thinking of the little girl. "I'm more than willing to take a shot and find out. What's the method of delivery?"

Micah turned to a table where various implements lay. "Like I said, we don't have much liquid copper." He picked up something that looked like a semiautomatic handgun. "We have a couple of these stun guns, loaded with hollow bullets filled with it. That's about it."

She took the gun from him and examined it. "Explain to me why we can't make more liquid copper."

"Because in order to make the charm, we need francium," Thomas answered.

Isabelle lifted a brow in question. "And this francium person can't come to the charm-making party or what?"

Micah rolled his eyes. "*Francium* is a very rare naturally occurring element. It's not like you can order vats of it over the Internet."

"Okay, sorry for not getting straight A's in francium class. I just wondered if you had enough left to make me up a syringe." She held her forefinger and thumb close together. "Just a little?"

Thomas took the stun gun back from her and set it on the table. "Do you plan on getting that close to him? Because I don't like that idea."

"The thing is . . . who knows how close we'll get? I've already been way closer to Boyle than I wanted to be twice. If we had syringes, maybe it could be a backup plan. A little something for just in case."

Thomas rubbed his chin. "I'll see what I can do. I don't think we'll be able to make enough for everyone, but I might be able to make enough just for you. I still want you to carry a gun, but the syringe you can carry in case of an emergency."

"Thank you."

He held her gaze. "Anything to keep you safe."

A smile spread across her mouth.

Micah made a gagging sound. "I'm leaving before I puke. Anyway, I need to brief Adam, Jack, and the others about the new weapons."

Thomas tore his gaze from hers to glance at his cousin. "We troll again tonight. Meet at the front doors at twilight."

"I'm going." There wasn't any liquid copper in Isabelle's voice when she said those words. It was all solid steel.

Thomas's big body stiffened. "Isabelle." Her name sounded like the snap of a whip.

"Uh, oh. I'm outta here." Micah gathered a few things from the table and left the room.

"Please, Thomas, I don't want to fight. You know you're going to have to tie me up to keep me from going and as much as I think you'd like to do that—and I might like it, too—I don't think you will. Just admit defeat now."

Sighing, Thomas pushed a hand through his hair. "The fact is I want to keep you safe. The problem is I don't know where safe is anymore, not with Boyle being able to enter and leave the Coven at will."

Ah, ha! Victory! She made sure her voice was soft when she replied, "Exactly, so there's no reason to fight with me in order to force me to stay here. All it does is sow discord between us."

Thomas's jaw locked and he closed his eyes briefly. "I'm going to make more liquid copper . . . if I can." He turned and stalked away, still limping.

Isabelle watched him go, the smile fading from her lips. The man really did care about her. For the first time in her life she had the beginnings of an actual relationship with someone other than her sister . . . and it was wonderful.

Too bad it couldn't last.

THOMAS VELCROED HIMSELF TO HER SIDE ALL NIGHT.

She rounded on him as they entered their fifth stop, The Black Cauldron, a popular nightclub for witches. It was somewhere they thought Boyle might be apt to frequent. "Look, if we meet up with the demon tonight, it will be *me* protecting *you*. You're the one with the injury. Please back off and give me some space."

Jack, Adam, Theo, Micah, and the other witches in their particular traveling party—Thomas had sent out several to search—had entered the recesses of the club, disappearing into the crush of the mostly witch crowd. The press of emotion and magick made Isabelle edgy because of the circumstances and she instantly regretted the harsh way she'd spoken to him.

Thomas turned and loomed over her, his face shadowed in the dim, pulsing light of the place. Suddenly that face she knew so well looked dangerous. He grasped her wrists and pushed her backward, making the other patrons move out of their way until she felt the press of a railing against her back. The man liked to trap her against things.

He lowered his mouth to hers and his breath teased her lips, warming her skin. His hand moved to the small of her back, pushing under the fabric of her V-neck black T-shirt. *"No."* His lips moved on hers as he growled the word. "Simple enough for you?"

His scent filled her nose, blocking out the slightly smoky, unwashed body smell of the club and replacing it with *Thomas*—clean soap, citrusy aftershave, and the inherent, indescribable scent of man.

Irritation flashed through her, hard and hot, but it was quickly followed by total desire. She'd never in her life had such a strong sexual reaction to a man the way she had to Thomas. It was pheromones, or something. Maybe it was just flat-out lust.

She pushed up on her tiptoes and pressed her mouth to his, parting his lips and pushing her tongue within to swipe. Isabelle felt more than heard the rumble that went through his body. He pulled her up against his chest and she gripped his shoulders as he plunged his tongue into her mouth like he wanted to consume her.

The people around them ceased to matter. They disappeared as far as she was concerned. Thomas pissed her off, it was true. He was protective to a fault. Yet it was nice to be cared about.

He moved, unbuttoning and unzipping her jeans and then sliding his hand down to stroke his finger over her clit through the material of her panties. She gasped into his mouth and her eyes rolled back into her head at the pleasure that rippled through her body. Isabelle moved her hips, grinding down against his hand for more of the exquisite sensation. Her sex warmed.

Lord and Lady, it was like she'd entered some kind of animalistic heat. All she wanted was for her jeans and panties to be off, for his thick cock to be moving deep inside her. The bathroom, maybe . . . anywhere would do . . .

"I need you," she whispered shakily against his lips. *In so many ways*. She wished like hell she could tell him how much.

"You need me to what? You need me to fuck you?"

She bit her lower lip at his base words. They excited her almost as much as the slow glide of his finger over the bundle of nerves between her thighs. Her underwear was wet from it and her clit pulsed, aroused and plumped.

She couldn't reply. *I need you to make love to me. I need you to tell me you care about me. I just need you, Thomas.*

"I need to feel you come, Isabelle," he groaned. "Right here. Right now." He moved the elastic of her panties to the side and dragged his fingers over her bared sex.

Her eyelids fluttered open to see a man nearby staring at her hungrily. Did he see what Thomas was doing to her right now? How could he in this dim light, in this great crush of people that made everything anonymous? Then Thomas pushed his fingers inside her and all those concerns ceased to matter.

He buried his face in the curve of her throat, licking, kissing, and nipping at her with his teeth. Her mind flashed back to the way he'd made love to her the morning before—how he'd pushed her facedown on the bed and taken her from behind like some feral animal. How he'd sunk his teeth into the nape of her neck just hard enough to force her to climax.

Thomas ground his palm against her clit and dragged his finger over her G-spot deep inside her. "Come on, baby," he growled into her ear a moment before he pulled her lobe between his teeth.

Her orgasm washed over her so fast and so strong all she could do was let out a sob of release. She felt a rush of moisture between her thighs as the pleasure slammed into her, wiping away every last coherent thought in her brain and making her knees go weak.

Thomas held her up and she splayed a hand behind her, fingers gaining purchase around one of the railings he'd pressed her up against. The fact that they poked in her back uncomfortably barely registered.

Once the ripples of her climax had eased and she hung there, breathing heavy, all dazed and confused, he zipped and buttoned her jeans once more. He leaned forward and whispered in her ear, "I hope that addressed your concern fully. You know, that one about me keeping my distance? Not happening."

He stared at her a moment longer, then turned and melted into the crowd.

Isabelle stood there stunned, too passion-slackened to think clearly. Then his arrogance hit her full force and annoyance bloomed. Pissed off once again, she peeled herself from the railing and headed after him, but someone yanked her back . . . *hard*.

Isabelle turned, half expecting to see the man who'd been staring at her before . . . but it was Boyle. Adrenaline spiked, sending a jolt of shock and primal fear shooting through her veins. *How the hell had he appeared right there all of a sudden*?

She heard Thomas call her name in the crush of people up ahead. Through the crowd, she saw the top of his head as he headed back for her. Ironically, he'd kept his distance after all, for about two seconds.

Apparently, that's all the demon had needed.

She opened her mouth to scream Thomas's name out of pure involuntary reaction, but Boyle clamped a hand over her mouth and dragged her to the left, toward the door.

TWENTY

❦

ISABELLE BIT HIS PALM AND BROUGHT HER BOOTED heel back hard into his shin. Boyle reacted as expected—hardly at all. He just jerked a little.

"She's had too much to drink," he said to the curious on-lookers with an unnatural lopsided grin pasted on his face. "She always gets rowdy when we go out." His accent when he said this was almost nonexistent and his speech was in the vernacular. No scent of demon magick clung to him either. Boyle was acting human this evening.

The people around them just stared, clearly not sure what to think. Obviously the club was short on heroic types tonight.

Instead of taking her out the door, as she'd expected him to do, he picked her up and carried her to the back, where he found another door that led out into the alley behind the building.

The demon pushed her through the doorway. She stumbled face forward into a dank smelling puddle. Water splashed and the pavement bit into her palms and scraped her knees. Behind them the metallic chunk of the door closing muffled the pounding music of the club. Not wasting any time, she glanced up at the mouth of the alley, looking for an escape. Finding one, she launched herself up like a track runner. It was reflex. Every molecule in her body screamed *flee*.

Boyle had her in an instant, wrapping his huge arms around her waist and whirling her around to land in the puddle on her hands and knees once more. The position was too much like begging for her taste, but this time she stayed there, motionless and breathing in the trashy, damp air of the alley in big gulpfuls. Her whole body hurt from being hurled to the pavement. Her hands and knees were scraped raw.

"So this is it, then?" She didn't look up when she asked the question. She stared at a piece of soaked, crumpled newspaper on the ground in front her. Her voice sounded bland and wooden to her own ears—resigned—but she still had one ace up her sleeve. She rocked back on her heels and incrementally moved her hand toward the back of her waistband, where the gun was tucked. "Time's up?"

The demon took three steps toward her and planted his massive booted feet on the pavement in front of her. "The head witch, I can feel his emotion for you. Behind the factory I mentioned you and his pulse raced, anger and fear flared. He does not like that I am even aware of your existence."

She shook her head and glanced up at him. "What?"

"When I fought with the leader of the witches, the one with the angel tattoo on his back, I saw that he has much emotion for you." He tipped his head to the side. "And I feel that you care for him, yet I feel reticence in you. I am fascinated by this."

This was beyond bizarre. What strange turn her life had taken that she should find herself discussing her love life in a back alley with her demon executioner.

Isabelle sat on her haunches in the puddle, enduring the sensation of the cold alley water seeping into her jeans, and placed her hands high on her hips, closer to her gun. "Why do you care?"

His blue eyes narrowed. "I'm interested in human behavior, even the behavior of the half-human, the *aeamon*. I followed you tonight to ask why you hold yourself in reserve."

Her mind fumbled. "You followed us tonight to . . . *You* followed *us*." *Fuck*.

The demon smiled and Isabelle shivered. A demon's smile wasn't a warm and fuzzy thing. Pointed teeth peeked from his peeled-back lips. "Did you think you were tracking me? No, *aeamon*. Your witches were lucky the other night, but you should know by now that you're outmatched. You can try to stop me, but you won't. Now answer my question."

"So you didn't come here tonight to put me in your stew pot? You just came to ask me this."

"I'm not ready to add your magick to the blend I need yet."

"So you're just playing with your food, then?" The question, spoken in a lighthearted tone, made her wince. It was good to keep him talking, though. She just needed a break in his concentration so she could pull the gun, aim it and fire. Isabelle wasn't sure exactly how to get that break, however. She doubted Boyle would fall for the classic *Hey! Look over there!* ploy. She had her syringe, too, tucked safely in a tiny holster inside her bra.

He grinned. "You are entertaining. It will be a pity to kill you."

"Uh-huh. Okay, why not tell you? I hold myself back from him because I know that soon you'll come for me. Giving into my emotions where he is concerned would only be cruel to both of us. He and I suffer from a horrendous case of bad timing. There. Happy now? Just tell your future meal one thing. Thomas isn't on your menu, right?"

"He doesn't possess what I need. Only you and a few others have that."

"Lucky us. Listen, you promise not to kill Thomas and I'll come with you willingly when you need me." *Of course that doesn't mean I won't try and kill you before you kill me.*

"You love him that much?"

"I *care* about him that much."

"I agree. I have no specific quarrel with the head witch. I have no reason to kill him if he doesn't get in my way where you are concerned. However, you would come with me willingly anyway because your alternate is your mother."

Shock rippled through her. "My mother?"

"Genetically, your magick is very strong. You and your mother have the same kind of magick, same level, same consistency. Both are exactly what I need for that particular component of this spell. Your sister had a similar level and consistency and was perfect for the earlier portion of the spell."

Rage rocketed through her. Her body shook from it. "You cannot have my whole family, you bastard!" she yelled.

She might have plenty of issues with her mother, but no way in hell would she allow her to become a victim to this monster the way her sister had. In the end, Catalina was her *mother*, dysfunctionality, selfishness, warts, and all. No matter what Isabelle may have said before about her, in this one moment that became crystal clear to her.

Isabelle couldn't wait for a distraction. She couldn't wait for anything.

Pulling the gun from the back of her waistband in one smooth move, she aimed and shot at Boyle. The sound ripped through her eardrums and echoed down the alley. With preternatural speed and reflexes, the demon twisted to the side and the bullet nicked him in the thigh, making him howl in pain and rage.

So close. She'd been so close. And, damn it, she *had* been close. Point-blank range, in fact, and he'd still dodged the bullet.

Boyle was on her in a flash. His weight pressed her into the pavement, compressing her lungs until she gasped. His big hand closed around her wrist and squeezed, trying to make her relinquish the weapon. She gripped it until she lost feeling in her hand, her arm.

Fighting as hard as she could under the demon's massive body, she kicked and clawed with her free hand like a feral cat. Boyle grunted and took the brutal treatment, pinning her to the ground with his tree-trunk-like legs.

A drop of Boyle's acidic blood from where her bullet had nicked him dropped onto her leg, burned a hole through her jeans and touched her skin. White hot pain seared through her.

Isabelle screamed.

Boyle recoiled in surprise and she managed to push up and aim the gun at him. She squeezed off a shot, but the demon pushed her hand at the last second and it went wide, ricocheting off a nearby wall.

"You have new weapons," Boyle hissed.

One hand pinned her wrist and the other came down over her throat as he straddled her. Her windpipe closed and her eyes bugged. The primal terror of having her breath cut off shut down her brain for a moment and made her thrash as hard as she could . . . to no avail.

Her hand went to his wrist, her fingernails digging in. The syringe was so close, but she couldn't reach down and pull it free, couldn't take her hand from Boyle's wrists in a desperate and futile attempt to grasp it.

But why wasn't he killing her?

Distantly, in the back of her mind, rationality flickered. He couldn't kill her. Not now. Not yet. Not this way.

From the mouth of the alley came the sound of pounding footsteps and yelling. It was about time. Granted, it was the dead of morning, but two shots fired and a woman's scream should have roused someone.

"I'm coming for you soon," he growled low. "This information I give you is a gift. Take advantage of the time you have left and make yourself ready to die."

A figure rose up behind Boyle and struck the demon over the back. Boyle grunted and backed away from her, rising and whirling around to roar at his attacker, still shadowed from Isabelle's view. Men yelled and shots rang through the air.

Boyle's charge on the witches was short-lived. Rolling to her side, she watched the demon scramble backward under the assault of copper-filled bullets. Likely, Boyle understood that the guns the attacking witches wielded were not ordinary. Boyle spared one last look at her, his expression intent, and then, instead of *poofing* through a doorway, he took off down the alley.

Isabelle lay on the ground taking in gulpfuls of bad air and watched Adam, Theo, Micah, and Jack run past her in pursuit of Boyle.

Thomas came down at her side. "Isabelle, are you all right?" All the blood had drained from his face and he looked exceptionally pissed off. Not at her, she presumed.

She coughed and snaked her hand into his lap. "I thought you said you weren't going to give me space?" she gasped, her voice raspy. It was a joke, but he didn't take it that way. A look of profound guilt passed over his face. She felt the pinch of it through her empathy.

She squeezed his hand and let a smile flicker over her lips. "Go, I'll be fine."

"I'm not leaving you."

Isabelle struggled into a sitting position and pointed down the alley after the others. "Go! Go help them, Thomas. If you want to protect me, don't let that son of a bitch get away."

He leaned in, kissed her and murmured, "I love you." Then he was gone.

I love you?

She sat for what seemed like a long time, stunned by his words, her hand covering her aching throat. He didn't mean those words. He couldn't. They'd probably just slipped out in the heat of the moment, maybe because he'd feared Boyle would kill her. She rubbed her fingers over her skin in an effort to ease the ache. Isabelle believed Thomas cared about her, could feel that he did. She knew he wanted to protect her . . . but love? Come on.

Although there had been a rush of pure, warm emotion emanating from him when he'd said it.

Isabelle had to admit that a part of her really liked the idea. *A lot.*

"What the hell are you smiling about? You just got your ass kicked by a demon."

She looked up to see Adam standing near her, doubled over and breathing hard, his palms braced on his thighs, and a quizzical look on his face.

Had she been smiling? Isabelle dropped her hand from her throat, swallowed and winced. "I guess I'm getting used to it." Her gaze locked on the mouth of the alley to see the others returning. "You didn't get him, did you?"

Adam straightened and gave a short, brutal laugh. "Hell, no. He was like a ghost. There one minute then, *poof*, gone. I think he made us chase him just for fun. Bastard."

"I think we injured him before he disappeared though," said Thomas, limping toward her. This little fracas probably hadn't helped his knee to heal any, though with the aid of Doc Oliver and some of the fire witches, it was rapidly improving.

He held out a hand and helped her to stand. "I got off one

shot that hit him in the upper arm." He paused and frowned. "I think."

Jack wiped a hand across his brow and spoke around his labored breathing. "I saw it. You hit him. That's when he *poofed* out of here. We chased him for a few blocks down these alleys. He dodged and weaved, hid behind stuff. None of us could get a clear shot, but Thomas managed to get him once."

Isabelle pushed to her feet, examined the damage done to her clothes, and grimaced. "That's something at least." She pursed her lips. "It sounds like he was just taunting us, like he enjoyed the chase."

"Yeah," Theo interjected. He had joined them a moment before, coming up the alley from the direction they'd chased Boyle. "He's not taking us seriously. That was hide-and-seek, demon style."

If they only knew how true that was. They were a game to Boyle, nothing more. Isabelle, in particular. Otherwise the demon wouldn't be following her around, asking her silly questions about her love life.

"*What happened?*" Thomas touched the hole in her jeans where Boyle's blood had burned through the cloth. Being choked had made her forget the low, throbbing pain of her leg, but now that it had been pointed out, it started to hurt.

"Boyle's blood isn't much fun," she said, fingering the eaten-away material around the hole.

Micah leaned in for a closer look. "Ow. That'll leave a scar."

"It will match the others he's given me."

Thomas took her arm and helped her to walk. Micah, Adam, and Jack followed. "Come on. I want you back at the Coven to see the doctor."

She tried not to lean against him because of his knee, but he pulled her against his body anyway and she stayed there because it felt good. The heat and scent of him calmed her frazzled nerves. Isabelle closed her eyes and melted against him.

Just for this moment she would pretend everything would be okay, because pretty soon these moments would be coming to an end.

TWENTY-ONE

—❧—

ISABELLE STOOD IN THE CONSERVATORY, FACE TIPPED to the glass ceiling above her so she could watch the rain pound down and the lightning flash. Every time thunder boomed, it shook the entire Coven.

It had been a week and there hadn't been a sign of Boyle anywhere. Had the copper bullet Thomas nailed him with done its job? Was Boyle dead? Or was Boyle still out there somewhere, biding his time before his next kill?

Tension dominated the overall mood of the Coven these days. The house vibrated with it. Micah spent his days monitoring the newspapers and morgues for some sign that Boyle's body had been found. They continued to patrol at night, but it had been fruitless.

Yet Isabelle knew Boyle was alive.

Being here in the Conservatory, sandwiched between the water in the stream running below her and the water cascading down on the glass above her, calmed her nerves. A chill had entered her bones and she couldn't shake herself free of it. It had lingered in the center of her for days—death with his hand on her shoulder. Isabelle wrapped her arms over her chest.

Soon Boyle would come for her.

He'd told her to get her affairs in order. Isabelle supposed that wasn't a bad idea. Just in case. She planned to go down kicking and screaming, but odds were . . . she *was* going down.

Someone touched her back and she jolted.

"*Shhh*, I'm sorry," murmured Thomas, his arms coming

around her. "I thought you heard me coming. I knew I'd find you here."

She snuggled back against him. Above them, thunder pealed. "I was thinking."

"Thinking about what?"

She licked her lips and decided she didn't want to lie to him. "Death."

"Cheery."

"Do you think it's a blessing or a curse to know that death is coming for you?"

He took a moment to answer. "I would say it's neither, just a fact of life. Death is coming for all of us eventually."

"I mean, what if you were given a certain amount of time to live. If someone told you, 'Get your affairs in order because you'll be dead within the week.' Would that be a blessing or a curse?"

"Where is this coming from, Isabelle?"

She shook her head. "I don't know."

Thomas turned her to face him. She stared up into his face and studied the shadows that shifted on it. Even in the darkness she could see concern in his expression. With Thomas she never needed her talent for empathy. His emotions were almost always clear to her. "Is there something you want to talk about?"

"Did you mean what you said in the alley? You know, when you said you loved me?"

Lady, why had she mentioned that? The words had just tumbled from her lips like she'd been asking him the time. It proved how badly she needed to know, even though this was a place she shouldn't want to go, not now.

He stilled and stared down at her. No sound but the storm crashing through the heavens reached their ears. Finally, he moved, brushing the hair away from her face and hooking it behind her ear. "I don't say things I don't mean."

"Say it again, then."

A long, heavy moment passed in which Isabelle kicked herself a thousand times. Finally, Thomas drew her close, wrapping his arms around her and enveloping her in his warmth, driving the chill of death from her bones.

"I love you, Isabelle." He whispered it near her ear. A hot rush of emotion flowed over her. "Don't leave when this is over, Isabelle." *Whisper.* "I want to keep you forever . . . Isabelle."

Tears pricked her eyes. She leaned into him, burying her face in his shoulder and inhaling the scent of him—the light woody note of his cologne, the clean aroma of his soap, the essential scent of Thomas.

Isabelle wanted to tell him that she loved him back, but her throat had closed up. Anyway, all her words were gone. They'd all been stolen by Boyle who was coming to steal her life soon as well.

They stood wrapped together in the Conservatory with the storm battering the glass ceiling and walls until Thomas tipped her chin up and stared into her face.

"I want to spend the night with you," she murmured.

Wordlessly, he took her by the hand and led her out of the shadowed Conservatory and through the sleeping corridors of the Coven.

Once in his apartment, he guided her into his bedroom and undressed her slowly in front of the window. Outside, the rage of the lashing storm provided a volatile backdrop. Isabelle soaked in his love as much as she absorbed the energy of the rain pounding down on the Coven. Her passion built with the fury of the storm.

Every inch of skin revealed by the removed clothing, he kissed, licked, and worshiped. Once he had her naked, Isabelle's whole world was only Thomas—his hands moving on her skin, the rough brush of his clothing against her flesh, the warmth of his breath, and the nip of his teeth on her shoulder, waist, and lips.

She sank to her knees and pushed the hem of his sweater up, running her tongue over his abdomen and unbuttoning his jeans. All she wanted was to drown herself in him, lose herself in this night and never return. Once she had his cock out, she stroked her fingertips over it. Thomas groaned.

He pulled her to her feet, hooked her leg over his waist and pushed his cock inside her roughly, as if he couldn't wait another moment to feel her. She gasped as his long, thick length slid deep within her. Holding on to his shoulders, she let her head fall back in ecstasy. Thomas was strong enough to take her whole weight, so she let him.

After a moment, Isabelle tipped her head forward and stared into his eyes. They stood still, intertwined and intimately connected.

Lady, she loved him back.

In the closeness of his bedroom, with the rain pounding outside his walls, and his body one with hers, she knew it. Her life would be perfect in this one moment if only she'd had the freedom to say it.

Without a word, Thomas picked her up. Her legs wound around his waist, his cock still deep inside her. He moved her to the bed, lying her down on the mattress and lowering himself on top of her.

He took her wrists and pinned them to the bed on either side of her, stared down into her eyes and began to thrust. His hips bumped hers on every inward stroke. Her clit, swollen and aroused, tingled and pulsed with the need to come.

When she closed her eyes and turned her head to the side, Thomas commanded, "Look at me." His voice was tender.

She turned her face to his and held his gaze, lips parted, while he stroked deep into the center of her.

"I love you, Isabelle." The words came soft and steady, his dark gaze fixed on hers.

The ripples of pleasure became waves. Her orgasm overtook her body and mind, just as Thomas had done. All Isabelle could do was ride it out. Pleasure coursed through her, making her back arch. She cried out his name and felt Thomas go, too, spilling inside her with a hoarse shout.

Afterward, they curled up together in the center of his bed—limbs and sheets tangled—and listened to the storm come to an end. Isabelle snuggled into Thomas's strong chest and closed her eyes as his arms circled her.

Despite the uncertainty of the future, she was happier than she could ever remember being. To make the warm feeling in the center of her chest remain for the entire night, she pushed the truth that it couldn't last far, far away.

Tonight she would hang on.

Tomorrow she had to pull away.

THOMAS SAT IN MICAH'S OFFICE, IN THE NORTH WING of the Coven. Micah and Isabelle sat at the same table, amidst scattered books and humming computer equipment. Tomes on quantum psychics, computer programming, and a variety of esoteric subjects stacked three rows deep surrounded them.

"We input what we knew about all four victims' magick and magickical capacities and the order in which Boyle is taking them. By running that information through the software I tweaked, we found five possible patterns." Micah slid a manila file folder across the table toward him.

Thomas flipped the folder open. Within were pages of data, graphs, and other information that Thomas couldn't make heads or tails of.

"Here." Isabelle flipped to the back of the file and pulled a couple papers out for him to read. "This breaks it down in normal people language. The rest of it is in Micah."

She wouldn't meet his gaze. Isabelle hadn't looked him in the eyes for the last three days, not since the night of the storm. He wanted to shake her shoulders, make her tell him what was wrong.

Isabelle was the most confusing woman he'd ever known. Hot one minute, cool the next. Her fears were getting in the way of the feelings Thomas knew she had for him and he grew weary of it.

"Thanks." He scanned the page. The second sheet simply had a list of names. Direct and to the point. That's exactly what Thomas wanted.

"They're forecasts," continued Micah, "using the data analyzed. Those pages you're holding list the names of the witches that might be at a higher risk of being taken by Boyle according to our calculations. Now, we don't even know if Boyle is still out there, but I think we need to work on the assumption that he is."

"He is," answered Isabelle in a flat voice. "Can't you feel him?"

Thomas glanced up to find her staring at the tabletop. "I can."

Isabelle looked up and met his eyes for the barest of moments, then turned her face away.

Gritting his teeth in frustration, Thomas ran his finger down the column. His trepidation grew. "This is a very long list."

"Yes," replied Micah. "Unfortunately there are many witches on it because of all the probabilities."

"Plus," added Isabelle. "These are just the witches in the vicinity. We ruled out witches that live far away since Boyle seems to have enough pickings around here without having to go elsewhere. However, there's really no telling if he would travel or not to obtain a victim, so that makes the results even less reliable."

"Great," Thomas muttered.

Micah shook his head. "He won't go out of the area. Why would he go to the trouble? It's not logical when he has such a wide selection here."

That was for sure. Thomas glanced up at Micah. "How many are there?"

"One hundred and fifty-one."

Thomas clenched his jaw and stared hard at the list. "One hundred and fifty-one possible next victims. That's a little under a quarter of the registered witches in Chicago."

"And," Micah put in, "those are only the witches in our database. As we know, not all witches are officially registered with the Coven."

Thomas tossed the papers to the table. "Then how helpful is this?"

Micah shrugged. "It's better than nothing."

He picked the papers up again and scanned the list of names. They couldn't ignore them. One of the names he looked at now might be the name of the person that Boyle was currently targeting. There was nothing to do for the witches who weren't registered, but somehow they had to find a way to cover all the witches on the list. "We'll figure out a way to monitor them." He scanned the list again. "Anyone we know on here?"

Micah and Isabelle didn't answer. Thomas raised his gaze

from the sheet and glanced at both of them. Isabelle was looking hard at Micah, who looked guilty. Anger flared. *"Tell me."*

Micah indicated the paper he held. "On that list there? No.
There's no one on that list directly connected to the Coven."

Thomas's fingers tightened on the sheets of paper. He
hated it when people tried to conceal things from him. "And
on the list *before* you cut out witches for location?"

Isabelle glanced at Micah. "My mother was on there."

Thomas raised his gaze and studied her. "But you took her
off because she's no longer in the Chicago area?"

"My mom left for California a couple of days ago."

Satisfied, he nodded. Folding the papers and sticking them
in his inside suit jacket pocket, he said, "You both did very
well to narrow it down to these names. I'm going now to see
how we might be able to monitor these people."

"I'll walk you out," said Isabelle to Thomas, rising. "I need
to meet Mira and Jack."

Together Thomas and Isabelle left Micah to his books and
computers and headed into the corridor.

Isabelle had leaked away a little the morning after the
storm. More and more of her had followed in the days afterward. When she'd refused to continue to sleep in his room,
even in the guest room, he'd wanted to push, *to force her*, but
he hadn't. These nights he slept alone.

He'd known when he'd admitted his love for her it might
scare her away. He'd told her how he felt against his better
judgment, but he'd done it anyway because Thomas had
sensed she'd needed to hear the truth.

He'd been right about her fears and now he paid the price.

She fell into step beside him.

"What's going on with you, Isabelle?"

Isabelle's steps faltered, but she didn't reply.

Thomas stopped in the middle of the corridor, grasped her
upper arm and turned her to face him. He knew he wore a
stormy expression. A storm had raged in him for weeks because of the demon and now because of Isabelle.

Now she met his gaze, only because he forced her to. Her
big brown eyes were wide and her lips trembled as she parted
her lips to speak. "I care deeply about you."

"I hear a *but* coming up."

She hesitated. "I don't want a commitment. You're a wonderful man and the last thing I want to do is lead you on. This is just . . . bad timing." Her voice shook with emotion. "I'm not ready for a relationship right now. You deserve better than what I'm able to give you."

"Bullshit. You're just afraid."

"I just want you to move on, please. For your sake. Just forget about me."

"I could never forget about you, Isabelle."

She glanced down, her eyes sheened with tears. Her voice came out a whisper. "I never wanted to hurt you, Thomas."

It wasn't the answer he wanted. A muscle worked in his jaw. "But you're going to anyway, aren't you?" He turned and walked away.

TWENTY-TWO

SHARP CLAWS SLICED THROUGH HER SKIN. THE PAIN was nothing compared to the hard suck in the center of her chest, where her power was being pulled from her like roots yanked out of the earth. Blood poured from her body just as she shed it psychically. She could do nothing, think nothing, move no part of her body—caught like a spider's prey with demon toxin running though her veins.

Trapped in the demon's close, dark embrace.

. . . clothing brushed her cheek and the musty scent of closet filled her nose . . .

Isabelle sat bolt upright in her bed, panting hard. Perspiration covered her. She put a hand to the center of her chest, sensing desperately for the pulse of her magick. She pulled a strand, just a trickle, teasing the slight amount of moisture in the air around her. Her heart pounded so hard she feared an attack and the gentle thrum of her power calmed her.

Scent tickled her nose—dry, earthy, a little bitter.

Demon in the room.

Isabelle went still and silent. Even her breathing stopped, arrested in her chest by perfect shock.

No movement. No sound.

Oh, Lady, she wasn't ready.

She opened her mouth, letting oxygen fill her. "Boyle? Are you there?" Her words fell into the quiet stronger than she expected. No quaver or shake to them. Apparently, all the quavering and shaking was going on inside her stomach.

"You have hindered my plans." The voice came from the corner and her gaze flew there to see a hulking shadow. "You guard my keys too closely."

The keys. The witches who were to come before her, yes. The ones on the list she and Micah had worked up. Isabelle had slipped her own data into the analysis, tweaking it so that the pattern ended on her exact magickal characteristics. It had narrowed the pool of potential victims between herself and the last two witches Boyle had taken from 375 to 151.

Micah had discovered her tampering, as she'd been sure he would, and she'd been forced to reveal her secret. For his cousin's protection, he had agreed to keep Boyle's ultimatum between them, although she'd had to argue with him loudly and at length to get his promise. He'd also agreed to remove her name from the pool. She and her mother had both shown up on the victim's list.

Thomas had made good on his vow to protect those on the roster. He'd brought all those into the Coven who would come, set guards on the rest. Isabelle imagined that Boyle was finding his pickings to be more challenging.

"But you have not stopped me," Boyle continued. "Your head mage cannot protect all the possible keys." His voice lowered ominously when he spoke next. "And he had better not try to protect you."

The shadow darted away. Boyle was gone. A soft rustling sound came from the direction of the window. The curtains moved a little from the breeze that blew. Isabelle hadn't left the window open before she'd gone to bed. It was Boyle's little way of letting her know he'd been in the room, watching her sleep . . . manipulating her dreams.

"I knew you weren't dead, you bastard!" she screamed toward the window. Her voice sounded harsh and filled with despair. A part of her had hoped so very hard that Thomas had killed him.

Isabelle pushed the blankets back, rose, and slammed the window closed, locking it. For a moment she stood, staring out into the early morning, across the front lawn of the Coven.

Soon.

Boyle would be coming for her any night now, any day. He would come and trap her, take away her freedom, render her mute, motionless, helpless. Put her in a small, dark place. All her biggest fears.

She closed her eyes. *Lady, she didn't want to die that way.*

Nausea rose up. She put a hand to her mouth and ran to the bathroom. After she'd finished, she sat on the floor and leaned her cheek against the cool porcelain of the bathtub, breathing heavily.

All she wanted was Thomas. She wanted to leave right now and go to his room, crawl into his bed and let him comfort her. But what if tonight was the night? If Boyle came back, then she would be putting Thomas in harm's way for her own selfish desires.

That was the problem.

The point was moot anyway. She'd burned that bridge. She'd done such a good job of putting distance between herself and Thomas, it was like an ice pick through her solar plexus every time he looked at her now. Sometimes her skills in empathy were not her friend.

It was time to return to her apartment in the city. If she left now, in the middle of the night, Thomas wouldn't even know she was gone. When Boyle came for her, she wanted Thomas as far from her as possible. Even though it killed her to keep him at arm's length, she did it for his protection.

Ironic, that.

Ironic that the man who wanted to protect everyone else was now the one she protected.

Isabelle dropped her hand to her thigh, where she kept the syringe filled with the spelled liquid copper sheathed at all times. At the very least, maybe she could take the demon with her.

She pushed up from the bathroom floor, brushed her teeth, and packed a bag. She'd been putting this off because, greedily, she didn't want to put this much distance between herself and Thomas. This was the second irony of the night since just a couple of weeks ago the very idea of Thomas made her feel trapped. Now all she wanted was to stay with him. But the time had come. This little visit from Boyle made that fact clear.

Apparently, settling in one place with one man simply wasn't in the cards for her. Maybe if she could defeat the demon. Maybe . . .

She shouldn't consider *maybes* at this point. They were dangerous.

She closed the door of her room at the Coven behind her and stepped into the corridor, bag in hand and copper knife in place in her wrist sheath. She didn't go anywhere without that or the syringe these days.

Just as soon as she'd heard the latch snick into place, the phone in the room rang. She stared at the door, wondering if she should answer it and decided against it. The ringing stopped, but in her pocket, her cell phone vibrated.

It was three in the morning! Frowning, she fished it out and looked at the caller ID. It was Adam.

She flipped it open. "Hello?"

"Isabelle." His breathing sounded exerted, like he was running while he spoke. "We need you. Boyle is in Gribben. He's going after Stefan." *Click.*

Isabelle dropped her bag and ran. Boyle was here. That meant she had another shot at killing him before her time was up. She would grab on to that chance with both hands.

Gribben sucked the magick out of her as soon as she crossed the threshold, making her lose a step and trip. She caught herself at the last moment and, dragging air into her suddenly starved lungs, righted herself and continued on. The guards recognized her and let her through without comment, telling her Thomas was in the bowels of the building.

They didn't have to tell her; she could feel Boyle. His very presence raised the hair on her body, and some kind of strange mixture of dread, terror, apprehension, and hope twisted her stomach. Lady, she hoped Boyle was as magickally hamstrung as they were in this place.

She was about to find out.

Isabelle reached the floor Stefan's cell was on, slammed the door open, and continued to run. She turned a corner and caught sight of Thomas and Adam. Thomas turned toward her. "What are you doing here?"

"Adam called me."

He turned and skewered Adam with his gaze. "Fuck, Adam! What are you thinking? Boyle gets her alone twice and that's not enough for you?" Thomas rounded on her and snarled, "Get out of here, Isabelle."

"You asked me to help hunt Boyle, Thomas. Remember? That's *my job* as defined *by you* at the beginning of this mess. I'm staying." She walked toward him, voice and steps steady. "Where's Boyle?" She noticed Stefan's cell door was open. Alarmed, she gaped for a moment before exclaiming, "Hell, where's Stefan?"

Thomas moved to the side and let her peer into the padded suicide cell. Stefan sat on the floor, head bowed. Blood pooled at his feet, dripping from a wound in his head. Rips in his gray prison-issued clothing exposed his leg and chest.

Why did Boyle want Stefan? Stefan hadn't been on the potential victims list, unless they'd done their analysis wrong. But with her plugged in as the last victim, there was little chance of that.

"We fought the demon off," answered Adam. "Boyle has disappeared and Jack, Ingrid, Theo, and the others went after him. We're guarding Stefan against his return."

Isabelle gave a short, bitter laugh. "We're guarding Stefan?" Then she yelled, "The Duskoff are the reason Boyle is here!"

"We have an agreement." Thomas's words whipped like a lash and made her wince. "He stays alive until Boyle is dead."

A roar from down the corridor behind her cut off Isabelle's reply. It sent a shiver up her spine and reminded her of all those horror stories Angela used to tell her when they were kids. The monster in the basement was real and coming straight at her.

Thomas took a couple of steps toward her, terror for her safety clear on his face. Another roar erupted behind her, closer this time. Thomas reached for her, but she pulled away from him. Boyle couldn't kill her. Not yet. She was the safest of all of them at the moment.

At the same time, Boyle appeared around the corner, radiating threat. Isabelle stared for a full moment, the stench of demon magick heavy in her nose. That answered whether or not he had magickical capabilities in Gribben.

She felt naked without her magick, stripped to the bone. Even though their power wasn't effective on Boyle, not having access to it at all in this place made her feel like tinfoil, easily crumpled.

Blood coursed from the demon's side, where someone had taken a sword to him. He looked at Thomas, but his gaze fixed on Isabelle, his massive chest heaving and his eyes red. "Stand aside. I have come for the warlock."

"You can't have him, Boyle," Isabelle said, her hand going to her sleeve, where her knife was secreted. She couldn't believe those words had just come out of her mouth.

He cocked his head to the side. "I don't understand. I'm killing him for you. You tried to kill Stefan, ergo you want the warlock dead. This is a gift."

Shock shot through her and her mind sputtered to a halt before revving into thought overdrive. A gift? He was trying to kill Stefan as a gift? For her?

"Where's Jack?" Thomas demanded from his position beside and a little in front of her. "Where are the others?"

"I came for Stefan. Not the *aeamon* who chased me."

"*Where are they?*"

Boyle didn't answer; he only raised a blast of demon magick and centered it at Thomas.

Isabelle screamed as power rocketed through the air. Thomas flew backward into the wall behind him and hit with a sick sounding thump. Dread pulled an icy knot in her stomach as he crumpled to the floor.

Boyle raised his power again and Isabelle whirled, screaming Adam's name. Surely Boyle meant to hit him next. But it was too late. Demon magick arced through the air, saturating her nostrils with the scent of old other-Earth. Adam went down, sprawled in an unnatural position on the concrete floor, while Isabelle watched.

"I do this for you, Isabelle Novak." The demon almost sounded hurt. As if he'd given her a gift that she'd thrown back in his face.

Her eyes wide and her chest heaving—how much stress could one take before one broke?—she glanced at Adam and then at Thomas. They both still appeared to be breathing, thank the Lord and Lady.

She turned her attention back to Boyle. "I did want to kill Stefan, Boyle. I wanted to kill him at first because I couldn't find you. I want to kill *you*, don't you understand? *You killed my sister!*" She screamed the last sentence.

The demon shook his head. "No, I don't understand. I have lived in your home for all these years. I have lived among you, passed for one of you, but I still don't understand you, *aeamon*." He looked off into the distance and almost seemed . . . sad. "I want to go home."

Isabelle remained unmoved. However, she did *move*.

Taking advantage of his distraction, she reached down, pulled the syringe free and rushed him. All she had to do was get the needle in him somewhere. Anywhere.

She'd taken him by surprise and managed to sink the needle through the fabric of his shirt and hit flesh, piercing his chest. Before she could press the plunger down and shoot the liquid in, Boyle roared, raised his arm and knocked her backward.

She went sprawling onto her ass. Her elbows hit hard. Pain exploded. She struggled to stare up at the demon, knowing that to take her gaze from him now meant lots of agony for her later.

The demon stared down at the syringe poking out of his chest, reached down and pulled it out. All of Isabelle's hopes crashed as Boyle tossed it to the side, like a piece of refuse. Involuntarily, she lurched forward and reached out as if to catch it and then collapsed in a heap at Boyle's feet.

Boyle stared down at her for a moment, his lips parted so she could see the tips of his double row of pointed teeth. His eyes blazed red. He raised his hand and magick pulsed through the air, coating the back of her throat with the dry, bitter flavor of it.

Staring up at Boyle, Isabelle could see her impending death. Inwardly, she groped for power and came up empty, all of it stripped away by Gribben. But these walls didn't affect

Boyle. His magick remained strong, vibrant. His desire to use it with killing force now stood clearly on his face.

Magick rippled and Isabelle felt something warm running over her upper lip—her nose had begun to bleed.

The demon moved his hand and she cringed, waiting for the blast that would end her life. Then he hesitated, lowered his hand. "I can't kill you now. Later. Soon."

He stepped over her, leaving her sprawled on the ground, and headed into Stefan's cell.

Isabelle lay for a moment, overwhelmed with relief that she'd dodged Boyle's temper . . . for the moment. Then she pushed up, hardly believing what she was about to do. How the hell had she'd gone from trying to kill the head of the Duskoff to trying to save his miserable life? She lunged after Boyle.

Isabelle careened through the space the demon had just oc-cupied and slammed into the doorjamb of Stefan's cell, breathing heavy. Raising her gaze, she stared into the empty room. Boyle was gone.

So was Stefan.

TWENTY-THREE

ISABELLE WHIRLED TOWARD THE TWO FALLEN MEN, but her thoughts whirled faster. Had Boyle pulled Stefan through a doorway to kill him at his leisure elsewhere? Or had Stefan taken the opportunity to flee while she'd feared for her life at Boyle's feet?

No matter now. Not while Thomas lay in a bloody crumple at the base of the wall, and Adam lay unconscious in the middle of the corridor.

Isabelle ran to Thomas and hauled him into her lap. Warm, sticky blood soaked through her jeans from the gash at the back of his head, but his breathing was deep and even. Fervently, she wished for her magick. By manipulating the water in his body, she perhaps could bring him to consciousness. Instead, she stroked her fingers down his cheek, silently willing him to come to.

After a minute, Thomas stirred and came awake. He groaned and his hand went to the back of his head, then he rolled to the side and looked up at her. "What happened?"

Relief rushed through her, making her lightheaded. She'd feared his head had been bashed in. Voice shaky, she told him.

Thomas pushed to his feet and pulled his cell phone from his pocket. As he dialed, he speared her with his gaze. "I want you out of here, Isabelle. *Now.* The demon might still be around, or he might return." His voice shifted, grew tighter. "Since it has been proven I can't protect you from him, I want you as far away from here as possible."

Of course, she'd expected as much. She shook her head, got to her feet, and went to Adam. "I'm not leaving until I've done all I can do to help."

"Isabelle, your job here is through. Consider yourself fired. *Go*." The force of his anger hit her like scalding water.

"No. Not yet." Isabelle refused to meet his gaze. She knelt at Adam's side, who was already rousing. Until she'd made sure Adam was all right, she wasn't going anywhere. He'd have to throw her out with his bare hands.

THOMAS SUFFERED THE ATTENTIONS OF DOCTOR Oliver for about a minute before pulling away from her.

"Thomas, you need to have this injury treated," the doc said, using her *I'm not taking any of your bullshit* voice. Doctor Oliver used that voice with him often. "You hit the back of your head hard against the wall."

"Thanks, doc, but later. Got other things to worry about now."

He turned away from her and headed down the corridor to where a group of prison guards stood receiving orders from Jack. Gribben was in lockdown and the prison was being searched from top to bottom for Stefan.

By Isabelle's account, it was possible the warlock had taken the opportunity to flee his cell when Boyle had rendered Adam and Thomas unconscious prior to his confrontation with her. If that was true, Stefan should not have been able to get out of Gribben. Not with all the checkpoints from his cell to the exit. He was caught like a mouse in a trap.

"He could have gone into the ventilation," Jack said as Thomas approached. "We've called in every available guard to search. Micah is studying the blueprints of the prison now and will brief you soon on how to proceed."

Thomas hung back, allowing Jack to take the lead. He and Ingrid were the heir-apparents for head of the Coven. Thomas liked having control and had a tendency to micromanage, but he had to force himself to step back and allow them to take the lead sometimes.

When Jack had finished directing the guards, he turned to

Thomas. "What if Boyle *poofed* Stefan through one of those doorways he can pull from thin air?"

Thomas gritted his teeth. "Then Stefan is free and this is a waste of our time. We can only hope the demon killed him somewhere beyond Gribben's walls."

"But I don't get it. Boyle went after Stefan to kill him, as if for sport. He didn't want him for his ritual. Why would he come here, to the heart of the Coven, to try and kill a warlock whose death doesn't matter in the scope of his plan?"

Thomas glanced at Isabelle, who stood a distance away talking to Adam. "Boyle told Isabelle he was killing Stefan for her."

"What?"

"Before the demon hit me and Adam, he said he was doing it because he thought she wanted Stefan dead. It was his gift to her."

Jack shook his head and rubbed his chin. "I'm not following this."

"Me, either. He's developed some kind of fixation on Isabelle, but Isabelle says she doesn't know why. She thinks it might be because Boyle killed her sister and now he feels some kind of morbid closeness with her. I think . . ." He trailed off, unable to say it aloud.

Jack said it for him. "A demon crush?"

"I don't know." The thought of Boyle having any type of fascination with Isabelle made his blood run cold, but the demon's words had made it sound as if he did.

"So maybe it is plausible Boyle snatched Stefan and took him beyond Gribben's walls to kill him."

"It's possible." Thomas paused. "But we're going to operate on the assumption that Stefan tried to escape on his own for now and search every inch of Gribben."

"You got it."

From the corner of his eye, he watched Isabelle turn to look at him, her expression forlorn. The woman made him crazy. The thought of her being harmed made him crazier. Then, Isabelle turned and walked down the corridor. Thomas had to stop himself from following her.

He ripped his gaze from her retreating form. "Damn it all to hell."

"We're already there, boss," came Adam's flat voice from his left.

Thomas glanced at him, his jaw tight. "Anything new on your end?"

Adam shook his head. "But if Stefan's still in Gribben, he's not getting out."

"Yeah." He stared into the depths of the building. They'd been there for hours now and it wore on him, wore on all of them.

"What's up?" Adam asked. "You don't think he's here?"

"My gut is saying no."

"Isabelle thinks Boyle got him out."

"We'll know soon enough. No one can stay hidden for long in Gribben." He debated asking and finally gave in. "Was Isabelle all right when you talked to her?"

Adam shrugged and glanced away. "She seemed kind of sad. Said you two weren't working out. Said she was headed back to her condo in the city, felt like she was safer there. Safer from the demon or safer from you, I wasn't quite sure which."

Thomas went still, absorbing that information. "Did she say when she was leaving?"

"I had the impression she was leaving now. Too bad. You were a lot easier to deal with while you were getting laid." On that note, Adam sauntered away.

So Isabelle had decided to leave the Coven in an effort to put some distance between them. Likely, she was afraid they were getting too close because he'd admitted he loved her.

The problem was he *knew* she loved him back. He sensed it every time she looked at him, spoke to him. He'd felt it downstairs in the corridor when she'd woken him up by running her fingers down his cheek over and over.

Isabelle was the best damn thing that had ever happened to him. She brought chaotic beauty into his existence. He brought stability and love to hers. No way was he going to let her run away from him. No way was he going to let her irrational fears ruin this for both of them.

Didn't she know by now that he wasn't giving her up without a fight?

WAITING.

Isabelle waited for death to come. Every tick of the grandfather clock in the living room brought it closer.

She rested her head against the back of the sofa and closed her eyes. She'd had about three hours of sleep in the last twenty-four, but dream time still eluded her. Though sleep was a thing she needed direly. She needed to be ready for Boyle. She curled her fingers around the syringe she'd plucked from the prison floor. With her other hand, she touched her knife in its wrist sheath.

They hadn't found Stefan inside Gribben. Adam had called to tell her. There was no sign—of course—of Boyle, either. Her chance to save herself had ended disastrously and now she was almost out of chances. She had one left and the odds were against her.

She pulled the comforter closer and inhaled the lingering scent of her sister's sweet perfume. The fear she'd felt before was almost gone. She would fight as hard as she could for as long as she could. She would protect as best she could those she loved. The rest lay in the hands of the Lord and the Lady.

Eventually, she dozed a little despite the ticking of the grandfather clock and the fact she'd left all the lights on. Pounding on the door brought her awake not long after, however. Bleary-eyed, she glanced up at the clock and saw she'd slept about a half an hour. Great. When the demon came she'd be in top physical condition.

She pushed off the couch and went to the door. At least she knew it wasn't Boyle. Demons didn't knock.

Isabelle checked the peephole, sighed, and rested her head against the wall. She'd wondered if he'd come. Of course it had been silly to think he wouldn't. Thomas Monahan wasn't a man to be put off easily. Yet she thought maybe she'd driven a hard enough wedge between them that he might stay away.

She had to get him out of here fast, but it was going to be hard to lie to Thomas. All her heart wanted was *him*—his presence, the scent of him, the circle of his strong arms, his husky voice in her ear. All her head wanted was to get him as far from her as possible.

Steeling herself, she unlocked the door and opened it.

He wore a pair of black pants and a white linen shirt. His hair hung long and loose over his shoulders and his dark eyes were hooded, but didn't look lazy; they snapped with fire. The normally sensual curve of his lips was set in a firm line. She recognized the body language; he was pissed.

Lady, he was sexy when he was pissed.

Her breath caught and her fingers curled a little, wanting nothing more than to slide under his shirt to touch the warm skin and hard muscle she knew lay there. Instead, she hid her reaction, kept a straight face, and simply walked back into the apartment.

The door slammed closed behind her and his hand came down on her shoulder. He whipped her around to face him. "You just leave? I don't even rate a good-bye?"

"You told me to go, Thomas," she reminded him grimly.

"To get away from the prison, yes. I didn't mean for you to leave the Coven."

"I don't want to do this again, Thomas. It hurt enough the first time." She sighed. "We both knew this wasn't going to work out long-term. It was just about the sex. The sex was great, but now it's time to let go." Such callous words, so easily uttered. Why did they feel like small blocks of ice in her throat?

And damn it, he didn't believe her anyway. She didn't even need her empathy, since doubt lay clear in his expression.

A muscle in his jaw worked. "You're not a good liar, Isabelle," he ground out. "You're just running away from me like you run away from everyone that gets too close to you."

She pulled away from him. "Thanks for the psychoanalysis, but you don't know the first thing about me." Of course, he did. She'd run away her whole life from any attachment or emotional anchor. It was only now she'd met Thomas and fallen in love with him that she didn't want to run anywhere but straight into his arms.

Except now was the one time in her life when she *had* to run. Sometimes fate sucked.

Her next words tore from the center of her, somewhere just left of the seat of her magick. She tried to keep her voice steady, but she had to turn her face away because she knew she couldn't master her expression. "Just get out, Thomas. Please, I don't want you here right now." Finally, a bit of truth, even if it hurt to say it.

"Why are you so afraid?"

She pressed her palm to her eye. "It's not fear—exactly. Moving around, it's just what I know. I can't stay in one place, with one person. It's just not who I am."

"Bullshit."

She sighed, rounding on him. The words she spoke now came from somewhere deep inside. "I don't want to screw it up, all right! Every time I form a relationship, find a good place to stay . . . it disappears. Nothing ever lasts! Maybe it's better to just not have it to begin with. Then I never have to worry about when it's going to vanish. Then I never have to feel pain when it inevitably dissolves."

"Isabelle—"

She cut him off, on a roll now. "When I travel, there's a fresh start at every arrival gate. New people. New places. Hotel rooms. Rented villas. Room service. All of it is . . . formless, nondescript, anonymous. Nothing to fuck up. Nothing to get attached to. Nothing to grieve for when I move on."

"Look at me."

"But the thing of it is . . . in the end, none of it matters. It's all just bullshit. I think I'm avoiding being cornered by emotion, by commitment, and by potential loss, but really it's just another trap. I know that because of my sister. She was the only person who ever really mattered in my life." *Before you.* A tear drop rolled down her cheek and she wiped it away. "When she died, I grieved so hard my soul twisted. It was the worst pain I've ever felt, but I would never, ever have given up loving my sister to have saved myself that pain."

"Isabelle . . ."

"So you see? It's a catch twenty-two. You either have nothing and feel nothing, or you have something and eventually lose it, thus feeling everything . . . in a bad way. You're damned if you do and damned if you don't." She laughed. It sounded harsh to her own ears. "And I'm really damned, Thomas. You don't know the half of it."

"Isabelle, *look at me*."

Slowly, Isabelle turned to face him.

Emotion moved over his face, breaking the anger into something like sorrow . . . or maybe love . . . for a moment. Her own emotions ran too high for her to get a read on his now. "I'm not leaving here and I'm not letting you leave me."

"Thomas—"

He pulled her into his arms. When she pushed at him, he only held on tighter. "I love you." He whispered it into her hair.

Isabelle made fists, trying not to grab on to him with both hands and never let go. Her fingernails dug into her palms. "Thomas, please don't do this."

"I love you, Isabelle," he whispered again. "I'm not letting you go. I'm never letting you go."

Her eyes filled with tears. The words just spilled out, easy as a river flows into the ocean. Nothing in the world—not even a demon—could've stopped them. "I love you, too."

He stroked her hair. "I know."

Isabelle clung to him for a moment, trying to gather enough strength to push him away and say something cutting, something so horrible it would make him leave. Possibilities polluted her mind. Each one she disregarded. Thomas saw straight through to the heart of her; anything she told him he would know was a lie.

Thomas tipped her chin up, forcing her gaze to his face, and kissed her. His lips slid over hers like silk at first, then the pressure grew harder and more demanding.

Isabelle's body reacted instantly. Her fingers closed around his upper arms, feeling the bunch and flex of his muscles as he dragged her up against his chest and slipped his tongue between her lips. She sparred with him, a low moan rising from her center.

"Please, I want you to go," she breathed against his mouth between kisses.

His teeth captured her lower lip and dragged. Isabelle felt herself grow warm and wet between her thighs. "Not until after I make every inch of you *mine*, Isabelle." His voice came out a low, needful growl.

Alarm shot through her, dampening her arousal. "No—we can't—" Her sentence ended in a yelp of surprise as Thomas swept her off her feet, literally.

"No?" he asked as he carried her to the bedroom. "Let me try and change your mind about that."

He threw her down on the mattress. Isabelle tried to get up and he came down on top of her, pinning her wrists. "Give it up," he breathed in her ear.

His mouth captured her words of protest. Once he'd kissed her so thoroughly her mind could barely form a coherent thought, he worked his way down her body, removing articles of clothing as he went. He found the syringe she kept in her bra and the knife sheathed at her wrist and placed them on the nightstand.

Lazily, he dragged her nipple between his lips until it popped out of his mouth. At the same time, he slid his hand down her thigh and found her clit. He circled it through the cotton of her panties, around and around. "Does that feel good?" His voice brushed like satin against her skin.

"Um." *Oh, yeah.* It felt so good she couldn't think. "We can't do this, Thomas. Not right now." The problem was that her voice came out all breathy and passion-soaked.

"Why not?"

She bit her lip, searching for a plausible reason why they couldn't make love. It wasn't like she could tell him the truth. And, Lady, she wanted this final good-bye with every fiber of her being. Couldn't she be allowed this one last connection with Thomas? Didn't she at least deserve that much?

When she didn't answer, he growled, "I thought so." Then he bit the waistband of her panties and drew them down with his teeth. Soon there wasn't one bit of fabric separating her flesh from his hands and mouth.

"Thomas—"

"I'm not leaving here until I fuck you senseless, Isabelle. I don't care what you say. I don't care if I have to tie you up to do it. Understand?" His finger stroked her clit as he spoke, sending ripples of pleasure through her body.

"You've made that clear." She sighed.

"So tell me right now. Last chance. Do you want me to fuck you, Isabelle?"

There was only one answer. "Yes."

"Do you want me to make love to you?"

"*Yes.*"

Holding her gaze, he hooked his hands under her knees and drew them up and apart, baring her most vulnerable body part to his gaze. Thomas looked his fill. "So sweet," he murmured before he lowered his mouth and closed it over her swollen, aroused clit. His tongue flicked it and then found the sensitive side and rubbed.

Isabelle bucked under his mouth and Thomas pinned her hips to the mattress, sealing his mouth over her sex. Her climax hit fast and hard. She gasped as it washed over her and then moaned out his name.

Thomas rode her through the explosive arc of pleasure, groaning in the back of his throat like he enjoyed her climax every bit as much as she did. When the orgasm still clung to her body, still made her toss her head in pleasure and moan, he yanked his pants down just enough to get his cock out and mounted her.

"Isabelle." Her name sounded ragged on his tongue, like a prayer or the word *water* from a desperately thirsty man. "I can't wait another moment. I need to feel you. I need to be a part of you."

In answer, she wound her legs around his hips and pulled him down on top of her, feeling the scratch of his pants against her ankles and calves.

He held her gaze as he pressed the head of his cock to her entrance, then gathered her wrists in one huge hand and pressed them to the mattress above her head. Then he held her hip with his other hand and thrust deeply into her, until she was completely filled and stretched by his cock.

Isabelle gasped and sank her teeth into her lower lip. Her clit pulsed and her sex rippled from the sensation of having him within her.

He rode her, taking her in long, steady, deep strokes that cleared every fleck of rational thought from her mind and made her body feel like melting butter.

When her climax came it enveloped her entire body in ripples that started small and then expanded outward. She arched back when it took her, her mind swamped with pleasure.

Thomas released her hands and sucked one of her offered nipples into his hot mouth, dragging it gently between his teeth. He answered her orgasm by groaning deep in his throat and coming.

"Thomas," she sighed, covering her face with her hands. What had she allowed them to do? How fucking stupid was she?

Thomas rolled off her and pulled her onto the bed. He dragged her against his body and stroked his fingers down her face. "You're mine, Isabelle. I'm not letting you go or letting you run. I'm not letting you push me away. And I'm *not* leaving here tonight. For better or for worse."

Defeated, tears stung her eyes as she turned and buried her face in the crook of his neck and inhaled. He smelled so good, smelled so much like Thomas. She slid her hand into his shirt to find warm flesh and hard muscle. "Get undressed then because I need to feel your skin on mine." Her voice sounded gritty from lack of sleep and emotion.

Together, they stripped his clothes off until his body brushed against hers, skin-to-skin. He kissed his way over her shoulder and down her arm, urging her to her stomach. Isabelle lay facedown on the bed while Thomas ran his fingertips down her spine to the small of her back over and over, lulling her to sleep.

"Isabelle," Thomas purred in a sleep-roughed and sex-satisfied voice, "why would Boyle kill Stefan as a favor to you?"

Her eyes shot open and she stiffened, but at least she could answer this honestly. "I don't know."

"Really?"

Isabelle turned onto her back and snuggled against him. She stared up into his face and brushed her fingers across his pects. "Really. I don't understand the demon mind. I find it incredible he could long for home, too, that a creature like him would have emotion that way." She shook her head. "I have no idea why Boyle would decide he needed to kill Stefan for me."

"What he said right before he knocked me out at Gribben . . . it made it sound almost as if the two of you have a relationship."

She raised her head and grinned, even though she hardly felt the levity. "Jealous, Thomas?"

"Hardly. Afraid for you, yes."

She took a moment to answer, carefully phrasing her response. "It's like I said before. I think he's seized on me because of my sister. He imagines that because he" —she had to pause and find the right words before she could continue— "he murdered her that he and I have a connection."

Thomas stroked his hand down her arm over and over until she sighed and her muscles let go of their tension. "That does make an odd sort of sense."

"I don't think demons make sense." Her eyelids drooped.

"Go to sleep, Isabelle. I can tell you need it."

She sighed and relaxed into him. Before she knew it exhaustion had towed her under.

ISABELLE WOKE UP FROM A DEEP SLEEP. FITTING HERself against Thomas's warm body, she smiled and closed her eyes again. By his side, she would always sleep well. For a moment she knew perfect bliss, and then she remembered. It leaked like toxic waste into her mind, poisoning her.

The demon was coming. Maybe not today, but soon.

Disturbed, she rubbed her eyes and glanced at the window, where the first strains of pale gray morning light stole through. She'd only slept an hour or two at most. What had woken her?

No scent of demon magick fouled the air. Not a sound could be heard. She wasn't too hot or too cold . . . then she knew it with utter certainty.

Dread curled itself like cold lead in the pit of her stomach. She pulled out from under Thomas's protective arm and slipped from the bed. Solemnly, she pulled on underclothes, a pair of jersey running shorts, and a long-sleeved T-shirt, then resecured her syringe and knife sheath. That done, Isabelle walked to the living room window as if drawn there by powers beyond her control.

Indeed, she probably was.

She pushed aside the curtains covering the living room window, and there, on the tree-lined street running past the apartment building, sat Boyle on his Harley—looking up at her. Metal and chrome, buffed to a high shine by loving demon hands, gleamed in the streetlight. Black leather covered Boyle from head to toe, and the morning breeze buffeted his blond hair.

She gasped, "Thomas," and turned to run and quickly try to get him out of the apartment. Instead, she ran smack into a very broad chest. The smell of leather and demon slammed into her nose.

Boyle stared down at her, his normally blue eyes already glowing red. "It's time."

Mute, she could only shake her head. It was time? How could it be time? It couldn't be time! Thomas was still in her apartment.

Boyle reached for her and she took a step back. He withdrew his hand. "Do you choose to place your mother in your stead? If so, let me know now. I don't have a long time in which to make this sacrifice."

"*I'm* the one making the sacrifice." Her voice shook. "And I won't allow anyone else to be put in my place."

"Very well." He held out his hand again. "Then we shall leave now."

Isabelle was amenable to leaving the apartment quietly, leaving Thomas to sleep in the other room . . . and not interfere. "All right." She went to the foyer, where her white Keds sat neatly side-by-side under the breakfast bar. She slid them on and turned to the demon. "I'm ready."

Boyle didn't *poof* her. He led her out of the apartment and downstairs to his Harley. Every step that took her farther away from Thomas made her throat constrict a little more. When they finally reached the street, Isabelle counted it a miracle she could still breathe.

The demon mounted the motorcycle. "It is a beautiful bike, don't you think?"

She only stared at him. Small talk wasn't something she could manage at the moment.

"I will miss this bike," he continued. "It is one of the only things I will miss about living here. So, we take my bike where we are going, instead of more direct transportation. It will be my last chance to ride."

"Is this the part where I'm supposed to feel sorry for you?"

He stared at her for a moment, his blue eyes glittering. "Get on." He turned the key.

The machine started with a muted purr, but she didn't move to obey him. She couldn't help but allow her gaze to stray down the street. Moonlit shadows played on the concrete of the sidewalk, dappled by the leaves in the trees. A soft, warm wind blew that made the limbs of the tall, beautiful maples shiver and creak. In the distance lights changed at an intersection and one lonely automobile traversed.

She did have on her running shoes.

"I know where your mother is." The demon's voice was low and sure. He knew what she'd just contemplated in the split-second she'd glanced down the street. *Of course he knew*. "I could be to her within the window of time I possess."

Sighing, Isabelle mounted the bike behind Boyle. Declining to encircle his waist to hold on, she gripped the seat instead.

"We're going to my warehouse."

Nausea rose in her throat. She wasn't wearing a helmet. Maybe they'd get lucky and have an accident before they arrived.

Actually, that was a good idea.

Isabelle knew that now she had the perfect opportunity to kill Boyle. If she could get the syringe out of her bra, she could inject the liquid copper into him while he drove.

Perfect.

Of course, if it worked they were going down. Isabelle, in

her Keds, running shorts, and T-shirt would be pretty much screwed in that case. But Boyle would be dead. That was the important thing.

"Put your arms around my waist," he commanded.

"Excuse me?" That would make it difficult to snag the syringe.

"Your arms. Put them around my waist and hold on. Do not remove them. I haven't come this far to lose you now."

Isabelle took a moment to collect her emotions and then slowly placed her arms around his waist. The muscles of a bodybuilder rippled under her hands. His torso felt like rock under the black leather he wore and Isabelle fought a gag reflex.

The bike lurched forward, along with her stomach. Isabelle closed her eyes and offered a prayer to the Lady. At the last moment, she looked up at the darkened windows of the apartment, where Thomas still slept.

Thomas.

TWENTY-FOUR

❧

"Isabelle?"

Thomas woke and turned over, groping for the warm body he missed. After finding only air and blankets, he cracked his eyelids. She wasn't in the room.

The hair on the back of his neck rose as his intuition kicked in. Something wasn't right.

He pushed the blankets aside, found his pants in the dark, and slid them on. Making his way carefully through the dimly lit apartment, he found the living room empty. He could feel that the entire place was empty except for him.

Outside on the street a motorcycle *vroomed* to life.

He knew the sound of that cycle.

Thomas rushed to the window in time to see Boyle pull away from the curb . . . Isabelle on the back. Just before Boyle accelerated, she looked up at the window wearing an expression of total desolation.

And then they were gone.

Clear, cold certainty quickly killed the jolt of shock that ran through his body. He knew Isabelle hadn't left with Boyle because she wanted to . . . and he knew exactly where the demon was taking her.

Thomas didn't waste time for anything but his car keys and cell phone. Barefoot and shirtless, he raced from Isabelle's apartment, dialing Jack and the Coven as he went.

* * *

THE WIND WHIPPED THROUGH ISABELLE'S HAIR AND blew up her shorts, making her shiver. Of course the shiver probably had less to do with the wind than it did the demon she rode with.

The bike ate up the streets between her apartment and the warehouse a lot faster than she would've liked. She watched the pavement fly by under her feet and wondered what it would feel like if the copper affected Boyle like she hoped. How did it feel to die in a motorcycle accident? Would she end up with gravel three inches under her skin? Would her head split open? She supposed if her head split open she wouldn't much mind the gravel under her skin.

Lady.

It was the only way and stalling any longer would be criminal. Now was the time. Her last chance. By doing this she'd save her mother, her sister would be avenged, and the worlds—both of them—would be rid of the likes of Erasmus Boyle.

All she had to do was move her hand, grab the syringe from her pocket, and shoot it into him. Then, if the copper injected straight into his body did as she hoped, she would die in a horrible, fiery motorcycle accident. *Piece of cake.*

She could do this.

She could.

Boyle flipped every stoplight they approached to green. Either that or he had some great luck at hitting the lights just right. Green light. Green light.

Green light.

They were getting near the warehouse and Isabelle knew she had to do it. It was time, past time. Her heart pounding so fast she thought she'd have a heart attack—preferable to the way she was about to die—Isabelle moved.

Boyle roared in protest as she took her arm from his body, but Isabelle ignored him. She plunged her hand down her shirt, sought the syringe, and yanked it out. Gripping the top between her teeth, she pulled the needle free, stuck it into the demon's neck, and pushed the plunger down.

The liquid copper shot into Boyle's throat.

Syringe empty.

Boyle gurgled. The bike wavered. Isabelle looked down at

the swiftly passing road beneath them. They righted for a moment and then the demon made a choking, snorting, screaming noise.

And they tipped.

The bike fell to the right and spilled Isabelle to the pavement. They'd been going about fifty miles an hour and in the split-second before Isabelle made contact with the road, her mind went completely blank—totally clear. Then she hit. No pain exploded through her. Nothing but softness met her head and body as she slid and rolled across the road and onto the sidewalk.

Isabelle lay on her side, motionless and aware. Clearly, she'd gone into shock and that's what had blocked the pain of the crash. If she looked down at her body now, she'd see blood, ragged flesh, and twisted limbs.

She decided not to look.

Instead she watched the bike scrape against the pavement, screeching in a fiery symphony of destruction down the middle of the street. Boyle went with it, his leg trapped under the twisted metal. The cycle came to a halt near the curb, the demon motionless.

Had she killed him? Was this nightmare finally at an end? She was still conscious. Did that mean she'd actually lived through the ordeal as well? Or was the numb coldness stealing through her body merely a precursor to death?

The sound of scraping metal once more filled the air. The motorcycle moved and Boyle shifted beneath it, groaning.

"No," Isabelle whispered, lifting her head. "Oh, no."

"Get up!" Thomas's voice. Strong hands under her arms, lifting her. "Isabelle, get up! He's not dead."

"What?" She pushed to her feet and glanced down. No blood. Not even a scratch. Not even her clothing was torn. "What's—"

"I cushioned your fall. Concrete is part of my dominion as an earth witch." He hauled her down the street as he spoke. "We have to get you far from here in case Boyle recovers and comes after you."

"Wait!" She pushed at him. "No, I can't run." Isabelle turned and headed back toward Boyle.

Thomas grabbed her and lifted her off her feet, carrying her up the street toward his still running car. "Have you lost your mind?"

She fought in his embrace. "No! You don't understand. Let me go!"

"You can explain it when we're five miles away, okay?"

Unable to break Thomas's iron-strong grip any other way, Isabelle focused on the water in his fingers, hands and arms, forcing it to momentarily heat up. Thomas yelped and dropped her.

Isabelle tumbled to the ground and righted herself, struggling to her feet. "I can't leave now. Boyle will pick another witch to take my place. Either he dies . . . or I die. I won't allow this to happen any other way."

Thomas stared at her for a moment before replying. "You made some kind of deal with Boyle? You either go willingly with him or he takes another witch in your place?"

She nodded furiously, her gaze straying behind Thomas to where Boyle was rousing from the ground. "*My mother*, in point of fact. He meant to take my mother in my place. Yes, I have issues with her, but I can't let Boyle kill her."

Boyle looked badly injured and hope flared within her. Judging from the way he moved Isabelle doubted he could get very far from his current location, which was comfortably distant from their own.

"Why didn't you tell me about this?"

She made a frustrated noise and clenched her fists. "Because I knew you'd do *this!* You'd rush in all *knight in shining armor* and let the demon kill you before he hurt me. I tried to keep you out of this so you would be safe. The Coven needs you, Thomas. Witchdom needs you. No one in the world needs me."

Thomas's response came swiftly. He reached out, grabbed her and crushed her to him. "*I* need you, Isabelle."

For a split-second she melted into him, closing her eyes at the emotion in his voice. Then she pushed away, putting him at arm's length. "Thank you for that, but I won't let Boyle put another witch in my place."

"No, you . . . won't." The voice came from behind her. Low. Rasping. Forced. In pain.

Boyle.

He put his hands on her shoulders. Apparently, she'd been wrong about Boyle's ability to move. Unfortunate.

Isabelle held Thomas's gaze for a moment. She knew she looked resigned.

Boyle *poofed* her.

SHE COULD STILL HEAR THOMAS'S AGONIZED BELLOW ringing in her ears when she suddenly found herself in the warehouse, her stomach roiling and her head pounding. Isabelle took two steps forward, staggered and went down on her hands and knees. Bile coated the back of her mouth and flooded her mouth with bitterness.

Her hands pressing into the cold concrete, she closed her eyes for a moment and concentrated on not passing out. Boyle's way of transporting people really sucked. She'd prefer a car to that any day.

Behind her came heavy, shuffling footsteps and a low groan. Keeping her head bent, she opened her eyes and stuck her hand up her sleeve, her fingers closing around the hilt of her copper knife.

"You won't live long enough to kill me, Boyle. You're done." Her voice echoed steady and harsh in the quiet of the warehouse. "It's in the sound of your voice and the cadence of your step. *Death*."

No sound. Not even a whisper of breath filled her ears. Isabelle hoped for one wild moment . . . then four shuffling steps toward her. Huge hands thrust under her armpits and lifted.

She'd expected to be yanked, thrown, hit, something violent. The demon's touch was gentle instead, almost caring.

"I'm going home," he whispered as he lifted her into his arms. "Don't you understand? I'm going *home*."

"Not if I can help it." Isabelle stabbed him in the throat.

Boyle dropped her. She fell to the concrete and this time Thomas wasn't there to cushion her fall. Isabelle hit her elbows, tailbone, and jarred her teeth. Boyle screamed and backed away from her, pulling the blade from his throat and tossing it across the warehouse.

Maybe his immune system had been weakened by the straight shot of copper into his body. Maybe he'd run out of "allergy shots." In any case, the wound she'd made with the blade smoked and popped, the gash growing larger. Acidic blood dripped and sizzled onto the floor.

Isabelle crab-walked back away from him, toward the door. She knew she couldn't leave until the demon was dead, but she went for the exit involuntarily anyway. Boyle held his hands to his throat, screaming, and tossing his head. She wanted nothing more than to get away from him, like a child needs to escape the monster in her closet that isn't imaginary after all.

She backed through the sticky part of the air that Adam had found. Her stomach lurched as the tendrils of half-baked magick pulled at her clothing, skin, and hair. Made up of the power from the murdered witches, the partially open doorway stung her nostrils like undiluted evil, like she'd snorted dark, bitter ale through her nose.

Isabelle gasped and shot backward, out of its range. It was much stronger than the last time she'd gone through it. Boyle's spell was nearly finished. She was the last key. Apparently, he'd taken another witch before her. They'd made it harder on Boyle with their list, but they hadn't stopped him.

Even free from its grasp, she couldn't shake the cling of the partially finished doorway from her skin and hair. Her breath came in short, brutal bursts as she waited—prayed— for Boyle to fall. For it be over.

Lady, please. She didn't want to be the last piece of that gateway of utter yuck.

Boyle turned and stared at her, as if reading her thoughts. His eyes glowed red and his lips parted, revealing razor sharp teeth. Slowly, he removed his hands and straightened, showing her clearly that his knife wound had healed.

Then he smiled.

Isabelle pushed to her feet. Base fear rocketed through her, burning down her veins and shooting up her spine. She wished she could be stronger, braver, but watching that demon smile at her made her whole body quake.

"Why won't you just die!" she screamed at him. Because, *Lady*, she didn't want to.

He took a step toward her and stumbled, his smile fading a little. "You don't understand my motivation. I'm leaving this place." He said *this place* like someone might say *maggot*. "I'm going home to my people, to the places I remember and love." He stumbled again, but then straightened and walked steadily for her, as if gaining strength from the very idea of returning home. "I refuse to die."

Isabelle backed up farther and farther. She simply couldn't stop herself. It took every ounce of her willpower not to run, just as it seemed to take every ounce of Boyle's not to die and keep slowly advancing on her. The bad thing was that she suspected Boyle's will was stronger than hers.

However, the copper she'd injected into him was taking its toll. If Micah's theory was correct, the copper was eating him up from the inside out. His body struggled to heal itself and regenerate tissue, just as he did with the external injuries inflicted with copper weapons. But copper taken internally would be far more harmful. Now it was simply a question of which was stronger, the killing effect of the liquid copper or his body's healing ability.

She kept her gaze on Boyle's shuffling feet as he neared her, completely unable to look up into those red, burning eyes—the ones that told her the end was near. "What tells you the sacrifice of five witches is all right? Because you have killed five, haven't you, Boyle? You took another one before me."

Shuffle. Pause. Shuffle. "Six witches. You haven't yet discovered the third I killed. The one after your sister.

Her stomach lurched.

"You are *aeamon*, only half-breeds. It's like slaughtering cattle, like hunting. It is nothing to kill you. Some *aeamon* I might take a liking to, like a human might care for a pet. I have taken such a liking to you." Shuffle. Pause. "But make no mistake; I will still kill my dog if it means I can go home."

Boyle stopped about five feet from her. Isabelle had backed herself up against the wall that had been farthest from him. The metal felt smooth and cool through her T-shirt.

"And the doorway? How does it work?" Her voice sounded hoarse and ravaged, as if she'd smoked a pack a day for the last twenty years. Really, she was just trying to stall, hoping the copper would do its work.

"I suppose you are owed an explanation. It appropriates the magick of the witches I sacrifice. Certain types of magick in certain amounts at certain times. Some witches I was able to take remotely, some I had to kill here. You, the last, must be killed in close proximity to the doorway."

Boyle covered the last few feet that separated them with more strength than he'd displayed since she'd injected him. The rest of Isabelle's hope died with a sick whine. The injected copper hadn't worked.

"Will you fight me?" he asked.

She stiffened and gritted her teeth. "How can I? How can I when I know you'll take my mother or some other witch in my place?" Even though every fiber in her body wanted to lash out at him, kick, punch, and scratch . . . then run for her life.

"That's why it will not give me much pleasure to kill you." *Much.*

Boyle pulled her into his arms like he might a lover. Her mouth pressed against the smooth black leather of his jacket. She tasted something warm and salty and realized she was crying. He cradled her in his arms for a moment, long claw-tipped fingers brushing through her hair.

Then he lowered his mouth to her throat and bit.

Demons were like spiders, their venom squirting from their mouths into their prey, rendering them paralyzed.

Boyle's sharp teeth pierced her skin like twenty needles. Pain shot through her body, making her twitch in something close to a convulsion. When she jerked against his teeth, it hurt even more so Isabelle went still and keened softly as blood ran down her neck. The demon groaned, as if in ecstasy, as if he loved the taste of her, and tightened his embrace.

The venom shot like acid straight into her bloodstream and Isabelle arched her back in agony, unable to do anything more. Her vision faded from color to black-and-white. The images she viewed were blurry around the edges.

Was this how Angela had felt?

No, she didn't want to think about Angela. Anything but Angela.

A coat brushed her cheek for the millionth time. Darkness had swallowed her whole. She didn't even know where the door was in the middle of the night when no light spilled beneath the crack. Hunger gnawed at her stomach lining. She'd gone through all the jacket pockets already and found nothing, not even any of those little plastic wrapped crackers from the restaurant. Her only comfort was Angela, slumped in sleep beyond the closet door, her breathing steady in the night.

The only steady thing in Isabelle's life. . . .

She came to lying in the center of the floor, not far from the doorway. Moving her limbs was fruitless, just as the involuntary scream that tore from her throat remained soundless, ineffective. Silent. Mute. Motionless.

Prey.

Just waiting.

Boyle lowered himself over her, her vision still in black and white. His mouth opened, but she heard nothing. The demon grasped her arms, cold fingers digging in. He lowered his mouth to hers and began to suck out the magick from the center of her.

Inwardly, she screamed. She writhed. She died.

Outwardly, she could do nothing but endure it.

Her heartbeat was the only thing she could hear. It beat loudly in her mind, growing slower. Her vision changed from black to white to blacker and then blacker still. Maybe she would be lucky and she would die before Boyle began to feast.

Had Angela died before that point?

Then Boyle was gone. The pressure on her chest eased and her magick snapped off where Boyle had bitten into it, sending a flash of searing pain through her and then nothing.

Unable to move, unable to see clearly, Isabelle only caught bits and pieces of the movement around her. Long black hair. Flashing copper sword.

Thomas.

Damn it. She'd known he'd show eventually. Fear for herself disappeared. Dread for Thomas replaced it. Movement flashed out of the corners of her eyes. Sword. Blood. Claws. Teeth.

Then, again, nothing.

Nothing but a pulsing, purring noise to go along with the beating of her heart. Soft at first, it grew louder and louder. Magick prickled against her skin, letting Isabelle know that the demon's venom was wearing off.

Where was Thomas? And what was that alien magick scraping along her body?

The texture of the power rippled and grew stronger. The same stink of evil teased her nostrils and then Isabelle knew what it was. She felt a tug on her body like tiny hands that grew stronger.

Somehow, the doorway had opened.

Thomas appeared over her, blood running down his temple and coating his long black hair. He scooped her up into his arms. "We've got to get away from here," he said, his voice sounding far away. "The doorway is appropriating Boyle's magick as he dies and it's opening, but it's unstable. Pulling . . . pulling us in."

Alarmed, Isabelle tried to move. It was like her arms had been wrapped in cotton, but she managed some mobility. Color now tinged the edges of her black-and-white vision, too.

Thomas dragged her a distance away, far enough that the pull of the doorway ceased, and lay her down. Isabelle sat up, scanning the room for the demon. Boyle lay a short distance away, on his stomach. Multiple stab wounds marred his back and his blood crackled and popped on the pavement around him. He still lived. His limbs twitched and a low, thick moan wafted from his throat.

About five feet away from him the doorway gleamed almost prettily in the air, a riot of shimmering colors that pulsed and flickered with magick. Isabelle was no earth witch, but even she could sense the volatility in the spell.

She glanced at Boyle and shook her head. "No, he's not dying. He doesn't die. He's like something out of a horror movie. You only think he's dying and then—"

Thomas *shhhed* and rocked her in his arms. "He's dying, believe me. He was more than halfway done for by the time I arrived. I just finished the job you started. It's over, Isabelle. It's over."

Could it be? It seemed like it had been forever since it had begun.

"Home." The groan came from Boyle. Bleeding and beaten, he pulled himself toward the doorway. He went inch by inch across the floor by willpower alone, leaving a trail of hissing blood behind him. "Home." This time it sounded more like a sob.

"Let's go," Thomas said, helping her to stand. "I don't know what that doorway is going to do."

She climbed to her feet and took a quick inventory of Thomas's wounds. His clothing and probably his skin were singed from Boyle's blood. Cuts marked his head, his cheek, and his chest. His own blood soaked his thigh from a gash, but she couldn't tell how deep it was. "Thomas—"

"Come on. We both need medical attention." He slid his arm under her waist and helped her walk toward the exit.

The door at the far end of the warehouse opened, revealing Adam and the rest of the Coven witches entering the building.

Adam's gaze focused on something behind her and Thomas. "Watch out!" he yelled and started to run toward them.

Isabelle glanced back and saw that Boyle had reached the doorway and was crawling through. The doorway had grown larger and brighter. Magick flared and rippled outward from the unruly, half-finished spell.

Light flashed and the pull intensified. Isabelle screamed as the thing sucked them in like some kind of black hole. Hell, maybe it was a black hole.

Magick, light, and sound exploded.

THOMAS CAME TO FACEDOWN IN A PATCH OF GRASS, his upper thigh throbbing in agony. His hand still gripped the handle of the sword. He had to physically force himself to relinquish it, one finger at a time.

Isabelle was no longer in his arms. He sat up and groaned, pain shooting though his body from his wounds. The pounding in his head had increased ten-fold and now nausea roiled in his stomach to boot. His hand went to his thigh and came away sticky and hot with his own blood.

He pushed all that away, pushed it back, and almost passed out from the effort. None of that was important. Only Isabelle was important.

"Isabelle?" he croaked.

It was dark. Wind creaked through tree branches not far away and the air smelled strange. Not at all normal. It smelled faintly of . . . *demon magick.*

"*Isabelle!*"

"I'm . . . here." She groaned and something thunked. "Damn it. I'm here."

Thomas groped toward the sound in the darkness and finally found warm flesh. He gathered her against his chest. "Are you all right?"

She took a moment to answer and when she did her voice sounded thin. "I can't take any more *poofing* today. It makes me sick."

"*Poofing?*"

"The transporting through unconventional means." She groaned. "*Poofing.* We went through the doorway . . . I think."

"I think so, too."

"Where do you think we are?"

He looked up, studying the night sky. It looked just like any other clear, perfect night sky—a few wispy white clouds and a whole lot of bright stars. Except . . . "Wherever we are, it's not Chicago." He pointed skyward.

"What?" Pause. "Oh, shit."

Above them hung two moons. One large and luminous, the other smaller and pale blue.

TWENTY-FIVE

"DO YOU THINK WE COULD BOTH BE HALLUCINATING the same thing?" Isabelle asked, huddling closer against his chest.

"I doubt it."

"How badly are you hurt?"

He shifted and the throbbing pain in his thigh shot to brilliant white-hot life. He gritted his teeth. "I'll be fine."

"Do you think Boyle is out there somewhere?"

Thomas took a moment to answer. His mind had been turning over that same possibility ever since he'd seen both moons shining in the sky. The thought of being trapped here, with no way to get Isabelle back home, sent a shot of ice water through his veins. The fear he felt for her would probably anger her, but he couldn't help it. He knew all too well she could take care of herself, but that didn't stop him from wanting to try.

He shook his head. "I don't know. If he is, he's probably dead by now."

"Maybe. Demons are like cockroaches, though. Hard to kill."

They sat in the dark for several minutes, absorbing their situation and listening to a strange bird cawing somewhere to their left. When Isabelle began to shiver, he wrapped his arms around her tighter. They needed to find shelter.

He had no way to judge the time, but light seemed to be getting brighter on the horizon, which logically meant it was nearly morning. Of course, in this alien world, who knew for certain?

Gripping the sword in one hand and using it as a sort of crutch, Thomas helped Isabelle to stand and led her to a small clump of trees on their left. At least they wouldn't be so out in the open. He hoped they weren't doing something dangerous, but he had no way to know for sure. His intuition said they were fine in the place he'd chosen and that would have to be good enough for now.

After they'd settled at the base of a huge tree, Isabelle turned to him and touched his face, tracing very lightly the cut on his head and the one on his cheek. "You're lying about being okay for my sake. Don't do that. Remember I'm empathic and can feel you're in pain. How badly are you injured?"

He hesitated before replying. "Boyle sliced me up with his claws. It's nothing serious except for the wound in my thigh. That one's a little deep, but I don't think he hit anything vital."

She snaked a hand to his left leg. It came away bloody, no doubt. "A *little* deep?" She'd tried to make her voice steady, but he could hear the quaver in it.

"It will be fine."

"Right." She made an exasperated sound and pulled her shirt over her head.

"What are you doing?"

"I'm using my shirt as a bandage. You take care of everyone else, so let me take care of you as best I can."

He grabbed her T-shirt before she could shred it. "You're going to freeze!"

"Then you're just going to have to keep me warm." In the semidarkness she glanced down at his bare torso and feet. "I'm wearing more than you anyway."

"Clothes weren't my first concern when I saw you on the back of Boyle's bike."

"Duly noted. Clothes aren't my first concern right now, either." She yanked her T-shirt from his grasp and tore it a couple inches up from the hem, making it into a long, ragged piece of material. "Now let me play nurse."

Leaning into him, she wound it around his upper thigh. He

took advantage, burying his nose in her hair and snaking his hands around her waist. "I told you, I'll be fine."

She finished by tying it tightly. He winced and stifled a yelp of pain. Then she pressed her hands to the gash to staunch the flow of blood. "Yeah, whatever. Maybe I can call you an ambulance. I'm sure the demonic emergency medical system is spectacular."

Thomas laughed.

"Damn it, Thomas. This isn't funny."

"I was just thinking about how I said I'd never traveled before."

She leaned her head against his shoulder and gave a low, soft roll of laughter. "If I had to get trapped on a demon world with anyone, I'm glad it was with you."

"Yeah, but we're not staying here. If there's a way forward, there's got to be a way back. That doorway has to still be open."

Isabelle leaned back on her heels and went silent for a long time. Finally, she said, "The doorway was already volatile. You felt it. Do you really believe it could still be open?"

"I have to." It was true that the doorway had been unstable. There was no telling what had happened to it. It may have completely collapsed once they were through.

Thoughts like that weren't welcome.

So instead he wrapped Isabelle in his arms, enjoying the contact of the bare skin of their torsos, and held her close, willing the pain in his side and all the uncertainty away. "I love you, Isabelle."

She sighed into his neck. "I love you, too, Thomas."

Somewhere in the darkened field in front of them Boyle groaned.

ISABELLE STIRRED FROM HER TWO-MINUTE INVOL-untary nap. Her ears twitched as sound carried across the clearing. Twigs breaking in the distance. Voices.

Many of them.

"Isabelle," Thomas whispered.

"I hear." She stiffened against Thomas's chest, where she'd fallen asleep. Her skin where they touched was warm, but her bare back—bare except for her bra strap—nape, legs, and arms were cold.

The morning light touched the iridescent green leaves and curling, vinelike vegetation of the alien outcropping of trees they'd taken shelter beneath. Even stranger than the flora was the staggered urban skyline in the distance.

A demon city.

A whole city filled with demons.

Isabelle's mind had stuttered to a halt at the idea—jagged and pointed alien skyscrapers full of *demons*.

There was a point where your mind could only hold so much. After that capacity was breached you either had to accept what you were seeing, or you would go crazy. She and Thomas had already passed that point before they'd glimpsed the skyline.

Thomas sat up a little straighter and pulled her along with him. The thicket concealed them, but who knew what sort of magick floated on this air. Neither of them could be certain they'd be able to hide themselves adequately from whomever or *whatever* approached.

Flicking out a small tendril of power, Isabelle tapped the morning moisture in the grass. Her magick flared instantly and shot out ten feet farther than she'd intended. "Shit!" she whispered. "My magick is a lot stronger here."

Power flared like velvet against her skin and a mild taste of earth skated against her tongue as Thomas tested the magickal currents. He grunted. "Mine is stronger, too, and it handles differently. The equivalent of going from manual to power steering."

"Different earth, different magick?"

"Or maybe—" He broke the sentence off. "Maybe it's not that our magick works differently here. Maybe it works different on our Earth. Maybe our power is stronger here because the part of us that's demon is . . . *home*."

"Don't say that. I reject that. I'm ignoring you now."

Cautiously, she added more magick, adjusting the way she handled it so it wouldn't rush out and alert the walkers to their presence. She sent it from one drop of water to the next, toward whoever walked on the far side of the clearing. She would probably only find out what they already knew—demons walked there.

After a couple of minutes, she found them and gleaned what information she could remotely. Around forty individual boots tromped through the wet clearing, so that meant something like twenty demons. All of them had large feet, which meant they were likely male demons.

Isabelle unhooked the tendrils of magick and withdrew. After she'd told Thomas what she'd found she added, "They're speaking some strange language, demonish, I guess."

He nodded. "I can tell they're coming right for us."

She stiffened. "Then let's get the hell out of here."

His hand closed around the handle of the sword beside him—the gesture of a man wanting action, but with none to take. "If we move now, they'll spot us for sure. I sense movement all around us, in all directions. Isabelle, we're trapped. In any case, they're moving slow, right? I don't think they know we're here."

Lady, they were like rabbits hiding in a thicket, hoping the fox passed them by. For a moment she balanced on the razor's edge of panic and fought to control it.

Once more, Thomas's magick flared along her skin. "They're all in lines," he added after a moment. "Like in a formation. You know how when a search party is looking for a body in the woods?"

"Yeah." She swallowed. "Think they're looking for us?"

"Or Boyle."

She closed her eyes and drew a breath. "Can you remember the location of the doorway?"

He scanned the clearing. "It was dark, but I noted how many steps we took to this tree and in what direction." He narrowed his eyes and scanned the immediate area. "Yes, I can."

She had him point out the area where he believed the doorway to be and she sent another tendril of magick out to search for remnants of the sticky yuck that could be their ticket home.

What she found was not heartening.

It took her a moment to form the words and once she managed it, they came out shaky. "I don't think the doorway is there."

Thomas said nothing, but his arms tightened around her.

"It could be simply that my magick, like yours, works differently here." She drew a ragged breath. "Maybe I'm just not detecting it." They both knew the truth. Her magick was much stronger here and the clearing was saturated with morning dew, making it even more effective.

If the doorway remained, she would have noticed it.

"Or maybe I can't remember the exact spot," said Thomas.

"It's possible, but I searched a pretty large area."

In the middle of the clearing, the demons made a racket. One group began shouting in demonish, or demonese, or whatever they called their guttural language and pointed at something in the grass. The other smaller search parties changed direction and hurriedly closed in on the yelling group. All the demons were moving now . . . all of them moving closer.

Thomas and Isabelle held their breath. They'd found Boyle, that was clear enough. Hopefully, they wouldn't search anywhere else.

A series a sharp yells and heated conversation met their ears. It was far too great a risk to peek their heads up to see what was happening, so Isabelle sent her magick out once more to try and glean information.

Oh, yes, they'd found Boyle all right. By the half-baked, fuzzy reflections she could get from the dew in the grass, he was nearly dead. The shouting grew louder and a thick, wet sound came from the direction of the demons. Isabelle flinched in surprise and her magick snapped back hard and fast like a rubber band.

He was now all the way dead.

"I guess Boyle is no longer a problem," whispered Thomas.

"Unless he can function without his head." Her voice came out barely more than a breath.

The yelling across the clearing lulled to almost nothing and then swelled. Isabelle and Thomas didn't need magick to understand the tromping of demon feet now moved quickly in their direction. Isabelle knew with a rising sick feeling in her gut they weren't getting out of this undiscovered.

Thomas pushed her facedown into the thicket with a harsh order to stay there, grasped the sword, and struggled to stand to greet the oncoming rush. Lady damn the man! He was injured!

She cast about for ways to use her magick as a weapon in this situation and came up empty since she couldn't use her ability directly on the demons. All she could do was watch in horror as Thomas took a wide swing and sliced into one of their attackers.

Rough hands grabbed her and pulled her up. She glimpsed the demon Thomas had wounded—tall, muscular and dark-haired. He'd collapsed to the thicket, holding his side and bellowing in pain as his wound smoked and popped.

Her captor swung her around to face the ravening horde. They looked human . . . well, except for their massive size. They wore leather, the lot of them. Boots, pants, and jackets. Almost like a uniform of some kind. The largest of them, a hulking demon with long red hair and brown eyes barked something at her in their language. She could only glare in response, her hands fisting.

Thomas had been scuffling with them beside her. Out of the corner of her eye, she saw three demons finally bring Thomas to heel, but not before he'd injured two of them. The demons wrestled him down, extracted the sword from him, and tossed it to the ground. Then they heaved him up fast and hard, making him groan in pain, and forced him to kneel next to Isabelle.

His hair fell over his face, concealing his expression, but anger rolled off him in biting, bitter waves. Blood soaked through the makeshift bandage her T-shirt made, dripped down his leg. Terror edged up her throat like a razor blade. He needed medical attention, damn it!

More shouting at them in the strange language.

"We don't understand you!" bellowed Thomas. He flicked his hair away from his face and Isabelle glimpsed his eyes, snapping hot black with ire.

A demon with short brown hair and a handsome face angrily pushed his way through the throng and shoved the redhead, barking something at him. The redhead barked back. The handsome demon gestured at her and Thomas, growing louder in his protestations.

Chaos ensued.

Demon turned on demon, shouting and shoving. They gesticulated at her and Thomas constantly. One of them tried to rush them, but was held back by his peers. Obviously, this was a serious disagreement.

Obviously, it was over their fate.

Thomas took her hand and squeezed it a moment before the redhead raised his hand and sent a blast of demon magick toward them.

The scent of it burned along her nose and throat, making her choke—triple stronger than on Earth—and blackness enveloped her.

ISABELLE AWOKE WITH A JOLT AND GRIMACED. THE redhead pulled a capsule away from her face and she saw he'd waved something that smelled bitter under her nose. She tried to move her hands, but quickly learned they, like her ankles, were bound.

They'd dressed her, at least. That was good because being clothed in just her bra around a bunch of male demons hadn't made her feel very warm and fuzzy. She now wore a dark blue tuniclike shirt in a soft weave of fabric that seemed a cross between silk and cotton.

The redhead said something unintelligible to her. She ignored him, too busy glancing around the room to locate Thomas. The room was surprisingly luxurious—soft dark green couches with tasseled pillows, granite tables, and plush throw rugs covering a polished stone floor. Gleaming swords decorated the walls. The décor appeared medieval and posh all at once.

It was a nice room, except for the fact Thomas wasn't in it.

"Where's Thomas? Where's my friend?" she asked, interrupting his fruitless attempts to communicate with her. She knew he couldn't understand her, but the question was involuntary.

"Pah, *aeamon*." The redhead waved a hand at her in a gesture that needed no translation, turned, and walked out of the room.

Isabelle fell back against the cushions in defeat. Damn it, she had to find Thomas. If they hadn't seen to his wound—and what was the chance of that?—he'd bleed out.

He'd die.

Her wrists were tied in front of her. She raised her hands and worried the rope with her teeth as fast as she could. Hell, she'd gnaw through them if she had to.

She'd managed to get the knots around her wrists undone and was busy laboring on the ones around her ankles when the door opened. Isabelle pressed herself back into the cushions, wishing she'd been able to work a little faster, and watched the new demon enter the room.

He stood close to seven feet tall and looked like a Viking on steroids—long blond hair, icy blue eyes, and a square, chiseled chin. Threat seemed to linger on the brutal curve of his mouth and sit all too comfortably in his eyes.

Viking demon didn't seem to notice, or care, that her hands were untied. Why should he? There was no way she could best this guy in a fight. She was completely vulnerable to him, locked in this room with him alone. It didn't matter if she were bound or not.

The demon stopped in the center of the room and studied her. She braced herself for another barrage of the foreign language. "Where's Thomas?" she repeated. She would ask until her throat was raw or he learned English, whichever came first.

"Safe." He paused ominously. "For now."

Relief flooded her, though she didn't like the *for now* he added on. She jolted as the second most important bit of information registered. "You speak English?"

He inclined his head a degree. "I speak many of the languages of your people. It is part of my job." His tone wasn't particularly hostile—more matter-of-fact—but the expression on his face remained icy. "My name is Rue. I am an ambassador to the *aeamon*."

She took a moment to reply, her mind wiped momentarily clean of thought. "Ambassador to the *aeamon?*"

His eyes glowed red for a moment and Isabelle lost her breath. "Why did you follow Ashe through the doorway?"

"Ashe? Do you mean the demon who called himself Boyle?"

The demon named Rue stalked toward her, shoulders hunched. Isabelle shrank back against the couch. "You know who I mean," he bellowed. "The *Atrika daaeman* we killed in the field."

Atrika demon? "Whoa! Hold on!" She held up a hand, as if that would ward him off. "We knew him as Erasmus Boyle, and we did *not* follow him voluntarily through the doorway."

The demon's massive hands came down on the couch at either side of her head, pinning her in place. The scent of demon magick came off him in cloying waves.

"You lie!" he snarled.

She startled backward, her head hitting the soft cushion. If she could get any farther back, she'd be inside the couch.

His teeth had started to lengthen and become pointed. "You came through the doorway to organize with the *Atrika.*"

Terror exploded through her body at the sight of his eyes, which now glowed a steady red. Isabelle knew with a vast amount of experience that glowing red eyes on a demon was never a good sign.

Isabelle sat forward, coming nose to nose with him, every muscle in her body vibrating with fear. "Look, I don't know what the hell an *Atrika* is, but if they're anything like Boyle, I want no part of them. An *Atrika* killed my sister. We were doing our best to return the favor. During Boyle's death throes, the doorway he was trying to open appropriated his magick, went wonky, and sucked us through." She drew a breath. "*We are not here by choice!*" She spat the last sentence and felt her face grow hot with anger.

He stared at her for a long moment, then turned, and stalked away. He crossed the room to a window that looked out over clear blue sky and stared out of it. Apparently, they were on a very high floor. She wondered which of the jagged gray skyscrapers that she'd seen before was the one she now found herself in.

"Tell me what an *Atrika* is," she said, finally. She needed some answers. Any answers.

Not turning toward her, he clasped his hands at the small of his back and glanced down as he answered. The gesture was so much like Thomas that a lump formed in her throat. "You know this already."

"*I do not.*" Her voice sounded low, cold and commanding. It was pure, unadulterated rage that made it that way. It filled the room like a general's might.

He turned to face her, anger on his face. "*Etaryi!*" He snapped out the word like a curse. "They are one breed of *daaeman*!"

She rubbed her wrists, where the skin had been bruised from the rope. Her hands were shaking. "There are different breeds?"

"There are four. Each have different characteristics. The *Atrika* are the most bloodthirsty, the most violent. They are illegal here. We hunt them down and imprison or kill them."

She looked up. "Demons so bad you had to exterminate an entire breed? Is that why you locked out Ashe?"

He stared stormily at her and she thought he wouldn't reply. Then he paced away and said, "Since the wars have ended and their services as soldiers are no longer needed, the *Atrika* have organized into a mercenary group. He was their leader until we caught him and put him in prison for his atrocities." He lifted his chin and sneered. "Then you foolhardy *aeamon* pulled him through."

"Hey, we weren't the foolhardy ones. The people who pulled Boyle through are like the *Atrika* in our world."

Rue's lips compressed into a firm line. His eyes glowed red, giving Isabelle momentary heart palpitations. "*If* that is true, there could be an explanation. You know that *aeamon* are bred from us?"

"Yes." She swallowed the *unfortunately*. It wasn't a good idea to insult a seven-foot demon to his face.

He nodded. "It is possible there are *aeamon* who have inherited the *Atrika* genetic traits. They can be like children, always grasping and wanting. They care nothing for the suffering of others and are slaves to their own selfish whims."

Inherited the Atrika *genetic traits*. Her mind reeled from that bit of information.

"What breed of demon are you?" she asked.

"*Ytrayi*. Leader class. We have strong magick to call and overdeveloped aggression, like the *Atrika*. Unlike the *Atrika*, we have the restraint and control to manage it. We have . . . honor."

This was all very interesting, but Isabelle had a far more pressing matter at the forefront of her mind. "So you understand that Thomas and I are not these people, right? We don't want to ever deal with an *Atrika* again. We're sorry we were pulled through the doorway, and, really, we just want to go home."

"This cannot be allowed." He turned once more, placidly hooking his hands at the small of his back and staring out the window.

Darn, and she thought they'd been making friends.

While his back was turned, Isabelle worked the rest of the knots around her ankles. Just as she was about to ease from the couch and pick up a long piece of jagged scarlet-colored crystal from a nearby table—a bit of artwork, she assumed— and bash him over his head, he turned to face her. "I should kill you now, but we may have need of you."

"Wait a minute!" Her mouth went dry. "We don't want to conspire against you or harm you in any way." *Like they could*. "My friend and I just want to go home. Please."

Talking to the piece of artwork she'd fantasized about whacking him over the head with would have had more impact. He strode past her and out the door. The lock turned on the other side, seeming to echo through the room.

Isabelle sagged against the couch in defeat, fighting a swell of nausea from being in a locked room. She drew a deep breath and squeezed her eyes shut. Now was no time for a panic attack. She pictured Thomas here in the room with her and her anxiety eased. Isabelle opened her eyes, steadier now.

But where was Thomas really? Had they left him to bleed out somewhere in this building? Had they decapitated him like they had Boyle? Nausea threatened once more.

She took slow, deep breaths in through her nose and out her

mouth. The demon had said they might need her. Logic said the same would be true for Thomas. Likely they hadn't killed him . . . yet.

With short, jerky movements, she pulled the rest of the rope around her ankles free and hurled it across the room with a bellow of pure frustration. That task accomplished, she slid from the couch and grabbed the heavy crystal sculpture from the table near her. Hugging it to her chest, she prowled the room, looking for a way out.

TWENTY-SIX

❧

THOMAS WOKE WITH THE STENCH OF DEMON MAGick in his nostrils and his cheek against something hard and cold. He pushed up, grit digging into his palms, and groaned at the pain shooting through his thigh.

When his eyes flickered open he glimpsed the interior of what seemed to be a cell in the dim light. An iron door with bars at the top. Concrete floor and walls. Ratty, folded-up blanket to serve as a bed.

He raised magick, power flickering over his tattoo and down his arms, tingling the base of his skull. It came weak and sluggish because of his injuries, even in this place where his magick was more powerful. All the same, the pavement near his head pulsed as he manipulated it.

Good. This place wasn't like Gribben.

A footstep sounded to his left. That's all the warning he got. A booted foot struck his injured side and Thomas's world went white hot with pain. He grunted, nearly tossed his cookies, and held onto consciousness with every last shred of willpower he possessed. Unconsciousness now could very well mean his death.

"We have your female," came a heavily accented voice. "If you cooperate, we will not hurt her."

Isabelle. Shit.

Thomas forced himself to turn over onto his stomach, agony spearing down his thigh and through his middle. At least that pain wasn't a quarter as bad as when the speaker had kicked him. He forced himself to focus upward, seeing a blond man staring down at him. "What do you want from us?"

"Why have you come to ally with the *Atrika*?"

He frowned. "The what?"

"Your female tried also to feign ignorance, but we know that's why you've come. That's the only reason any *aeamon* comes here."

His mind whirled at the influx of information. Did that mean witches had come here before? No, warlocks, most likely. Not witches. Had they achieved it?

Thomas's vision blurred. He blinked and the demon came back into focus. "We came here accidentally. When we fought Boyle with copper, the spell he was cooking to open a doorway became unstable. We were caught in the maelstrom." He drew an unsteady breath, feeling lightheaded. "There is no attempt on our part to ally with any *Atrika*." *Whatever the hell that was.*

The demon took three menacing steps forward, his boots crunching on the grit of the floor. "Do you think we don't understand your goals? You forced the demon to open the doorway and then tried to kill him once you had no more need of him."

If Thomas had not been bleeding to death and at the mercy of a seven foot demon in an alien world, he would have laughed. "You think we forced Erasmus Boyle to bring us here? You actually think us capable of that? We just spent the last three weeks trying to *stop* Boyle from doing whatever he wanted."

"Ashe, this demon you know as Boyle, would never have returned willingly. He knew we would track and kill him as soon as he set foot on our soil again."

Thomas touched his thigh and winced. His hand came away red, warm and sticky with his blood. The wound had reopened. "He was . . . homesick," Thomas replied on a tired sigh. Speaking cost him. All he wanted was to slip into unconsciousness.

"Homesick?"

"He would've risked anything to get back here, even death." Thomas paused to drag some ragged gulps of air into his lungs. "Boyle was killing witches to get home. The only way to stop him was to poison him with copper, but it only did the job three-quarters of the way. We were pulled through the doorway and you finished him off in the field. That's what happened. Why would we do our best to kill the demon before coming through the portal?"

Silence.

Desperation edged into Thomas's body, more painful than his wound. Isabelle was alone somewhere with these creatures. What was happening to her?

"So you could weaken him," the blond demon replied. "Weaken him long enough to come through and then kill him. So you could prove to the *Atrika* that you are powerful enough to kill their former leader and gain their respect. But something must have happened to prevent you from killing Ashe on this side of the doorway."

Thomas closed his eyes. The demon didn't believe him.

"We will get the information from you, believe me, *aeamon*. We will obtain the truth. From you or from your woman." He toed the wound on Thomas's thigh, making him gasp and see stars. "It will not be pleasant . . . *for you or the female*."

"Let Isabelle go. Keep me. She's an innocent in this." So was he, but they didn't want to believe that.

"You have no bargaining chip here. We have you both. We will keep you both."

Thomas raised his head and snarled, "*Fuck you, demon*. If you have any sense of honor, you'll let her go free."

The demon stiffened at the word *honor* and his eyes narrowed. "Do not insult my people," he growled.

He'd touched a nerve purely by accident. Not one to waste opportunities, Thomas played it up, trying to appeal to him as best he could. He knew nothing about their culture, but he'd use whatever was at hand in his goal to see Isabelle safe. He raised his head a little to hold the demon's gaze. "In *our* world, *we* protect those we care about. It's a code of honor we have . . . a code between warriors. Keep me and let the innocent female go. She knows nothing and you have no need of her."

"*Aeamon,* do you know the deal you strike? You will never see your world again."

He closed his eyes, on the verge of passing out. He nodded, his focus centered in one and only one direction. "Just make sure Isabelle does."

THE DOOR OPENED AND ISABELLE SWUNG HER WEAPON, only to find her wrist caught painfully. The sculpture was torn from her grasp, dropped to the floor, and shattered. Rue growled low at her and tugged her forward, through the doorway and into the corridor.

"Where are you taking me?" she demanded, fighting him and allowing her gaze to eat up her surroundings at the same time. Polished dark green floor and smooth black walls. Many doors. Lights embedded in the ceiling. No other demons in sight.

"Home."

She stilled, in shock at the sudden turn of events. Earlier it had sounded as though they might torture her for information she did not possess. Failing that, they would kill her. "What about Thomas?"

"We have need of him. He stays." He dragged her forward, down the corridor.

Isabelle exploded into motion, pulling her arm back where he grasped her wrist, punching him with her free hand, kicking and screaming. She flailed against him, hurling every swear word and insult she could think of. Lady, she felt so tiny and insignificant in the face of his bulk. A gnat going toe-to-toe with an elephant.

The demon turned, his eyes glowing red. "The head mage will not return. He has agreed to stay willingly if we set you free. Forget him and count yourself lucky. You will go back to your people and know we have been merciful with you."

He turned and pulled her once more down the corridor. Against his superior strength, she had no option but to be dragged along.

All she desired was Thomas, to touch him and know he was okay, to fit her face into the curve of his neck and inhale the scent of him.

Isabelle now understood the meaning of the word *despair*.

Emotion swelled within her, hot and hard. In the center of her chest, her magick pulsed in response, stronger here than it would have on Earth. Impulse made her act, to reach out for the only strength available to her. Tendrils of magick shot from her in all directions, seeking any moisture in her immediate area.

The pipes in the walls, under the floor, above their head in the ceiling all began to bang. The small amount of moisture in the air coalesced on her demand, creating a mist around their heads.

Her captor slowed, staring around him. Water erupted and sprayed down from a light fixture above their heads as it found any tiny crack or throughway to obey her call. To their left a pipe burst, sending liquid running down the wall.

Somewhere in the building she found a large pool of water. Its calm depths purred at her for a moment before she yanked it toward them. Her magick was amazingly strong here. What would have zapped her energy on Earth only made her feel energized on Eudae.

The roar of water approaching down the corridor behind them caused the demon to turn and scowl at her. "I have given your mage my word I would return you," he yelled at her over the roar of the oncoming rush. "But he remains."

The wave of water turned the corner at the end of the corridor and rocketed toward them. Isabelle focused all her will on directing it past her, straight at the demon. She would escape him and find Thomas. "If he stays, I stay!"

The demon stared at her grimly, his gaze holding hers. Then, right before the wave hit, he raised his hand and parted the sea. The water rushed past them both, barely wetting them.

Isabelle closed her eyes against the swell of disappointment and grief rising from the center of her. Her knees went weak and she had to catch herself before she collapsed.

Rue reached out, snared her wrist, and dragged her forward.

Her feet slid on the wet floor as she resisted, but nothing could halt her relentless progress until the demon stopped in front of a large carved wood door. A monster with horns cavorted there, chiseled by a demon hand. It looked like a cross between a ram and a huge man. Rue waved his hand and the door opened. He pushed her through.

The circular room had no decorations to speak of and seemed wholly utilitarian. The walls were of polished dark stone and the floor was also stone—dark green, marbled black, and marked with strange symbols in a circular pattern. Cabinets stood along the edges of the room and she wondered what filled them, what purpose they served.

The chamber stank of demon magick.

She could not only smell the demon magick, but feel it along her skin. It pulsed with a subtle light all along her body. Like walking into sunshine without the glow.

Under the stink of demon magick lingered the lighter scent of herbs. Immediately it made her think of earth magick. She glanced more closely at the room and glimpsed bowls set in what seemed to be strategic locations. Very possibly the smell emanated from them in a sort of magickal potpourri of dried plants.

Symbols marked strategic places on the floor at her feet. Cold inched up her spine at how closely it resembled a warlock's demon circle. In the center, Isabelle could feel the subtle pulse and pull of a doorway.

"*Aptry domini*," he uttered.

Light shimmered in the gateway, growing brighter.

Thomas. Oh, Lady, she couldn't leave him here.

The demon placed a hand on her shoulder, as if to guide her to it. "I'm not leaving without him!" Isabelle shrugged him off, turned, and used every ounce of physical strength she possessed, going completely berserk. Still, he wrestled her kicking, screaming, and biting, as though she were a mosquito, into the circle, and pushed her through the doorway with not even a fare thee well.

Isabelle fell.

"THOMAS!" ISABELLE LUNGED INTO A SITTING POSI-tion and immediately doubled over and dry heaved.

"Whoa! Whoa! Calm down, Isabelle."

Adam's voice. That had to be Adam's broad, warm hand on her back, too.

She opened her eyes and saw shoes all around her, the toes pointed in her direction. Isabelle lifted her head, palms and knees biting into the concrete floor, and looked up at the witches who'd apparently been in the warehouse when she'd reentered.

She remembered nothing from the time the demon had pushed her through until she'd dry heaved. Her body seemed to remember, though. She shivered and bitterness crept up the back of her throat, like she had the flu.

"Damn it, Isabelle, you're scaring me." Without preamble, Adam scooped her into his arms and lifted her like a doll. Isabelle was too out of it to protest.

Micah's concerned face entered her view, but she couldn't focus on it. Nor could she stop shivering. He put his palm to her cheek and grunted. "We need to get her warm and hydrated. I think she's going into shock."

"My SUV is outside. Let's get her back to the Coven. Jack and the others can wait here in case that thing spits Thomas out." Adam walked toward the door.

Thomas. They still had Thomas!

Isabelle moved, struggling against him. "Wait! I can't leave. Let me down—"

"All right, all right! Calm down already." He set her to her feet.

She nearly collapsed and he offered an arm to steady her, which she grabbed on to with both hands. Her teeth chattered as she spoke. "They kept him. They kept Thomas."

Micah took her by the shoulders and forced her gaze to his. She shuddered and tried to get her eyes to focus. After a moment his face came in clearly. "Who are *they*, Isabelle? What do you mean?"

She drew a breath and closed her eyes, arranging her jumbled, panicky thoughts. "We were pulled through the doorway, ended up in Boyle's world, on Eudae. In the morning, the demons found Boyle and killed him, then located us somehow even though we were hidden." She shook her head. "Maybe

Boyle told them where we were as a final fuck you. I don't know."

Micah tightened his grip and shook her a little. "Stay focused. The demons found you?"

She nodded. "An *Ytrayi* demon sent me home, but said they intended to keep Thomas there."

"*Ytrayi* demon?"

Ignoring Micah, she whirled—and nearly fell down— toward the place where the doorway had stood. "Out of my way," she said as she pushed a couple people aside.

"Isabelle?" Adam asked, right on her heels.

She walked through the area, got down on her hands and knees and felt the floor. No trace of the doorway remained. Thomas was not coming through.

Maybe he was never coming through.

Adam touched her shoulder. "He can take care of himself." His voice was the gentlest she'd ever heard from him.

She stood, turned into him, and let him wrap his arms around her. "Damn it, Adam. I don't want to lose him."

"None of us wants to lose that bastard."

"We have to open another doorway. We have to go back through and get him."

He set her at arm's length apart. "We can't do that, Isabelle, and you know it."

A small sob escaped her throat. She knew it. Only an *Atrika* demon could open a doorway, either that or a powerful, highly knowledgeable witch with the soul of a serial killer. Or maybe the Duskoff could do it. They'd be willing to murder to wedge the doorway open a crack.

She shook her head. No, they could do nothing to get Thomas back.

Thomas's cousin, Mira, appeared on her right with tears brimming in her eyes. Mira placed her hand on Isabelle's shoulder and Isabelle finally lost it. She turned into Mira's arms and allowed the other woman to comfort her.

During the course of the next two hours, many of the witches began to trickle out—heading home or back to the Coven. Finally, only the core remained—Adam, Jack, Micah, Mira, and Theo.

"You need to get back to the Coven, Isabelle. Get some sleep and food," said Micah. He sat a short distance from her on the cold concrete floor.

She shook her head and pulled the blanket they'd put around her shoulders a little tighter.

Micah sighed. "You can't stay here all night."

"Why not?" She continued to stare at the empty space that had been the doorway as if her will alone could bring him back.

"Because you need rest and food," Mira interjected. "Without these things, you'll get sick."

Isabelle glanced at the pregnant air witch. She was beginning to get a lovely baby belly. "*You* need to get back, Mira. Not me. I'll be fine." She turned her head and speared Jack with a hard stare. "Get her out of here. Get her home and fed. This dank building is the last place she needs to be. While you're at it, take the rest of these witches with you."

"We don't want to leave you alone," Jack answered.

"Do it anyway. *Please*."

Silence.

Isabelle resumed willing Thomas back into this dimension with only the power of her mind.

Finally Micah spoke. "Tell me about that shirt you're wearing." His tone was downright covetous and she'd seen the way he'd been staring at it all evening.

"On the other side I used my shirt to wrap Thomas's wound. Since they found me topless, one of the *Ytrayi* demons dressed me in this. It's yours at first opportunity, Micah. I promise you I never want to see it again." Sorrow sliced through her stomach like a surgical blade.

Micah opened his mouth, but Mira shot him a chilling look from across the room, and he closed it again. Isabelle would've bet every cent she possessed that he'd been about to ask more about the *Ytrayi* demons. She'd tell him all she could . . . later.

More silence. More staring.

Adam cleared his throat. "Listen. I'll stay with her. The rest of you can head back."

"I don't need anyone to stay with me," she responded woodenly.

"Please, shut up. You're not as tough as you pretend to be," answered Adam. "Now go on the rest of you. We'll let you know if there's any change."

Isabelle barely noticed when the others left. She heard their low conversation, but understood none of it. It reminded her of the time she and Angela lived with Martha Newcomb, one of her mother's rich friends, for the summer. Martha's aunt had died that season and her funeral had been like that— low, hushed voices, slow-moving people, long faces.

Adam sat down next to her with a heavy sigh. He drew a random line with his finger on the concrete floor. "We all love him."

She turned to look at him. "I just found him, you know? The horrible thing is that I thought I was going to have to let him go anyway, but I thought *I* was the one who was going to die."

"He's not dead, Isabelle."

She chewed her lower lip. "No. You're right. He's not dead." Isabelle stared hard at the empty air in front of her. "And he's coming back soon. If he doesn't return on his own, I'll find a way to break him out."

"You really do love him, don't you?"

"Yes." She swallowed past the lump in her throat. "He told them he'd stay willingly if they let me come home."

Adam sighed. "That's Thomas for you."

In the morning, Isabelle woke up wrapped in the blanket on the cold warehouse floor, with a crick in her neck. Adam lay sprawled nearby.

Thomas hadn't returned.

TWENTY-SEVEN

⟣

ON THE STOVE, THE TEAPOT WHISTLED. ISABELLE pulled it off and poured steaming water into her coffee cup, then turned and leaned against the kitchen counter to sip it. Letting the mild flavor of the lemon balm tea fill her senses, she glanced around at the wreck that was her kitchen.

These days she wasn't home much. Every waking moment was spent at the Coven, with Micah, trying to get back into hell. Together they had read every word of the texts forward and backward, tracking down and cross-referencing the information they found with anything else they could locate about Eudae and demon magick. Desperately, they looked for any way to open a doorway that didn't involve the cold-blooded murder of a series of witches.

By digging far and wide into non-magickal ancient texts, they'd discovered a wealth of information they'd never known existed. But it took a lot of time to separate the wheat from the chaff. She'd started her search the day after she'd returned and had worked every day and every night since, averaging about four hours of sleep per night.

Isabelle glanced around her kitchen again, curling her lip at the sink full of dishes, the hand towel discarded on the counter, and the trash can that definitely needed to be emptied. Nothing mattered but her research. She came home late every night, made dinner, maybe some tea, then got a meager amount of rest.

Her mother had come back from California when she'd heard about Thomas. She was actually being supportive and unselfish, which was . . . strange, but also welcome. Her mother had hired a cleaning service to come in starting tomorrow and Isabelle hadn't declined. It was a good idea under the circumstances, and Isabelle was pleased that her mother was making an effort with her.

Isabelle would be up in a few hours and back at the Coven to work at the first sliver of dawn on the horizon. Jack and Ingrid kept insisting she just sleep at the Coven, but she couldn't do that . . . not yet.

There were a few leads, a few ways they might be able to get back to Eudae without using blood magick. The problem was that only one way was viable for those of a non-demon persuasion, and it was beyond complicated. They were still researching some of the steps of the spell. Once it was determined they could do it at all, then would come the complex ordeal of gathering what they needed to cook it up. Even if it did work, it would take a long time to complete.

She leaned against the counter as a wave of grief swamped her. The heaviness of it always sat in her chest. Throwing herself into her work didn't help. Nothing helped. The only thing that would lift the constant weight in her heart and eradicate the lump from her throat was Thomas's return.

And she would work toward that goal until the day she died.

The phone rang. Isabelle set her cup down and stretched to pick up the cordless handset from the breakfast bar. "Hello?"

Silence.

"Hello?"

Nothing.

She punched the Off button and stared at it thoughtfully. She needed to have caller ID installed so she could catch the prankster who kept trying to get a rise out of her. There had been calls like that once every night at this same time for the last week and she grew weary of them.

In her darkest moments, she imagined it was Thomas trying to contact her. Then she pulled herself back from the shaky edge of grief-induced insanity and reminded herself that interdimensional communication wasn't possible.

The phone rang again, right in her hand, startling her. She punched the On button. "Listen, punk—"

"Isabelle."

She knew that voice, that accent. Shock ripped through her like an electric charge. "I thought you were dead."

Long pause. "No. I did look into the eyes of death, however." Breathy, low voice. "Much the same way I did back in that limo with you."

"You can only mean you looked into Boyle's eyes. He got you out of Gribben, didn't he?"

"*Oui* and he meant to kill me. I believe he was a bit besotted with you. Meant to kill me on your behalf, Isabelle."

"Why the hell didn't he?" she snarled into the phone. That Stefan should be calling her while Thomas languished in the demon dimension killed a part of her.

Another long pause that Isabelle didn't like one bit. "Alternate plans were made."

All thought momentarily fled her mind. That sounded ominous. She swallowed hard, a bit of her bravado gone. "Well, then it's a damn good thing Boyle is dead."

"Yes, a pity." He drawled it.

She found a long, loose hank of hair at her nape and pulled at it while she paced the kitchen. "Other than to share with me the glorious news of your continued existence in this world, did you have another reason for calling me this evening?"

"I wanted to say I forgive you."

She stopped short and actually sputtered for three seconds. "F-forgive me? You forgive me? You—"

"Last year I lost the only father I ever had. I understand you lost your sister and so I have absolved you of your sin. I will not seek retribution."

"Well." *What the hell?* "Uh. That's incredibly big of you, Stefan." Her voice dripped sarcasm.

"This is the first and only free pass you will get from me."

"Wow. I can hardly contain my gratitude." She drew a breath, mastering her anger. "You know we'll keep hunting you."

She could hear the smile in his voice when he answered. "You can try, but I have become wary of beautiful redheads of late. You will not find it easy."

"Nothing worth achieving ever is."

Click.

Isabelle held the cordless phone in her hand and stared at it, cold dread inching its way up her spine. Stefan remained in this world while Thomas had been expelled from it. Was there no justice?

After a moment she replaced the handset and turned back to the counter. Damn it. Her tea was cold. She picked up the mug and set it near the sink, then leaned against the counter and closed her eyes. Lady, she wanted Thomas back. With every fiber in her body, with every breath she drew.

Impulsively, she grabbed her keys and left her apartment, letting the door slam shut behind her.

No way was she getting any sleep tonight anyway, and there was a stack of half-translated texts at the Coven just waiting for her.

CLAIRE ENTERED THE CELL, LETTING THE DOOR STAY open as long as she could without drawing suspicion because she knew the light made the earth witch, Thomas, content. On the bad days, on the days his body was wracked with fever, he said it made him think of a woman named Isabelle. He talked of her constantly when he was delirious.

Now, the delirium had passed. There weren't any more bad days, either. Not real ones, anyway.

The door closed with a metallic thump and darkness closed around her tight as a fist. Water trickled in the far corner of the small, dank cell. The *drip, drip, drip* must drive the prisoners crazy.

The man, the first *aeamon* Claire had seen since the death of her mother, knelt on the floor, his arms strung out on either side of him by heavy chains, chains that were resistant to this one's magick. His powerful body had been brought to heel as much as the *Ytrayi* could bring a witch such as this to heel.

They'd shorn his hair because the *Ytrayi* knew it held power. His once long, beautiful hair now stuck up in uneven tufts. But they'd left the tattoo alone. She had thought they might cut it from his back, but they hadn't bothered. The only reason for that was they underestimated him and his magick.

Just as they had always underestimated her.

It was ego. The *daaemon* thought themselves to be superior in every way to the *aeamon*. What the *daaemon* didn't understand was that the spell that been cast to allow the birth of witches so long ago had been born of Eudae and had linked the *aeamon* eternally to this land. Witches were more in tune with the *daaemon*'s own planet than they were.

Thomas looked up and moved his arms, his muscles flexing. A beard shadowed his face, but Claire knew he was handsome under the hair. Strong chin, black eyes that held heat and anger barely banked, full lips that seemed made for traveling over a woman's skin. She responded to him like a woman did to a man. She couldn't help it. He was the first eligible male she'd ever encountered. Eligible, but a prisoner.

Selfishly, she wanted to keep him, to seduce him. She wanted something here, *someone* who was totally hers. But this man didn't see her, not the way she would have him *see* her. His whole heart and mind was centered on *Isabelle*.

And Claire was going to do all she could to see he got back to her.

She'd been sent to tend Thomas and act as translator because she was the only person besides Rue who spoke his language. Soon the *daaemon* would realize what a mistake that had been.

"Claire," he greeted, his voice strong and sure. Good. When she'd first been sent to him, he'd been sick and broken.

She nodded, walking near him and setting her burdens to the floor—a bucket of hot, soapy water and a rag. Secreted on her person she also had a razor, a package of food, and medicine rolled up in a bit of cloth, even antiseptic wash for his mouth.

Claire had been instructed to care for Thomas, to keep him alive—barely alive—so that the questioning and beatings they put him through during the day didn't kill him. She'd been doing her job.

Well.

Much better than the *Ytrayi* had ever intended.

His magick was fierce and strong, fiercer and stronger here on Eudae than on Earth because his homeland fed him. The *daaemon* wanted Thomas weak enough that he couldn't use his power. *She* wanted him strong enough to break out of here. And tonight she had everything in place.

The *Ytrayi* thought they had her under their thumb. It was time she showed them how mistaken they were.

Smiling to herself, she dipped the rag into the water and placed it to his skin. Carefully, she wiped clean the grime and dried blood from his body. Every night she did this, wiped away the evidence of the beatings he received and tended his wounds. She took her time, took her pleasure in the hard satin stretch of his body and the way his skin quivered under her touch. Undoubtedly, he fantasized it was his lover who caressed him. Claire didn't care so long as *she* was the one with her hands on him.

Isabelle could have him tomorrow. Until then, he was hers.

Tonight, she did not speak. Normally, in soft, hushed murmurs, she tutored him in ways to use his magick against his captors. Claire had learned a lot in the twenty-five years she'd been trapped on this rock. She'd learned far more than Rue realized.

When she picked up the razor and set it to his face, he jerked away from her. "You've never shaved me before," he rasped.

She smiled and her face hurt from it. Claire couldn't remember the last time her mouth had moved that way. "For Isabelle," she admonished him. "You don't want to go to her looking like . . . what is that creature? I can hardly remember . . . a yeti?"

He swallowed hard. "Is it time?" He sounded like a starving man being offered a three-course meal.

Her smile lingered in response to the barely leashed eagerness in his voice. She slid the razor over his face, ridding it of the three week's worth of hair. "Your magick is curled deeply in you now, trained by me and ready to strike. I believe you're ready. Have you been acting weak and broken in front of Rue and the others?"

He nodded.

"Have you been casting the glamours I've been feeding you to make you appear dirty and injured?"

"Yes."

She smiled. Smiling felt nice once her muscles grew accustomed to it. "Good."

After she'd fed him the flatbread and meat she'd tucked into her pockets, let him wash his mouth, and administered the final dose of high-powered medicine she'd had to steal daily from the doctors, Claire stood and backed away from him. "Demonstrate," she commanded.

Magick prickled along the nape of her neck. Her own earth magick responded to his tap with a low purr in the center of her chest. She closed her eyes and sighed into it. Around her the entire cell pulsed, breathed like a living thing for a moment. The walls expanded outward and then inward. The ceiling cracked. Dust and rock rained down and the floor beneath her feet rumbled.

Claire opened her eyes, shivering a little at the display of power. "Yes, you're ready to take on the *daaemon*."

Even in the dim light of the cell, his expression tightened and his eyes glowed with eager threat. She'd fed him charms over the course of the last three weeks, so many that he should have enough tricks up his sleeve to make it from his cell to the doorway. Everything was ready.

When Rue had put her in charge of keeping Thomas alive, she'd answered him with properly downcast eyes . . . but in her mind, she'd begun planning this.

They'd never broken her, the bastards.

She tapped her magick, drawing it straight up from Eudae herself, and the chains binding him snapped. Thomas couldn't touch those chains . . . but she could.

Thomas straightened his long, broad frame just as the guards threw the door open. His show of magick would not have gone unnoticed. The two hulking *daaemon* stopped short just inside the doorway and Thomas struck like a lightning bolt, raising power and directing it at them. It pulsed along her skin, tasting of a place she couldn't remember but missed with all her heart, tasted like *home*, and then the guards were down. Dead, Claire had no doubt.

Losing no time, they stepped over their bodies and raced down the corridor of the prison before more guards arrived.

At the end, they turned the corner and ran straight into an entire group of *daaemon*.

TWENTY-EIGHT

～

ISABELLE LEANED OVER A SHEAF OF PAPERS IN THE library, squinting against the exhaustion that had overtaken her. The room was dark, but for the light illuminating her immediate area. Micah and the others helping them on this project had long since retired.

She was no scholar, didn't even have a college education, but since Thomas's disappearance she'd had a crash course in lots of esoteric subjects she'd never had cause to be interested in before, like the nuances of Aramaic and the delicate intricacies of earth magick.

Until now the Coven had had no reason to delve into historical documents kept by non-magickals, but since their witchy origins had been revealed, Micah had been procuring them and scouring them for any information that might fit in with what they'd received from the Duskoff. In the process, knowledge that needed to be closely guarded from the warlocks had been discovered. If Thomas hadn't been trapped over there, they would've let it stay buried forever. It was *quite* practical and some of it very dangerous.

Mumbling to herself, she read the line giving her trouble for the fiftieth time and then double-checked the three translations she had, trying to figure out which one fit with rest of the text.

She sat back, rubbing the bridge of her nose and closing her bloodshot eyes. "I really need to let Micah handle this," she mumbled to herself.

They were growing closer to a breakthrough for getting

back to Eudae every day, giving her just enough hope to continue on. She tried not to think about how long Thomas had been over there or that the odds grew slimmer every day that he still lived. Those were not things she could dwell on.

Isabelle leaned forward and laid her head on the papers in front of her. Sleep pulled at her, but she resisted. Just needed to rest her eyes a bit. . . .

A warm hand closed around her shoulder. Her breath caught in her throat, arrested by the familiarity of the touch. She would know the warmth of that hand anywhere, the weight of it. Her eyes opened slowly.

"Isabelle?"

His voice. Her name on his lips.

She had to be dreaming.

Isabelle lifted her head, tears stinging her eyes. This couldn't be real. She pushed the chair back, rose and turned around.

Thomas stood before her still dressed in the same drawstring pants he'd been wearing three weeks ago. His hair, tangled and matted, stuck up in tufts around his head. Someone had cut it . . . badly. His now short hair threw his brutally handsome face in angular relief. He'd lost at least twenty pounds. Someone had tried to clean him up, but dirt and grime still marked his skin, as well as a profusion of cuts and bruises. He smelled heavily of blood and demon magick.

Isabelle didn't care.

She stepped toward him, hand outstretched, trying to gain a foothold on the moment. Blinking, she said, "I fell asleep. I'm dreaming."

Thomas stepped toward her and yanked her into his arms. "You're not dreaming, Isabelle. Do you think anything in this universe could stop me from getting back to you?"

Then he lowered his mouth to hers and proved to her that he was, indeed, flesh and blood. His warm lips skated over hers softly, then pressed down possessively. His tongue speared between her lips and rubbed against hers with a ferocity that stopped her breath in her throat. His fingers curled into her hair, his arms strong around her body.

He held her like he'd never let go.

Isabelle sobbed against his lips, tasting her tears as they

ran into her mouth. "How?" she murmured. Her fingers found solid purchase around his shoulders. "What did they do to you?"

"I'm okay." His voice came out scratchy but strong and steady. "They just roughed me up a little and showed me some demon hospitality when I refused to share information with them."

Fudging the truth for her sake. She could feel it. As usual, even now, he tried to protect her. "I don't believe you."

He took a moment to answer. "They didn't like it when I refused to share every aspect of Coven business and our dealings with the Duskoff."

"They tortured you." Her voice sounded angry and flat to her own ears, accusatory. "You told them to let me go and keep you."

He nodded. "I did. I love you, Isabelle."

She swallowed hard. "Why did they send you back?"

"They didn't. I escaped. I had help on the inside, a woman named Claire. She slipped me extra food, treated my wounds, gave me charms to make me seem more injured and sick than I was, taught me—"

"Taught you?"

"She had earth magick like I've never felt before. Strange and powerful. She taught me how to use my magick against the demons. With her help, I gained enough strength that I broke myself out. It was dicey getting from the cell to the doorway, but we managed to get through all the obstacles in our path."

"Who was she?"

"I don't really know. I could never get her to say much to me. I don't know why she was there or how she got there in the first place. At the end, I tried to get her to come with me, but she refused."

"She wanted to stay?"

"I don't think so, Isabelle. I don't think she felt like she had a choice for some reason."

Poor woman. Isabelle would forever be in her debt. She thought about their research on opening another doorway. Maybe she could repay this woman for what she'd done.

She dropped her head to his shoulder and held onto him like she was drowning. "I can't believe you're back."

He brushed his fingers through her hair. "It was the thought of you that sustained me while I was there."

She raised her head. "I'm glad the thought of me got you through hell and back, but you shouldn't have done what you did."

He shook his head. "Not even another word." His voice had an edge of steel to it. "When I saw an opportunity to free you, I took it."

She pushed away from him a little. "Thomas, you never stop—"

He dragged her up against him and she angled her head to brush his lips. The taste and feel of his mouth was like sunshine on her skin after a year of constant night. "Don't pull away from me," he whispered. "Not ever."

She smiled against his lips. "I'm not going anywhere."

THOMAS SLIPPED HIS HAND TO ISABELLE'S WAIST, reveling in the warmth of her skin radiating through the fabric of her shirt and into his palm.

"You need to see the doctor," she murmured into his neck.

His arms tightened around her. "I am seeing my doctor."

She raised her head. "I'm serious, Thomas."

He touched her cheek. "So am I. Look, I'll be fine. I just want to spend some time with you now. The doctor and the rest of the Coven have me tomorrow. I want to be yours tonight."

She looked up at him with a raised eyebrow. "Mine tonight? Baby, you're mine forever."

"Then let's go upstairs. I need a good bath and then I need you."

"Healing waters I can do. Stay here a moment and give me a head start." She leaned up and kissed him tenderly. He closed his eyes at the sweet pressure of her mouth on his, his body going tight as a bowstring with the need to be one with her. She broke the kiss with a slow groan and murmured, "I'll see you upstairs."

When he opened his eyes, she was gone. For a moment he saw the inside of his prison cell in his mind's eye. He heard the *drip, drip, drip* of the water. Smelled blood and demon magick. For a heartbeat he wondered if this was just another dream, one of many he'd had in the dark of night while he'd been tucked away in a place somewhere between *here* and *there*. Then the library came into focus and he sighed in relief.

He stepped forward, sifting through the papers that Isabelle had been leaning over. Apparently, they'd been trying to find a way to get back to Eudae and break him free. He let his fingertips rest on the texts, his thoughts straying to Claire and how wistfully she'd looked at the doorway while absolutely refusing to step through. Isabelle looked exhausted. Apparently, she'd been working nonstop, but maybe their labor hadn't been in vain.

Those were serious considerations for tomorrow. Tonight he just wanted the woman he loved.

Thomas made his way upstairs to his room to find she'd left the door open a crack for him. He pushed it the rest of the way, stepped inside, and breathed in the familiar scent of his Coven apartment. Nothing except Isabelle had ever smelled so good. Steam rolled from the bathroom doorway.

He walked into the puff of the steam, then stopped short just inside to take in the best sight he could imagine—Isabelle naked in a pool of water, waiting for him.

Life didn't get better than this.

"What are you waiting for?" she asked. Water lapped at the curves of her breasts and beaded on her throat. He wanted to lick those water beads off, one by one.

He shed his clothes and slid into the welcoming heat of the bath with a groan of pure satisfaction. Instantly, the water moved in ripples and waves around him, massaging the lingering ache of abuse from his body. That was one of the benefits of being in a bath with a water witch.

Isabelle moved across the tub and fitted herself against him. Slick wet skin slipped across his, tightening his every muscle. She started with his hair, dripping shampoo into her palm and massaging it through the uneven length. "Bastards tried to strip your power."

His hand covered her wrist. "They didn't succeed because they didn't take you."

Warm smile playing on her lips, she lathered her hands with soap and then eased them down his arms, over his shoulders and back. Thomas let out a low groan of satisfaction as she washed him from head to toe, her lips trailing on his now-clean flesh as she went. Every bruise and cut seemed to heal a little just from her touch.

Even better was her mouth when it found his.

Her lips fluttered against his tentatively at first. He nipped her lower lip and dragged it through his teeth while he slipped one hand down her waist and over her thigh to just under the sweet back of her knee. He pulled her leg up over his hip, enjoying the feel of her wet skin against his.

She parted her lips and allowed his tongue to slip within her mouth and ground her sex against his aching cock. Wiggling her hips, she sought his crown and slid down over the top of it.

All his nerve endings shot to brilliant life. He tipped his head back and groaned at the way the warm, silken muscles of her sex rippled and pulsed along his length as she impaled herself.

One with Isabelle, *now* he was truly home.

He pressed her down onto the top ledge of the tub that rose an inch above the water's surface and sank as deeply within her as he could. She wound her legs around his waist and her arms around his neck, burying her nose in the curve where his shoulder met throat. There she laid a series of kisses and gentle nips of her teeth.

Thrusting in and out of her soft, tight heat, he slaked the weeks-long need he'd had of her. Inserting his hand between their bodies, he used his wet fingers to rub her clit until she shuddered and came beneath him, sinking her teeth into his shoulder.

This was hard and fast lovemaking, urgent. Once he'd sated himself, he'd put her in his bed and do it again, slower, sweeter. Lather, rinse, and repeat . . . for as long as she'd have him.

He sealed his mouth to hers as his climax overtook his body, thrusting deep within her as he came.

Once it was over, they slipped into the water, tangled up in each other. For a long time, they did nothing but touch one another, kissing along smooth, wet skin.

She bit her lower lip and traced a bruise on his shoulder. "How bad was it?"

His arms tightened around her. He didn't want to tell her about the beatings he'd received every day. If it hadn't been for Claire patching him up and giving him glamours, he probably would've died there. "Bad. It could have been worse, though."

She rubbed her lips against his shoulder. "Stefan is alive."

He gritted his teeth, but didn't reply. Score number two for the Duskoff. That was the second time he'd escaped them.

"He told me he struck some kind of deal with Boyle," she continued.

Thomas rubbed his palm up and down her arm and murmured, "Considering we witnessed Boyle's beheading, I'd say all negotiations he made are probably void."

She snuggled against him, her body soft and warm against his, but her voice was hard. "Let's hope we never get an *Atrika* on this side of the doorway again."

But they would. Maybe not tomorrow or the next day, but one day the Duskoff would pull another through.

"Let's forget about all that for now. The future will take care of itself. Let's live in the present. Or, better yet, let's talk about our personal future . . . together."

She frowned up into his face. "You're not going to do something dumb and ask me to marry you, are you?"

"I want you to stay, Isabelle. I love you."

"I love you, too, Thomas, and the only place I want to be in this world is with you. I would've said yes, you know."

Pleasure warmed him from the tips of his toes to the top of his head. "In that case, will you—"

"Yes." She kissed him. "Yes, I will. Thank the Lady you finally got around to asking. I've always wanted to be a queen."

"What do you mean?"

"Well, for all intents and purposes, you're the king of witchdom."

He smiled. "And you're definitely my queen."

ALEJANDRO LEANED AGAINST THE BAR AND WATCHED the crush of dancers gyrate to the pounding beat in the Blood Spot. Lights flashed through the dark interior of the building, periodically illuminating bodies clad in almost nothing.

Blood hunger stirred within him. He was restless for a drink that had nothing to do with the imported bourbon in the glass he held. This place was rich with promise for a vampire. All those young bodies flushed from the energy of the music and their dancing, it was nearly irresistible.

It would be so easy to pull one of the lush women from the crowd, lead her into the velvet darkness of the back of the bar, ease her head back, and drink from her throat. He'd make sure she liked it. He'd make sure she climaxed while he drew the blood from her veins. His *veil* was strong when it came to giving pleasure.

His gaze focused on a twentysomething brunette, whose hips twisted and snapped to the frenzied music. She had beautiful tanned skin—the kind of woman typically found out here on sunbaked Darpong. The dark part of Alejandro whispered, *You could make her beg for it.*

Hell, most of the patrons were here because they hoped they'd find a Chosen to bestow on them the dark kiss. The bite of a vampire was a rush to a human, like a drug. The venom secreted by a fully Chosen's fangs caused their victim to relax and become aroused. Too much of the venom could kill them, or turn them, but most were willing to take the chance for the high.

A Chosen's *veil*, their ability to twist the mind, further intensified the pleasure.

The Blood Spot was known as a place where willing human donors and vamps could meet up. The Chosen and humans alike came from miles around to this desolate location for just that purpose.

That little brunette out there would probably welcome his bite. In fact, she was probably looking for it. He could press her back against the wall, slide her skirt up to her waist, part her thighs, and ease his cock inside her while he drank. She'd feel so smooth, soft, and hot around him, and her muscles would ripple and tighten as he made her come.

Alejandro swore under his breath and stared down at his glass to distract himself from the thoughts that assaulted his mind. He downed the remaining liquid, letting the alcohol burn down his throat.

Blood hunger twisted in his gut and he pushed it away. It remained tamped down for the moment, but he doubted his ability to keep it that way. He didn't deal well with temptation. Never had. Not even before he'd been Chosen.

He was here on business for the GBC, the Governing Body of the Chosen, not to avail himself of the willing donors who surrounded him. He could resist. He had to.

After ordering another drink, he settled back against the bar and watched the dancers with heavy lidded eyes. The bourbon wouldn't make him drunk, but the enticing morsels shaking themselves in front of him could.

A redhead in the crowd caught his gaze and smiled flirtatiously. He looked away.

Maldita sea!

He was supposed to be meeting Daria here. Where the hell was she? If she didn't get here soon, all his self-control would dissolve.

Alliance law decreed that vampires were supposed to feed from only the *succubare*, the class of Chosen that gained their sustenance from sex instead of blood. They were humans who'd been Chosen, but hadn't made it through the arduous process. They were not *fully* Chosen, only halflings.

As long as vampires fed from willing human blood donors, the law wasn't typically enforced. Basically, it was a consensual crime without punishment.

However, the Governing Body of the Chosen, the law making organization for all Chosen had the same law and they were strict. They were especially hard on the vampires who worked directly for the GBC. They were not allowed to feed from a human, no matter how willing that human might be.

He swirled the bourbon in his glass and tried not to stare at the redhead who still endeavored to catch his eye.

Yeah, he had a problem with the regulation placed on him by the GBC. He craved human blood, wanted to feel a human body crushed against him when he drank. He was driven to fill the hole it created inside him. Some humans found being bitten by a vamp an addiction, but he found taking their blood just as big an enticement.

Human blood was sweeter than the blood of the *succubare* and far more intoxicating.

The redhead broke away from the crowd and approached him on long, shapely legs. A short black skirt sheathed her from the waist to mid-thigh. Red stiletto heels, the same color as her filmy, almost see-through top, encased her slender feet.

The fashion was retro these days—Earth at the beginning of the twenty-first century. Out here in the Nabovsky Galaxy, named for the astronomer who'd discovered it, the settlers had a lot of nostalgia for the home planet.

An expensive ruby pendant nestled in the smooth hollow of her throat. More rubies hung from her delicate earlobes. The woman who approached him now was probably rich and slumming it out here in the outreaches of the lawless Logos Territory on Darpong, looking for a thrill or two. He'd bet any amount of money she had a wealthy husband back on Angel One.

"You look lonely over here," the redhead purred at him. She touched his chest with long, manicured nails. They scraped his skin through the material of his shirt. Her voice lowered predatorily, her eyes lighted with speculation. "You're a vamp, aren't you, handsome?"

DARIA MORRIS PUSHED THE DOOR OPEN AND STEPPED into the Blood Spot. Her pupils adjusted to the dim light and her nostrils flared at the heavy odor—a combination of Darpongese booze, the bitter smoke from *rashish* cigarettes, and the metallic scent of blood. The pounding beat of the club's music assaulted her eardrums.

There were vamps in here. She could feel them. This sleazy club in the outreaches of the Darpong was well known as a place where veilhounders, blood donors who were psychologically addicted to a vamp's *veil* and physically addicted to the chemicals secreted by a vamp's bite, hung out, waiting for a vampire to grace them with their presence . . . and their fangs. The edges of her mouth curled down in disgust.

If it were up to Daria, veilhounding would be illegal everywhere. She found the practice abhorrent, despite the supposed joys of having a vampire sink his or her fangs into you and unfurl their illusions within your mind.

There were addiction clinics all over the Angel System. For the love of the quad planets, you'd think people would learn not to get their kicks this way.

There were even isolated cases of vampires trafficking in the sale of addicted humans they called blood slaves. Sometimes they abducted veilhounders from places just like this one and sold them into it.

She shook her head, glancing around at the people that filled the building. *The fools*.

Daria's hand rested on her patrol-issued pulse disruptor, a weapon capable of briefly preventing muscular impulses or causing the cessation of synapses firing in the brain, depending on the setting. The weapon worked on most species, even the Chosen. She was not a willing blood donor and she'd be damned if anyone mistook her for one.

Her pupils finally adjusted to the dim light and she sought out Alejandro Martinez. She hadn't seen him in over seven years. All the same, she spotted him right away since he still looked like sin made flesh.

A black leather dune-biker jacket sheathed broad shoulders and his muscular arms and chest. Thick black hair framed a face hewn in masculine lines, with a strong chin, chocolate-brown eyes, and a mouth made for kissing . . . and other things. She filled in from memory what she couldn't see, since his face was currently buried in the neck of a tall redhead.

Daria hung back, watching him sway and dip the woman in his arms, a veilhounder most likely, his pelvis moving sensually against hers. The rhythm to which they danced was a lot slower than the music. They looked like they were in the throes of a slow, pleasurable fuck, oblivious to everyone around them.

Daria shook her head. It had been far too long since she'd had one of those. Everything looked sensual to her these days. Although, Alejandro had always exuded confident sexuality, even before he'd been Chosen.

What the hell was he doing biting a human? That was against GBC regulation.

She worked her way around the edge of the room, picking past entangled vampires and donors and stepping in sloshed beer and other substances she didn't care to identify. Finally, she entered the crush on the dance floor and elbowed her way to him.

"Alejandro?" she queried loudly, competing with the music. "It's me, Daria."

No reaction. Just that irritating sway and thrust.

"Alejandro," she repeated, louder this time.

He raised his head. His dark eyes were heavy lidded, and a hank of black hair had fallen across his forehead. Dark stubble graced the square jut of his jaw and shaded the skin around his well-formed mouth. Those beautiful lips twisted. "Your turn?" he drawled in his Spanish accent.

He released the veilhounder redhead who stumbled back drunkenly with a smile on her face. Daria stepped away, but he grabbed her around the waist and drew her close.

Her protest died on her tongue as his hot breath caressed her throat. Some strange quirk of vampire chemistry made a

Chosen's breath consistently sweet. Their nonhuman bodies took the blood they drank and transformed it into pure energy, pure life. Scientists had hypothesized that it acted as a mild tranquilizer, lulling their human victims.

Daria held her breath, trying not to inhale it. Alejandro bussed his lips across the bare skin between her collarbone and shoulder. The hard rake of fangs followed the sensation.

That broke her momentary stupor. She pushed him away and hooked her leg around to sweep his legs out from under him. He went down hard on his back, scattering the bar's patrons around them.

Daria knelt beside him, drawing her pulser and pointing it at his temple. It whirred up, readying to fire. The light on top that was connected to her brain wave patterns flared red. "I told you, Alejandro. No fangs."

Someone to their immediate left gasped, another screamed. They all backed away. But Daria knew that in this place a ruckus wasn't uncommon. They'd go back to their drinks and dancing soon enough.

Alejandro blinked. "Daria? Jesus, I didn't recognize you."

Self-consciously, she touched her hair with her free hand. She'd undergone a lot of cosmetic work for this operation. The face of the person she'd been when she'd known Alejandro was now permanently altered. Her dark chestnut-colored hair was now blond, and her jaw was square instead of delicately pointed. Her lips were fuller and her cheekbones more prominent.

The only thing she'd left untouched from the neck up were her eyes. They were still a dark blue. When she went undercover, she'd turn her blue eyes brown with an ordinary pair of colored contacts. There'd be no way her quarry would recognize her even without the added precaution of the contacts, but there was no sense in taking chances.

Sante used to say he loved the color of her eyes, the bastard.

"*You* haven't changed at all," she said. "Don't sink your fangs into me, got it? No biting. No fangs."

"That's kind of ironic considering what you want me for. How do you think this is going to work, anyway? I can't Choose you without taking your blood."

A fine tremble in her hand shook the pulser. "I know." She

was still in denial about that part. She'd do it, but until that time, she didn't want to think about it . . . or talk about it. "But that's for a good reason. I don't want you to bite me just for kicks. I'm not a veilhounder."

He stared at her for a moment before speaking. "You're not ready for this at all, are you?"

She ignored the question and cocked her head to the side. "What the hell are you doing breaking GBC law, anyway? Are you blood drunk?"

"What makes you think that?"

"You let me spill you on your ass, Alejandro, and me a puny human and all." She smiled. "You a lush now, big guy?"

With the kind of speed achieved by only the fully Chosen, he disarmed and flipped her in one smooth motion.

She tried to strike out at his throat and eyes, but he grabbed her wrists and pinned them to the floor.

"If I was blood drunk," he growled, "would I have been able to disarm and restrain an agent of the Allied Bureau of Investigation so easily?"

"You son of a bitch, Alejandro. I could've killed you if I wanted to. Your brain was only a trigger squeeze away." She lifted a brow. "If I didn't need you for this mission, I'd report you to the GBC for your little . . . *slip*. I wonder how often you're slipping these days?"

Fear flashed through his eyes and he clenched his jaw before responding. "Such fire, Daria. I don't remember you being like this. It's so arousing." He lowered his mouth and brushed his lips across hers. "I might have to change your mind about not allowing my"—he inhaled her scent and groaned—"*fangs* to sink into you."

His accent rolled over her and tingled places that hadn't tingled in a long time. God, she loved his accent and his voice. The two together were magic. She ignored her response. "Some things never change," she said. "Not after thirteen years, not even after you've been Chosen. You think all the women will just fall at your feet."

He smiled. "Didn't you?"

"That was before you were Chosen and the circumstances were . . . strange. It wouldn't happen now."

White teeth flashed, making him look feral in the half-light. His fangs were retracted, thank God. "It would be even better *now*."

It had been fantastic before.

She could still remember that night, the taste of him in her mouth and the feel of him moving inside her. He'd brought her to climax hard and fast at first, and then he'd taken his time with her, drawing out two more orgasms before he was finished.

He'd been better than Sante had ever been, and Sante had been Chosen when she'd slept with him, even though she hadn't known it.

She'd used Alejandro that night. He'd known it and hadn't minded. She'd needed him to help her forget what had happened, to drown her in lust so she wouldn't drown in sorrow. He'd done a good job. For that one night, he'd been like a knight in shining armor to her damsel in distress.

Daria shivered as his mouth came down on hers. His lips slid over hers like silk, in just the lightest brush. Pure desire shot down her spine straight to her sex.

Damn him!

She was still attracted to him after all these years. And, of all the things he could be, he was a *vampire*. She bit his bottom lip and tasted blood. It spread across her tongue like silk and wine. She resisted the urge to spit.

Swearing, he jerked back and Daria rolled away. She snatched up her lost pulser and stood, wiping the floor yuck from her clothing with a grimace. "Get up, Alejandro. We need to move." She offered her hand and he took it.

Once he was on his feet, she turned on her heel and headed straight for the bar. She needed to take a minute to settle her nerves.

"Rocks?" the bartender asked.

She gave her head a shake.

The bartender served her the shot and she downed it. There was nothing like Darpongese whiskey. It was a little like Earth whiskey, but stronger with a slightly bitter flavor and a smooth finish.

Alejandro touched her shoulder. "You okay?"

She shrugged him off. "I'm fine." She set the shot glass

back on the bar and closed her eyes for a moment. It was a lie, one she was desperately trying to believe.

Two years of service in the Galactic Patrol, seven years in the Allied Bureau of Investigation, two medals of valor, numerous undercover operations and hundreds of busts and she still wasn't sure she could handle what was to come.

"LET'S GO, HUNTER." CORMACK STEPPED BACK FROM the open cell door, his voice gruff to disguise any hint of favoritism. "Move your ass!"

Marc held out his wrists, relieved to see Cormack was putting him in standard-issue police cuffs instead of a four-piece. Marc had pleaded male pride, telling Cormack that the idea of being seen by a pretty woman while wearing full restraints was humiliating.

"I haven't been near a chick in six years, man," he'd said. "I don't want to shuffle in there like some fucking loser."

"I'll see what I can do, but you're classified red, you know. They can't do nothing to you they ain't already done, but *me* they can fire." Cormack had pointed a thumb at his own chest. "You hurt that lady, and it's *my* ass that'll be on the line. I got kids to feed."

It was too bad about the kids, but Marc had people depending on him, too.

He'd allowed himself to look insulted. "I'd never hurt a woman. Besides, why would I do anything to her? I need her help finding Megan."

Obviously, Cormack had believed him.

Cold steel touched Marc's skin, the handcuffs closing with a series of metallic clicks. Then, sandwiched between Cormack and another guard, he walked down the long hallway and through the first checkpoint, ignoring the shouted warnings, obscenities, and threats that followed him.

Marc felt his pulse pick up as they left the maximum-security wing. He tried to tell himself it was just the thought of what he was about to attempt that had his adrenaline going, but he knew there was more to it than that. It was also the thought of seeing Sophie again.

What would she think when she saw him? What would she think of the man he was now? Truth be told, he didn't want to know.

It had been twelve years since that night at the monument, twelve years since they'd sipped sodas and shared their dreams, twelve years since she'd made what had probably been the biggest mistake of her young life and given him her virginity. He'd always wondered how she felt about it afterward, whether she'd had regrets. He certainly hadn't. Memories of that night had helped him get through boot camp, sustained him through the freezing cold of Afghanistan, and brought him back to Colorado when his term of enlistment was over.

No, he hadn't forgotten her.

Tension drew to a knot in his gut as Cormack led him through the last checkpoint and into the visitor's area. He was lower than a snake's ass for even thinking of putting Sophie through this. But she was his only ticket out of this place, and Megan and Emily needed him. Hopefully, the fact that Sophie knew him would give her some measure of trust and keep her from becoming too afraid—or putting up a fight. Then again, if she reacted too strongly to seeing him or was friendly, the guards would get suspicious.

And then he'd be fucked.

"You taking it from here, Kramer?" Cormack motioned Marc through the next gate and stepped aside.

"Yep." Kramer adjusted his leather belt with its Glock 21 .45 caliber and looked at Marc with obvious disgust. "Why anyone wants to talk to this piece of shit is beyond me."

Some of the tension inside Marc settled. He liked Cormack and hadn't been looking forward to roughing him up. But he had no qualms about kicking Kramer to hell and back.

"Over here, Hunter." Kramer led him toward one of the visitation rooms. "You got thirty minutes. And just in case you got ideas about putting your hands on that sexy bit of gash, just remember I'll be standing right behind you."

Then through the Plexiglas window, he saw her.

He quit breathing. His step faltered. His mind went blank. He didn't notice Kramer opening the door or ordering him inside or shoving him into a chair, one beefy hand on his shoulder.

He was aware only of Sophie.

She was even prettier than he remembered—not a teenage girl, but a woman. Her strawberry-blond hair was still long, and she wore it up in a style that was both feminine and sophisticated. Her gentle curves seemed fuller, softening the professional cut of her navy blue blazer and skirt. Her face seemed even more delicate, her cheekbones higher, her lips more lush, her eyes impossibly blue.

Fairy sprite.

He fought to clear his mind, to think, to relax. He needed to focus, to rein in his hormones, to control his emotions. Anything else would get him killed.

She seemed to study him, her expression detached, her hands folded in her lap. She wore no rings—no engagement ring, no wedding band. She reached to shake his hand. "I'm Sophie Alton from the *Denver Independent*. Thanks for agreeing to meet with me."

That's when it hit him.

She didn't recognize him.

The realization came like a fist to the gut, cutting short his breath, the force of it taking him completely by surprise. It had never occurred to him that she might not remember him. It didn't seem possible, but he could see in her eyes that it was true.

He willed himself to speak, took her small hand in his, tried not to look like a man whose world had just imploded. "My pleasure."

Helluva blow to the ego, isn't it, dumbass?

But it was more than that.

It meant that she would be terrified.

He looked at her sweet face, saw the girl he'd made love to—and wondered how he was going to bring himself to do this to her. Then he thought of Megan, alone and running for her life, Emily in her arms, and he knew he had no choice. He'd already lost his sister once. He wouldn't risk losing her again.

Sophie pulled her hand back, feeling strangely uncomfortable. There was something about the tone of the inmate's voice, something in the way he looked at her . . .

She set her digital recorder in the middle of the table, cleared her throat. "Since I can't have my notebook or pens here, I need to record our conversation. I hope that's all right with you, Mr. Hunter."

He nodded, his gaze focused entirely on her. "Whatever you want."

Marc Hunter wasn't what she'd expected. She'd known he'd be tall because his sister was tall. But Megan was also fragile and out of shape, the result of heroin addiction, a sedentary life, and years of prison food. There was nothing fragile or out of shape about Marc Hunter.

At least six foot three, he was athletic and well built, his orange prison smock stretched across a broad chest, the sleeves of his white undershirt rolled up to reveal powerful, tattooed biceps, the U.S. Army's eagle and shield on his right arm and a Celtic band on his left. His brown hair hung to his shoulders, thick and wavy. A dark beard covered the lower half of his face, concealing most of his features, emphasizing the hollows in his cheeks and his high cheekbones, and giving him a threatening look that was lessened somewhat by a full mouth. His eyes were a piercing green that seemed to see beneath her skin.

Even if she hadn't read his criminal record, Sophie would have known he was dangerous. He had an air about him—intimidating, menacing, aggressive.

A killer.

She pushed the record button and struggled to compose her thoughts. "Um . . . As I'm sure you know, I've been following Megan's situation since—"

"I've read the articles," he said, adding, "obviously."

She hadn't revealed to DOC officials that her interest in this interview had originated with an anonymous caller sent by the inmate, sure they'd refuse to grant her request under those circumstances. She wasn't going to acknowledge that fact now, either, not with Lieutenant Kramer listening. Mr. Hunter might not care whether he aroused their suspicions, but she did.

"What you might not know is that I care very much for Megan and Emily and haven't been able to think of anything else since they disappeared. I was hoping you might have some idea why she vanished or where she's gone."

His lips curved in a slow smile. "And here I thought you might be able to tell me."

Confused, Sophie stared at him. He had contacted her, hadn't he? The man who'd called had told her that Marc Hunter would be able help her with Megan. And yet Hunter was sitting here saying that he hoped *she* had information. It made no sense.

His smile faded, and his expression grew serious. "Megan is a very troubled young woman, Ms. Alton. She's been fighting drug addiction since she was a teenager, and every time I think she's made it, she relapses."

No news flash there. Sophie had already reported this in her articles. "Are you saying you think that's what has happened this time?"

"That's what your article led me to believe." He stretched out, his muscular leg brushing against hers beneath the table.

Growing annoyed by this purposeless, circular conversation, Sophie found herself glaring at him. What kind of game was Marc Hunter playing? She glanced up at Lieutenant Kramer, who looked like his mind was a thousand miles away, then back at Hunter. "Is there anything about Megan you'd like to tell me, Mr. Hunter?"

He started to speak, his words cut off by a coughing fit. He raised his cuffed hands to cover his mouth, croaked out, "Can I get . . . some water?"

Lieutenant Kramer nodded, and Sophie realized he expected her to get it.

"All right." Biting back a retort about middle-aged men and sexism, she stood, crossed the room to the water cooler, and filled a little paper cone.

Why had Hunter wanted her to come down here? If he had something to tell her about Megan, why didn't he just tell her?

He'd known a C.O. would be present during the interview, that he wouldn't be able to speak with her privately.

She carried the water back and held it out for him.

It happened all at once: the splash of cold water against her wrist as he exploded out of his chair, hands somehow free, feet flying; her own scream as Lieutenant Kramer fell, unconscious or dead, his weapon out and in Hunter's hands; Hunter's iron grip as he grabbed her wrist and yanked her roughly against the hard wall of his chest.

Their gazes collided, his green eyes as hard as jade and unreadable.

Light-headed, her body shaking, her pulse frantic, she gaped up at him, tried to jerk away. Then her splintered thoughts drew together, formed one word. "N-no!"

"Don't fight me, Sophie!" He wasn't even out of breath. "I don't want you to get hurt."

From outside in the hall came shouts and the shrill peal of an alarm.

They knew. The guards knew. They would stop him.

Stay calm, Alton. Stay calm.

Even as the words entered her mind, she found herself spun hard about, her back crushed against his ribs, his arm locked around her shoulders. She heard him rack the slide on the gun, felt the cold press of steel against her throat, and then she *did* understand.

You're his hostage, Alton. He might kill you. He might kill everyone.

She shuddered, felt her knees turn to water.

This couldn't be happening. It could *not* be happening.

Marc felt Sophie's heart pounding, saw her lips go white, and hated himself for doing this to her. Then she did something that made him hate himself even more.

"Pl-please don't! I-I h-helped your s-sister!"

It was nothing less than a plea for her life, a desperate appeal to his conscience.

Too bad he no longer had one.

"I know." He pulled her toward the door, almost lifting her off her feet. "And now you're helping me."

He heard a key in the lock, and every muscle in his body

tensed, ready for whatever came through the door. He knew he had one chance—one chance to convince the guards he was serious, one chance to escape, one chance to find Megan. He was betting his ass on this one. If he fucked up, if the guards didn't buy it, his sister would pay the price.

The door flew open.

Russell, Hinkley, and Slater filled the doorway, weapons drawn.

"Drop the steel and back off, or I'll blow her the fuck away!" Marc yelled it like he meant every word of it.

Russell's nostrils flared, and a muscle clenched in his jaw. "Ain't going to happen, Hunter. You might as well let her go and drop—"

"Do it!" Marc's shout made the guards jump and drew a terrified shriek from Sophie, who trembled, almost legless, in his arms. "Do it now!"

"P-please do what he says!" Sophie's voice quavered, barely audible above the harsh blare of the alarm. "I-I don't want any of you t-to get hurt!"

Russell glanced at Sophie, and Marc could see that the old man was fond of her, a weakness that would make him easier for Marc to control. Marc watched the shifting emotions in Russell's eyes as the guard weighed his options—and broke.

"You win, Hunter." Russell bent down, put his weapon on the tile floor, then backed away, shouting over his shoulder. "You heard him! Lay down your weapons! Clear the hallway! We've got a hostage situation!"

The other officers followed Russell's example.

But Marc knew he hadn't won—not yet. "Get on your radio and have them order the snipers out of the towers. I don't want to see a single uniform between here and the highway. If I do, she pays the price. And have someone kill that fucking alarm!"

Russell did as Marc asked, conveying Marc's demands via the radio clipped to his shoulder. "Done. No one is going to stop you. But if you hurt her, so help me God . . ."

The alarm fell quiet, the silence almost startling.

Marc nudged Sophie forward, took a step toward the door. "You're a good man, Russell. You may have saved her life.

Now back up, lie facedown, head toward the wall, hands behind your head. You know the position."

"There's still time to rethink this." Russell lay on his stomach now. "Let her go. You'll still have the weapon, and we're unarmed now."

"When I'm safely away, I'll let her go, but not until then." Marc glanced out into the hallway, saw no one. He reached down, grabbed a second Glock off the floor. "Come on, sweetheart. Visiting hours are over. And don't forget your purse."

CLUTCHING THE ARM THAT IMPRISONED HER, SOPHIE struggled to keep up as Hunter pushed her down the empty, silent hallway, gun near her cheek. Her mouth had gone dry, and her heart beat so hard it hurt, her sense of unreality growing with each forced step.

This couldn't be happening. It couldn't be real.

It was only too real.

It seemed to her she watched from outside herself as he drew her through the checkpoint, down the hallway, and through Lieutenant Russell's station with its metal detectors, ink pad, and black light scanner. She felt an absurd impulse to hold out her hand and run it under the scanner as she always did on her way out.

You're in shock, Alton.

That must explain why she couldn't think straight, why she was stumbling along with Hunter like a puppet, why she hadn't tried get away from him. Well, that—and the fact that he'd threatened to kill her and had a gun to her head.

And to think she'd come here to help his sister.

Rage, hot and sudden, burned through Sophie's panic and fear. She twisted, kicked, scratched, brought her knee up hard. "Let . . . me . . . go!"

"Son of a—!" His curse became a grunt as her knee met his groin.

In a heartbeat, Sophie found herself pinned up against the wall, the hard length of his body immobilizing her, her arms stretched over her head, his forehead resting against hers.

His eyes were squeezed shut, breath hissing from between

his clenched teeth, his face contorted in obvious pain. He drew a deep breath, then opened his eyes and glared at her, his expression shifting from pain to fury.

"I'll give you that one because, God knows, I deserve it. But *don't* try to play rough with me, Sophie! You'll only end up getting yourself hurt!"

He seemed to hesitate for a moment, then his gaze dropped to her mouth.

For a split second, she thought he might try to kiss her, and a completely new fear unfurled in her belly. "Don't!"

He thrust her in front of him and pushed her down the hallway. "I'm a convicted murderer, not a rapist! Besides, now isn't the time. Move!"

Her rage spent, she did as he demanded, trying not to trip, trying not to cry, trying not to throw up. Just ahead lay the lobby and beyond it the front entrance and visitors' parking lot.

They passed the abandoned registration desk where Sergeant Green had checked her in, and hurried through the now vacant lobby. And then they were outside.

He surprised her by stopping just outside the door and drawing her back against the brick wall with him. "Give me your keys! Which one is yours?"

"Wh-what?"

"Which car?"

"The blue Toyota. But you can't—!"

"There's no time for this!" He covered her mouth with his hand. "Listen close, Sophie. The moment we step away from this building, a dozen snipers with high-powered rifles will sight on my skull. Perhaps that idea pleases you, but it makes me a little nervous. I don't have time to call a cab, so we're taking your car. Understand?"

He lifted the hand from her mouth.

She nodded, her pulse skyrocketing. "Y-yes."

He was *kidnapping* her!

No! No! Please, no!

She swallowed a sob and fumbled in her purse for her keys.

Marc heard Sophie's breath catch, felt her body jerk, and realized she was crying.

*Goddamn it! God*damn *it!*

He fought the urge, so instinctual, to reassure her. He couldn't afford to think about what she was feeling. Not now. Not yet. One mistake out here, and he'd be a dead man.

She drew her keys from her purse and held them out for him, metal jangling. "P-please just take my car and leave me!"

"No can do, sweetheart." He grabbed the keys from her hand, glancing from the parking lot, which was flooded by search lights to the lobby, where a dozen C.O.s had gathered, waiting for him to slip and offer them a clear shot. "Go!"

Her car was parked nearby—the first space in the second row. He fought for footing, skidded into the door, his knees crashing against metal as the first shot rang out.

Sophie screamed, and for one terrible moment Marc feared she'd been hit. Then he felt it—searing pain in his shoulder.

"Shit!" He slipped the key into the lock, jerked the door open, then shoved Sophie through the door and piled in behind her. "Scoot over!"

An explosion of weapons fire.

A barrage of bullets.

The driver's side window and mirror shattered, glass spraying through the air as rounds shredded the door where he'd been standing a split second ago.

Keeping low, he slammed the door, slid the key into the ignition, and gunned the engine. Then, both hands on the steering wheel, he fishtailed out of the parking lot and toward the highway. "Put on your seatbelt, sweetheart. This ride is likely to get rough."